JOHNNY-BOY

ALSO BY A. F. CARTER:

The Yards

All of Us

The Hostage

Boomtown

JOHNNY-BOY

A. F. CARTER

THE MYSTERIOUS PRESS
NEW YORK

JOHNNY-BOY

Mysterious Press
An Imprint of Penzler Publishers
58 Warren Street
New York, N.Y. 10007

First Mysterious Press edition

Interior design by Maria Fernandez

Library of Congress Control Number: 2024912091

ISBN: 978-1-61316-580-5
eBook ISBN: 978-1-61316-581-2

10 9 8 7 6 5 4 3 2 1

Printed in the United States of America
Distributed by W. W. Norton & Company

JOHNNY-BOY

CHAPTER ONE

JOHNNY-BOY

Johnny-Boy Witten stands in the shower, allowing the water, as hot as he can bear it, to pepper his body, dipping his head to soak his hair, raising it to soak his torso and his groin. He stays that way for several minutes, his eyes closed, before turning to let the water pound his back. The bathroom is dark, like the rest of the small farmhouse he's renting. Johnny-Boy prefers the dark, always has. Darkness provided relative safety when his mom's train left the rails, as it did every time she drank and dropped, which was pretty much every night of the week, month, and year.

Johnny-Boy had a sister, Katie-Girl. Some claimed she was retarded, or possibly brain damaged from the beatings. For sure, she didn't know how to hide until Mommy passed out, or until one of the uncles came by and took Mommy into the bedroom. Hidden outside at the edge of the forest surrounding the shack Mommy called a house, Johnny-Boy could hear Katie-Girl's screams. Still can, for that matter.

Well, better her than him, better anyone than him.

Johnny-Boy no longer calls himself Johnny-Boy. Hasn't in many years. Just now, as he shuts the water off and grabs a towel, he's Paul Ochoa. Ochoa's a Basque name, carefully chosen. It means wolf and fits Johnny-Boy's self-image nicely. A hunting wolf never stops moving, covering mile after mile, relentless, uncompromising. Here I come, ready or not.

And how many miles has Johnny-Boy covered over the years, how many states, how many cities? He's kept no diary, no record, and for obvious reasons. But maybe later, after he's caged or killed, which he almost surely will be. There are so many ways a project can fail. A cop happening along at the wrong time, a hidden security cam, a bit of evidence left behind. Eventually, the unforeseeable will close its jaws around the rest of his life. Which won't be all that long if he's nabbed in a death penalty state. Like this one.

◆

The task ahead challenges. Johnny-Boy arrived in the little city of Baxter three weeks ago, come to commit a murder, which is how he makes his living. Contract killer wasn't a profession he sought, but over the years he's become a thorough professional. These days, a double cutout protects his identity. The buyers contact a facilitator named Braulio Montez who contacts Johnny-Boy's agent, a man named Sol Cohen. Neither the first cutout nor the client, or even Sol Cohen, knows Johnny-Boy's real name or the name he's currently using. Sol's knowledge is limited to an email address in Malaysia and an offshore account in the British Virgin Islands.

Johnny-Boy accepts about half the contracts that come his way, but has few absolute rules beyond no cops, no children. And the why, the motive, doesn't particularly interest him. He likes killing things, always has, and the pay more than keeps him in groceries. It frees him to pursue his other interests, though murder figures into both, into the business, into the pleasure.

This latest job, the job that's brought him to the little city of Baxter, included a wrinkle. Johnny-Boy has a recent photo of his target, but knows only that Theo Diopolis migrated to Baxter three months ago, along with several thousand others, seeking work on a Nissan factory in the early stages of construction. If he's to be killed, he must first be found.

◆

Johnny-Boy steps out of the shower and towels off. He dresses quickly, adding a bomber jacket to jeans and a T-shirt before leaving through the back door. Behind him, on the other side of the house, Baxter's lights are strong enough to cast a faint, distorted shadow of the house over the soybean field before him. Johnny-Boy entered the city only days after a particularly bountiful harvest. The last harvest, apparently. Baxter's extended its city limits to include this slice of Revere County to the north, as well as a slice of Sprague County to the east. Just as well, because most of the farmland had been purchased by developers before the agreement went through.

Off to Johnny-Boy's left, a sickle moon barely penetrates the lacy sweep of the stars, leaving the Milky Way to run from horizon to horizon like the ghost of a rainbow. Johnny-Boy grew up on the Florida Panhandle, out in the boonies. He'd spent many a night away from the shack his mother called a house. Not stargazing exactly. Johnny-Boy fancied himself a hunter, and his slingshot weapon the Hammer of Thor. He stalked rodents for the most part, but also owls perched statue still on branches, and raccoons who rose up to examine the intruder, maybe imagining that thirty yards was sufficiently distant to ensure their safety. It wasn't.

Johnny-Boy takes a deep breath as he watches a shooting star, then another, then a third, streak across the sky. Nodding to himself, he recalls a drunk late one night in a bar he tended. The bar was a no-name dive on Hamilton Street in Racine, and Johnny-Boy was cleaning up as closing time approached. A regular, the drunk had his ass on a stool and his head on the bar. Johnny-Boy was assuming he'd have to carry the jerk out the door when the drunk sat up. Glassy eyed, he'd waved a finger at Johnny-Boy.

"Hal," he announced, the name Johnny-Boy was using at the time, "it's all bullshit. The astronomers, the physicists, the Webb fucking telescope. There ain't no trillions of burnin' stars out there. There's only one light and it's hidden behind a cloth fabric stretched around the earth." He stopped to look up at the ceiling for a moment, his hands flat on the bar, then returned to Johnny-Boy. "Them lights you see? Them dots you call stars? They're nothin' but pinpricks in the fabric of the sky. One light, Hal. Only one fuckin' light. The light of truth."

◆

Behind him, Johnny hears, barely, the wail of a train's air horn. The action never stops at the construction site. Or in Boomtown, or in Baxter. Call it construction fever with developers in every neighborhood fighting to finish their projects. No small feat with construction material in short supply, with the grid and the water system barely able to keep pace, and no guaranteed access to either. At the same time, skilled construction workers have the upper hand and they know it, demanding midproject raises, threatening to walk up the street if their demands aren't met.

None of that matters. Baxterites are optimists, as Johnny-Boy finds them, one and all. Forget the cost of upgrading the city's infrastructure, or the cost of new schools to educate a swelling population. Baxterites share a vision, a vision of prosperity they embrace as fervently as Pentecostals embrace the Holy Spirit at a midsummer tent revival.

Johnny-Boy pulls the chilly air down into his lungs. Yes, he's here to work. If not for the job, he wouldn't know Baxter exists, the city nothing more than an obscure pinprick on an unfolded map. So, here he is, money deposited in a bank nearly as far away as one of those stars, and truly dedicated to a positive outcome. For Johnny-Boy, at least. But the contract only explains his location, not his true mission. Nor his motto: all work and no play makes Johnny a dull Boy.

Johnny-Boy's momentarily distracted by a pair of coyotes loping across a field of alfalfa stubble. They're several hundred yards away, pale silhouettes, and unaware of his presence. Driven by hunger, they weave through the stubble, noses down, in search of a rodent that's only searching for a dinner of its own.

◆

The property he's renting on a month-to-month basis includes the house, a storage shed big enough for a plow, and a partially collapsed barn. The barn was beyond repair, but the storage shed was in decent shape when Johnny-Boy took residence. Positioned a hundred feet from a gravel-topped farm road, it measured twenty by thirty feet before Johnny-Boy got to work. He used wood scavenged from the barn to add several layers to the shed's inner walls, only stopping when no scream or cry for help could be heard. Even if someone made the half-mile drive from Route 23 to the house at just the wrong time. Which nobody has, not even the mailman. Johnny-Boy pays the rent in cash and the utility bills online.

Johnny-Boy's imagination runs full-out as he walks to the shed. These days, he demands a life story. Pain for words, for revelations whether real or concocted. That's the promise, though he never adheres to his end of the bargain. He doesn't have to because they go on and on despite his lies. Proving, he supposes, that hope springs eternal. Or maybe not, because in the end they fall into a stupor, failing to react despite his determined efforts. They're alive, yes. He can watch their chests expand and contract, feel their hearts beating beneath his palm. But they're no fun at all.

◆

The boy in the shed is imprisoned by a cable that runs through the wall to an eyebolt on the shed's exterior. Inside, it feeds into a leather cuff secured around the boy's wrist by a combination lock made of molybdenum. This arrangement allows the boy quite a bit of free movement. Enough to put up a fight.

The boy's name is Case Dixon. Fifteen, but small for his age. He couldn't have weighed more than 120 pounds when

Johnny-Boy came across him, stoned out of his mind at three o'clock on Saturday morning, his back and head resting against a tree. It took Johnny-Boy less than twenty seconds to get him into the van, so gentle the boy did little more than groan.

Johnny-Boy uses a key to unlock the door Case Dixon can't quite reach. Last time, the boy came at him with a piece of board he'd somehow torn from the wall. Stupid, really, because even if he succeeded in killing Johnny-Boy, the cable would hold him prisoner until he starved or died of thirst. Stupid also because Johnny-Boy outweighs him by more than a hundred, tightly-muscled pounds.

◆

As a teen, Johnny-Boy spent hour after hour in his foster father's weight room, and that's when he wasn't taking classes at his foster father's MMA studio. But diligence be damned, he'd never acquired the sculpted body he liked to imagine. He'd thickened instead, in the chest, neck, arms, and thighs, a refrigerator with legs and the power of an NFL lineman. In the gym, he routinely benched four hundred pounds. In the cage, he just wasn't quick enough to avoid the fists and feet of his opponents. But on the street, against the unsuspecting, he's near invincible. Not that he threatens, or appears threatening. His broad face is nondescript, his small features evenly spaced and almost always composed. Just another poor jerk making his way in the world.

Yanking the door open, Johnny-Boy steps back, prepared to deal with whatever the boy throws at him. He needn't have bothered. The boy somehow wrapped the cable around a protruding nail on the wall, then around his neck, finally sagging down.

Death hadn't come quickly. No, not at all. The boy's tongue hangs over a slack jaw, his eyes bulge and his fingernails are a deep blue. He'd strangled himself, and slowly, the pain of the cable preferable to the pain Johnny-Boy planned to deliver.

◆

Johnny-Boy's pissed and frustrated, but there's nothing he can do, no one to punish. Still, he kicks the boy in the ribs, watches him jump and settle, a bag of suet. Then he goes to work. He enters a numerical code into the padlock, pulls it free, then unwraps the cable, exposing a narrow wound cut deep into the boy's neck. Johnny-Boy feels no pity, nor any true regret except for the lost hours. He grabs the boy's heels and drags him out of the shed, across the mix of grass and weed that covers the yard around the house, all the way to the barn. Disposal is a crucial part of Johnny-Boy's calculations. If at all possible, bodies should never be found, and Johnny-Boy's located a dumping site in Sprague County. Unfortunately, dawn is on the way, a dim glow on the horizon. The shift change at the Nissan site is only an hour away and he needs to get to the bar he tends.

A large freezer, its sides rusted, its cord and plug missing, rests in the shadows against a wall. Johnny-Boy drags the kid across the floor, opens the freezer, lifts the boy, and dumps him inside. The body will begin to smell as the day warms, attracting carrion eaters like those coyotes he saw earlier. Crows, too, even vultures and rats. As Johnny-Boy closes the lid, he decides to have a little fun when he returns from work at 2:00 A.M. He'll set the body out behind the barn and wait, suppressed rifle in hand. Johnny-Boy's good with a rifle, especially one powerful enough to drive a bullet through one side of a coyote's body and out the other.

◆

An hour later, his Johnny-Boy persona shed, Paul Ochoa's sitting on a stool inside the Coolwater Bar & Grill on the southern end of Boomtown, that strip of chaos on the eastern side of the construction zone. Paul Ochoa tends bar at the Coolwater seven days a week, a schedule he chose. As Ochoa, he's reliable, efficient, and keeps his hands out of the till, the last a big plus in his manager's eyes.

The Coolwater's a drinker's bar, designed to accommodate ordinary working men usually content with a shot or a beer or both. That's good because Paul Ochoa's not a mixologist or anything close to a mixologist. If pressed, he can put together an old fashioned or a Manhattan, even a half-assed martini. But Moscow mules, mojitos? He'd have to consult a recipe book.

Paul Ochoa's come to the Coolwater, a bare-bones storefront business, ostensibly to get the bar ready to open. That's what he'll tell the Coolwater's manager, Matt Browner, if Browner shows up, which he rarely does. The bar's a small fish in Matt's pond, one of the reasons Paul Ochoa likes the job. The rest of the staff, two women, will arrive ten minutes before the bar officially opens. They're never early, which allows Ochoa to sit, as he is now, on a barstool tucked in the shadows behind the front window, pressing a pair of self-focusing binoculars to his eyes, relentlessly sweeping the Nissan's worker-entry gate as the workers pass through. Looking for Theo Diopolis, who's yet to show his face.

Find Diopolis, kill Diopolis, move the fuck on. The story of Johnny-Boy's life, the only story he wants to tell.

CHAPTER TWO

DELIA MARIOLA

We're at home. Me, my son, Danny, his girlfriend, Fetchin' Gretchen, and my partner, Zoe Parillo. I'm the city of Baxter's chief of detectives, which sounds exalted, but Danny and I live in a two-bedroom house, a cube with a sloping roof. Living room and kitchen are jammed into one space with the living room divided, one side for the living part, the other for eating. Our single bathroom takes a fair chunk out of Danny's bedroom, though neither bedroom is very large.

While Danny was still young and my cop/mom life barely allowed time for a deep breath, I'd more or less ignored the aesthetics. My home was clean and the furniture on the better side of shabby, but that was the best I could do. Now, with Danny able to care for himself and my salary a good deal higher, I've bought a new leather couch with matching chairs and a dining room table that doesn't wobble like a drunken flamenco dancer. Two posters hang on the wall behind the couch, crime-movie posters. They've been up for years, but I recently added a pair of drawings purchased at what passes for an estate auction in Baxter. Done by the same hand, they're unsigned, sparsely sketched views of an anonymous prairie in winter. I find one especially compelling. In the foreground, the withered remains of last season's goldenrod bow toward the earth. In the distance, a single buffalo, its breath steaming in the frigid air, grazes on whatever dried grass it can uncover with its hooves. A weak sun hangs at the horizon, whether preparing to rise or set I can't tell.

Surely intended by the artist, the scene speaks to perseverance, to patience, to endurance. But maybe not intended, I sense a dogged unrelenting loneliness that mocks the noise and bustle of my city. We're all about gung ho in Baxter, full speed ahead, cash and dash. There's a car factory to build, jobs for all, money to spend, new cars and homes to buy as fast as they can be constructed. What's infinity compared to all that?

◆

A gigantic smart TV that's about as the dumb as the mutts I deal with every day rests on a sideboard across from the couch. Danny's always been a serious child, forming goals and the means to achieve them. Now he sits for hours after dinner, baseball in hand, watching videos on the art of pitching. Which is what we're about tonight. The art of pitching, what it means, what it takes to master the craft.

When the doorbell rings, Danny's at the sink, rinsing and stacking dishes in the dishwasher. It's Danny's turn, simple as that, and while he didn't beg off, he doesn't want to be seen with a sponge in his hand when our visitors come through the door. That would be Jack Harmon, coach of the Goldman High Warriors, and a man named Gene Famello. Danny shuts off the water, then grabs a dish towel and dries his hands.

Gene Famello played minor league baseball, rising briefly to the triple-A level before injuries, as he tells it, drove him from the game. These days he runs Aspirants Baseball in California, a camp with close connections to Stanford University's Division I baseball scholarship program.

◆

I watch my son cross the room. He's what another generation would call strapping, already six-two and still growing. Meanwhile, I'm remembering him at three, climbing into my bed after a nightmare, clutching the stuffed bear that kept him safe.

Coach Harmon is Coach Harmon, a middle-aged man with a ready smile who loves the game and his players equally. In college, he was an occasional starter at second base for Michigan's baseball team, but that's as far as it went. He strides in now, smile in place. The man with him, Gene Famello, outweighs Harmon by fifty pounds, most of it in his gut. A role model he's not, yet between the twinkly blue eyes and firm jaw he projects a casual confidence that reminds me of a criminal defense lawyer before a jury. But I'm not sensing grifter, and for good reason. After the appointment was made, I assigned one of my cops, Clyde Norman, to research Aspirants Baseball. As Baxter's police department has expanded, some of our veterans have demonstrated unusual talents. Clyde's our data czar. Marriages, divorces, deeds, taxes, lawsuits for and against. If it's there, Clyde will find it.

According to Clyde, Famello's camp is well-known and well-respected. And fully booked by late April. He doesn't need our money.

◆

Introductions are made and hands are shaken. This afternoon, Danny worked out for coach and Famello. The session was private and I was not invited.

"What you have to do, Mom, is go with your stuff," Danny had explained over breakfast. "Whatever you have, you have. You can't wave a magic wand and suddenly get better."

Now we'll find out whether Danny's "stuff" met expectations.

I'm serving coffee and an assortment of mini-pastries from a new bakery, Cunning Confections, one of four to open on Baxter Boulevard in the last six months. There are strawberry tarts, napoleons, lemon meringue mini-pies, and tiramisu cups, all bite-sized and neatly arranged. They lie on a platter next to a pot of coffee, French roast. I'm half expecting Famello to offer some unctuous comment about the house, or even how much he's enjoying our little city, but the man, as he sips his coffee, appears tired. He's come to Baxter on Coach Harmon's suggestion, but only because they played college ball together.

"Your son is very talented," he tells me. "Most high school pitchers throw eighty to eighty-five miles an hour. A few touch ninety, but they're seventeen and eighteen. Danny's sixteen."

I'm tempted to remind him that I know Danny's age, this jerk who's come to take him away from me. Stanford is fifteen hundred miles from Baxter. It's true, though. Toward the end of Goldman High's baseball season, Danny's fastball had been virtually unhittable. When he got it over the plate.

◆

"Do you think he can win a scholarship?" This from the always practical Gretchen Somerset. A mommy type with privileges.

"I don't make promises." Famello shakes his mostly bald head. "Or maybe I can make this promise. The sessions are two weeks long. At some point during those two weeks, scouts from Oklahoma, Notre Dame, Texas, and a half-dozen others will show up. A scout from Stanford attends every session. I expect Major League scouts, too, looking at players who want to enter the minors out of high school. That much I can promise."

I'm not having it. I like Gretchen, even admire her, a girl as goal directed as my son. But a direct reply is in order. "That doesn't answer the question, Gene. As I understand it, you charge attendees eight hundred for the camp. The rest is on the camper. Hotel, meals outside of lunch and transportation costs. So, I'm not asking you to make promises. On a scale of one to ten, how would you rate Danny against other pitchers at your camp?"

"Against all the kids, about an eight. Against sixteen-year-olds, a ten." He pauses long enough to pop a napoleon into his mouth, then smiles. "That's really good." He casts loving eyes on a tiramisu cup before continuing. "Here's what struck me this afternoon, watching your boy pitch. Danny throws with conviction. There's nothing tentative. He must've been nervous, right? How could he not be? Only he was so tightly focused on each pitch that I couldn't see it. That's a big deal." He turns to Danny after a short pause. "You have a fair way to go, Danny, before you're ready to face hitters at a Division One school. You're tipping your pitches, for example, by drawing your arm back farther on your fastball than on your changeup. College coaches will spot the difference before you finish your warm-ups. Also, your two-seam fastball has good movement, but it runs straight across the plate. You need tilt and we can show you how to get it."

Danny listens quietly, not showing emotion. Maybe he's already aware of these imperfections.

"What about Mike?" he asks.

Danny and Mike Taney have been friends for years, the tightest of tight buddies. At Danny's insistence, Mike was included in this afternoon's workout. Now he's insisting again. He won't allow Mike to be ignored.

Famello sighs and look down at the pastries for a moment. I have the feeling he's been here before. His tone, when he speaks, is quiet, but firm. "Mike's a talented kid, Danny. He likes playing baseball, but I don't . . . I think he lacks the drive for perfection that pushes you forward. That said, if he signs up for the camp, we'll improve him. A scholarship isn't off the table." Famello reaches up to scratch the back of his neck and his eyes reach toward the ceiling. What to say next? "Think about this tonight, Danny, before you go to sleep. Last year, more than 480,000 kids played high school baseball. Almost 35,000 played college ball. Exactly 906 men played in the majors. In my mind, even to have a chance, you need to commit yourself. Totally."

My phone rings as Famello glances at his watch. It's Detective Blanche Weber. I stand up. Blanche knows about Danny's showcase, so whatever's happening, it needs my attention. "I have to take this. Give me a couple minutes." I carry the phone into a clear, crisp night before answering. "Hey, Blanche, what's up?"

"Got a body, boss. In a field off Route 25."

"In Sprague County?"

"In what used to be Sprague County before we expanded. It's ours now." She hesitates for just a moment. "Boss, it's Case Dixon."

"I'm on my way."

◆

I pocket the phone and head back inside, explaining even as I come through the door. "Sorry, folks, but duty calls." I glance at Zoe. She'll keep an eye on things in my absence. "Stay as long as you want."

Famello rises. "Actually, I have a plane to catch at an airport fifty miles from here. So, Danny, if you decide to come, do yourself a favor. This spring, during the season, don't throw anything off-speed. We'll teach you to throw curves and sliders without hurting your arm."

"Okay, I got it."

"And one more thing. If you're thinking Stanford, you'll need combined SATs touching fourteen fifty." Famello glances over at Gretchen. "Keep his shoulder to the wheel, Gretchen. You can't major in push-ups at Stanford."

To Gretchen, right? The girlfriend, not the mother?

◆

Zoe follows me outside. She knows me well enough to know when I'm worried. Which I am. Case Dixon's parents reported him missing three days ago. A good kid, they insisted, who slept in his own bed at night.

"It's bad?" Zoe asks.

"They're all bad, honey."

But this one could be a lot worse. We get several missing-teen reports every week. Almost all turn up after a couple days and we don't make much of an effort to locate them in the short term. Nor am I briefed on every missing kid unless we have reason to suspect foul play. Did we do anything to locate Case Dixon, missing for three days? Case's father, James Dixon, operates a lumberyard close to the construction site and sits on the board of the local Chamber of Commerce. A man of influence, no doubt, influential enough to merit a face-to-face with the chief of detectives. Afterward, I'd assigned one of our newer detectives, Stuart Harrison, to investigate. The bad news is that I have no idea what Stuart may or may not have done.

Zoe gives me a hug. "You look worried. About the call? About Danny eyeing a school in California? Which?"

"All of the above." I take a step toward my car, then turn back. "I'm supposed to want what's best for my child, right? And I know my child has a dream. And I know the camp will move him toward his dream. But Stanford? Scholarships? Major League scouts? I don't see a place for me in all this."

"Delia, do you know what Danny told me the other day?"

"Nope."

"He wants to use any bonus money he gets to buy you a new car. A Porsche."

"A Porsche?" Somehow, I can't imagine myself tooling down Baxter Boulevard in a Porsche. A Jeep, maybe, but not a Porsche. Old men drive Porsches when they're out to impress young women who should know better. "Let's dump the pity party. I have a body to attend."

"Don't you leave crime scenes to your detectives?"

"Not this one."

CHAPTER THREE
BLANCHE WEBER

The scene could only be worse if there was a kid involved, although you could reasonably say that Case Dixon's still a kid. I don't turn away, though, unlike Patrolman Jake Nurine. Nurine's a prime example of what I've been whining about for the past few months. The Baxter PD's expanding at warp speed. And yes, I can understand why. Ever since Nissan chose Baxter for the location of its new plant, the city's been soaking up newcomers like a dry sponge in boiling water. And the city was surely dry before that announcement, just another Rust Belt disaster, the population shrinking year after year as not only our best and brightest, but even our CFAs, our complete fucking assholes, deserted the ship.

More residents, more cops. Simple, right? Or so Baxter's city council decided. And the fact that our new residents were transient construction workers only made the need more urgent. More cops, and then more cops, just what the voters ordered.

You don't have to be a Harvard scholar (hated above all others in these parts) to predict that among those hastily hired recruits, men with the mentality of Russian prison guards would find their way onto the job. The description fits Jake Nurine perfectly, right down to the blond hair, the low forehead, and biceps as big as his head. His default expression is a sneer, a man who doesn't get out of your way, a man you walk around.

The better news is that right now, as we speak, the knucklehead's vomiting onto the grass by the side of road. We've got a body, and, yeah, as murdered bodies go, this one's seriously ugly. But Jake wouldn't be here if he wasn't a CFA. Jake should be with the two patrol officers directing traffic around my crime scene. But Jake barged right in and now he's contaminated the scene, an indiscretion for which my boss, Captain Delia Mariola, will surely make him pay.

◆

Speaking of which, Delia pulls up while Jake's wiping his mouth. We're buddies, sort of, me and Delia. Or at least we've worked together several times without her bullying me, or making a pass at me either. Unlike many of her male counterparts on the force.

Delia's quick, always has been. She's on Jake Nurine almost as soon as she ducks under the tape and walks onto the scene. I mean right in his face.

"What the fuck is this?"

"Hey, I . . ."

"No, I take that back. Why are you here? Why aren't you on the other side of the tape?"

"I . . ." Jake stutters away, probably hoping Delia will supply an answer of her own, which I know she won't. His eyes tighten for a moment, then relax when his small brain happens on a response. "I thought I might know him."

"And what?"

"I thought I might help with an ID."

"So, you just ducked under the tape, walked across the scene, and took yourself a long look?" Delia glances at the puddle in the grass. "Or a short look, as the case may be."

"Hey, I'm sorry . . ."

Delia shakes her head. "I want you to go back to the house and wait for me. I don't care how long. Wait."

◆

This isn't how weak little women talk to Jake. Not to massive Jake, the juiced-out knucklehead firmly committed to the doctrine of might makes right. And then, technically, Delia is chief of detectives, while Jake's a patrol officer working under Saul Rawling, our chief of patrol.

I can see the gears revolving inside Jake's tiny brain. All our new hires are probationary employees for their first six months. They can be summarily fired, no explanation necessary, and no appeal to a higher power. It's already happened. And did I mention that the force isn't unionized?

"This ain't right."

Delia points to Jake's puddle. "Our coroner will need a written report to explain this mess. Have it ready. Did you touch anything?"

"No, I . . ."

"Good, then we'll only need an imprint of your shoe soles in case we find impressions at the scene. Now take off."

Jake's eyes narrow and his mouth tightens as he displays a pre-attack threat posture that falls as flat as his IQ. Delia doesn't flinch. Fight or flight? The jerk decides to walk through door number two.

◆

It's a beautiful night, crisp and clear, with the stars veiled by lacy clouds drifting slowly from west to east. We're at the new border between Baxter and Sprague counties. If Case Dixon's body had been found on the other side of Route 25, the case would belong to the Sprague County sheriff. On this side, it's ours.

I approach the body alongside Delia, neither of us speaking. As I said, we've worked together before and we commonly study crime scenes independently before comparing notes. Delia takes her time, squatting alongside Case Dixon without touching him. The boy's naked, lying on his back, left arm above his head, right jutting out, legs crossed at the ankles. It's obvious at a glance that he wasn't killed here. Pulled by gravity, blood settles in the parts of the body closest to the ground after death. The process is called lividity. So if a corpse is left on its back for a few hours, the backs of the legs, the back, and the buttocks will take on a purple color deep enough to be easily recognized. Once completed, the condition is permanent.

In this case, Case Dixon's blood has settled almost entirely into his lower back, his buttocks, and the bottoms of his thighs. His upper torso and lower legs are white. I'm thinking he was sitting in a chair and strangled from behind, say with an electrical cord. Narrow and deep ligature marks around his neck indicate strangulation, but cause of death will be finally determined at his autopsy.

It wasn't the lividity, though, or the ligature marks that caused Patrolman Jake Nurine to drop his dinner inside the crime scene. Case Dixon was tortured. Chunks of his flesh have been torn away from every part of his body, with some of the wounds obviously fresher than others. His suffering must have been immense, a nightmare that wouldn't end. This is not something I want to think about. No, better to step back, reduce the victim to an autopsy chart with the wounds indicated here, there, and everywhere. No room for empathy, only for anger, revenge being the order of the day even knowing that no penalty open to government, even the lethal, will come remotely close to balancing the scales. At the same time, I can't stop imagining what I'd do to this perp if I had the time and the right.

◆

"Blanche." Delia calls my name without looking up. "The cop assigned to the missing persons investigation. It was Stuart Harrison, right?"

"Yeah, Stuart." I'm about to add that I've found him reliable in the past, but Delia cuts me off.

"Call him into the house, pronto. Like right now, Blanche. I don't care if he's in midstroke. We'll be going back in a few minutes and I want him waiting."

Delia has what's called command presence. She orders, you comply, but this time she adds an explanation. "The family has to be notified and I want to make sure we get there first." She gestures to a passing car. "Before somebody figures out what's happening here and makes a phone call."

I back off and take out my cell. I don't have Stuart's phone number handy, but it only takes a moment to get it from the duty sergeant. Stuart answers on the second ring.

"Hi, Stuart, it's Blanche Weber."

"Hey, what's up."

"Mariola wants you in the house forthwith. Like yesterday."

"Am I in trouble?"

"Only if you're not there when she gets back. That'd be a half hour from now."

◆

I turn back to Delia as Arshan Rishnavata, our cardiologist/coroner, pulls up. We've been trying to recruit a trained medical examiner for some time, but as we don't have our own pathology lab and our city's almost dead center in the country's flyover zone, trained applicants have been hard to come by.

Arshan leans under the tape and steps onto the crime scene, only to be stopped by Delia. "He's dead as dead can be, Arshan. The paramedics have been and gone. I don't want you to touch him until the Crime Scene Unit processes the scene."

"He's been identified?" Arshan wants to know.

"Not your problem, not yet. But you might consider this. Everything we do is liable to be second-guessed. And by we, I mean you and me and the Baxter Police Department. And, oh yeah, the mayor and the entire city council."

"And a pleasant evening to you, too, Delia."

Delia shakes her head. "The whole city's gonna be lookin' over our shoulders. We have to get it right. You can come back later, if you want, or wait in your car. But I want you off my crime scene until it's processed."

My crime scene? I can't say I like the sound of that, or that I can do anything about it, the chain of command being forged of unbreakable links. At least in the minds of superior officers.

◆

"Look, Blanche, I'm sorry I told Arshan that I was in charge. It's your case and I'm gonna let you run it. That way, if the shit rolls downhill, I can blame you." Delia's sense of humor is always a little off base. Most times I'm not sure that she's kidding. "But with Arshan, you have to be firm and direct. The guy rationalizes every impulse that jumps into his head."

I let that sit for a minute, then ask, "What do you make of the scene?" We're in Delia's car. One of the uniforms will drive my unit back to the house.

"The ligature marks on his right wrist," Delia responds. "Why?"

"That's how he was restrained."

"Yeah, surely, but one thing bothers me."

"Why only one wrist? And why no sign of restraint on his ankles."

"What else?"

We're running fast, the GPS guiding us from state road to county road and back to state road until we pass over the northern end of the Nissan construction site and onto Baxter Boulevard. I don't care for the interrogation, but I can understand the urgency. Case Dixon's father, Jimmy Dixon, is a world-class jerk, a self-made man whose rise in life has gone to his head. He knows everything about everything, especially when he's been drinking, a nightly habit that begins after work in Randy's, a club on the northern end of Baxter Boulevard.

"I don't wanna jump to any conclusions, Delia, but maybe whoever kidnapped the boy wanted him to fight back. Not get away, because he probably couldn't, but to struggle . . ."

"Why?"

I don't like the answer that jumps into my head, but as it's the only answer I have. "Because it was more fun that way." Delia's staring through the windshield, eyes fixed on the road ahead. "A thrill killing? I mean we can hope it was about revenge, that we can connect Case with his murderer. But we can't rule out a serial killer. There's no way."

"Those two words, Blanche? Serial killer? I do not want you to say those two words out loud to anyone but me. If the public needs to be informed, I'll inform them. Me or the commissioner."

◆

Delia pulls into her parking slot at Baxter PD's headquarters behind city hall. We're out of the car almost before she flips the key and pulls it from the ignition. Sergeant Pascal's manning the desk, a sharp-eyed veteran of twenty years. He nods once, then says, "Harrison's waiting in the squad room."

That would be Detective Stuart Harrison, assigned to investigate Case Dixon's disappearance. We find him standing by the coffee machine, filling his personal mug. On one side of the mug, a giant stands with his right fist curled around the top of an oil well. On the other: OKLAHOMA PRIDE. Tall and lanky, Harrison projects a rather lazy image. The impression is misleading. He's not the fastest worker in the squad room, but he's meticulous, crossing those t's before they get crossed for him.

Delia motions Harrison into her office. She waits for him to pass, then for me, before closing the door behind her. "Case Dixon, Stu, tell me you investigated his disappearance."

"Yes, ma'am, I did." Harrison's words come slowly, his drawl pronounced. His eyes are watchful, though unafraid.

"What have you got?"

"The boy is far from the dutiful son his daddy described. 'Bout as far as you can get." Harrington sports a mustache that curls to the edge of his mouth. He tugs at one end as he considers his words. "You want, I'll get my notes. Might get the names wrong if I have to fall back on memory alone."

Delia raises a hand. "Let's rely on your memory for now, but I'll need copies of your paperwork and your notes on my desk. Tonight, Stuart."

"A done deal, captain. Now, first thing Monday, I interviewed the boy's guidance counselor at Goldman High. His math teacher, as well. The counselor told me the boy was truant so many times, the school would've kicked him out if his father hadn't threatened to sue. Way it is now, this counselor—her name was Consuela something—figures the boy'll flunk out anyway. The math teacher's name was Mack something. He confirmed the counselor's evaluation. Said Case ran with a gang of slackers. Not violent, right, not criminal, more like a loser's club."

"You leave it there?"

"No, ma'am. Mack something named a few names, other kids in the club, and I went right after 'em. Found his girlfriend, or so she claims to be, and I didn't have to ask about the drugs. Lola is what the girl calls herself, and she had a hard time standin' up when I spoke with her. Told me that her, Case, and more than a dozen of their buddies partied together on Friday. Startin' in midafternoon at a vacant shack out in Oakland Gardens. I had to wiggle it out of her, but she admitted they were combinin' mushrooms with Ecstasy when Dixon caught himself a bad trip. Took off around midnight and that's the last she saw of him. Two other kids, boys, told me the same thing. A party with drugs aplenty. Case was there and then he wasn't. Wasn't there the next day, either, but nobody thought much of it. Seems Case Dixon's conversation was generally confined to how much he hated his father and how he planned to run away soon as he put a few dollars in his pocket." Another twist of the mustache. "That's about it, captain."

Delia takes a seat on the edge of her desk. "Case Dixon's dead, Stu. Murdered, which I want you to keep to yourself until his parents are notified. But I gotta say, you did a good job. Real good. Thanks, I was afraid I'd have to face the family empty-handed."

CHAPTER FOUR
BLANCHE WEBER

We drive north along Baxter Boulevard, our silence interrupted by a train whistle off to the east. These days, as much construction material arrives by train as by truck. The outer walls on the factory are up, the roof as well, just in time for winter. Inside, plumbers and electricians run pipe and wire as the work moves into a new phase. Many of the workers who toiled on the outside have left for home. Others with different skills arrive every day.

And what if among these strangers, these ghosts here and gone a few months from now, there's a man who kills because he likes to kill? I know it's too early to draw any conclusions, that I'm peering into a crystal ball designed to induce paranoia. Maybe the case will go down in a few days. Maybe Case Dixon had an enemy whose hatred left him with no restraint, but I'm not holding my breath.

The Behavioral Unit at the FBI has been studying thrill killers for decades now and they generally refer to these murders as sexually motivated homicides. The obvious being the obvious, I have to conclude that thrill killers kill for the thrill. They like it, the terror, the panic, the screams, the disappearing life in their victims' eyes. It turns them on.

◆

"Tell you what, Blanche," Delia taps the wheel. "I'll take the lead with the family. Let them come to me for updates. Complaints too. That'll give you room to operate without James Dixon looking over your shoulder."

"Will I be working alone?"

"No. Take any two detectives you want. More if you need 'em."

We turn left on Howe Street, a cul-de-sac on the edge of Baxter Park. Halfway around, Delia pulls to the curb in front of a two-story Colonial. It's not the best house in the city and I think the Dixons could afford better. If better was available.

"I'm gonna check," I tell Delia as she shifts into park, "for any open homicides with injuries close to Case Dixon's. I'm thinking no, but it won't hurt to look. If the killer is new to the city, it might help to narrow things down. If that doesn't work, I'll try ViCAP."

ViCAP is the FBI's Violent Criminal Apprehension Program. They have a database of unsolved homicides designed to link related murders occurring in different jurisdictions.

◆

I hate notifications. Walking up to someone's house, knocking on the door. Hey, guess what, your father, mother, son, daughter is dead. No, I'm not callous, but it amounts to the same thing. Usually, the news hits so hard and fast, there's no wording sensitive enough to cushion the effect.

James Dixon answers the door. His wife, Maureen, stands behind him. A small woman with a perpetually resolute expression, she lays a hand on her husband's shoulder.

"Mr. Dixon, Mrs. Dixon," Delia says. "May we come in?"

James Dixon wears two faces. When he's courting the big contractors who've descended on the city, he's quick with a joke, a hale and hearty type. The rest of the time, he's a bulldog, head forward, lower lip pulled over the upper, dark eyes eternally suspicious. Now he seems caught in between and he hesitates for a second before stepping away from the door.

The Dixons lead us into an all-American living room. There's a gigantic eagle on a throw draped over the back of the sofa and a flag above the mantle. Another flag, decked out in what I assume to be rubies, sapphires, and diamonds, dominates the ring finger of Dixon's right hand.

"I'm sorry to have to tell you this," Delia says. "We found Case's body an hour ago. Near Sprague County."

Maureen lifts clenched fists to her chin and begins to tremble. She needs her spouse, but James Dixon retreats, his anger obvious. This can't happen to me. I'm James Dixon.

"How?" he demands.

"Homicide."

"He was killed?" Again, the offended tone.

"Pending an autopsy, we're investigating his death as a homicide. I don't expect that to change."

"I reported him missing a week ago."

In fact, the report was filed three days ago, but Delia's expression doesn't so much as flicker. Probably she saw it, or something like it, coming. "And we've been looking for him."

"But you never found him?"

Delia knows that any details shared with a belligerent loudmouth are likely to be repeated, perhaps to reporters. What does she want him to know? What does she want him to share?

"Case was at a party on Friday night. According to multiple witnesses, he left shortly before midnight by himself. So far, we haven't located anyone who's seen him since."

Dixon's mouth opens. He's about to make some further demand, but Maureen chooses that moment to cry out. Her wail pops the little bubble established by Delia and her husband. He turns to his wife then, startled, as if remembering her for the first time. Then he surprises me by taking her in his arms and whispering something I can't quite hear. His touch is gentle, loving, caring, and I can't make myself believe he's faking. James Dixon loves his wife, as he probably loves his son. That he's also a loudmouth jerk is like saying he's also balding, front to back.

"You provided us with a list of Case's friends when you reported him missing," Delia says after a moment. "Did he have any significant enemies?"

Wrong question. Dixon's eyes roll upward as he seizes on the possibility. Somebody did this, somebody has to pay, and he knows just who that person is. He's in charge again. He's in control. I read all this in face as his eyes open and his chin comes up, as he visibly calms in a matter of seconds.

"Yeah," he tells Delia. "A boy named Bard Henry. Trailer trash, detective. Father in prison, mother a drunk. When he got caught threatening kids for their lunch money, he blamed Case.

Called him a snitch and vowed revenge." Dixon shakes a finger. "Bard's almost eighteen, a senior. He's a giant compared to Case. Start with Bard Henry and I'm thinking you won't have to go much further."

Delia nods agreement, and, yes, we'll tap Bard Henry. But Case Dixon's injuries tell a long-term story. Some of his wounds were fresh, others had started to heal. We're talkin' days, not hours. We're also talkin' about a place to hold him while it went down. We're talkin' about careful preparation because a safe house has to be secured in advance. How likely is it that a schoolyard bully could pull that off? A shotgun blast, yeah? A knife in the gut, yeah. But several days of torture?

◆

I leave Delia, who's already calling her boss, Commissioner Taney. Our Crime Scene Unit's on scene and Delia's agreed to monitor their progress. I went through the immediate area when I first arrived and I doubt there's anything to find. A car stopped, four wheels on dry asphalt. A body was dumped. A car drove away. My only real hope was that the perp left shoe prints in the hard earth at the side of the road. He didn't.

Back at the house, I find Stu Harrison. His tall, bony frame is draped over his desk as he deciphers handwritten notes. He sits up when I approach, his long face serious.

"What's up, Blanche?"

"I'm tapping you for the investigation." I smile, but Stuart only nods. "The party Case attended last Friday. Did you get an address?"

"Uh-uh. The house ain't no more than a shack. Hasn't been lived in for years. Doesn't have an address. But I had Case's girlfriend take me past."

"Let's take a ride. I want a look at that shack."

◆

The shack's in Oakland Gardens, the neighborhood bordering the construction site. Before Nissan, it had fallen apart year by year, mirroring the decay of the whole city. Its houses leaned to one side as their foundations crumbled. Roofs sagged, windows were broken or covered with sheets of plywood, candles flickered at night as junkie squatters prepared their evening fix. The Yards, the neighborhood closest to the packing plants, was already gone, with Oakland Gardens next on everyone's list. It needed demolition, a chance to start over, but a dying city couldn't find the money for a decent burial.

We're past that phase in the history of Baxter. As I turn right on Caseman Avenue, we enter a block lined on one side with attached, three-family town houses. All brand spanking new, all clean red brick and bright windows that reflect the newly installed streetlights. Already sold too.

"How stoned was Case when he left the party?" I ask as we cross into an unimproved block. Most of the homes have been demolished or collapsed on their own, leaving rubble-strewn lots behind. The few still standing are empty except for one unit where candles flicker behind broken windows. Our reigning pols predicted that once the Nissan construction produced jobs for all, the drug epidemic would at least slow down. That hasn't happened. Our tiny narcotics squad's making as many arrests as ever.

"Case was blasted, according to his girlfriend. Ecstasy and mushrooms, a stimulant with a psychedelic. According to Lola, she begged him not to go off alone. He agreed, then disappeared ten minutes later."

"Did anyone look for him?"

"Nope." Stuart pushes his feet into the fire wall as he stretches out. "See, these kids, they see themselves as losers. Always were, always will be. It's sad, ya know. Givin' up when they're so young. But they're all about piercings and tattoos and stayin' stoned on anything they can swallow or put up their nose. They have no expectations."

The housing stock in Oakland Gardens has a sameness to it, even broken-down. Small, single-story homes, three bedrooms at most, tiny yards. The party house where Case Dixon was last seen is distinguished only by a low, chain-link fence lying on a sidewalk that's little more than tilted concrete slabs.

"You go inside, Stuart?"

"Just took a quick look from the front door."

"And what did you see?"

"Garbage piled in a corner—they weren't sittin' in it—and paraphernalia, wrappers mostly, on a plank table near a car's rear seat they were usin' for a sofa. Also, a rat. 'Bout as big as a steer. Didn't move a muscle, right? Just stared right back at me. Like a dare." He tries to cross his legs, but there's not enough room. "You wanna go inside?"

"Uh-uh. I want you to call in to the sergeant. I think Denny Pascal's on the desk. Tell him you're working a homicide and you need a car to sit on the house overnight. I'm gonna let CSU work it first." I pause until Stuart nods, his bony chin bobbing up and down. "Tell me, did any of the kids you interviewed mention a boy named Bard Henry? Supposed to be Case's enemy."

"Matter of fact, Bard Henry's name was mentioned. Not in a serious way, though. Wasn't at the party either."

"What about the father and mother? They gave you a list of Case's friends. Did either mention an enemy?"

"It's like with the kids. Bard Henry's name was mentioned, but more casual than anything else."

CHAPTER FIVE

JOHNNY-BOY

It's eight o'clock and customers at the Coolwater should be standing two deep at the bar. Instead, three men and a woman huddle before a TV. They're watching a baseball playoff game as they nurse their drinks. Jim Beam White Label, beer chasers for the most part, a C&C highball. The woman squeezes a wedge of lime into her rum and Coke.

Nobody's paying attention to the man behind the bar, the man they know as Paul Ochoa, not even Sherman, the middle-aged man seated as far away from the television as he can. Sherman's the Coolwater's resident dealer and he's nursing a bottle of Bud, waiting patiently for the day shift to finally clock out. Overtime on the site is mandatory. They say, you stay.

For Johnny-Boy, it isn't about the money. Not so the two women sitting at a table out front. Bar girls both, they're focused on the tips they're not earning. Wondering if they'll make rent at the end of the month.

◆

When the door opens, all eyes turn, perhaps expecting a parade of thirsty construction workers. Instead, they get Matt Browner, the Coolwater's manager. Browner's gut precedes him as he crosses the room. He's a tall man, and broad, but too out of shape to be personally threatening. Much to his regret.

Johnny-Boy doesn't know who owns the Coolwater. Only that Browner, despite jowls that start at his earlobes, speaks with an assurance that guarantees the sort of backing Johnny-Boy doesn't need to encounter. Meanwhile, Browner's huffing away, the short walk from the parking lot to the bar taking a toll. Johnny-Boy figures the man's got ten years at most till his heart gives out.

"Where's the action, Paul?"

"Mandatory overtime. They'll be along pretty soon."

"Hope so. We're not doin' so good. The rent here's off the fuckin' charts."

"I'm pourin' as fast as I can," Johnny-Boy says, "but if you wanna raise prices, I got no problem."

"Raise the price? You kiddin'? We're already at six bucks a pop."

Browner stares at Johnny-Boy as if he expects his bartender to disagree, but Johnny-Boy's expression doesn't change. The conversation's over as far as he's concerned. It's already gone too far. He's the bartender. He pours the drinks. The rest of the bullshit's up to the boss.

"Awright," Browner says, leaning forward, "the man to my left. What's his name again?"

"Sherman."

"Well, Sherman's dealing meth and coke inside the bar. And don't ask me how I know. I know."

"In the toilet," Johnny-Boy says, "not out in the open."

"You think what? That an undercover won't get to him? You think the toilet's some kind of protection? You think the fuckin' city won't shut us down if there's open dealing in the bar? My people have connections inside the cops and their strategy has changed. Like they've become a lot more practical. Their drug eradication program was a total flop. They took out the top crew, but now there's a dozen crews feeding the city." Browner stares at his bartender for a moment, but Johnny-Boy only nods. "The cops have decided on the next best option. Arrests, Paul. Lots and lots of arrests. Lots of aggression too. When the good citizens of Baxter complain about crime, the pols counter with the stats. The city's one and only jail is overflowing, the courts are months behind, and there's no money to expand. Anybody for a tax increase?"

Johnny-Boy wonders if Browner's aware of the conflict. Workers come into the bar, most after a day of reasonably hard labor. They have a couple drinks, they get tired, they start thinkin' about dinner and bed. Unfortunately, they have no family to greet them when they get home. Only a bed, sometimes in what amounts to a dormitory. So, what they do is snort a line or two of coke or meth, and fast as you can snap your fingers, they're wide awake and ready to pay for a few more drinks.

"You want me to get rid of him?"

"That's exactly what I want."

Johnny-Boy drifts along the bar until he's face-to-face with Sherman. He beckons Sherman with a finger and Sherman responds by leaning across the bar. As he comes forward, Johnny-Boy hits him, hard and very fast, a right hand that catches Sherman just below his left eye. Sherman flies off his stool to land on his back. He's staring up at the ceiling and his eyes are open, but he doesn't attempt to get up for a moment. Then he rolls onto his knees and pauses, his body listing from side to side, until he rolls onto his back for a second time. In no hurry, Johnny-Boy ducks under the service station at the end of the bar. He walks over to Sherman, grabs him by the collars of his shirt and his jacket, drags him out the door.

When he returns to the bar, all eyes follow him, including Matt Browner's. He advances a few steps before fixing his gaze on the workers. "No dealing inside the bar. Nowhere, right? You wanna get stoned, take it outside." He pauses here. The men and the one woman are staring at him, seeming as stunned as poor Sherman. In truth, Johnny-Boy felt absolutely nothing when he drove his fist into Sherman's cheekbone. A job to be done, like fetching a keg of beer from the storage room in back, like pressing glasses into the glass washer, like rinsing and putting them away.

Johnny-Boy flashes a quick smile, equally free of emotion, then says, "Next round's on me. Belly up."

◆

Johnny-Boy serves the drinks without contributing to the buzz. The important thing is that Browner and the patrons are looking at him with new respect. They know that he had a reason to hit Sherman, that the violence wasn't random, though it did come out of nowhere. Their bartender's not crazy.

Matt Browner shakes his head when Johnny-Boy finally approaches. The punch was unexpected, but that's not where Browner's focused. The speed of the punch? The power? Browner recognizes talent when he sees it. Nevertheless, he can't allow himself to be intimidated.

"I didn't tell ya to do that."

"I know, boss. Sorry."

"What do you hope to accomplish?"

When two men walk through the door and take a table for six, one of the bar girls, Sharon, leaps out of her chair. Finally.

"The customers at the bar will tell the ones comin' in now. About Sherman and no dealin' in the bar. Word will spread and that'll be that. We'll still have dealers inside, only these dealers will do business in the parking lot."

"Yeah, you hope so, but keep an eye out anyway. Hear me?"

"I'm on it, boss. No worries." Johnny-Boy endures another hard-ass stare. Browner needs to pound his chest at every opportunity, this man who can't walk across the room without wheezing. Johnny-Boy understands and is perfectly willing to pretend he's impressed. Means to an end is what it's all about. And truth be told, he has needs of his own. "How about whores?"

"You get whores?"

"On and off. They're not takin' their business into the toilet, but they're definitely makin' dates."

Browner runs his right hand, palm and fingers over his face and jowls. "These men, they're a long way from home. Ya gotta figure . . . no, forget it. The cops are bustin' the whores on the street, like in busloads." He leans forward. "Boomtown ain't gonna last forever. A year from now, the factory'll be finished and that'll be the end. For the workers and us. We can't afford a shutdown. The whores wanna drink, okay. They wanna trick, throw 'em out."

◆

The Coolwater heats up fast after Browner leaves, the mandatory overtime only contributing to the collective thirst. Mostly men with a sprinkling of women, all in work clothes, dusty and ready for a shower. But not before havin' a couple drinks and maybe even gettin' lucky. It's like Browner said, "These men, they're a long way from home." Only he left out the women, who are also far from home. Johnny-Boy bears witness every night, the flirting, just enough hookups to make the possibility possible.

Johnny-Boy maintains a steady pace even when the Coolwater's at its busiest, ignoring the two girls, Sharon and Glory, who complain every time they approach the pickup station. Hustle it up, get the lead out. But if Johnny-Boy's not the fastest bartender in Boomtown, he's tireless, and by eleven thirty, the crowd thins. A quiet night with a single exception. Two men got mouthy at one point, but Johnny-Boy stepped in before a punch was thrown. He quietly ordered them to take their dispute to the parking lot and they cooled off in a hurry. Now he stands behind the bar, his remaining customers pretty far gone. At this point, he's expecting a regular named Sam to unburden himself. It happens almost every night.

"You got kids, Paul?"

"Uh-uh."

"You married?"

"Once."

"Didn't work out?"

"Nope, didn't."

One for the money, two for the show, three to get ready, and four to go. It's a monologue from here on. His wife, his kids, his mom and pop (sadly deceased), his dog, his home, his hometown, Thanksgiving, Christmas, and the Fourth of July. How he misses them, one and all, and equally.

The lament washes over Johnny-Boy without affecting him. He's always had a tolerance for addiction. Drugs of choice, in this case alcohol, become impossible to resist if indulged often enough. He oughta know because he tried to kick his own addiction way back when. Only to have the pressure build until he felt like he'd explode. The release when he finally caved was exquisite.

◆

The sad-sack story ends abruptly as Sam drops into a semi-stupor and lays his head on the bar. That's enough for Johnny-Boy and he's about to send the man home when Theo Diopolis walks through the door. The square head, the high brow, large eyes so closely set they remind Johnny-Boy of an owl's. A scar on his jaw is deep enough to pass for a cleft chin.

It's a *Holy shit!* moment, for sure, and Johnny-Boy tenses up, but only for a few seconds. Then he draws a mug of Coors for a customer at the end of the bar before approaching Diopolis.

"What can I get ya?"

"Jack, rocks. Water back."

Johnny-Boy pours and serves, trying to think of some way to open a conversation. He can't. And Diopolis doesn't engage with any of the Coolwater's few patrons. He chugs his Jack, follows it with a sip of water, finally nods to the barkeep before walking out the way he came in. So long.

◆

Johnny-Boy leaves the Coolwater at 2:45. He's cleaned the bar and the sink, dumped the wedges of lemon and lime, washed and dried the small bowls that held the thirst-inducing peanuts. He'll restock the speed rail and the beer fridge and the garnish station tomorrow. Another excuse to come in early.

The van's alternator light glows red for a moment when Johnny-Boy twists the key. A loose belt, which he'll tighten tomorrow morning. Then he's off on what has become a nightly expedition. Johnny-Boy isn't one of those serial killers who read serial killer books, but he's looked at a few, and what he's doing now is called trolling. He's never liked the word. There's no bait on the end of his hook. No hook for that matter. Nevertheless, his search for Case Dixon's replacement has begun.

The news came through at ten o'clock when KBAX broke away from the ball game to report a body discovered in the weeds off Route 25. No details, but Johnny-Boy knew who it was alright. He'd been on his way to the dump site when he was stopped at a Baxter PD checkpoint. This was exactly the unforeseen circumstance he'd been fearing from the beginning. If the cop who examined his license and registration had taken a close look at the rear of the van, Johnny-Boy's career would have come to an abrupt end. But the cop had only leaned close enough to smell alcohol or weed in the vehicle. Finding neither, he'd waved Johnny-Boy forward.

That was enough, though, to spook Johnny-Boy. He wasn't going to hang at a dump site, digging a grave, hoping his van wasn't spotted behind the trees. On the other hand, he couldn't take the kid, who was already beginning to stink, back to the barn. The obvious solution? A quick stop, drag the bitch into the weeds, goodbye and good riddance. And that's what he'd done.

◆

Now it's back to business, which in this case is mixed. He's looking for his next conquest and for Theo Diopolis. Johnny-Boy wants to get the last part out of the way and he cruises Main Street in Boomtown, stopping in at the few bars still operating. Just a quick look around. No questions, and no luck either.

Main Street is quiet with most of the clubs, brothels, and mini-casinos dark, but the road is well-lighted by activity in the construction zone. A giant Nissan logo—it has to be fifty yards across—is being attached to the facade. The sign dangles from a pair of cranes while workers in cherry pickers prepare the side of the building.

Johnny-Boy barely glances at the construction as he passes. He's much more interested in what's happening on a street that's far from deserted. The hookers are out, as they are every night, and if customers are few and far between, that's only led the girls to cluster on corners, waving to him as he passes, most in miniskirts that rise over their butts whenever they move. A few spin around to shake those butts at Johnny-Boy, who has zero interest in the willing. He continues on, exploring numerous side streets. No luck here either.

At this point, Johnny-Boy's not in a hurry. After a successful project, the intensity lowers, say from a raging scream to a nagging hum. And the trolling helps too. It's a message he sends to whatever demon drives him. I'm out here working. I haven't forgotten you.

◆

Johnny-Boy's mind drifts, though his eyes never stop moving. These days he often returns to the sequence of events that led him to his foster father, Garrison Granger. Those events began to unfold on the day he was born, his mama insane, his daddy unknown, the chaos even worse than the beatings. Waking up in the morning too young to tie his own shoes, wondering if he'd be fed.

Enough explanation, he tells himself, for an FBI profiler. The genes, the environment, the perfect storm. But his brain doesn't want to take Garrison Granger out of the equation. More than likely, without Granger, Johnny-Boy would have been just another dumb cracker. Maybe he'd rob a store, or burglarize the wrong house, or punch the crap out of the wrong citizen. Off to prison, on parole, back to prison, all the days of our lives.

◆

Garrison altered the fate of the twelve-year-old given to his care. No doubt, no questions to be asked. That was after Mom went off on Katie-Girl once too often, this time with cast-iron pan that crushed an already-dented skull. Katie-Girl never woke up despite the surgeries.

With plausible deniability off the table, Mama went to prison after a very short trial. That left Johnny-Boy to be delivered by Uriah County's Social Services into the care of Garrison Granger. Then promptly forgotten.

The sex was unpleasant, at least at first, but Johnny-Boy didn't fight it. He'd never known anything approaching mainstream culture. Under Mom's roof, big dominated little, simple as that. With Garrison, on the other hand, there were many compensations. A clean bed in a clean house, food whenever he wanted, jeans that weren't torn, shirts that weren't stained, and no beatings. His life became stable, order in lieu of chaos. Rigid order, true, but order nonetheless, and no school, which is what Garrison's version of homeschooling amounted to.

Johnny-Boy thrived.

◆

Johnny-Boy pilots the van along the street running across the top of the construction zone and into Oakland Gardens. Further on, near Baxter Boulevard, construction projects dot the neighborhood. This far east it's a wasteland, every house a shack, most of the shacks abandoned to vagrants and druggies. Vacant lots and yards are rubbish-strewn, everything from refrigerators to stripped cars to piles of garbage bags long ago torn open by rats. And there are many rats in Oakland Gardens. Johnny-Boy watches several rummage through a heap of something he doesn't quite recognize. A black hump next to one of the many saplings that have sprung up since the lot was cleared, nature on the rebound.

Johnny-Boy angles the van toward the curb so that his headlights reach into the lot. Then he knows. He's looking at a body, legs drawn into its chest, the fetal position marking the end of its days. He can't tell if the stiff is male or female, not from this far away, and he has no desire to come any closer. Not that he's squeamish. No, not at all, but it's none of his business. He puts the van in reverse, backs into the center of the street, straightens up. Then he's on his way. Still hunting.

CHAPTER SIX

DELIA

I start my workday in conference with Commissioner Vern Taney. We're in Vern's office, surrounded by memorabilia from his years as a high school football star. A half-deflated ball from the state championship, Vern shaking hands with Aaron Rodgers and Eli Manning at a cop conference, a long shelf bearing his many trophies. A pair of blue love seats face each other across a wooden coffee table. We take seats on either side.

The rumor mill would have Vern running for mayor or the House in a few years. Both are currently occupied by very elderly politicians. Time for new blood.

Vern's the commish and I'm a lowly chief of detectives. That I'd be the one to stop at Lena's Luncheonette for coffee and frosted crullers still warm from the oven was a simple given.

Vern takes a long pull at the coffee, seeming almost amused. "Why is it that we only meet these days when there's a problem? Didn't we used to be partners?"

We did, true, but as partners we had access to the same information at the same time. No more. Vern sits above us working cops, which makes him dependent on whatever info we decide to share. As no messenger wants to be executed for delivering bad news, there will always be news that isn't delivered. Of course, Vern knows I'm here to discuss Case Dixon, but he decides to begin casually.

"This guy from the baseball camp," Vern says.

"Gene Famello."

"Yeah, him. You think he's straight?"

Most likely, Vern wants to be told that Famello's a money-grubbing fraud. Sorry, Vern. "I had him checked out, him and the camp. Famello doesn't need our money. The camp's fully booked most of the year."

"Then why'd he come all the way to Baxter?"

"He and Coach Harmon played ball together in Michigan. That's one reason. Beyond that, I think Famello loves the game and the camp is a way of staying in it. Two boys who came through his camp are playing in the majors. That makes him relevant."

Vern reaches behind him to lift his championship football. "I had NFL hopes once upon a time. Until my father passed and I had to help support the family. So, you could believe me when I tell you that I don't want to step on Mike's dreams. He's my only son. But, Delia, I figure between the tuition, the plane fare, and the hotel, we're lookin' at five grand. With no guarantees."

"No argument, Vern, but a year at an in-state college will set us back twenty thousand dollars. Myself, I'm not thinking the camp's biggest benefit is the training. I'm thinkin' it's the college recruiters with scholarships in their wallets instead of cash."

I don't have anything to add. It is what it is. Vern replaces the football after a moment, then gets down to business. "Case Dixon. Where are we?"

"The missing person investigation went to Stuart Harrison. Lucky for us. Harrison interviewed Dixon's teachers and his counselor at Goldman High. Vern, the kid was a serious fuckup, barely holding on. According to friends, also interviewed by Harrison, Dixon attended a party in one of the abandoned properties in Oakland Gardens on Friday night. A party with mushrooms and Ecstasy on the menu. He left by himself around midnight, the last time any of his pals saw him. Or will admit to seeing him."

"Can I assume he was stoned out of his mind when he left?"

"Yeah, completely blasted. The other kids at the party claim they tried to talk him out of leaving."

Vern's a large man. As a boy, he would have been called hot by the cheerleading squad, but he's matured now, adding a few pounds to his waistline. His face has broadened as well, swapping his good-old-boy looks for something more reserved. Zoe calls it gravitas. Me, I'll settle for command presence.

"The autopsy's scheduled for an hour from now," I continue. "But I was at the crime scene."

"You mean the disposal site."

"Call it what you want, I'm near certain the boy was tortured for a long time before he died."

"Before he was murdered."

"Or killed himself."

"Seriously?"

"Just prepare yourself for either manner of death. And for James Dixon. When I did the notification, he was already claiming that we sat on the missing persons report."

"But we didn't."

"Unless we make a quick arrest, I doubt that's gonna matter." I pause, but Vern doesn't dispute the claim. "Okay, we'll begin by dragging everyone Stuart already interviewed into the house, along with a kid named Bard Henry. Supposedly, the boy threatened Case. I'm not thinking he's a viable suspect and I want to eliminate him, if possible, before James Dixon throws him to the wolves."

For the next few minutes, while Vern processes the details, we dig into our crullers and chug down the coffee. Lena makes all the pastries at her luncheonette. She generally arrives at three in the morning to bake the day's goodies, then opens whenever she's finished.

Vern breaks the silence. "What're you thinking, Delia? Who are we looking for?"

"Case Dixon was a gentle kid according to his friends. Yeah, he was a fuckup, but he wasn't robbing stores or dealing drugs. In fact, if you can believe his friends, he spent most of his time wasted."

"So, he had no real enemies?"

"None, who'd do . . . no, scratch that. It's too early to speculate and I'm gonna be late for the autopsy, which I don't want to start without me. The kids we plan to interview are already being picked up. They'll give us other names. I want to cover every base before I start lookin' for someone who kills for fun." I raise a finger. "Before I start lookin' for that needle in the haystack. And given the number of out-of-town workers in Baxter, we're talkin' about enough hay to fill a barn."

◆

I stop outside Vern's office to phone Saul Rawling, our chief of patrol. When he answers, I don't mince words. I'm already headed for the parking lot.

"I'm calling about one of yours, Saul. Jake Nurine. Last night, he walked onto my crime scene. A homicide, understand. And prominent too."

"Case Dixon?"

I shake my head. It's already out there. "Yeah, Case Dixon. And get this, he approaches the body, then pukes in the grass."

"He did this on his own?"

"Yeah, ducked under the tape. And caught an attitude when I chewed him out. Saul, the asshole's bad news."

"I'll talk to him."

"How 'bout firing him instead. He's probationary. All you have to do is find his performance unsatisfactory."

"Not that easy, Delia. He's my nephew." Rawling chuckles, a rumble that begins low in his chest. "What's it they say? Happy wife, happy life? I'll talk to him."

◆

I find Blanche Weber and Arshan Rishnavata in the basement/morgue at Baxter Medical Center. Arshan's a cardiologist by trade, a coroner only because the city couldn't afford a medical examiner when he was hired. That's changed and we'd have a qualified pathologist if we could lure one to Baxter. We've reached out to several, but thus far no takers. For some reason, they don't want to work in a poorly equipped hospital basement.

In his defense, I have to say that Arshan's improved over time. He's read the books, watched the videos, even taken a course or two online. A small man with black saucers for eyes, he seems eager today. Blanche only appears resigned. Her heavy jaw is locked, her lips compressed.

In a group, we move to a gurney and the body covered by a sheet. Arshan removes the sheet and slips it into a large evidence bag. Later, it'll go to the state forensic lab. I step forward to examine the body. Blanche follows.

Case Dixon's lying on his back, looking very young and very frail. His wounds are obvious enough, but my first take is the dirt covering him from head to toe. Not soil, but the kind of dust and debris that reminds me of the workers coming off the construction site. The dirt, in that case, is on the workers' clothing. Here it's on his skin and speaks to him being unclothed in a dirty environment for an extended length of time.

"He must've been kept inside," Blanche tells me. She's almost whispering. "The temperature's been down in the low forties at night. He wouldn't have survived outside through the first night."

I'm not too sure about that, but I know Blanche has the inside part right. Small gray splinters have attached themselves to some of his wounds. The sort of splinters I associate with a deteriorating wood floor. But you can find a hundred deteriorating wood floors in Oakland Gardens, or in the many abandoned farm buildings outside town.

"These splinters, Arshan, collect as many as you can."

"Yes, of course." Arshan's lips curl into a pout. The man's intensely vain, his greatest flaw, and I'm not surprised when he changes the subject. "The ligature mark on his wrist." He produces a ruler and measures the width of the wound. Its depth speaks to how tight it must have been. "Nearly four inches wide. So, this is not from a handcuff or a zip tie."

"A shackle then?" Blanche asks.

"A close look and you will notice the injury is not smooth, but deeper in some places than in others. Therefore, the cuff was probably not metal. Canvas, perhaps, or leather."

"Nice to know," Blanche observes, "but the real question is why only one hand. His left wrist is untouched."

"This is why you are a detective and I am a simple physician. But there is a bigger question here for me. I have examined the body before you arrived, front and back, and I can find no indication of wounds from a knife, a bullet, or blunt force trauma. Of course, I will perform the autopsy and perhaps something unexpected will come to the surface."

"But as of now?"

Arshan points to the ligature mark on Case Dixon's neck. It's narrow and very deep and could certainly be the cause of death. That's not the point, though. Manual strangulation with a ligature generally leaves a track that runs in a circle around the neck. The front and back will be very close to the same point on the neck, a choker necklace, only for real. Ligature marks left by hanging generally don't follow that pattern. They may begin at the same point on the front, just below the larynx, but the weight of a hanging body pulls the back of the ligature to the base of the skull, leaving a wound noticeably higher in back than in front. That's the case here and it presents a problem, especially for Vern when he holds the unavoidable press conference. If Arshan classifies the cause of death as strangulation, but the manner of death suicide or undetermined, Vern will have a lot to explain.

Blanche leans closer to the wound on Case Dixon's neck. "This here, these shiny spots. Am I looking at metal?"

Arshan's pissed off again. This is something he might have spotted himself. Still, with no choice, he fetches a heavy magnifying glass and peers through it for a moment. "Yes, metal. So, the ligature probably wasn't rope or fabric. A thin cable, maybe. The lab will narrow it down."

Using tweezers, Arshan collects perhaps ten of these slivers and bags them. He takes his time, perhaps because the only thing left to examine is so gruesome. There are wounds along Dixon's arms and legs, on his ears, his fingers, and his toes. The injuries are small, perhaps an inch long, but are so numerous and so deep they could only have been intentional. Worse yet, about a third have begun to scab over while other appear fresh.

"Do you see this?" Arshan finally asks. He points to one of the fresher wounds, this one in the back of Dixon's left arm. The flesh has been crushed, and the damage seems equally distributed on both side of the damaged area. "If you look closely, you will see a corrugated effect in this crushing injury. The pressure was delivered with an uneven device. Toothed perhaps."

Blanche jumps in. "Or grooved, like pliers."

"Yes, perhaps." Arshan's annoyed again. The man lives for an opportunity to demonstrate his own expertise. Now Blanche has upstaged him twice. "I will photograph the injuries and send them out for analysis." He stops as one of his assistants walks into the room. "Finally. Now we can move the body to the dissection table."

That's enough for me. Tomorrow morning, we plan to raid three homes, one in the opulent Mt. Jackson neighborhood. Drugs are being sold at each location and our search warrants are rock solid. Over the past year, as workers flooded the city and the department added officers, undercover work has become easier and easier. Dealers can't know their customers personally. A simple recommendation is enough to get prospective buyers through the door and for the arrests to keep coming. The drugs too. The drugs, the arrests, the prison sentences, the ruined lives.

CHAPTER SEVEN

BLANCHE WEBER

I've witnessed more than a dozen autopsies. They're all grisly, every single one, but I'm no longer timid. I don't frown, cringe, or react to the stench. I can watch Arshan slide a scalpel in a semicircle around Case Dixon's skull, then pull the boy's scalp down to cover his face. I can watch Arshan take a Mopec autopsy saw, remove the top of the boy's skull, and lift out his brain. I can watch Case's organs removed, one at a time, watch them inspected, measured, and weighed, watch the specimens as they're taken, watch the leftovers dropped into a blue plastic bag and placed in the kid's now-hollow abdomen.

Maybe I can handle all this because it's necessary, or because I know that Case Dixon's beyond feeling pain. Or maybe because I'm still focused on the other part, the injuries done to him before he died. What runs through the mind of a sadist? I imagine dark pathways in the brain leading to an empty cavern that can only be filled with the suffering of another. And I witnessed sadism many times when I worked patrol, usually visited on wives or children. But these men, these husbands and fathers, had a goal. They wished to dominate by inducing a fear so terrible it precluded any attempt to escape.

That's not the case with Dixon's abductor. The boy could not escape. He was bound by the wrist to whatever space was allotted to him while his captor delivered incredible pain over an extended period of time.

◆

"I'm pronouncing time of death between 8:00 P.M. Monday and 2:00 A.M. on Tuesday. This is consistent with the temperature of the liver and the discoloration of the skin."

I tune out the rest of Arshan's explanation. Time of death is notoriously hard to determine unless the body is examined soon after an individual passes. So, yes, on average a body will cool 1.5 degrees per hour. That's why pathologists generally start with an average body temperature of 98.6 degrees and work backward. The only problem is that an average is just that, an average. Normal body temperature can run a degree higher or cooler for any individual, and bodies cool more slowly in a warm environment than a cold environment. How much more slowly? Well, that depends.

An art, not a science. That's how any honest pathologist will describe estimated time of death in bodies discovered more than thirty-six hours after death. For the detective, the longer the span, the better. Suspects, in this case, will have to provide a six-hour alibi to be eliminated. Room to work.

"What else, Arshan?"

"You are in a hurry?"

"As a matter of fact, I am."

Arshan frowns, his expression petulant, a child called in from play. Most likely he can't imagine any tasks on my schedule being more important than his professional wisdom.

"Well, then, I will be brief. First, the subject's organs are normal for a boy of his age. Second, I have discovered no trace of disease with the possible exception of minor scarring on his lungs consistent with cigarette smoking. Third, his stomach was empty. He hadn't eaten in at least four hours and I suspect for longer still. Fourth, fissures in the anus indicate violent sex, perhaps twelve hours before death. I have not observed the presence of semen, but have taken swabs of the anus and mouth to be examined. Finally, I cannot determine the cause of the many wounds on the subject's body, except to say they are not bite marks."

I want to scream at Arshan: He has a name, you asshole, and it's not Subject. I don't, my so-called hot temper already an accepted fact inside the department.

"The manner of death, Arshan?"

"Strangulation, certainly."

"That's cause of death." Which Arshan already knows.

"I'm not seeing homicide with certainty."

"But it could have been. Imagine strangling someone from behind with a ligature. The victim slips and the perpetrator yanks up to contain the additional weight. Wouldn't the ligature slide up at the same time?"

"Yes, this is possible. But I still cannot state homicide. I will rule undetermined until additional evidence should surface." A sly smile now, sure to precede a dig. "If it ever does."

I left for the autopsy before breakfast and I've got a long day ahead of me. Or we, meaning myself and the detectives on the case, have a long day ahead of us. Though I'm half-nauseated, I need fuel and I stop at a fast-food drive-through for an egg-and-cheese sandwich on a toasted English muffin. I eat it quickly, follow with a cigarette. I don't smoke all that much, just enough to foil every attempt I've made to stop.

I've ordered Stuart Harrington to pair up with another detective, Patrick O'Malley. Accompanied by several uniformed patrol officers, they're presumably at work rounding up Friday night's partygoers. Patient interviews will yield still more names. And maybe we'll get lucky. Maybe one of the kids stepped outside to get a breath of air and saw something, anything, that'll lead us to Case Dixon's kidnapper. But I'm not holding my breath. And I won't stop there either. There are dozens of abandoned buildings in Oakland Gardens and a scattering of abandoned buildings in other neighborhoods. We don't need a search warrant to inspect the interiors and I intend to have each one searched.

Somehow, while I'm driving, I manage to punch a number into my phone. My boyfriend's number. Owen Walsh has a lot going for him. He grew up poor in an Alabama family that sharecropped the same patch of land for generations. Almost by sheer force of will, he'd graduated from high school at the top of his class, worked his way through the University of Alabama, then on to dental school.

Personally, I think the effort was heroic, but I'm not a man. I only know that the ways of men are equally mysterious and stupid. That's because Owen has an adequacy problem whenever he's around other cops. He feels diminished in the face of their macho posturing; that posturing is the reason I don't date other cops. My own opinion? Male cops are damn near as insecure as Owen. They need to flex their testosterone whether or not it's called for. I've been propositioned too many times to count, like it's written into the training manual. Prove your manhood by asking your co-worker for a quickie in the back seat. Or bent over the hood of your cruiser. Or the trunk. And catch an attitude when she turns you down. Like how could any *real* woman resist my abundant charms?

"Hey, baby." Owen's voice is light and cheery. "What's up?"

"Work. I'm the primary on the big one."

"That kid?"

"Yeah. I don't know when I'll be home. Not by dinner, for sure."

Owen's voice is tighter when he responds. "All right, fine. Anyway, I have to get back to work. The Queen is here."

The Queen is a standing joke between us. Owen came to Baxter from Lexington, Kentucky, shortly after the Nissan deal was announced. He'd been working in a clinic ever since he graduated, paying his dues. But Owen's nothing if not ambitious. To say that Baxter (pre-Nissan) was medically underserved is to minimize the condition by plenty. Nissan turned that on its head. Baxter is now the land of opportunity. Gold Mountain. Owen invested every penny he had and borrowed more to open a practice inside an almost abandoned strip mall on Baxter Boulevard. That was two years ago. Now every store in the mall is occupied, its flagship a Starbucks, the only one in town.

Owen's practice is going well. He's essentially a friendly guy, and almost entirely nonthreatening. Still, debt service takes a big chunk out of the monthly receipts and Owen works as many hours as there are appointments. Nobody gets turned away, especially the Queen.

The Queen has a name. Mrs.—don't call me Ms.—Leila Nolan. At sixty-eight years old, having neglected her mouth for decades, she appeared one day in Owen's examining room. Owen fitted her with dentures after a series of extractions, root canals, and crowns. The Queen has been in pain ever since, with each twinge an emergency that must be instantly addressed. This morning if possible.

We both know that Mrs. Leila Nolan, broad shouldered, broad chested, will sweep into the office, accompanied by her entourage, an equally imposing sister and two daughters. Nobody says no to the Queen, and Owen won't either. He'll fiddle with the dentures, put them back, fiddle again when she finds his adjustment unsatisfactory, keep fiddling until she finally goes home.

"Good luck, then."

"You too, Blanche."

"Thanks for that. I'm gonna need luck to put this one down. I don't know if you've heard, but Case Dixon's murder is now in the public domain. All over KBAX and the *Bugle* on their website. We'll be doing a press conference later in the day."

CHAPTER EIGHT
BLANCHE WEBER

The situation in the squad room is approaching chaotic when I come through the door at noon. Most of the kids who attended the party were easy to round up. They were intercepted as they arrived for school. But you can't formally interview kids, not on the record, without notifying a parent or guardian. If they ask to be present, you must include them. In this case, collecting those parents and guardians proved difficult. Many were at work. Some refused to leave, others couldn't. Then we made ourselves clear. Though none were active suspects, the kids weren't going home until they were interviewed. If parents didn't want to attend, their children would be interviewed outside their presence.

Some parents showed up and now they're angry at the inevitable delay. Tough shit. We only have three interview rooms and they're filled. We'll get to all the kids eventually, but for now it's sit and wait. There are four uniformed officers in the squad room, with the kids and their parents lined up on a long wooden bench. The uniforms are there to encourage civility.

A lone detective, Cade Barrow, waves me over to his desk.

"What's up, Cade? We about to have an uprising?"

He jerks his head toward the bench. "The kids are okay. They want to cooperate. The parents are the assholes. But we're ongoing. Two of the kids at the party are in the box. That'd be rooms one and two. We have the other one, Bard Henry, in room three."

"Anybody talk to him?"

Cade shakes his head. "Waitin' on you, but . . ."

"But what?"

"Boy's a hard case." He gestures to one of the uniformed officers standing by the bench. "Smacked Kevin Gomez over there when Gomez ordered him into the cruiser."

Kevin notices us staring at him and smiles. He's got a mouse beneath his left eye. It's just beginning to discolor.

"We notified Bard's mom," Cade says, "but she about told us to go fuck ourselves."

"Any good news?"

"Yeah, Bard's seventeen."

The state considers seventeen-year-olds mature enough to be interrogated without notifying a parent or guardian. Juries commonly have other ideas. But the fact that we contacted Bard's mother and she refused to act in her capacity as his parent should help us if it ever comes to a trial.

"I'm gonna get started, Cade. Make sure we get photos of Gomez's eye. A stop in the emergency room wouldn't hurt either."

◆

The door to room one opens while Cade and I are talking. A young girl, looking all of fourteen, walks out, followed by an older woman, then Stuart Harrington. All appear relaxed and I assume the interview was successful. I'm not expecting anyone to confess. At this point we're still gathering information. This evening, probably after dinner, we'll sift through the results to determine our next moves.

I wave Stuart over. He crosses the room in a few strides. The man has to be six-three, in contrast to my five-seven. A quiet man, his smile is affable and patient.

"Stuart, have you had a chance to check out Bard Henry?"

"Had a quick call with his guidance counselor at Goldman. The boy's been suspended three times for fightin', and twice for threatenin' a teacher."

"What about Case Dixon? Did Bard threaten Case?"

"I believe he did. Case's father complained to the school, it's on record, and every kid we interviewed knew about the threat."

"Did anybody witness the threat?"

"Yeah, two. Kid named Vince Factor and Dixon's girlfriend, Lola Dunn."

"The phrasing?"

"'I'll rip your balls off and make you eat 'em, you fuckin' snitch.'" Stu drops his butt onto the edge of the desk. "Bard Henry's what you might call an equal-opportunity thug. He bullies kids out of their lunch money, or any money they have in their pockets. Younger kids, mostly, or smaller kids like Case Dixon. And Henry already has a conviction for beating the crap out of a classmate. He was sixteen at the time and prosecuted as a juvenile. Caught six months' probation, which he only cleared a few weeks ago. A second offense would earn him some time."

◆

There are no windows, not even a two-way mirror, in our interrogation rooms. Instead, there's a monitor on the outside displaying video generated by a camera on the inside above the door. Personally, I like the arrangement because it heightens a claustrophobic atmosphere that encourages the impulse to do anything, even confess, in order to get out.

Bard Henry doesn't appear particularly impressed by the atmosphere. He's leaning his chair against the far wall. The boy seems older than seventeen. His mustache and pointed goatee are dark and thick, and faint lines radiate from the corners of his eyes. A spiral tattoo curls up the right side of his neck, tiny skulls that disappear beneath his long hair.

When I open the door and step inside, Bard Henry brings his chair down. He's handcuffed to a bolt on the arm of the chair. Both hands.

"You hungry, Bard? Thirsty?"

"I gotta piss."

"Sorry, but that's off the list for now. So, hungry, thirsty?"

"Fuck you."

I sit down on the far side of a well-gouged wooden table. Shabby by design, like the unpainted walls and the graffiti. You're nothing, you don't deserve better. That's the message and it's had plenty of time to sink in. Henry's been sitting here for two hours, but the only emotion I'm reading is anger and I have to assume that's his default, how he resolves any and all conflicts. I also have to assume that he's stupid as well. He's just off probation, that second chance so many refuse to take, but he decided to assault a cop. Did the inner rage that drove him to attack Kevin

Gomez also lead him to avenge himself on Case Dixon? I don't think so, but I can't discount the possibility altogether.

◆

Bard Henry's left eye is swollen almost shut, courtesy of Patrolman Gomez. He was checked by paramedics before being transported to the house. They offered him a free ride to Baxter Medical Center's Emergency Room, which he refused. More stupidity.

"All right, I know that your rights have been read to you, but I'm gonna read 'em again." With the camera running, so there can be no later denial. I remove a card from my pocket and read the whole thing off, rapid-fire. Finished, I tuck the card in my pocket and lay my hands on the table.

"Do you know why you're here, Bard?"

"Don't know, don't care. You wanna charge me with smackin' that pussy you call a cop? He hit me first."

"Is that what the dashboard camera's gonna show? How 'bout the body cam?"

Henry draws himself up, forgetting about his cuffed hands. He remembers again when they bring him up short. Hardened criminals usually don't take offense after they're arrested. Been there, done that, so how do I take this hook out of my mouth? But Henry's still unseasoned and he simply repeats himself.

"Fuck you."

"Bard, wake up, the only one fucked here is you, and the saddest part is that you fucked yourself. But that's history and I'm not here about a confession. The lump on the patrolman's face is more than enough evidence to charge and convict you. As an adult, of course."

I drop my hands to my lap and give Henry some time to think it over. He looks to the right, then the left, as if for an escape hatch, then down at his hands. Reality making an appearance? His voice is quieter when he finally speaks.

"What do you want? The prick who arrested me wouldn't tell me why."

"The officer wasn't arresting you, Bard. We only wanted to talk with you."

"About what?"

I sense genuine puzzlement as Henry eyes meet mine. Add another chip on the innocent side of the pass-fail line. "Case Dixon."

"That asshole?"

"Yeah, that murdered asshole." I give it a couple beats. "You sure you don't want anything? I'm gonna run to the vending machine for a Diet Sprite." Another pause, again no response. Henry's looking down at his hands, trying to figure it out. I walk to the door, pull it open, then turn. "We have witnesses who heard you threaten him. No more point denying it than denying you assaulted a cop."

"I don't have to talk to you. Go fuck yourself."

"I'll be right back."

◆

I take the time to confer with Stuart Harrington. The interviews are still going well. Though no witnesses have emerged, names are being named and one name has come up repeatedly. Caily Martin, Bard Henry's off-and-on girlfriend.

"The girlfriend ain't no girl, Blanche," Stuart tells me. "She's in her late twenties, ten years older than Bard. A druggie, which you might expect, with a charge currently pending. She's sittin' right now in the Sprague County Jail."

"That charge, would it be a felony?"

"Sold an eight ball to an undercover. Just last night, as it turns out."

"She have priors?"

"Down twice. Probation the first time. Three years the second. Been out about six months."

An eighth of an ounce of cocaine. Three and a half grams. Worth about $300. The offense may seem petty, but if she's convicted in this state, Caily Martin's lookin' at a ten-spot. That makes her likely to cooperate, but cooperation doesn't necessarily guarantee the truth. This is a lesson I've learned the hard way. And more than once.

◆

Bard Henry's where I left him, his attitude unchanged. He's got a sharp nose and he jabs it at me as I set my soda down and take a seat.

"I heard about the asshole gettin' clipped," he tells me. "It was all over the news when I woke up. But I didn't have nothin' to do with it. I ain't seen him since . . ."

"Since when?"

He drops his head, but continues to look at me out of the corner of a gray eye. It's the look of a child who's trying to outslick a parent. "Since I seen him in school last week."

"Is that when you threatened to . . . ?" I leaf through my notes. "Rip his balls off and make him eat them?"

"Hey, I never touched the kid."

"But you're not denying that you threatened him?" With no answer coming, I jump to the meat of the matter. "You could save us both a lot of trouble if you have an alibi. Start with Sunday afternoon, say around five."

"Until when?"

"Six on Tuesday morning."

"I'm supposed to what, account for every minute?"

"Just in general. Where you went, who you were with." I want him on the record, knowing that given time, we'll uncover any lies he decides to tell. "You don't have to be too specific. We can narrow it down later."

Henry straightens in his chair, his mouth twisting into a sneer. Yeah, defiance. Defiance and anger.

"Okay, about six o'clock? You wanna know what I was doin'? Well, if I remember correct, I was fuckin' your daughter in the ass. Now, I want a lawyer. Understand? I ain't got a goddamned thing left to say."

And there it is, the magic word, and I have no wiggle room with the video running. The questioning has to stop. I rise, leave the room, turn off the video, and come back inside. Henry finally opens his mouth a second before I punch him in his already-swollen eye.

"That's for the daughter I don't have."

CHAPTER NINE

BLANCHE WEBER

I grab Stu and pull him to the side. "The asshole wants a lawyer. I had to shut it down. But I want you to keep him here as long as possible before you book him for assaulting Gomez. If I can get back, I want to brief whatever prosecutor's doing arraignments."

"Where you goin', boss? In case I need to get in touch."

"Bard Henry's girlfriend, Caily Martin. I wanna reach out to her before Bard or one of his friends does." I wait for a nod, then say, "Anything happening here that I should know about?"

"Lotta new names, lotta work ahead. Nothing substantial, but it's still early."

"Then get to it."

◆

I head for Delia's office, pausing at her open door until she waves me inside. Her office isn't much, a desk, shelves, a computer, a keyboard, a printer. I take a seat on a wooden chair and cross my legs. I want to light a cigarette, but know better.

"So, what's up, Blanche?"

"Bard Henry's got a girlfriend, older than him. Her name's Caily Martin and right now she's sittin' in the Sprague County Jail. Sold an eight ball to an undercover, her third offense."

Enough said. Delia's eyes light up. "Anything I can do?"

"Are you friendly with Sheriff Fletcher?"

"Fact of the matter, Blanche, Sheriff Pickford Fletcher hates my guts. Also happens he's running for reelection and that election'll come off a bit under a month from now." She lifts her cell phone and scrolls through her directory for a moment, then punches in a number. "Captain Mariola in Baxter. Calling for Sheriff Fletcher."

The responding "please hold" is expected. About a year ago, the Baxter PD stepped all over Sprague County's turf to confront a mob from New York. Adding disrespect to disrespect, that particular stretch of Sprague County, Boomtown, has since been ceded to Baxter by the county's board of supervisors. Baxter's media had been quick to label this development a tacit admission that Sheriff Fletcher was unable, if not unwilling, to police his home territory.

The man, by all accounts, was not pleased.

"Tell you what, Blanche. I'll most likely have a wait here, so why don't you go outside and have the smoke you're dying to have. I'll meet you in the parking lot. I think it's best if we go together."

◆

When your boss is right, your boss is right. I am truly in need of a nicotine fix and I head for the parking lot behind our headquarters. As I come through the door, I reach for my smokes, failing to notice the uniformed cops standing about a hundred feet away. But their laughter draws my attention and I turn my head to discover five cops, all men, looking directly at me. Jake Nurine is among them.

My first impulse, to walk over and punch one of them in the face, passes quickly. There was definitely a time in my career when I might have done just that, consequences be damned. I'm cooler these days, more centered. Of course, I know cops with longer tenures resent my promotion to detective. And my increasingly close relationship with Delia Mariola hasn't helped either. I've partnered with Delia in the past and now she's put me in charge of a high-profile investigation.

The possibility of merit, that I got the job because I'm the better cop, would never occur to these assholes. In fact, two of the cops, Costello and Purington, propositioned me in the past, Costello more than once. Now, the latest rumor is that Delia and I are getting it on in her office. How else could an undeserving female rise so fast except by having sex with another undeserving female?

Costello's looking directly at me when he mouths the words *Jersey Girl,* the implication being that anyone raised east of the Ohio-Pennsylvania border is some kind of elite, like those New York–based assholes who turned Baxter upside down last year. The rank and file on the Baxter PD hated them as much for their city of origin as for the many crimes they committed. After all, we had our own criminals, homegrown with long years of disservice to the community. The sudden appearance of New York mobsters was viewed as a calculated insult. Like my turning Costello down.

In truth, elite wasn't even a dream in the Weber household. My father's a mechanic. He's been working for twenty-plus years at Serie Oil. The company ferries home heating oil from the tank farms near Elizabeth to hundreds of homes and apartment houses further inland. The fleet includes thirty tank trucks that must be up and running throughout the fall and winter months. My dad and the other mechanics make that happen.

After my brother and I started school, Mom took a bookkeeping job in Serie's office. She had almost no experience and her wages reflected her ignorance. So, yeah, there was food on the table every night, and new clothes when we outgrew the clothes in the drawer. But there was nothing elite about any of it, and only enough extra money to help me through two years at a junior college.

◆

I'm finishing my smoke when Delia comes out. She takes in the situation before the door closes behind her. Expressionless, her eyes jump from one man to another, settling on Nurine. She's taking names, obviously, and four of the five turn away. Maybe they realize that Delia has a pipeline into the office of our commissioner, Vern Taney. The two were partners for years, and remain close friends. But Nurine hasn't absorbed the concept of chain of command or come to grips with his precarious hold on his job. Or maybe he doesn't care. He continues to look in our direction, smirk firmly in place.

"He needs to be gone," Delia says, her tone matter-of-fact, as though she was commenting on the weather. "Before he infects the whole force."

◆

We stay mostly silent during the half-hour ride to the Sprague County Jail in Kendrick. Located beside a small railroad depot, Kendrick's grain elevators anchor the town's economy. A pair of unadorned gray cylinders with domed caps, they remind me of old-time whiskey jugs. Steel tubes from a towering grain leg reach to the tops of the elevators. This is who we are.

Twelve thousand people reside in Sprague County, most on farms, and the crime rate is fairly low. That's probably why the jail shares space in a two-story brick building that also houses the sheriff and his deputies. It's also why the county wanted no part of Boomtown and its many vices, why Sprague's board of supervisors eagerly parted with both. Effectively policing Boomtown would have required a substantial tax increase, along with a degree of urbanization residents rejected out of hand.

Delia's phone rings as she backs into a parking space a block from the jail at the northern end of Kendrick Avenue. She answers, listens for a moment, finally hangs up.

"Found a body in Oakland Gardens," she tells me. "Syringe still in his arm. Cade's handling it, but there's no sign of foul play. Except for the rat bites."

We step into a chilly October afternoon. The sky above is the color of lead and there's just enough bite in a steady breeze to hint at the oncoming winter.

"I want you to run the interview," Delia tells me. "I'm only here in case some deputy catches an attitude."

On one level, it's the truth. On another, Delia's told me how much she misses street work. True, the money and the prestige don't hurt, but they can't replace the relentless pursuit, the hunt, the final takedown. There's nothing quite like putting the cuffs on a seriously bad man or woman. The experience can lift you for days.

"Where do you wanna go with it?" Delia adds.

"Have to get a look at her first. But if she decides to alibi her boyfriend, I'll make her account for every minute. On the night Case was murdered, and the night he was kidnapped. If it matches Bard Henry's account, all to the good, because I'm not thinking the jerk has the brains to pull off the kidnapping."

"And if she doesn't?"

"Provide him with an alibi?"

"Yeah."

"Well, if he's not excluded, he's included. We'll just have to live with it. And you're assuming she'll talk to us. She might be as big an asshole as her boyfriend."

◆

Over the phone, Sheriff Fletcher promised to keep Caily Martin on ice until we arrived. We didn't want to give her time to prepare. But there she is, tucked into a small interrogation room, uncuffed, smoking a cigarette, a Coke and a bag of chips on the table in front of her. Her thin face with its knife-blade cheekbones is expressionless, but her dark eyes are watchful and intelligent. She's not dope sick either.

Though I don't think it's necessary, I introduce myself and Delia. "We're with the Baxter Police Department." I hesitate, but Caily's obviously been tipped off and she doesn't respond. "You're not a suspect in any crime. We've come to talk with you about your boyfriend. That would be Bard Henry."

Caily draws on her cigarette, then speaks before exhaling, her voice a soft hiss. "Boyfriend?" she tells us. "That'd be a stretch."

"Not a boyfriend? How would you describe the relationship?"

"Boy toy. I kept his nose filled and he filled something else."

When I laugh, she draws back. I'm sure she meant to shock me, but I've reached the point where almost nothing a mutt says can rock my little world. Some years ago, I sat across from a burglar named Scott Yeager as he described murdering an entire family, including two children as they slept. He went through it second by second, staring up at the ceiling as he relived the events.

"Can I assume you were together often? You know, discharging your mutual obligations?"

"Yeah, we spent a lot of time together."

"And where would that be?"

"I'm rentin' a trailer in Revere County." She stubs her cigarette into a battered metal ashtray, then leans back in her chair and crosses her legs. Caily's wearing an orange jumpsuit, standard jail wear, but seems comfortable and confident. I know that she's in serious trouble, and she knows that I know it. But she's been in the system too many times to reveal what's happening inside. You get the outer shell and nothing else.

"I know why you're here. This is about the kid who's been all over the news. What's his name again?"

"Case Dixon."

"Yeah, Case Dixon. Bard had a beef with Case. Thought Case snitched on him. Don't know what it is with Bard, but he's got a serious hard-on for rats. Me, I figure it's only part of the game. Like, for instance, me and you talkin' right this minute. You want me to help you out. I want you to help me out. The game goes on."

Great idea, but we don't have anything to offer. Any deal would have to come from the Sprague County prosecutor. Personally, I'm not holdin' my breath. But if Caily's tale is compelling, it's still possible. The tale, of course, that we've yet to hear.

I turn to Delia and gesture with my chin at the video camera over the door. "You think we can get that shut down?"

Delia nods once before leaving the room. A moment later, the red light on the camera winks off. I wait for Delia to find her chair, taking my time, then return to Caily.

"I'm not gonna spar with you, Caily. You been around too long. Long enough to know that you're not gettin' shit until we hear what you have to say. Also, you were read your rights when you were arrested and you have a lawyer you haven't asked for. So, let's get to it. You got something to sell, then sell it."

"Off the record, right? You can't make me testify."

Actually, we can, but I'm not going there. "Off the record, Caily."

Caily runs her fingers through her stringy brown hair and shakes her head. "I guess the first thing you need to know, Bard was out lookin' for the kid on Friday night. Started out around eight and didn't come home until the next morning. I asked him if he had any luck, but he just looked at me. Not a word, right? But I'm willing to swear that the stains on his sweatshirt weren't strawberry jelly."

Again, I'm supposed to be impressed, but that's not happening. "So you live in Revere County."

"Like I said."

"And you live there with Bard Henry?"

"Part-time. See, Bard likes to be alone and he likes to move around. Sometimes he stays with his mom, but mostly she doesn't want any part of him. That's because he starts fights with her boyfriends."

"Did he ever attack you?"

"You're thinkin' all wrong here. Bard Henry's seriously fucked up. In the head, right? Like he gets into a fight every other day. Don't matter how many times he gets his ass kicked. Don't matter if it's a wimp like Case Dixon or half a dozen shitkickers in a biker bar. But not women. Women don't set him off. If that sounds crazy, that's exactly what Bard Henry is. Crazy."

I make a note to check her claim, maybe with Bard's probation officer. I'll need to know if he's ever been treated for a mental illness anyway.

"So where does he stay when he isn't with you or his mother?"

"Mostly in one of the abandoned houses. You know, in Oakland Gardens."

The neighborhood, Oakland Gardens, rings the bell I'm sure Caily meant it to ring. Case Dixon was partying in Oakland Gardens on the night he disappeared.

"He ever take you to one of these abandoned houses?"

"More like the opposite. Me droppin' him off when his car broke down, which was like every other day. But here's the thing, Detective Weber. Bard knew Case Dixon was gonna party in the Gardens. In fact, the way Bard told it, half the high school knew that Case and the loser brigade were gonna party on Friday night. Knew where and when."

Another claim to check. "Your trailer, Caily. Will you give us permission to search it?"

"Sure as hell, detective. The sheriff's already been there, so I don't know what you'll find. But go ahead. I been hit with a forty-thousand-dollar bail and there ain't no way I'm gonna make it. I won't be goin' home anytime soon."

"Unless you cut a deal with us."

"Yeah, unless." Caily squares her shoulders. "Another thing, detective. A thing Bard told me after word got out that Case Dixon was missing. 'The rat got what was comin' to him.' That's what he said."

"But he never out-and-out confessed?"

"Now, see, that's somethin' we should talk about at a future date. Like after you take what I gave you to the prosecutors. You know, let's make a deal. And I'll make sure to have my lawyer present if we do."

◆

The last part stays with me as we return to Baxter. Delia's behind the wheel, humming a tune I can't quite identify. "She's good, Delia."

"Yeah, she is."

"Can't tell whether or not she's lying."

Delia smiles. "Nope, can't tell."

"But I do know this. She'll say anything we want her to say if it'll save her from a decade in state prison."

"There is that."

It's six o'clock when we cross the northern end of the construction site and hit Baxter Boulevard. I need to phone Owen because I won't be going home until I huddle with my detectives to examine the partygoers' signed statements. That done, we'll develop a plan of action for tomorrow. That plan will have to include Bard Henry. I'd hoped to eliminate him, but I can't.

"Ask you a question, Delia. An imagine-this question. What do you think was likely to happen if Bard Henry ran into Case Dixon after Dixon left the party?"

"You mean the Bard Henry who attacks bikers in biker bars?"

"Yeah, that one."

Turns to me as she slows for a red light. "I imagine an immediate attack, immediate and vicious. I don't see Case snatched off the street and held prisoner for days. That's not how Bard operates."

"And we both know the man who murdered Case Dixon was a sadist."

I don't have to state the obvious. Neither of us believes that Bard Henry tortured and murdered Case Dixon. Does it matter? I report to Delia. She reports to Vern Taney, our commissioner, who will report to Mayor Venn and Tommy Atkinson, our district attorney. A final decision, to prosecute or not to prosecute, will come from those higher powers. As for Caily Martin, everything she told us about the party on Friday and Bard's hard-on for Case was public knowledge.

"You hungry?" Delia asks.

CHAPTER TEN
JOHNNY-BOY

It's early evening, barely eight o'clock, and Johnny-Boy's standing at a bar on the lower end of Boomtown, not far from the Coolwater. Tonight's his one day off, but there's nothing leisurely about it. Johnny-Boy's eyes, and the eyes of everyone else in the joint, are glued to a press conference playing out on a TV above behind the bar. The police commissioner's there, along with the dyke, Mariola. She's standing off to one side, eyes alert, sweeping the room as if she expects Case Dixon's murderer to rise up and confess.

As for the conference itself, James Dixon, the kid's old man, beat them to it. His interview with KBAX's Jane Theroux took place at six o'clock in the Dixon home. According to Daddy Dixon, Case was a hardworking, sober lad whose bright future was virtually guaranteed by a higher authority. Dixon sat upright as he spoke, ready to go. In contrast with the devastated wife who sat beside him on the couch, slumped over, blank eyes swollen.

Johnny-Boy had watched, stone-faced, though he laughed inside. Case Dixon hated his father, spent his entire waking life stoned, and the only higher authority deciding his fate was named Johnny-Boy.

◆

On the screen, Commissioner Taney gives way to Captain Mariola, Chief of Detectives. She opens with the usual spiel. Case Dixon's killing has become a priority and major resources are now devoted to apprehending his killer. Interviews with friends and personnel at Goldman High are being conducted. Those interviews will continue indefinitely and the Baxter Police Department appreciates the cooperation it's already received. Nevertheless, a suspect has yet to be uncovered.

"We know that Case attended a party in Oakland Gardens on Friday night. He left about midnight, then disappeared. If anyone in the community saw him, or even think they did, or noticed anything that seemed out of place, please contact our hotline."

The man seated next to Johnny-Boy at the bar whacks his glass against the top of the bar. "Everybody knows who fuckin' killed the kid." He glares at Johnny-Boy, who doesn't react, not even an eye blink. "Fuckin' kid named Bard Henry, that's who. Believe me, I grew up in Baxter. My kid goes to school with Bard Henry. He's psycho, man. He's fuckin' crazy."

For the next few minutes, Johnny-Boy listens to his neighbor's rant. The asshole's locked into the belligerent phase of his alcoholic evening. An hour from now, he'll be crying in his beer.

As Johnny gets up to leave, his offended neighbor reaches out to take his arm. Johnny-Boy ignores the restraint, and the man lets go after glancing into Johnny-Boy's eyes. Johnny-Boy emerges into the Boomtown night to confront a pack of hookers, male and female, standing by the curb. They call out to him as he passes, offering various pleasures that fail to entice. How much, he asks himself as he opens the van's door, would they charge to be held captive for a few days before being killed? The question amuses him, but doesn't alter the equation. He has no time to indulge his passion. In fact, if he hadn't committed himself to the Diopolis job, he'd already be on the road.

◆

Twenty minutes later, all trace of amusement abruptly vanishes. Johnny-Boy's driving along Poplar Street in Oakland Gardens where every abandoned house on the block has a red X spray-painted on the front door. He'd been in Florida when Hurricane Irma ripped the state apart. Afterward, rescuers went from home to home, searching for people trapped inside. They spray-painted a red X on the front door after they finished. This building's been searched, don't waste your time searching again.

Johnny-Boy's working harder than ever on his day off, looking high and low for Theo Diopolis. But the abandoned house to abandoned house search has him as worried as he ever gets, which isn't very. First thing, every house on that block of Poplar Street was searched, indicating a systematic approach that'll continue until every abandoned house in the city has a red X on the door. At one time, that would've kept the house he's renting in

Revere County off the table. Or what used to be Revere County, now part of Baxter.

So how long before Captain Mariola orders her troops to take a closer look at dwellings beyond the old city limits? How long before Mariola realizes that the many abandoned barns and homes in farm country are perfect spots to hold a victim indefinitely? Mariola can't be underestimated. Johnny-Boy read that in her eyes as she stood behind her boss. His home, of course, is not abandoned, but it's far from the main drag, well-concealed behind a small woodlot. And while the arid, mainly blank landscape in this Midwestern state doesn't resemble the lush Florida Panhandle, both share characteristics when it comes to roads. A four-lane state road, maybe two, a few more county roads, two-lane but also paved, and dozens of unpaved roads, gravel-topped or plain dirt, that wandered through the interior. The road leading to Johnny-Boy's rented home falls into the latter category. You have to drive a long way and come around the trees in the woodlot before you reach Johnny-Boy's little domain.

There's only one play on this gameboard, Johnny-Boy tells himself. Find Theo Diopolis, kill Theo Diopolis, leave Baxter in the rear-view. Or maybe this kid, Bard Henry, will take the charge. That would buy Johnny-Boy some time, but it won't let him off the hook. After all, Bard Henry is innocent. And Johnny-Boy will kill again, whether or not he moves on.

◆

The evening progresses, much of it spent in shifting the van from place to place. He'd move faster on foot, but he can't be sure he won't need the van if he should happen on Diopolis. So he parks the van, hits the closest bars, in most cases merely peeking inside, then moves the van again. As he goes, he reminds himself of the name he's chosen. Ochoa is a Basque word meaning wolf and wolves, in sharp contrast to cats, are not ambush predators. As often as not, their prey sees them from a distance, and are usually faster than wolves in an all-out sprint. But the wolves never give up. They keep coming until the creature they pursue collapses from exhaustion. The outcome, from that point, is never in doubt. The prey can only hope the wolves don't begin to feed until after it's dead.

The effort pays off a few minutes after midnight when Johnny-Boy walks into Farrow's Tavern on Baxter Boulevard, a faux-Irish bar appropriately decorated with shamrocks, harps, and leprechauns. He doesn't ask himself what Diopolis, surely a Greek, is doing in an Irish tavern. He strolls up to the end of the bar farthest from where Diopolis hunches over a mixed drink and orders a beer. His only goal at this point is to leave the bar without being noticed. If he hadn't been halfway to the bar when he recognized Diopolis, he'd have backed off immediately. As it is, he keeps his own head down as he drinks his beer, tips the bartender, and walks out the door ten minutes later.

◆

Johnny-Boy's sitting behind the wheel of his van with the engine off. He's parked across from Farrow's Tavern, waiting for Diopolis to emerge. There are fewer pedestrians on Baxter Boulevard than on Main Street in Boomtown, but traffic is still brisk and the cops are out. Three cruisers have come past since he took up his watch thirty minutes ago, yet he somehow fails to notice a uniformed foot cop until the cop raps on the window. Johnny-Boy allows himself to briefly startle, then throws the cop a broad grin as he lowers the window. The cop leans forward and his nostrils flare. He's checking for the distinctive odor of marijuana. He doesn't find it and moves on to scan the seat and the floor, most likely in search of a weapon or an open bottle. He discovers neither. Nor, when he looks, does he find the keys in the ignition.

The cop's name tag reads DOYLE. He's big and beefy, his cheeks and nose reddened, a throwback to a different age. When he demands to see Johnny-Boy's license and registration, Johnny-Boy complies. Both are forgeries, but good enough to pass.

"You been sittin' here for a long time," the cop says.

There's no question mark at the end of the sentence, but Johnny-Boy responds with another grin. "Maybe had one beer too many," he explains. "I don't sober up soon, I'm gonna call a cab."

Doyle fails to return Johnny-Boy's smile. He straightens up and takes a step back. "That'd be a real good idea," he announces. "Better safe than a drunk tank. Especially our drunk tank."

CHAPTER ELEVEN
JOHNNY-BOY

Diopolis emerges five minutes later. As luck would have it, he crosses Baxter Boulevard and slides into the front seat of a brown Honda parked two cars ahead of Johnny-Boy's van. Johnny-Boy pulls out a few seconds after Diopolis, expecting to head east into Boomtown. Instead, Diopolis turns west, riding through Norwood and into a neighborhood simply called Westside. Far from Boomtown and the Yards, which preceded the construction zone, Westside's residential streets and avenues are lined with modest, well-kept houses. Most are single-family, with a few two-family homes scattered haphazardly throughout the neighborhood. Diopolis parks in front of a two-family on Tulip Street. He gets out, and points his remote at the Accord, locking the car.

Johnny-Boy's brain is in motion before Diopolis reaches the door. Lower level? Upper? The lights in the front room of the first floor are off, the lights of the second on. A moment later a woman rises inside the upper apartment and Johnny-Boy assumes it's to greet Diopolis. The quarry in its burrow.

Johnny-Boy continues down the street. He measures sight lines as he goes. What appears to be a small park several hundred yards away first catches his attention. Johnny-Boy isn't a special forces sniper. He can't kill from a thousand yards distant, but he's accurate up to three hundred yards. The little park is well within that range, but the cover it offers is meager and even now, after midnight, he finds a man walking a dog. There'll be a lot more dog walkers out in the morning before Diopolis heads off to work.

So, not here. Johnny-Boy continues to reconnoiter the neighborhood until he comes upon Thomas Jefferson Public School, a two-story building significantly taller than the surrounding homes. From the school's flat roof, he'll have a clear view of the Diopolis front window, but not the yard or the doorway. That means he'd have to fire through the window. Not a problem for him, but if the woman's in the room, she'll never forget.

Johnny-Boy uses a Sig Sauer Cross suppressed rifle for this kind of work. Retail, the Sig, with silencer and 10X sight, runs about seventeen hundred, but Johnny-Boy wasn't stupid enough to buy it over the counter. He'd invested considerably more, but the investment has paid for itself over the past few years. Firing subsonic ammo, it gives off a thin, metallic clack when the weapon's fired. Even if heard, it sounds nothing like gunfire.

Johnny-Boy circles the school. In the back, he discovers a standpipe, maybe six inches in diameter, held to the school's brick facade by steel straps. He's sure he can use the pipe to scales the wall and get to the roof, even carrying the rifle in its backpack case. One problem, though. The sides of the school are covered by security cameras. Come in ninja style? Body and face covered? The first cops on the scene when Diopolis goes down will have no idea where the shot came from. As long as he doesn't leave a shell casing behind, they might never be certain, but even if they do pinpoint the shooter's location, he'll be long gone. Unless, of course, the security cameras around the school are being monitored.

No sleep for the wary. Johnny-Boy spends the next two hours hunkered down in the back of the van, sitting at an angle so he can see through the windshield. The lights inside the school remain off, which makes twenty-four-hour security inside the building unlikely. In addition, the single patrol car that drives past the school does not slow down.

◆

Still unsatisfied, Johnny-Boy makes another pass by the Diopolis residence. Diopolis is driving an older Accord, its brown paint sun damaged. Large white patches on the roof and hood make it easy to identify. Spotting the Honda parked on a Boomtown street will not be a problem. Nor will following it home. Johnny-Boy need only wait until Diopolis parks and starts to get out. Then it's pop, pop, pop, over and done.

Johnny-Boy laughs to himself. If it seems too easy, that's because it is. He doesn't spot any security cameras as he drives along Tulip Street, but that doesn't mean there aren't any there. He'll have to steal a car, take out Diopolis, drive a few blocks to where he's parked the van and switch vehicles. Risk, risk, risk. Like the possibility that Diopolis doesn't live on Tulip Street, that he's just visiting and won't return anytime soon.

Minimize risk, maximize reward. The secret to success in the business of killing.

◆

Johnny-Boy takes the long way home, along County Road 10. Barely two lanes wide and gravel-topped, it meanders through farm country. Homes here stand between acres and acres of brown fields, or meadows populated by dairy cows, or steers headed to the slaughterhouse. Johnny-Boy has no interest in the animal population or in the vegetables, whatever they may be. He's drawn to a small house fronted by a well-maintained picket fence. Sharon Cowl, one of the Coolwater's bar girls, lives here. Lives alone for the most part.

Sharon's sad story is well-known to Johnny-Boy. She's told it often enough. An alcoholic, she'd first lost her husband, then custody of her children, a boy and a girl. Deserved, she admits. She didn't care for them, didn't nurture them, though she never stopped loving them. Or so she claims.

Now her life is about regaining custody. She's attends AA meetings almost every day, hasn't a had a drink in more than a year, never misses a shift at the Coolwater. Hell, she's never even late.

Johnny-Boy listened to her tale of woe as he listened to all the sad stories recounted by the Coolwater's patrons, drunk or sober. Listening is part of his job. That's not the point tonight. The point tonight is that Sharon lives alone and Johnny-Boy wants another trip to the plate before he leaves town. Yes, it won't be satisfying, an appetizer when he wants a four-course meal. He won't have more than a couple hours with Sharon, but any port in a storm.

Or maybe it's make hay while the sun shines because the Case Dixon investigation is sure to produce rain in the future.

A half mile farther down the road, Johnny-Boy comes upon a woodlot. When he first arrived in Baxter, he'd wondered about these forested parcels. Why are they here when the land could be used to grow crops? The answers, when he posed the question to a local, were simple enough. Back in the day, before farm homes acquired central heating, the small groves provided firewood to keep families warm and timber to build and repair the homes and barns. They also acted as a windbreak, screening homes from the unrelenting winter wind.

Johnny-Boy stays low as he crosses the fields between the woodlot and Sharon's isolated house with its pitched roof and tiny front porch. He's almost reached a cut in the earth with a stream, dry this time of year, when he spots headlights in the distance. No problem, he simply flattens until the vehicle, a crew-cab pickup, slides by. Then he drops into the cut.

Careful despite a solid cloud bank that's produced conditions approaching a blackout, Johnny-Boy lifts his head to the top of the little gully. No more than a hundred feet away, he watches two women sitting on a couch in the living room. Sharon and her co-worker at the bar, Glory Simms. They stare off at what must be a television, then break into laughter.

Johnny-Boy's disappointed but not surprised. The Coolwater closed about an hour ago. It's early evening for bar workers like Glory and Sharon. Still, he's tempted to take them both. Maybe kick down the door and kill one of them with the handgun stowed behind a panel in the rear. That should make the survivor eager to comply with his demands, despite knowing that she'll be next.

For a long moment, Johnny-Boy's overwhelmed with lust and an excitement beyond lust, an excitement that he can't name. Then he calms and his natural caution reasserts itself. Kick the door down? Sounds easy, but without knowing the door's strength, or the strength of the lock, he's as likely to break his knee as gain entry. And it's possible, maybe even likely, this being gun country, that Sharon has a weapon of her own.

The best move on the table is to be inside the house when she gets home. That shouldn't present a problem because he intends to quit his job now that he's located Diopolis. He'll have plenty of time to prepare.

So, Johnny-Boy's happy with the night's efforts as he makes his way to the van. He'll sleep well tonight and wake up rested. Energized as always when plans fall into place. Or, if not exactly into place, at least as they begin to jell. A week from now, he'll be headed west, to Taos, New Mexico, where he maintains what passes for a permanent residence. There to await the next call to action.

CHAPTER TWELVE
DELIA

I love my job for the most part, but not today. Not this morning when the Baxter Police Department has secured a warrant to search the home of Grayson and Amelia Bridger. Two kilos of cocaine are hidden somewhere in the house, not by Grayson or Amelia, but by their sixteen-year-old son, Malcolm.

In with the wrong crowd? A bad seed? Whatever, there's no doubting the bottom line. We've got an undercover inside a small drug crew. Meth, cocaine, dope, whatever comes through their pipeline. That crew's time in the free world will come to an end this morning. We're going to hit four locations. We have arrest warrants for ten individuals.

I'm not leading the charge this morning. Cade Barrow's running that show. But Grayson Bridger owns Bridger Hardware on Baxter Boulevard. Bridger Hardware's been sponsoring a Little League team for decades and the Bridgers contributed significantly to the renovation of St. Andrews Presbyterian Church. An animal lover, Amelia heads the local Humane Society.

Good guys, right? Respected in the community, right? Salt of the damned earth.

The four warrants will be served at the same time. At three of the locations, one of our cops will scream *Police!* a split second before another cop separates the door from its hinges with a battering ram. At the fourth, the Bridgers', I'll knock politely.

And that's because I'm sure to blast a hole in their hearts when I handcuff their son.

◆

Speaking of sons, I'm still at home when my own son, Danny, strides into the room. I generally believe my son to be without flaw, with one exception. In the morning, while I hunch over a cup of coffee, sleep in my eyes and drool at one corner of my mouth, he's already the Energizer Bunny. Just now he's dressed for his morning run. Wiser than either of us, Zoe's still asleep.

"Hi, Mom."

My grunt doesn't discourage Danny, who's accustomed to the greeting. He pours himself a mug of his own, then takes a seat on the other side of the table.

"You arrest Bard Henry yet?"

"Bard's under arrest, but for assaulting a police officer."

"Yeah, I remember. But for Case Dixon?"

I walk to the coffee maker and refill my own mug. My back's turned to my son when I ask the question. "You've already convicted him? That it?"

"No, Mom, but that's what's goin' around. I mean, I know Bard Henry from school. Him and Case Dixon. Bard's crazy, mom, and Dixon's . . . I mean was. Dixon was halfway suicidal. Mostly, I avoided the both of them."

"Did Bard ever . . . mess with you?"

"He's not that dumb."

I ignore the macho display. Late yesterday afternoon, Blanche spoke with Cleo Baldwin, Bard Henry's former probation officer. An MRI taken as a condition of probation detected abnormalities in several regions of his brain, including the amygdala. The result of traumatic brain injury? Probably, not certainly, but it leads to the conclusion that Bard Henry is unable to control his violence. And makes his threats all the more ominous.

"Case was in one of my classes," Danny continues. "He had a good sense of humor, especially about himself."

"Did you ever hang out with him?"

"No, never. Case and his gang, they're losers. All of 'em."

◆

As I ring the Bridger doorbell, I feel like I do when I'm about to notify a family that a loved one has passed. The hurt this time might be even worse. There's finality, after all, in death. The wound I'm about to open will be reopened a hundred times as Malcolm Bridger winds his way through the criminal justice system. His parents are entirely ignorant here. Unbeknownst to his parents, the boy fell in with a crew who filled his nose with coke, who tossed in a little sex, who insisted that storing two kilos of cocaine in his parents' home carried no risk.

Grayson Bridger finally comes to the door. "Who is it?"

"Police, Grayson," I say. "We have a warrant. Open up."

"What?"

My demand, most likely, has bounced off his brain. Search warrant? It makes no sense. What does search warrant have to do with Mr. Straight Arrow?

"It's Delia Mariola, Grayson. We have a warrant to search your house. Open the door."

Grayson Bridger complies a moment later. A heavyset man in a terry-cloth robe, he's obviously bewildered. His eyebrows are so narrowed they form a straight line across his forehead.

"Delia, what . . . ?"

I pass him a copy of the search warrant, as required. "We believe there's a large quantity of cocaine stored in the house."

"That's ridiculous . . ."

"By your son. By Malcolm."

As Bridger absorbs the message, his wife, Amelia, comes down the stairs, followed by their three children. I know Malcolm by sight. He's sixteen, the oldest. The other two, a girl about ten and a boy about five, hide behind their mother.

"There must be some mistake," Amelia declares as she turns to her son. "Tell her she's made a mistake."

I'm walking a fine line here. At what point does Malcolm become a suspect? At what point do I have to read him his rights? He's not under arrest, but he soon will be. Even worse, if he doesn't admit to his guilt, his parents could be arrested alongside him. It's their house.

Malcolm shrinks under his mother's stare, shoulders folding, knees bending. His mouth opens, but he doesn't speak. I can't read his mind, but if he believes that remaining silent will help him, he's mistaken.

"We've hit them all, Malcolm," I announce. "Itzy's, the Harley House, Rooster's." I give it a few seconds, then say, "I want the coke you brought here two nights ago. I want the coke, but I don't want to tear the house apart. You need to help me here."

Grayson Bridger finds his voice. "Did you do this? My God, did you do this to your mother? To me? To your brother and your sister?"

"Dad . . ."

Grayson wants to say something that I'm sure won't help. The time for family discussion is long past. "All right," I tell the four cops with me, including Marie Colangelo, who's lugging a video camera, "as we discussed. Begin upstairs, room by room. Be thorough."

Malcolm Bridger's a small kid, small and very frightened. But he's smart enough to recognize the only course open to him. Or maybe his conscience is actually bothering him. Now he finally lifts his chin.

"In the basement," he announces. "Behind the furnace."

◆

Twenty minutes later, I'm standing in the living room with Grayson and Amelia. Malcolm's in the back of a cruiser, hands cuffed in front. The room reminds me of my own living room, though it's a good deal larger. A trike in one corner, games on a folding card table, well-used furniture of good quality. Family photos reaching back through the generations crowd the mantle above the fireplace.

"Did you really need to arrest him?" Amelia asks.

"Yeah, I did. Depending on purity, the cocaine in your house has a street value of somewhere between a hundred and two hundred thousand dollars. The charge against Malcolm will be first-degree possession with intent to distribute."

Amelia begins to weep. "Are you saying my boy will go to prison?"

I can see the wound, already open, as it deepens. They had such hope for Malcolm, the firstborn. Justified hope on the one hand. The boy's grades put him the top 10 percent at Goldman High. His scores on the PSATs put him in the top 10 percent of the country. That's all gone now. The road back, if there is a road back, will be long and steep.

"It's a definite possibility," I tell the Bridgers, husband and wife. "Look, first thing, contact a lawyer. I'll see that Malcolm's arraigned today. Given his clean record, his bail will be reasonable. In the meantime, I'll make sure he's kept in a cell by himself. Away from the general population, right?" I watch Amelia lay a hand on her husband's arm. Grayson hasn't completely shed the bewildered expression, but I'm a pretty sure he'll come around. Business owners tend to be pragmatic. "Bottom line, only Malcolm can help Malcolm. Testifying against his co-defendants would go a long way. And I can't dismiss the possibility that he was coerced, or perhaps blackmailed. He might have been motivated by fear. There's probably more to the story."

I'm planting seeds. The Baxter Police Department would prefer not to reveal the identity of the undercover who broke the case. That can only happen if somebody flips, somebody inside the crew. Malcolm Bridger can do a lot of good, for himself and his family, and for us, if he's that somebody.

◆

I emerge into a cold morning, with the temperature in the mid-thirties. It's windy as well, another reminder of the winter to come. Malcolm Bridger's sitting in the back of a cruiser to my right. He comes alert when he sees me, jerking his head several times. His mouth moves though I can't hear what he says.

"He wants to speak with you," Marie tells me. "Asked for you right away." Then she shakes her head. "How the fuck can a kid so smart be so stupid?"

"Doesn't matter now." I hand my weapon to Marie, then open the rear door. By design, the back doors on police cruisers are designed to open only from the outside. "Move over, Malcolm."

Malcolm's been read his rights in front of his parents and five cops. There's no room for denial and he hasn't asked for a lawyer. Anything he tells me can be used against him, but it's not the cocaine he wants to talk about. Not at all.

"Bard Henry, I saw him. You know, that night. Friday."

"You've got my attention," I tell him. "Let's hear the rest."

Malcolm Bridger's a handsome kid, sharp-eyed and eager. His hands move as he speaks and I'm reminded of preachers at the start of their sermons. Engage instantly.

"Okay, first thing, I knew about the party. Everybody did. Big party, lots of drugs, stoned-out girls, like crazy wild. I didn't really buy the hype. Case and that crew were strictly down-side. You hang with them, you end up on Prozac or some other shit." He stops for a second, perhaps thinking the word shit will offend me. I don't react and he continues. "Like Friday was boring. Rooster and Itzy were out doing business somewhere and my sort-of girlfriend was grounded by her parents. I tried a spot I know in Boomtown and that totally sucked. So, I finally headed for the party in Oakland Gardens. Case Dixon's party. I walked in about eleven thirty and stayed for maybe ten minutes. Psychedelics are not my thing and the assholes were laid out everywhere. Tripping, right? But get this. I walk back out and see Bard Henry sitting in his mother's Jeep Cherokee. It's, like, red and you can't miss it. Bard's not doin' anything, right? Just sittin' behind the wheel. Alone."

CHAPTER THIRTEEN
BLANCHE WEBER

"You gotta see this," I tell Delia as I walk into her office. "I found this taped to my locker."

I hold up a photo of Snooki, a character on the reality show *Jersey Shore*. She's wearing a gaudy dress, the bodice reaching below her waist, her breasts all but spilling out. Across the bottom of the photo, in block letters: HOME SWEET HOME.

Delia sighs. Not what she needs, obviously, but not what I need either.

"You know who put . . ." She points to the photo. "You know who taped this to your locker?"

"Nope, and there are no cameras in the locker rooms, the men's or the women's. Plus . . ."

"Tell me."

"The lens of the camera in the hallway leading to the locker rooms has been spray-painted. Pink, of course."

Delia slows for a moment, then asks, "Anybody else see this on your locker?"

"Yeah, Fran Underwood. In fact, Fran was the one who told me it was there when I came in this morning."

"She saw it before you did?"

"I just said that."

Delia ignores my sharp tone. "You're being harassed." She points to Snooki's breasts. "Sexually harassed. You can file multiple complaints. We have our own board, if that's where you want to go. But the city of Baxter and the state also have harassment divisions. Personally, I think the sooner you're on the record, the better. We can stop it, even if the man who put it there is never identified."

Delia's certain it was a man. Me, I'm skeptical. The sisterhood has traitors too. Doesn't matter, though. "I'm not gonna file right now, boss. I'm gonna take a shot at finding out who did it. I'm thinking the department's too small to keep a secret for long."

I'm expecting a lecture about my temper. My temper and my inability to control it when provoked. Doesn't happen, though. Delia has too many other problems on her plate. She's seen the evidence, advised me, over and done.

"News, Blanche," she announces. "Good or bad, I'm not sure. You know about the raids this morning."

"Yeah, how'd that go?"

"Smoothly, no violence. But one of the people we arrested is named Malcolm Bridger, age sixteen."

"Malcolm Bridger? As in Bridger Hardware?"

"Yeah, somebody convinced him to warehouse coke. Two kilos."

"Warehouse, not sell?"

"That's right. He had it hidden behind the furnace in the basement." Delia shrugs. Dumb is an old story in the cop business. "Maybe he wanted to impress someone. Maybe he liked the drugs they fed him. Maybe it was too much rap, too much bad-boy fantasy. What matters is that he's lookin' for a way out. He told me he went to that party on Friday night. Case Dixon's party in Oakland Gardens. He arrived after eleven thirty and left right away because the scene turned him off. As he walked back to the car, he noticed Bard Henry parked across the street. A hundred percent sure, Blanche."

"You think he's telling the truth?"

"I'm gonna let you decide. And don't take him for an idiot. He's dumb, but he's not stupid."

"How 'bout scared? Is he scared?"

"Yeah, underneath. I promised his parents I'd keep him isolated until his bail hearing and I kept my promise. I put him a cell by himself. But he had to walk past the drunk tank to get there."

◆

Neither of us speaks for a moment as we process the obvious. We're building a circumstantial case against a suspect we believe to be innocent. Finally, I bring up the conversation I had with Bard Henry's former probation officer. Old news, but all the more relevant now.

"Look, Bard's MRI showed damage to parts of the brain that control violent impulses. If we can also put him outside the party fifteen minutes before Case Dixon left, prosecutors will eat it up. Even without physical evidence."

"But me and you, Blanche? We don't think he's a murderer."

"I can imagine Bard Henry beating someone to death. Or using a knife or a baseball bat. I can't imagine Bard holding someone hostage for three days first. And I can't imagine him finding and preparing the private space he'd need." I shift in my seat, suddenly calm. "You're gonna take this upstairs, right? To Vern Taney? And most likely, our commissioner will cover his ass by taking it to our district attorney and we both know what comes next. Tommy Atkinson answers to the public every four years, the same public demanding a quick arrest. Delia, once that ball starts rolling . . ."

◆

Malcolm Bridger has every reason to be afraid. When I step inside the interview room, I find a boy in the process of becoming a man. Unfortunately, he's a long way from completing the transformation. At perhaps five-nine, he's slightly built and underweight, a good-looking boy with deep blue eyes and fine brown hair long enough to cover his ears. He'd have a tough time in a juvenile institution. Put him in an adult prison, he'll be wearing lipstick within a week. But I'll give him this. When he looks up at me, his expression effectively conceals whatever he's feeling inside. His gaze is frankly evaluating and I can't help but think he's got a hole card to play.

"I'm Detective Weber. I understand you have something to tell me about Case Dixon's murder."

"What about Mariola?"

"It's Captain Mariola to you, asshole. And this is my case. It's me or nobody."

"Jeez, you don't have to catch an attitude. I'm tryin' to help."

"An attitude? I'm givin' you one minute to tell your story." I lean forward to poke him in the chest. "You don't convince me you're worth talkin' to, I'm gonna put you back in a cell."

I finally hit a nerve. Most likely, Delia was gentle with the boy in front of his parents. I'm the bad cop.

"Okay, simple. That party in Oakland Gardens? Case Dixon's party? I showed up a little after eleven thirty . . ."

"How do you know exactly when you arrived?"

"I know it was after eleven thirty because I was at a friend's house, just hangin'. His parent's kicked me out, me an' everyone else, at eleven fifteen. That's what they said. 'It's after eleven. Go home.'"

"You're positive?"

"I mean, I can't tell you to the minute, but I'm sure it was after eleven thirty when I got to the party."

"Tell me what you saw when you arrived."

"Stoned-out freaks. Tripping on mushrooms and communicating with the great unknown. That crap's for losers. Staring at the walls and the ceiling. But Case Dixon was there. Lookin' just as fuck—just as messed up as everyone else."

"So, you did what?"

"Walked back through the door. That's when I saw Bard Henry sittin' in his mom's Cherokee. Right across the street with the headlights off. And if the engine was runnin', I didn't hear it."

"You didn't speak to him?"

"Hell, no. The guy's crazy, detective. One minute he's a nice guy, the next he wants to crack your skull. And you have no idea how you pulled his trigger."

◆

I back off. We've interviewed a dozen of the kids who attended the party, some briefly. Malcolm's the only one to mention Bard Henry's presence. Still, it makes sense. According to Bard Henry's girlfriend, Caily Martin, Bard knew about the party and was actively searching for Case Dixon on the night Dixon vanished. So, where else would he search, if not at the party?

"You know how much time you can do for possessing two kilos of cocaine?"

The question catches him off guard, especially because I ask the question matter-of-factly. He flinches, and I can almost watch his thoughts whip through his brain, like the hearts and cherries on a slot machine.

"Let's say I believe you, Malcolm. So what? You have a good reason to lie, which is what Bard Henry's lawyer will tell the jury at every opportunity."

Malcolm brightens visibly and I know he's been waiting for just this minute. He's gonna play that hole card.

"Yeah, I get the point. Only I didn't go to that party alone. See, I was grounded that weekend. Not a big deal because my bedroom's on the first floor. I climbed out the window and took off about ten o'clock. My brother and sister were asleep and my parents were in their bedroom doing whatever. The point is that I didn't have a car and there was no way I could get anywhere on foot. So I called a buddy. He picked me up ten minutes later and we cruised."

"And this buddy?" I don't want to ask the question, but I have no choice. "Can I assume two things? That he, too, noticed Bard Henry, and that you didn't speak to him after your arrest?"

"Yes, to both parts. I've been in a cell by myself since I got here and I haven't made a phone call. To anyone."

"All to the good. Now, let's hear the name of your friend."

A happy smirk. "I think I should wait for my lawyer."

"And I think I should put you in an isolated cell with a pair of serial rapists."

"C'mon."

I walk over to the door, open it and shout across the room to Cade Barrow. "Yo, Cade, I need a favor."

Malcolm breaks in quickly. The smirk's gone now, replaced by anger. I've spoiled his power fantasy. "Okay, I get it."

Cade's staring at me, an amused smile playing across his great stone face. I don't have to tell him the name of this little ploy. He's surely used it himself, and probably more than once. We both nod and I shut the door.

"A name, Malcolm."

CHAPTER FOURTEEN

BLANCHE WEBER

"His name is Benny Cooper. He lives a couple houses from mine. We've been friends since forever."

"How old is he?"

"Coop had a birthday last week. He's seventeen."

"Does he go to school?"

A nod. "Baxter Prep."

Enough for now. Benny Cooper's most likely in school, it being a Friday. If not, we'll find him. But I want it done fast. I head for the door, pausing only to inform Malcolm that he's headed back to his cell. He stops me, though.

"Were you gonna do it?" he asks. "What you threatened?"

"Nope. I have strict orders to keep you isolated until your bail hearing."

"That's what I thought." A smile now, thin and rueful. "But I couldn't take the chance."

◆

The squad room is busy this morning. Delia's raids produced numerous arrests. Six are clustered at one end of a long wooden bench. I know they're Delia's because they're handcuffed. Clustered at the opposite end, as far from these criminals as possible, four kids and their parents wait to be interviewed. At least a dozen detectives and uniformed officers, some wearing the body armor used in the raids, add to the congestion. Their tours will end before the paperwork is completed.

Stu Harrington's standing near a young couple, patiently addressing their complaint, undoubtedly the same complaint we've been hearing for days. We need to get to work. When will you finally be done with my son or daughter?

I motion Stu over. "Twenty minutes, Stu. In the conference room downstairs. I want updates. On the interviews and the trace evidence. Let's decide where to go next."

"Got it."

"One other thing, and we need to pull it off as soon as possible. A kid named Benjamin Cooper. He goes to Baxter Prep and he was supposedly at the party on Friday night. Get someone out there to bring him into the house. He's seventeen, by the way, and definitely not a suspect. You don't have to notify his parents."

Stu nods once and I head for the parking lot and a smoke I feel I deserve. I'm reaching for the smokes in my jacket pocket when that little voice tells me, for maybe the millionth time: *You're killing yourself.* That done, I take a cigarette from the pack and rummage in my pocket for my lighter. That's when I notice the shithead standing about fifty feet away at the edge of the building. The shithead would be Jake Nurine and he's positioned himself in one of the few corners of the parking lot not covered by security cameras.

As I light my smoke, he mouths the words *Jersey Girl.* The taunt's designed to provoke and it works. I'm not big on take-it-like-a-girl. But I manage to keep my anger to myself as I approach Nurine. I've been studying martial arts for many years, and while I eased off last year, I still hit an MMA gym at least once a week.

Nurine assumes the pose when it becomes obvious that I'm not about to slow down. Legs apart, hands on hips, chest out, chin up, smirk firmly in place. Most likely, he's expecting a lecture, no little girl, in his mind, having the courage to challenge him. That's okay with this little girl, perfectly fine. With no warning, I launch a snap kick that tracks between those spread legs to collide with the family jewels. He drops to his knees, the pain overwhelming, but I'm not through. His hands are between his legs. They offer no protection when I punch him in the face hard enough to mark him.

◆

I take a step back, still silent, as I light my cigarette. I'm feeling, faintly, the onset of hothead remorse. I'm not afraid though. We're both armed and I don't think he'll want to go that route. Then a cruiser holding a pair of uniformed cops pulls onto the lot. Nurine's still on his knees, trying to hold his balls and his face at the same time.

No chance, now, to keep this between me and Jake. I walk back to the doorway and finish my cigarette. The word's gonna spread, and quick. That's okay. A message has been sent and I doubt that

Nurine will make a formal complaint. Formal complaints are for weak and defenseless girls, or for the male equivalent thereof.

I don't think it's finished though. I'm not a fool. Some form of retaliation is sure to follow. Meanwhile, there's work to do. I head upstairs to our conference room. Talk about the bare minimum. A gray table made of reclaimed wood, eight chairs, a sector-by-sector police map on the wall, state and American flags separated by a podium. The room is another one of those improvements to come, but this morning I find it utterly charming. Not for anything inherent, but for a box of doughnuts from Lena's and eight extra-large containers of coffee. Laid out and ready for consumption.

There are six officers besides myself in the room when I enter, four detectives and two uniformed cops. I expect to hear from two of them, Stu Harrington and Patrick O'Malley. Stu's been running the interviews, while O'Malley's been following the trace evidence as it wends its way through the state lab. While the others have been involved in the investigation and I don't want to shut them out, I do want them to quietly observe unless prompted by a higher authority. Either Stu or Patrick should be aware of what they've turned up. If not, I have a problem.

I add cream and a packet of sugar to one of the coffees, then stare into the doughnut box for a moment. There's a slice of crumb cake that's calling out to me, but I know what's gonna happen if I bite into it. My navy blazer is right out of the cleaners. It doesn't need to be speckled with crumbs. There's my team-leader dignity to consider. I settle for a glazed doughnut.

"Patrick, why don't you lead off?"

Patrick's in his late forties, a tall man with a belly to match. He's been around long enough to be careful and now he consults his notes before he begins. "So, the small wood splinters recovered from Case Dixon's body are fragments of pine flooring. Very old pine flooring with only traces of an original brown varnish still present. We've recovered similar flooring from the car belonging to Bard Henry's mother, which we know he regularly drove, and also from the trailer rented by Caily Martin."

Jesus, two more nails for the coffin. Caily Martin gave us permission to search her home. That's not a problem. Anything we find can be used at trial. But Caily also told us that Bard regularly spent time in one or another of the abandoned houses in Oakland Gardens. He could have picked up the splinters at any of them, but I have a feeling that District Attorney Atkinson will see it differently. Oakland Gardens was the second neighborhood to develop in Baxter, after the Yards. This was in the 1880s when Baxter Meatpacking opened for business. Most of the homes were built at the same time. Built quickly to house workers, the construction often shoddy. Pine floors would likely have been universal.

Meanwhile, James Dixon was on TV again this morning, insisting that the police have a suspect and should already have made an arrest.

"Anything else?" I ask.

"Yeah, the metal slivers we found are stainless steel and probably came from a thin cable."

"Probably?"

"I spoke to a captain at the lab named Barton. They're hedging their bets. They wanna send everything to the FBI lab at Quantico in Virginia." He stops there to review his notes. "Some of the lab work from the autopsy came through. Case Dixon's tox screen showed traces of THC, nothing else. That only makes sense if he was held without access to drugs for several days." He looks down again. "One last thing, the instrument used to inflict the wounds on Dixon was probably a pair of tongue-and-groove pliers."

Tongue-and-groove pliers are my tool of choice for home maintenance. Their jaws can be widened or narrowed by sliding the lower jaw along a channel. That allows you to do anything from a pull a nail to loosen the nut on a bolt. Their long handles also produce tremendous torque. What they'd do to human flesh . . .

"Barton seemed pretty sure, captain, but the state lab wants its conclusion confirmed before they're willing to testify."

"Confirmed by the FBI?"

"Exactly."

◆

"Stu?" I nod to Stu Harrison. He's been overseeing the interviews. Time for an update.

"Same old story, captain." Stu's sitting back in his chair, legs crossed at the knee. His tone is steady, his drawl pronounced. "Near everybody knew about the party. Near everybody knew about Henry's threat. We have more than a dozen kids on the record. Written statements, captain. Signed."

"Any of the kids notice Bard Henry in front of the party house?"

"Nope. But given as how they were completely stoned, I'm not sure they'd notice if their shoes were on fire. Somethin' did turn up on the hotline, though. I'll let Jennie Cordoba tell you about it."

Jennie can't be more than twenty-three or -four. Young and eager, she's the first Latina to join the force. But times are changing, and quickly. A farm in Maryville County, twenty miles west of the city, has been turned into a barracks for Mexican and Guatemalan construction workers. They don't work at the Nissan site. Instead, a contractor supplies them, as needed, to commercial and residential projects throughout the city. Are they being trafficked? The farm lies outside our jurisdiction. We don't have the authority to investigate.

Jennie Cordoba interlaces her fingers and leans forward. "Three calls, captain. Anonymous, right? But I'll get to that later. All three remembered a white van cruising through the neighborhood around midnight. This van, it had no rear windows, which is what caught their attention. That would make it a commercial model, what they call a panel van, and you'd expect to find the name of a business somewhere on the doors or the sides. The sides and the doors on this van were blank."

I slow her down with a wave of my hand. "That seems a little thing to notice. A van with no signs."

"That's where the anonymous part comes in. Ask yourself, what would these callers be doing in that part of Oakland Gardens near midnight? Except looking for drugs in one of the drug houses or sex in one of the brothels operating in the neighborhood."

The sex part rings a bell. These are like prostitute rave events. The pimps move from one house to another, setting up for a few days action, spreading the word to the Nissan workers, reaping a quick profit before closing up. We know from our snitches that it's happening, but priorities keep it on the to-do list.

"According to the callers, the van was 'cruising' through the neighborhood. Not like somebody on the way home. Like somebody looking for something. Or somebody."

"You said the calls were anonymous."

"Yeah—as one caller admitted, he wanted to help us, but didn't want his reasons for being in Oakland Gardens examined."

One more item on the menu and it resolves itself as we attack the doughnuts and coffee. The door opens following a single knock to reveal Detective John Meacham, universally called the Dink. Delia dislikes Meacham for reasons she hasn't bothered to explain, but whatever his transgressions, he appears to have reformed. Uninspired, but competent, he's the perfect second to a primary detective. Whatever you tell him to do, he does. Like fetch Malcolm Bridger's pal, Benny Cooper. Cooper's supposed to confirm Malcolm's claim that Bard Henry was parked outside the party house on the night Case Dixon vanished.

"You have him?" I ask.

"Actually, no. I found him at school, but the school wouldn't let him leave until they called his father." He shrugs. "I couldn't just drag him out of there because he hadn't committed a crime." He stops again, staring at me through brown puppy eyes, until I wave him on. "So, his father's a lawyer. Real estate mostly, but he got there in a hurry. When I told him what I wanted, without mentioning Bard Henry, he talked it over with his kid for a few minutes."

"And then?"

"Then the kid went through his movements last Friday evening. How they hung out at another kid's house until a little after eleven. How they went to the party and saw Case Dixon. How they came out and spotted Bard Henry parked across the street." Meacham brightens noticeably. "I had him write it out, Blanche. Write it and sign it. There's no going back."

CHAPTER FIFTEEN
BLANCHE WEBER

I finish my afternoon at another meeting. This one in our commissioner's office. Delia and Vern Taney are ex-partners and longtime buddies. Me, I have my doubts about our leader. Too much football-star memorabilia, amplified by a smile that's a little too ready, a little too folksy. Taney was appointed by Mayor Venn and confirmed by the city council. He can be easily replaced should he displease either. And then there's a persistent rumor that has him running for mayor should our current mayor retire.

We make small talk as we wait for our last guest. That would be District Attorney Thomas Atkinson. The meeting is at his insistence. That he'd also be last to arrive goes without saying.

Physically, Atkinson is Vern Taney's polar opposite. Taney's a large man with the beginnings of a belly. What you might call a man of substance who still looks good in a uniform.

The three stars on either epaulet gleam, even under fluorescent lighting. Tommy, as he comes through the door, is all energy. Maybe five-nine and wiry, he strides up to shake our hands, then drops his briefcase at his feet as he settles onto one of the two love seats framing a coffee table. Vern Taney, at twice his size, sits alongside. I'm sitting beside Delia, across from Atkinson.

"People to see, places to go," our district attorney says. "But don't spare the details."

◆

I'm expecting Delia to lead the presentation, but she catches me by surprise. "Detective Weber's the primary, Tommy. She's up to date."

Three sets of eyes turn to me, but I'm not intimidated. I run through the first part, Bard Henry's threats, the party, Henry knowing the party's location and announcing his intention to seek Case Dixon out at the party.

"This info's coming from a woman named Caily Martin, Bard Henry's girlfriend according to multiple witnesses. Martin's sitting in the Sprague County Jail, charged with selling an eight ball to one of the sheriff's undercovers. A third offense, right? She's lookin' at a dime, so there's no way she's gonna testify unless she gets a deal."

"An eight ball versus a murder," Tommy says. "I'll work it out. You said something about a witness seeing Bard Henry outside the party?"

"That would be Malcolm Bridger."

"Ah, I see. Grayson Bridger's kid. I assume he also wants a deal?"

"He does, but he claims he was with a friend named Benny Cooper and both of them noticed Bard Henry sitting in his mother's Jeep outside the party sometime after eleven thirty. That would be very close to the time when Case Dixon left the party."

"You've interviewed this other kid?"

"We've got a signed statement, made in the presence of a parent, confirming Malcolm Bridger's account."

"Excellent." He rubs his hands together. "Am I right in thinking that Benny Cooper hasn't been accused of a crime?"

I get the point. If Cooper's a witness, not a suspect, he can be compelled to testify. No deal necessary. "He hasn't."

Atkinson waves me on. "More good news, please."

"Both Henry's mother's car and Caily Martin's trailer were searched. The trailer wasn't used to imprison Case Dixon. Too small, too neat. We did recover individual hairs from the car and the trailer. The hairs were microscopically examined and they could not have belonged to Dixon. At least according to the state lab. More important, slivers of wood found on Case Dixon's body have been identified as very old pine. Slivers of wood found in the car and trailer are also of aged pine. Minute traces of floor varnish appear on samples from all three sites."

"Are you talking about a match?"

"No, the state lab's not willing to go that far. They're only saying that comparisons don't exclude the possibility that the samples came from the same floor. The samples are very similar, the wood dried almost to the point of crumbling, indicating great age and exposure to extreme temperature variations. But there are dozens of abandoned homes in Oakland Gardens with pine floors, and many abandoned barns and homes outside the city limits. A true match is unlikely, but the state techs hope the FBI lab can do something with the traces of varnish."

Atkinson waves me off. "A jury hears you can't exclude the possibility the samples came from the same floor, they're right away thinking match. I'd save that news for later. First, I'll establish the threats through as many witnesses as the judge will let me call. Then the girlfriend, what's her name . . ."

"Caily Martin."

"Yeah, Caily Martin." Atkinson's sitting bolt upright, both hands moving as he works through his fantasy case. "Henry set out to find and kill Dixon on the night he disappeared. Henry knew about the party. Henry was spotted by two witnesses parked outside the party shortly before Dixon's kidnapping. Wood splinters found on Dixon's body can't be distinguished from splinters found in the car Henry drove or the trailer where he lived. There's nothing not to like."

I can't let it go. I want to wipe that smug, satisfied grin off his face. "One last thing. Bard Henry took an MRI of his brain while he was on probation. At the insistence of his probation officer, by the way. The scan showed damage to his frontal cortex and the amygdala, possibly resulting in violent impulses he can't control. He might go with an insanity defense."

"Please, detective. Insanity defenses are wildly expensive. You need expert witnesses every step of the way. And Mr. Henry, he's not gonna have an OJ dream team. He's gonna have a public defender with a limited budget." Atkinson finally leans back in his seat. "Besides, once a jury hears the words 'uncontrollable violence,' it won't just be another nail in the coffin. It'll be dirt landing on a coffin already in the ground."

CHAPTER SIXTEEN

JOHNNY-BOY

Last night, Johnny-Boy drove past the Westside house where Diopolis spent Thursday night. Drove past twice with no sign of the man or his beat-up car. So, who lives in the house? A steady girlfriend? Not steady enough for the Greek to show up two nights running. So, maybe the hookup was entirely casual. And maybe the hours Johnny-Boy spent crisscrossing Boomtown's streets without spotting the Greek's Honda were equally meaningless. After all, he hadn't started until the Coolwater closed. But one thing is inescapable. He can't spend most of his days and nights tending bar and still mount an effective search. Time to quit, like today.

◆

Just now, it's seven thirty, the sun barely up, and he's inside the Coolwater, watching the worker bees arrive for another sweat-of-the-brow day. And there goes Theo Diopolis through the gate, his brown Accord with the sun-damaged paint as easy to spot as Johnny-Boy expected. But there's no completing his assignment inside that particular beehive. Even if he managed to gain access, which you can't do without a pass, getting back out would be all but impossible.

Johnny-Boy's not a paranoid type for the most part. Nevertheless, his thoughts move to the great flaw in his methods. He's far removed from the men who hire him. If that means they don't know much about him, not even his name, it also means that he doesn't know much about them. Worse yet, he doesn't know much about his targets. Who did Theo Diopolis offend? How did he offend? Is he a putz, or a hardened gangster on the run? More to the point, has he been warned? That's not impossible. It's not even far-fetched. Maybe some interested party whispered into the Greek's ear: *Look out, kid, they know you're in Baxter.*

Johnny-Boy watches the Honda as it follows a steady stream of vehicles into the site's huge parking lot. He continues to watch until Diopolis parks it somewhere in the middle of the lot before breaking away.

◆

Inside the Coolwater, Johnny-Boy loses himself in the familiar setup routine. The floor has been swept and mopped by a porter who comes in after closing time. The porter cleaned the room's perimeter first, then lined the bar's tables against the walls before loading the chairs on top. Moving at the steady pace that defines his working life, Johnny-Boy slides the tables into place and sets out the chairs before turning to the bar. The stock first, the beer fridge, the wine racks, the shelves behind the bar. His labor is mindless and he finds himself drifting, as he often does, to his life back in Florida and Garrison Granger, his foster father.

Daddy Granger died long ago, murdered in Raiford Prison where the state sent him after his relationships with young boys became so flagrant they could no longer be ignored. No fool, Johnny-Boy took off right after Granger's arrest. Before the state could place him in a group home that closely resembled a prison, the residents commonly referred to it as the Joint. He was sixteen, big for his age, but still unformed. Inevitably, the predators he encountered on the road mistook him for easy prey, an error in judgment Johnny-Boy quickly reversed. His response, at times, was brutal enough to land grown men in the hospital.

Johnny-Boy drifted from city to city for two years. Twice, state authorities consigned him to a group home from which he promptly escaped. He had sexual encounters along the way, with men and women, sometimes trading his body for a few nights' shelter and dinner on the table. Throughout, he had no direction and took whatever work came his way. He wasn't exactly searching, but couldn't shake a sense that he was missing something. Something that should have been obvious.

Johnny-Boy's quest came to a head in Fort Wayne, Indiana, a few weeks after his eighteenth birthday. He'd more or less blundered into a relationship with a woman in her early forties. Johanna Hopkins had a long-running fondness for young men and Johnny-Boy fit the bill. His wealth of experience was an asset, and Johanna had a warm heart that allowed her to play both the seductress and the nurturing aunt. She also owned the Hoosier, a bar in the Memorial Park neighborhood.

As plain as the Coolwater, Johanna tended the Hoosier from its opening late in the afternoon until closing. She took to training Johnny-Boy in the fine art of running a dive bar, her aim perhaps to keep an eye on him. Or so Johnny-Boy thought. He didn't mind though. The work was simple enough. He carried drinks and pitchers of beer to the tables, lugged stock up a set of basement stairs, spent enough time behind the bar to get the hang of the trade. It beat sleeping in laundromats.

The training continued for a couple months, until one afternoon shortly after opening, with the bar empty, a man pushed through the door. Johnny-Boy's first thought, what with the bulging eyes, the grinding teeth, and the deep sores at both corners of the man's mouth? The man had to be crazy, one of those wandering psychos who haunt the streets of every city. But the man, whose name turned out to be Matt Fleming, wasn't psychotic. Fleming was a tweaker at the far end of a three-day binge. Broke and desperate, he seemed to be unaware of his surroundings as he strode to within a yard of Johnny-Boy, then pulled the ancient .38 revolver tucked into his belt.

That last bit, the unaware part, proved his undoing. The revolver left his grip to enter Johnny-Boy's in less than a second. And there the confrontation might have ended. Deprived of his only advantage, the tweaker froze, offering no resistance as he processed the turn of events. And Johnny-Boy, in fairness, considered the obvious alternatives. Tell the asshole to move on. Call the cops. Smack him a couple times to make a point.

Johnny-Boy chose none of these options. Instead, he lifted the revolver and pulled the trigger, sending a bullet through Fleming's forehead, through his brain, through the back of his skull. As he watched Fleming topple backward, Johnny-Boy experienced an epiphany, though he didn't (and still doesn't) know the meaning of the word. He'd found his calling.

Johanna notified the cops right away, dead bodies being too inconvenient to ignore. When they arrived, she remembered only the basics. An armed man, a struggle, a gunshot. That wouldn't have been enough to satisfy the detectives who questioned her, but Johnny-Boy caught a major break. Fleming was on the run from a warrant issued in Little Rock. During a carjacking, he'd killed an eight-year-old girl. Good riddance being the appropriate response to bad rubbish, they pronounced the shooting to be in self-defense. Not only wasn't Johnny-Boy arrested, he was treated to coffee and doughnuts by the cops in the local precinct.

CHAPTER SEVENTEEN

JOHNNY-BOY

Johnny-Boy's called back from his reveries when Matt Browner walks through the door. The man's sweating, as usual, though the outside temperature's in the forties. "Whatta ya say?" he says, one bro to another.

"Hey, you're early."

"Yeah, we gotta take an inventory."

"Okay, Matt, but I have some bad news for you. Somethin' came up and I have to quit."

Johnny-Boy's tone is blunt and final. There's nothing to debate, yet Browner, somehow, doesn't get the point.

"Who's gonna tend the bar?"

"Who covers for me on my day off?"

"Sharon."

"Use Sharon. She better than me anyway."

Outside, a line of cement mixers, their drums turning, contribute to a constant rumble. The cement is for the interior floors that have to support the weight of the many robots soon to follow.

"The fuckin' noise," Browner finally says. "All day, all night. I don't know how you stand it."

"Practice makes perfect."

"So, okay." Browner gives his jowls a shake as he decides that it's for the best. This guy, Paul Ochoa? There's definitely something weird goin' on here and Browner's not all that anxious to find out what that something is. "Sharon? She's off tonight, so I'm askin' for one more shift. Then we part company on good terms."

Johnny-Boy's had enough of the Coolwater, but he's cautious by nature. Accommodation is in order.

"One more night, boss," he says. "You got it."

◆

Johnny-Boy's last night goes smoothly enough. He pours the drinks, listens to the stories, evicts an overly aggressive hooker, watches the clock. It's Saturday, the day after payday, and the Coolwater's busy. Johnny-Boy doesn't lock the door behind him until nearly two, but finds Boomtown still booming when he steps onto the sidewalk, the hookers out in force.

"Yo, Paul."

Johnny-Boy turns to find the woman he eighty-sixed a few hours before. Still in her teens by the look of her, she's smiling a no-hard-feelings smile that reveals the broken teeth of a crackhead.

"Hey," she tells him. "We could make some money together."

"How's that?"

"Use your imagination. You have a back room. Put in a cot, call it quickie heaven." She reaches out to touch his shoulder. "And if things are slow . . ."

Johnny-Boy doesn't recoil, not physically, but everything about the girl turns him off. He's reached the point where sex with the willing offers only minimal satisfaction. Of course, he could invite her back to the farmhouse he rents. Especially if he offered cash or drugs as an inducement. And he might do just that except for potential witnesses.

"What's your name?" he asks.

"Fatima."

"Well, Fatima, you're wastin' your breath. Tonight was my last night in the bar."

Instantly indifferent, Fatima turns away. Johnny-Boy watches her for a moment, something like a smile pulling at the edges of his mouth. Daddy Garrison had been as antidrug as a Baptist preacher, though not for the same reasons. Addiction of any kind inevitably led to the loss of volition. Good or bad, addicts went to whatever place their addictions took them. Control your own life is what Garrison preached, unaware, apparently, of his own addiction, one that led him to a bloody end in Raiford Prison. He was forty-seven at the time.

Despite the late hour, Johnny-Boy begins a search for Theo Diopolis. The man should be home by now, wherever home is, with his car parked nearby. Johnny-Boy starts in Westside, at the house of the girlfriend who's apparently no girlfriend. The lights are off and the brown Honda is nowhere to be found. He works Boomtown next, covering the side streets, past the RVs, the Quonset huts, the single wides, the bars, and the brothels. No Honda.

Johnny-Boy doesn't give up. He decides to work Oakland Gardens, a decision he immediately regrets. The number of doors bearing that red X, the one that means the dwelling's been searched, has doubled. The cops . . . no, make that Detective Weber, whose name was all over the news this morning, has grasped the obvious. Given the damage done to him, Case Dixon must've been held captive for a length of time. If they uncover the where, they'll uncover the who. And maybe they'll realize that it can't be the kid Bard Henry.

Early this morning, Johnny-Boy read about Henry's violent background in the *Baxter Bugle*. Multiple stories covering multiple pages. He also watched the extended coverage on KBAX, again with multiple reporters, one of whom was punched by Henry's loving mom. Bottom, bottom, bottom line? The kidnapping of Case Dixon required planning and self-discipline, both of which Bard Henry obviously lacks. Most likely, Weber and Mariola know it already, the only issue being whether they'll throw him to the wolves anyway.

◆

It's nearing 4:00 A.M. when Johnny-Boy gives it up and heads home. Tomorrow morning, he'll park within sight of the construction zone and hope that Diopolis drives through the gate. The construction zone runs full-out from Monday through Friday. On Sundays, only technical personnel, mostly engineers, along with a few tech workers, can be found inside.

Johnny-Boy stops for a light. He's on Baxter Boulevard, cruising past City Hall Green. The meandering path that belts the park is well-lighted by ultrawhite LED globes. The path has become a magnet for joggers. Even now, a man runs through the night, his breath pluming in the fall air. Johnny-Boy would like to join him. He'd like to shake off a little voice that's getting bigger all the time. He needs to be gone, obviously. But if Diopolis, four hours from now, doesn't show for work, the man won't return until Monday morning. Johnny-Boy's plan, to follow Diopolis when he leaves in the afternoon, will have to be abandoned. It's back to a random search.

◆

Johnny-Boy's at the very northern end of Baxter Boulevard, headed for Route 23 and home, when he spots the woman. She is sitting with her back against the wall of Spotless Laundromat, one of four retailers clustered inside a tiny strip mall fronted by a narrow parking lot. There's one car in the lot, parked at an angle, apparently empty.

Effortlessly, Johnny-Boy enters into calculation mode. He's been here many times, cruising along some obscure road, presented with a sudden opportunity. And these moments are always the time of greatest risk. A witness or a camera unseen, a cop on a routine patrol that puts him in the wrong place at the wrong time. Johnny-Boy's brain is running full-out, but there's no allowing for unforeseen contingencies.

Johnny-Boy's eyes jump to the side mirrors. He finds no oncoming vehicles and no trailing headlights. The woman comes next. He can't even guess at her age, not staring into the shadows, but doesn't care anyway. What's important is that she's not moving. On the far side of Baxter Boulevard, the lights are out in the single home on the block. A small construction site directly across the road is also dark, with no sign of a security guard or even a camera.

Johnny-Boy laughs to himself. If the woman's hurt, and not just too drunk or stoned to move, he can dial 911. That would make him a hero. A man who cares. But salvation, unfortunately for this woman, is not Johnny-Boy's game. Neither is impulsivity and he continues past the strip mall for a half mile before reversing course. Still no traffic, in front or behind. The woman appears to be exactly as he left her.

He makes a quick left into the narrow parking lot fronting the stores, then he's out of the car, approaching the woman, totally committed. The stink of alcohol greets him first and he immediately puts it together. The car parked at a crazy angle is hers. Drunk, she managed to leave the road before she passed out. Then for reasons he hopes to learn, she left the car and staggered as far as Spotless Laundromat before she lost it.

"Hey, you all right?" Johnny-Boy leans over her. She's young, in her early twenties most likely, and as drunk as he expected. Pretty, too, despite the slack jaw and a thin line of drool from the left corner of her mouth. "You need to get up, honey. You'll freeze if you stay here all night."

Johnny-Boy's surprised, but pleased, when he gives her arm a gentle tug and she sits up. "C'mon, I'll drive you home." She staggers to her feet after a gentle tug, then takes a few steps.

Sixty seconds, Johnny-Boy tells himself. Sixty seconds until she's in the van, until she's thoroughly disabled, until he owns her. Those expectations fall apart only a moment later when he presses a button on the vehicle's remote and the side door begins to open. The woman is suddenly awake, in a frenzy, screaming, "Noooooooooooooo." What with there being a house across the street, he's got to shut her up, and fast. He spins her in a half circle and drags her several feet before smashing the top of her head into the store's brick facade. Now silent, she drops, face-first, onto the sidewalk, then lies unmoving. Johnny-Boy drops to one knee and turns her onto her back. Her eyes are open, but fixed. When he touches her neck in search of a pulse, he feels nothing. Ten seconds later, he's pulling out of the parking lot, on his way home.

CHAPTER EIGHTEEN

DELIA

It's nine o'clock on Sunday morning and I'm supposed to be off duty except for emergencies. I don't know if the crap on my plate meets the emergency threshold, but deal with it I must. Lemonade from lemons. That's the challenge.

I'm at the home of my boss and friend, Commissioner Vern Taney. Lillian Taney, Vern's wife (also my friend) is in the kitchen with two of their children, Mike and Cora. Vern and Lillian's adopted daughter, Emmaline, sits on my lap. Emmaline's going on about her twice-a-week trips to Little Darling Daycare. Lillian's a stay-at-home mom, perfectly able to care for Emmaline, but they want the girl to have more contact with kids her age.

Vern and I partnered for several years, back when the city was on the brink of extinction. We've expanded our horizons since then, but the plain fact is the job of commissioner was first offered to me. I turned it down because I didn't want to sit in an office all day and I'm glad I did.

The job's changing Vern. Half administrator and half politician, he spends too much of his time either defending the force or negotiating the budget. The media expect a response to anything newsworthy, while the pols on the city council protect their flanks by also demanding answers. The murder of Case Dixon is a prime example. The boy's father continues to push for a quick arrest, the *Baxter Bugle* runs profiles of Bard Henry, the pols on the Public Safety Committee want to know when the arrest will come. I believe they're truly frightened by the suffering Dixon endured, and they won't breathe easier until Bard Henry is charged.

◆

"Sorry to drag you over here on a Saturday morning," Vern tells me when Emmaline finally slows down. "But I was busy yesterday." He grins, the smile apologetic. "I had a talk to give. To the Baxter Boosters, if you can believe that. Delia, not a single one knew anything about policing, but each and every one had an opinion."

"Par for the course, Vern. Opinions are cheap."

"True enough." He leans back in his chair, then shakes his head. He knows I'm not gonna like what he has to say, but he has to say it anyway. "Atkinson's decided to indict Bard Henry for the murder of Case Dixon."

"When?"

"As soon as he can work a deal with Caily Martin's lawyer. Could be as early as tomorrow. The middle of the week at the latest."

Caily Martin is prepared, for a price, to testify against her lover, her motive obvious enough. The deal hinges on the Sprague County prosecutor's willingness to cut a deal.

"Vern, I need more time."

"You don't think Henry's guilty. I know that, Delia, and I have doubts myself. But our opinions don't amount to a hill of crap. Deciding guilt or innocence isn't what we do. We collect evidence and pass it to prosecutors. The decision to indict or dismiss belongs to them."

"C'mon." I wave his comment off, my irritation obvious. "If there's a trial, Blanche will be called as a witness. Suppose she's asked whether she believes that Henry's guilty?"

Emmaline's had enough. She drops off my lap, takes a few steps toward the kitchen, then turns, hand on hips. "Stop fighting," she tells us. "It's not polite."

We laugh, all three of us. Time to bring the temperature down. Vern drops his hands to his thighs as Emmaline disappears into the kitchen.

"First thing," he says, "Bard Henry has a violent history. Going way back, Delia. Second thing, Henry threatened Case Dixon many times. We can produce a dozen witnesses to back the claim. Third thing, Henry knew about the party. Fourth thing, Henry left Caily Martin's home intending to confront Dixon. Fifth thing, we've got Henry outside the party in Oakland Gardens minutes before Dixon vanished. That's motive and opportunity. Sixth thing, we've got wood splinters in Henry's home and vehicle that can't be distinguished from the splinters found on Case Dixon's body."

"But not just anyone can hold a boy prisoner for three days without being discovered. His restraints included some sort of leather cuff and enough steel cable to strangle him. We can't tie Henry to any of it, the safe house or the cable or the cuff."

"I'm sure his lawyer will point that out." Vern glances at his watch. He's adding a bedroom to his house and the workmen are supposed to show up at nine thirty. "Anyway, it's not up to us, to me or to you. That said, there's nothing to stop you looking for wherever Case Dixon was held. It's expected." Another hesitation, then the real reason I've been summoned. "Something else, Delia. Late yesterday afternoon, I learned that Blanche Weber assaulted a patrolman named Jake Nurine. You should have reported the assault to me as soon as you found out. As it happened, I was blindsided by Saul Rawling. You remember Captain Rawling, our chief of patrol. Nurine's his nephew."

Called to the carpet by an old buddy, my ex-partner. No fun, but maybe deserved. "I spoke to Nurine, Vern. He told me that he didn't want to file a complaint. Plus, there were no witnesses to the actual confrontation and Nurine didn't allege that he was attacked. From what I could tell, he wanted to let it go."

"Yeah, well, now the prick maintains that he's disabled and can't work for the next two months. Or maybe forever." Vern stops for a minute to run the fingers of his right hand over his face. He's tired, more tired than he should be, considering that he spends his days behind a desk. "For the time being, I'm putting both of them, Blanche and Nurine, on paid leave. Nurine'll stay home in any event. Blanche will have to join him."

"For how long?"

"A week, at most. That's what I'm hoping, anyway."

"Does she have to surrender her gun and badge?"

"Nope." Vern leans toward me. "Look, if it gets any worse than a paid vacation, I'll fight for Blanche. She's a damn good detective and Jake Nurine's an asshole. But I'm hoping that time will cure all wounds. In the meantime, I want you to run the Dixon investigation. Personally and cooperatively."

◆

I stop in the kitchen on my way out. Emmaline's giving me a suspicious look. How dare I upset the harmony of her happy household. The girl spent her first three years as the daughter of a drug dealer. Chaos defined her life and she has a strong nose for disorder of any kind. Mike, though, is all smiles.

"Your son is dragging me to the gym again," he tells me. "Just when I was looking forward to a lazy, unproductive Sunday morning."

Unproductive? The kids, Lillian's and mine, are growing up, and fast. Meantime, I'd love a cup of coffee and some leisure of my own, but that's impossible. I've already called Blanche. When I told her to stay home, that I'd come to her, she had to know this wasn't gonna be good. As she has to know it's not only about Jake Nurine. It's also about her quick temper. We've spoken about her temper in the past. Unproductively.

◆

A cold wind catches me off guard when I leave the house. Winters throughout the Great Plains are long and cold. With no obstacle between the Rockies and the forests to the east, the winds become unrelenting from November into mid-May. What we're getting this early in October is a preview. And not a sneak preview. With the temperature in the midforties, this preview is a slap in the face.

I'm on my way to give Blanche Weber the bad news when I receive a phone call from a detective named Sam Barret.

"Sorry to bother you, chief," he says, "but you asked to be notified in case of a homicide."

Barret's in his midtwenties and smart enough, but his apologetic tone sometimes grates. Like now, when I've got enough on my mind. "Details, Sam. And quick. I'm jammed at the moment." Right away, I know I made a mistake. Barret reacts poorly to anything that sounds like a rebuke.

"So, we've got a body?" I add.

"Not exactly, not yet, but I'm at Baxter Medical Center and the docs are pessimistic. The name on the victim's Oklahoma driver's license is Mila Wegson. She's an accountant according to a business card, but she must've been partying last night. Her blood-alcohol level was nearly three times the legal limit when she was admitted."

"Sam, please . . ."

"Okay, okay. So, she was found last night in that little strip mall at the north end of Baxter Boulevard. A dry cleaner, a nail salon . . ."

"I know it."

"Well, someone smashed her head into the outer wall of the dry cleaner's. Brick, right." He pauses, but I've nothing to say. "One time, one injury. At four o'clock this morning. No robbery, either. A diamond pendant and a purse with a hundred and twenty dollars inside were both recovered at the scene. Plus, her unlocked car was in the parking lot with the key in the ignition."

"She's alive, though?"

"Yeah, I couldn't find a pulse when I first arrived, but the paramedics did. So, she's alive, but barely, and she probably wouldn't be except a neighbor across the street heard a scream. He's an old guy, right, like in his eighties, and it took him a minute to raise the shade on the window. He saw the woman lyin' there and called 911."

"Her attacker was gone?"

"She was alone in the parking lot, but the neighbor, Carl Hurt, saw a vehicle, a white van, on Baxter Boulevard. Headed north toward the old city line."

"Not in the parking lot?"

"No, on Baxter Boulevard."

"I'm assuming he didn't catch a plate number."

"Too far away."

◆

I pull to the curb, my attention captured. I can hear Barret's breathing on the other end of the connection. He's waiting for instructions and I want to make sure that mine are clear.

"Is Mila Wegson conscious?"

"She's in surgery."

"Then there's no reason for you to stick around. You can check back later. Did you work the crime scene?"

"Yeah, the vic was removed to Baxter Medical by the time I arrived, so there was no real urgency. I found blood and hair on the wall."

"Any sign of a sustained attack?"

"No, and what with her purse not being touched, it's pretty likely the perp had a personal motive for the attack."

"A good place to start. And again, there's no sense remaining at the hospital. You can check in later. Let's find out where she was living, if she had a boyfriend, or even a husband. That shouldn't be too hard if she was working at the construction site."

"I'm on it, boss."

◆

Blanche isn't all that happy to see me. That jaw, large by any standards, is pointed right at me and thick enough to pass for the barrel of a shotgun. She's pissed off but stymied at the moment. I rang the bell just as Owen Walsh, her partner, was leaving for work. Now we're all smiling politely.

"Off to work, Owen?" I ask.

"Sunday, busiest day of the week."

"Well, happy drillin'."

"No worries there. I'm always happy. My patients, on the other hand . . ." Another smile before Owen heads out to his car.

I've only met Owen a few times, but I like him. He's friendly, and basically gentle. Blanche leads me into a large eat-in kitchen. The appliances, including an enormous, two-door refrigerator, are stainless steel.

"You want coffee?"

I stare into the back of Blanche's head as I remind myself that she dug the hole she's in. "No, had enough for one morning."

"So, get on with it." She turns to face me, her dark eyes blazing. "Will I be shot at sundown or sunrise?"

"Neither. You're being put on administrative leave. Paid leave, Blanche. You'll have to stay away from the house."

"Did the asshole file a complaint?"

"That's what you should have done, Blanche. But the answer is no. Instead, he's claims that he's disabled. He's already filed for workers' comp."

"And he's blaming me?"

"Who else?" I'm expecting a smart-ass response, but for once Blanche has nothing to say. "Nurine hasn't filed a complaint. Not yet, anyway, but even if he does, there were no witnesses to the actual confrontation. You can claim self-defense. Myself, I don't think it'll come to that. Vern expects things to cool down in a week or so. But if it does go bad, he told me that he'd fight for you."

Blanche lays her hands on the kitchen table. "Yeah, he said that?"

"He means it too."

"What about my gun and badge?"

"No change there, and no change to your policing powers. Just stay away from the house."

Blanche looks at me for a moment, then gets up and pours coffee for us both. With no choice in the matter, I add sugar and a little milk before taking a sip. I'm meeting Mike, Danny, Lillian, and Zoe at the newly opened Code Red Gym and I'm already late. Praise the Lord.

"Spill it, Delia," Blanche says, her tone equal parts amusement and exasperation.

"Bard Henry's arrest solves too many problems for too many people. He'll be indicted by the middle of the week unless we produce another suspect. And before you get pissed, Vern told me that he has doubts too. In fact, he's putting me in charge of the investigation, whether I like it or not. But he did offer me some advice. Find out where Case Dixon was held for the last three days of his life. Find the where, find the who."

"And that's it?"

"Maybe not." I summarize the first part of Sam Barret's report, the ferocity of the attack, the early morning hour, the valuables left behind, the victim's blood-alcohol level. "According to Barret, she's not expected to survive."

"What does any of this have to do with me?"

"There was a witness, a man named Carl Hurt who lives across the street. He heard a scream and went to the window. Not fast enough to witness the attack, but he did see two things. First, Mila Wegson—that's the vic's name—lying unconscious. Second, a white van traveling north on Baxter Boulevard. Didn't catch a plate number and can't identify the driver, but if I remember right, there were several calls to the hotline mentioning a white panel van."

"Yeah, with no business signs on the sides or the door. Was there a sign on the van Hurt saw?"

"Barret didn't ask. No reason he should. Now I'm leaving it up to you. By the way, Wegson had a business card in her wallet. She's an accountant. I sent Barret to investigate her private life, including her employment. He'll check in with the hospital from time to time, but there's no reason why your investigations should cross paths."

Lemonade from lemons.

CHAPTER NINETEEN

BLANCHE WEBER

I follow Delia outside and light a cigarette. Though we split the bills, the house belongs to Owen and there's no smoking inside. It seems that smoking is death to gums and teeth, even secondhand smoke, even secondhand smoke magically filtering through a closed door in a far corner of the house. Except for the smoking, Owen's not very demanding, but I see trouble ahead. Owen craves stability, normality, community, roots. He wants children and I'm not the motherly type. Worse yet, in a sense I've betrayed him by applying to major police departments far from Baxter. If an offer comes through, I can't see myself declining, though I'm sure I'll be going alone.

Delia drives off without looking back. I've received my marching orders and I suppose I should be rejoicing. The whole business with the shithead could have gone worse, a lot worse. For instance, our beloved commissioner, Vern Taney, might have covered his ass by suspending me. He might have ordered me to face a disciplinary board. Instead, he told Delia he'd fight for me.

Skeptic that I am, especially when it comes to bureaucracies, I do believe the man will keep his word should a fight develop. This time.

◆

It's cold outside, but I continue to suck away as I settle enough to consider the job assigned to me. The Wegson attack bears strong similarities to the kidnapping of Case Dixon. I'm not talking about the white van. I'm not a profiler, but I'm not uninformed either. Impulsive serial killers are caught early. The ones who kill for years are extremely careful. They patrol their territory on an almost daily basis, searching for an opportunity that presents as little risk as possible. The means to control their victims, along with a place to bring them, are always close at hand. It's that first move, though, from the street into a vehicle, be it car, van, or SUV, that worries them. That's because there are no second chances for men like them and they know it.

Case Dixon left the party stoned out of his mind. He didn't have a car and couldn't have driven in any event. So, he's on foot in Oakland Gardens where there's not a single occupied house on some blocks, and where more streetlights are broken than working. At the same time, a murderer trolls the neighborhood, having chosen it precisely because it's dark and deserted. He moves from street to street in search of the helpless.

It's 4:00 A.M. and Mila Wegson, her blood-alcohol level three times the legal limit, is utterly helpless. A white van passes, on one level a coincidence, on another an inevitability given the days and hours the man invests in his obsessions. Either way, he knows this is his chance. All he need do is get her into the van without being seen. But drunks are unpredictable, and this woman is almost beyond drunk, yet for some reason she screams. Now he's got to shut her up and get away. After all, there's a house across the street and he's on Baxter Boulevard. With no time to spare, he slams her into the wall, then jumps into the van and heads for home.

The van sighting adds fuel to the fire, of course, and gives me a place to begin, but I'm not locked on to one possibility. Given her blood-alcohol level, Mila Wegson had to be out partying. Assuming Barret runs the location down and interviews her companions, an obvious perpetrator may well emerge. Myself, I avoid tunnel vision.

◆

I finish my cigarette, crush it on the flagstone path leading to the sidewalk. I'll carry the butt into the house and drop it in the kitchen pail. As I stand up, a green SUV pulls to a stop in front of the house. Detective Laura Udell is first to emerge, followed by Detectives Marcus Goodman and Cade Barrow. Formerly special forces in the military, Cade heads our SWAT team. He's smiling as he approaches.

"Hey, Blanche, how ya holdin' up?"

"I've been better."

"We've come by to offer support. For what it's worth."

Marcus Goodman steps in. He's the only Black cop on the force. "I dealt with it, too, when I first came on board," he tells me. "Blackface cartoons taped to my locker. Or worse, NO MONKEYS ALLOWED—."

"What'd you do about it?"

"I stayed cool until a cop challenged me in public. Broke the man's jaw is what happened next."

"Were you suspended?"

"Nope. But that's because I filed a number of complaints before I threw that punch. If Chief Black suspended me, he would have found himself explaining why he didn't address the problem earlier. Say, at a deposition."

I get the message. File complaints, with documentation, immediately after an incident. Cover your ass, which anybody with a modicum of self-control would have done without thinking twice.

"Listen," Cade tells me, "you want, I'll have a talk with Nurine. I've measured him and I think he'll fold if he's confronted. I know you can't do it yourself, the position you're in at the moment."

Mostly, Cade's easygoing. Quick with a smile or a pat on the shoulder. On missions, though, he becomes the polar opposite. Totally focused, he's often first through the door, and God help the asshole who decides to put up a fight. I have no doubt that he can intimidate the likes of Jake Nurine. But I met Cade's wife, Annie, at a BBQ this summer. Annie lost a hand serving her country, which hasn't slowed her down for a second. I remember her with a baby in one arm, the one with the prosthesis, while she flipped burgers with the other. I can't ask Cade to fight my fight.

"Let it go, Cade. Delia's got my back. Taney too."

I hope, I hope, I hope.

◆

I change into white slacks and a dark brown sweater. On warm days, I add a blazer, but not today. I slip into a wool coat that drops almost to my knees. Better still as it effectively hides the Browning behind my right hip. Call me paranoid, but I always carry a backup gun. In this case, a Seecamp .32 with no sights, total weight 11.5 ounces. The weapon's designed for close-up use and won't snag when you pull it from your pocket. I think of it as more of a panic gun than a backup gun. When you have to have a weapon in your hand, like right now this very fucking second.

I drop the Seecamp into my coat pocket as I head out the door. It's still cold and the sky overhead is slate gray with only a few hazy breaks in the clouds. I hop into my car, a 2018 Jeep Renegade. And, yes, it's a big-boy car, and, yes, Owen wishes I'd tone it down. Maybe I will someday, but this Jeep has earned my loyalty. Call it luck of the draw. The car runs as well today as it did on the day it came off the assembly line.

First stop, the crime scene, of course. Barret told Delia there was nothing to see, but I want to look for myself. You never know.

The mall's up and running when I pull into the parking lot, with a dozen vehicles parked in front of the four businesses. Thus, despite several potholes with dirt bottoms, tire impressions are off the table. Six feet from the door to the Spotless Laundromat, yellow crime-scene tape, guarded by a Baxter PD cruiser, blocks off a portion of the wall. I pull into a parking space as far from the cruiser as possible. I can't approach that tape without announcing myself to the single, uniformed officer in the cruiser. Technically, it's still Barret's case and my appearance, a cop on leave, would be reported back to him.

Would Delia be upset? She wasn't explicit. Yes, the investigations, mine and Barret's, would run in parallel, but are there to be no interactions? The juices are rising, as they always do when I start an investigation. There's a bad guy at the other end who needs to be separated from society. Once upon a time, I had a boyfriend who labeled himself a 'true libertarian.' The relationship didn't last long because liberty, to him, meant the liberty to screw any woman who'd have him. But he told me that maintaining enough order for people to mostly go about their business reasonably securely was a legitimate function of government.

Mostly, I think my ex was right. All cops do is keep the lid on. Despite reports to the contrary, I think we do a pretty good job. Now I need to keep the lid on myself. I want to jump out of the car and start with a close-up examination of the nearly black stains on the wall and the concrete sidewalk, but I don't. Instead, I let the window down and light a cigarette as I try to imagine what I'd gain from a close examination. The cop in the cruiser is undoubtedly waiting for the CSU to arrive, and he's probably half-asleep. No sense in waking him up.

That doesn't mean there's nothing to learn in the mall, only that I need to explore without attracting attention. There are no security cameras on the exteriors of the businesses, but what about inside? Maybe protecting the stock and the cash register seemed more urgent than a view of the parking lot when the stores first opened. From north to south, there's Soonai Nail Salon, Spotless Laundromat, FreshPet Dog Grooming, and MaxHealth Nutrition. Two, Soonai and MaxHealth, have steel housings designed to contain roll-down steel shutters at the roofline. I'll do these first, but I'm not expecting much. Shutter systems aren't cheap, to buy or install. Nobody makes that investment, then leaves the shutters rolled up at night.

◆

I step out of the car and head across the street. First the witness, then the follow-up. The man I want to speak to is named Carl Hurt. Hurt's an older man according to Barret, but it's a child, a young boy, who answers the door. He stares up at me, his green eyes suspicious, until I show my badge and ask, "May I speak with Mr. Hurt?"

"Daaaaaad, the cops are here."

A man in his thirties wearing designer sweats appears a moment later. He rubs the boy's head before saying, "You want my father-in-law. He's in the sunroom. Let me show you."

He leads me through the living room and a large kitchen to a room at the back of the house. A pair of skylights and the glass doors leading to the backyard would let in a good deal of light if there was much light to let in. It's too cloudy today, but I get the point.

A book in his hands, a man in his seventies lies on a chaise longue. He puts the book on a side table, drops his legs over the side of the chair, and sits up. Carl Hurt's painfully thin, his cheekbones are hollow and as prominent as his brow, the skin below nearly translucent. I'm guessing that he's been sick, but sick or not, his blue eyes are alert and confident.

"Detective Weber." I offer my hand, which he takes.

"Carl Hurt." He gestures to a wicker chair. "Have a seat. You want coffee?"

I take the seat but refuse the coffee. "I won't take up much of your time, Mr. Hurt."

"Time's all I have these days. How's that woman doin'?"

"Mila Wegson. She was in surgery last I heard. The injury was very severe."

"Ah, too bad."

The man who brought me into the room, Hurt's son-in-law, breaks in. "I have chores to do, so if you don't mind, I'll get to them. Anything you need, just give a yell."

Carl waits until we're alone before saying. "Do you think it's a betrayal when you like your son-in-law better than your daughter?" A sly grin lights his face.

"I don't have a daughter, Mr. Hurt, or a son-in-law, but I suspect it's a matter of taste."

Hurt raises a finger to his lips: "Shhhhhh."

"Your secret's safe with me." I smile, but it's time for business. "I know you've done this before, but would you please go over your experience last night? I want to hear it firsthand."

"Sure." He stops for a moment, turning his eyes to the left as he collects his thoughts. "Okay, so you hear a lot about intelligent design. Like humans are so perfectly designed they could only have been created by God. Well, there's nothing perfect about wrapping the prostate around the urethra. That's called a design flaw, and it's the reason I was awake last night when I heard the scream. It was after my second trip to the bathroom and I was lying in bed, drifting off, but not asleep. That scream, detective? Terror, that's what I heard. Terror."

He stops for a moment, then sighs. "If I was a little faster . . . see, I have a bad back. I'm okay if I get out of bed slowly, like one piece at a time, but if I jump out of bed quick, I'm halfway to crippled by the pain. All I'm sayin' is that it took me a little time to get to the window and pull the shade to one side. I noticed a car, first thing, parked at an angle in the middle of the lot, then the woman. She was lying against the laundromat's front wall. Not movin', detective, not at all. I called 911 straight away, then got dressed and crossed the street. Poor woman didn't look any better up close. Fact is, I thought she was dead."

"Is that it, Mr. Hurt? Is that all you told Detective Barret?"

"Except for the white van."

I nod. "Please."

"The van was on Baxter Boulevard, close to the northern end of the parking lot. Not movin' slow, not movin' fast, just a passing vehicle. There ain't much traffic, that hour of the morning, but there's some."

"Do you know the make of the van?"

Hurt raises his eyes to the ceiling as he struggles to recall some element he's all but forgotten. "I'm no good anymore when it comes to makes and models. Gave up my license two years ago. But there was one thing about the van that caught my attention when I first saw it. I don't know if it's important."

"Just tell me what you saw."

"There were no windows in the back or on the side. A panel van, right? Not a family van."

"Used for business?"

"Yeah, I guess so."

"Did you notice the name of the business?"

Another pause, then. "Not exactly sure. I'm just seein' a plain white van."

"That's great, Mr. Hurt. Now, when you heard the scream, what time was it? If you remember?"

"I remember. It was four forty-three when I heard the scream."

"Exactly? Are you sure?"

"I am. See, I've got a digital clock with big red numbers on my nightstand. I use it for a night-light when I need to hit the head. Forty-three minutes after four o'clock. Exactly."

CHAPTER TWENTY
BLANCHE WEBER

There are cars in the lot when I cross the street, and gawkers out of their cars, pausing to take a quick photo of the dried blood. They can't get close enough for a selfie, but it'll make for a good story over dinner tonight. Even as I make my way to the nail salon, a KBAX news van pulls onto the lot. I turn my head away after a glance at the two women and the man who emerge. I don't recognize them, all to the good.

I hit Soonai first, then MaxHealth. Both have security cameras inside and both assure me that their shutters were drawn last night when they left for home. My reception at FreshPet is less than enthusiastic. Operated, apparently, by a single worker, a woman with a soapy dog in a tub, she points to a pair of leashed dogs near a grooming table.

"I spoke to the cop already, the one sleeping outside. You wanna know what I said, ask him."

And the woman who now lies in a coma? Does she count so little that you can't take a moment to speak with the cops? I leave the questioned unanswered because there are no security cameras in the store.

Spotless Laundromat comes next, my last chance at what was a longshot from the beginning. I move quickly because there are now three BPD cops in the mall. They're gathered around the bloodstained wall at the far end of the laundromat, taking samples, blood and probably hair. Apparently, the state CSU copped out. Personally, I don't believe there's a shot in hell they'll find any trace of the attacker, but the effort has to be made. Otherwise, a defense lawyer is sure to pronounce the investigation sloppy.

I manage to get inside the laundromat without being seen. That's my first lucky break. Three more follow. A counter bearing a cash register and a gallon container of fabric softener rests against the wall near the front of the store. Above and behind the counter, a sleek camera projects into the store. That's two. The third, perhaps the most important, is that I know the woman behind the counter. Her name is Helen Wojcik, which she pronounces Woe-chick. We met at a BPD fundraiser a couple months ago. I remember Helen first for her accent, not impossibly heavy but definitely there, and for her railing against government aid of any kind. She, herself, puts in ten hours days, six days each week, and why can't they do the same?

Helen was more than a couple drinks ahead of me that day, and I recall patiently absorbing her ire only because she and her family tend their teeth in Owen's office.

"Ah, Blanche," she says, sober now, "terrible, terrible. What happens last night. This woman, she will live?"

"Touch and go, Helen." I watch the woman nod, as if I'd said something important. She's in her late thirties, a sturdy woman with broad shoulders and an erect bearing. She looks to her right, at the three women handling laundry dropped off earlier. Latinas all, I wonder if they've come from the compound in Maryville County. Helen's looking at them as if she expects one of them to run off with a washing machine.

"Was that working last night?" I point to the camera.

"Yes, always. They break in one night and try to steal from the change machine. This I empty every night, so these morons only break machine. Then they try washing machines, then dryers. How many cars drive by with nobody noticing broken front window which cost hundreds to replace?"

I stop her before she can list every penny of damage. "So, why not install shutters like your neighbors?"

"For what? More than fifteen hundred for cheapest kind and shutters don't protect from robbery." She glances fondly at the camera. "Video runs to computer in storeroom and then to Cloud."

"The video, Helen, what does it include?"

"Lens is wide angle." She touches her right eye. "Camera sees entire laundromat."

"That's good, because I need to review whatever the all-seeing eye saw last night between four forty and four fifty A.M."

Helen nods once, then bawls, "Teddy."

At the far end of the room, a head pops out of the opened front of a washer. A boy about sixteen rises to his feet, then trots up to the counter. "What's up, Mom?"

"Here is Detective Weber," Helen replies, putting emphasis on the detective part. "She needs to see video from last night."

"No problemo."

Helen takes another look at her workers. "Speak English," she tells her son.

◆

Teddy leads me to a door at the back of the laundromat. He opens the door to reveal a shallow room that runs the width of the store. Drums of detergent sit next to a wet/dry vacuum against the wall. Shelves above hold bleach, softener, and dryer sheets. To my left, a row of filing cabinets is topped by open files. To my right, a computer sits on a small desk with a chair in front. I'm tempted to ask why they still use paper files when my eye happens on a patch of mold near the ceiling above the cabinets.

"Black mold," Teddy declares. "I spray it with bleach every few days, but it keeps comin' back. What we need is better exhaust fans for the dampness. It's growin' in a couple other places too." He shrugs, then changes the subject. "What happened last night, it hadda be real bad from the mess out front. I heard the woman died."

"Last update I had, she was alive, Teddy."

"I mean, what was she doin' in the mall anyway? It was after four in the morning."

"If she wakes up, we'll ask her." I gesture to the computer. "Meanwhile, I need to check out the data from four forty to four fifty this morning. Tell me, does your camera use a motion detector?"

"Nope, it runs full-time."

"And the data flows to the computer?"

"To the computer and to the Cloud. You can store a lot of data in the Cloud if you're willing to pay for it." He taps a key, bringing the computer to life. "The computer's programmed to delete the data after two days. Up in the Cloud, it stays in place for a year. Now, tell me the time again."

A minute later, I'm looking at a live shot. Teddy will start from here, then scroll backward. I want to take a closer look before he begins and I ask him to hold it for a moment. Helen was wrong. The camera's field doesn't extend all the way to the back of the laundromat, but it does include the front window. Carl Hurt places a white van heading north on Baxter Boulevard immediately after he heard a scream. Now I'm trying to place the van inside the mall's parking lot. Two problems though. Four signs of various sizes block much of the window. Neither does the image, clean as it is, stretch any great distance into the parking lot.

As Teddy scrolls back through the hours, I imagine a sequence of events that's little more than a wish list. A predator spots a victim inside a mall parking lot. He pulls into the mall, grabs the woman, but things go wrong and he needs to get out fast. He has a problem though. The mall lot has a single entrance and he's facing away from it. In a hurry as he turns the van around in the narrow parking lot, he brings the van close enough to the store's front window to be recorded.

I'm holding my breath as the video rolls forward from 4:40. I let it out when the time stamp passes 4:43. I don't stop watching, though, and my patience is finally rewarded at 4:47.

"What's that?" Teddy points to a shadow that passes the window from right to left. When I don't respond, he rolls the video backward, then watches in slow motion. "You see that?"

"What do you think it is, Teddy?"

"It's too long to be a car. I'd say we're lookin' at the bottom edge of a van."

"What color?"

"White, definitely white."

◆

Outside, I move away from the news crew and the BPD cops before calling Delia. I'm excited by my discovery, but Delia eventually drags me back to earth. She listens patiently while I brag about putting the van seen by Hurt inside the parking lot immediately after the attack on Mila Wegson.

"Great work, Blanche," she tells me when I finally slow down. "Did you copy the data?"

"To a thumb drive. It's in my pocket."

Overhead, the skies are lightening. I glance north along Baxter Boulevard as I wait for Delia to speak. The van was headed north, out of town, when Hurt saw it. That jibes with a judgment I've been reaching for the past couple days. We're searching abandoned buildings in Oakland Gardens, hoping to locate Case Dixon's little prison. But even in Oakland Gardens with its abandoned homes and dark streets, Dixon's killer would be taking a big risk if he operated in the neighborhood. Most of the abandoned homes have doors long unlocked by squatters. Sheets of plywood cover some windows, but not all. And a space, if only a bedroom, would have to be escape proof and soundproof. Could the necessary modifications be made without somebody noticing? And who's to say that one of the many drug addicts who haunt the neighborhood wouldn't wander up to the house, stoned out of his mind, while Dixon was inside? On the other hand, there are many isolated structures out in the farmland surrounding the city, including farmhouses for rent and abandoned barns that could be converted with far less risk. One had been used in a kidnapping/extortion scheme two years ago.

"You know, Blanche, this doesn't help Bard Henry unless we can tie the attack on Mila Wegson to the death of Case Dixon. Right now, we can't. Keep in mind, Wegson is a woman, Dixon was a man."

"I know. As a general rule, heterosexual killers murder women, gay killers murder men. It's all about the fantasy. But there are definitely exceptions, like Dennis Rader, the BTK killer. He killed men, women, and children. The Night Stalker too. I can't remember his name."

"Richard Ramirez. And you're jumping to so many conclusions that I've lost count. What do we actually have? A few anonymous phone calls mentioning a white van, which is now associated with a probable kidnap attempt. But any connection to Cade Dixon or Bard Henry is mere speculation at this point."

"Okay, Delia, I get it. And what I'm gonna do is find and arrest the asshole who attacked Mila Wegson. Just now, I'll take a ride along Baxter Boulevard, see if I can locate an outdoor security camera with a view of the road. I want to get a better look at the van. I won't get a plate number, but there might be a distinguishing mark, a scrape or a dent, that'll allow a positive ID when I run the van down."

"Sounds like a plan. Good luck."

◆

I'm in the car lighting a cigarette when my phone beeps, announcing an incoming text message. I don't recognize the name or the number, but I surely get the point.

Hello you fucking whore. You're a disgrace to your job, you and your fagget boyfriend. Maybe you're thinking how you got over real good yesterday, but your time is coming. My advice, don't ever be the first one through the door because there ain't nobody gonna follow unless it's your dyke bitch boss.

I'm not shocked, not even surprised. No, what I do, remembering the kind advice I received from Marcus Goodman, is forward the message to Captain Delia Mariola and go about my business.

CHAPTER TWENTY-ONE

JOHNNY-BOY

Johnny-Boy's been driving all night, south and east to Indian Hills, a suburb of Little Rock, where he maintains a small base. He's now sitting across from Mike Sedgwick, universally called Sedge. There's a wooden desk between them covered with files, empty coffee containers, fast-food wrappers, and a pile of car keys, most with remote fobs attached. An oversized coffee rests within easy reach of Johnny-Boy. He needs it.

"The van didn't work out?" Sedge asks.

"Too many tickets," Johnny-Boy replies. "No windows, right? That makes it commercial. But a commercial van has to have a business sign on both sides in some states. And cops, when they can't see inside after a stop, usually decide to take a closer look." He crosses his legs and flashes a brief smile. "Times when that's inconvenient, Sedge. As you can imagine."

Sedge Sedgwick does understand, about the van, about Johnny-Boy. Johnny-Boy can read that much in the man's dark eyes, a quick flash in all that sludge. "Your point is taken, Paul. And you got a right to be left alone, too, like every born American."

In fact, Johnny-Boy hasn't picked up a single ticket, and even when he was stopped at that checkpoint, with Case Dixon's body in the back, the cop hadn't said a word about the van. On the other hand, he can still hear the woman's scream, totally unexpected, and maybe not even related to him, but to some alcohol-inspired memory. More to the point, as he drove away, a curtain in the upper story of the house across the street moved and a narrow slice of a human face appeared. Johnny-Boy was already on Baxter Boulevard, safe probably, except for the van. Too distinctive, it has to go.

◆

Two flags hang beneath a small sign on the wall behind Sedgwick. The sign reads SEDGWICK MOTORS. The red flag on the left bears the crossed bars of the Confederate battle flag. The flag on the right is a fifty-star American flag hung upside down. Johnny-Boy has always imagined himself a solitary predator, the outside world his territory. He claims no more responsibility for his environment than a pack of hyenas at a water hole. Sedge's political sentiments are merely amusing, the sort of commitment Johnny-Boy will never be stupid enough to make.

"So, whatta ya lookin' for?" Sedge asks.

"A straight swap."

"Nah, can't do it. I gotta charge a fee." Sedge's neck sits almost on his shoulders, a mushroom on a decayed stump.

"How do I know what you did with the van? You coulda killed someone. I mean, would you tell me if you did? Would I wanna know?"

Johnny-Boy doesn't dispute the possibility. No point. Sedge is as greedy as a weasel in a chicken coop. "How much?"

"A grand oughta do it."

"Not a problem, Sedge, but I want it done quick. The registration, the plates, everything."

Sedge looks at Johnny-Boy for a moment, saying nothing until Johnny-Boy goes into his pocket. Johnny-Boy's visited several ATMs on his way to Indian Hills, anticipating this development. He counts out ten hundreds, passes them over, watches Sedge stuff them in his pocket as he rises.

"Okay, let's roll. You need a rush job and I'm gonna see you get it."

◆

Sedge leads Johnny-Boy out of the office and onto the lot. Maybe a hundred cars sit in uneven rows and Sedge winds his way between the rows to a garage at the back of the lot. He steps inside and calls out, "Cammy, come over here."

A moment later, Cammy appears, a young Black man who might've walked off a professional basketball court. Obviously in shape, he's well over six feet tall.

"Hey, Paul," he says to Johnny-Boy, "what's up?"

"He's tradin' in the van," Sedge tells Cammy. "Find him one the same price. Not more, right?"

Cammy's big enough to crush Sedge's head with one hand, but he only nods, expressionless. "Got it, boss."

◆

Johnny-Boy slips a C-note into Cammy's hand as they walk away from the garage. He doesn't have to say why.

"So, what you need, Paul?"

"A van with tinted windows. Not too dark."

He leaves it at that. They've been here before, and Cammy knows that Johnny-Boy puts reliability at the top of his must-have list. He doesn't know why and doesn't ask as he leads Johnny-Boy to a 2018 Dodge Caravan. The van doesn't have a sliding side door, a definite negative, but the windows along the side and in the rear are dark enough to block a casual glance. There's a small dent on the back fender, a tear in the driver's seat back and the green paint is slightly faded. All to the good.

"Don't look like much," Cammy admits, "but it runs nice. Surprised me when it first come in. Tranny's doin' its job, brakes are near new and the steering's tight. I put in shocks and changed the plugs, but that's it. Didn't need nothin' else." He pats the Caravan's hood. "Two hundred and eighty-three horses, and they're all pullin'."

◆

An hour later, Johnny-Boy drives the Caravan off the lot. The plates on the back were taken from a wreck, the registration's a near-perfect forgery, the VIN on the dash a fake. Driving the van anywhere in Arkansas would certainly present a risk. But Johnny-Boy's headed for Baxter, where out-of-state license plates are more common than local plates. True, if a cop decides to run the plates, or check the registration, he (or maybe the cop) will be in trouble. But the phony reg on the old van has already passed scrutiny and he's not really worried. No, what's bothering Johnny-Boy is returning to Baxter at all.

Hit and run. That's been Johnny-Boy's modus operandi since he first heard the term. A target constantly moving. But there's still Theo Diopolis. Theo and Johnny-Boy's reputation for extreme reliability. Once he accepts a contract, it's as good as done. So, it's back to Baxter after a night without sleep. If all goes well, he'll arrive soon after dark, in time for a long rest before he takes up his surveillance of the construction site.

Two hours into his ride home, he pulls into a fast-food court on I-55. Pizza, burgers, tacos, and doughnuts, the usual, available at various stalls inside a featureless building that reminds Johnny-Boy of an airplane hangar. Just beyond the doorway, he hesitates long enough to sweep the building in search of threats or prey. There are no threats in sight. How could there be? On the prey side, though, his eyes are quickly drawn to a young boy sitting by himself at one of the tables scattered throughout the building. The boy appears to be about seventeen but could be younger. That's not the point. No, between the tousled, sandy-blond hair, the wisp of a goatee, and the torn, obviously soiled jeans, his appearance screams runaway or throwaway. But whether he fled or was summarily tossed to the wolves doesn't really matter because Johnny-Boy's already lived that life. After Garrison Granger's arrest, he'd been forced into a world he barely understood. He did have that one advantage, the skills he'd acquired in Garrison's gym, but the rest of it was a blank slate.

How to get an apartment, a job, open a bank account, acquire a driver's license and a car, find friends he could trust, allies he could rely on. Everything had to be learned with imposed penalties for any failure, any wrong turn. And this bewildered kid, with his pale blue eyes and slumped shoulders? Most likely, he doesn't have a dollar in his pocket or a place to lay his head.

Johnny-Boy walks past the kid to a food stall. A few minutes later, he returns with two doughnuts, a large container of coffee, and a handful of napkins. He's wearing a tan zip-up jacket over a white T-shirt, and khaki trousers. His expression is mild, as always, his power well-hidden by his blocky frame. He takes a table six feet from the kid, sips at his coffee, and begins to work on a glazed doughnut. He's sure the kid will speak first, drawn by a pressing need to be somewhere else. Probably dropped here by a traveler headed the wrong way, he has to move on before he's confronted by security guards or cops. So, he'll take a chance he shouldn't take, but has to take. He'll reach out.

The breakthrough comes a few minutes later as Johnny-Boy's wiping his fingers. "Hey, mister."

Johnny-Boy makes the kid repeat himself before responding. Then he looks up, pulled from his thoughts, his expression mild.

"You goin' north by any chance?" the kid asks.

"North to where?"

"St. Louis maybe."

Johnny-Boy returns to his doughnut, every nerve alive on the inside, showing nothing on the outside. At some point, Johnny-Boy needs to head west, but he could stay on I-55 as far as St. Louis. The interstate runs through sparsely populated farm country along the west side of the Mississippi River. An alternative route is more direct, but involves a spider's web of state roads through numerous small towns. Towns with local cops who protect their turf like warlords.

"I could get you close," he tells the boy. "Close to St. Louis. What's your name?"

"Sloan."

Johnny-Boy stares into Sloan's almost colorless eyes for a moment, then pulls a small roll from his pocket and peels off a ten-dollar bill. "Here, get yourself something. You can eat in the car."

Sloan hesitates again and Johnny-Boy can see the boy's thoughts as they dance through his brain. He doesn't trust this stranger, doesn't and shouldn't, but he's broke and hungry. And he'll have to trust somebody because he's almost surely running from the kind of beef that can only be resolved by flight. Otherwise, he might've (and probably should have) remained wherever he's from. However hard that little world, he at least understands it.

◆

"So, kid, you runnin' away or what?" Johnny-Boy waits until they're cruising north on I-55 before asking the question. Traffic's light and he's set the cruise control to 72 mph.

Sloan lifts his chin. "Nah, I got dumped. My mom found a new boyfriend who didn't like me. He told her that one of us had to go, her child or him."

"And she picked him?"

"What could I say—I don't know your name."

"Paul."

"Yeah, well it was like this. He was the one puttin' the junk up her nose. I was the snotty kid who needed dinner."

There's more to it, but Johnny-Boy doesn't push. He wants to put the boy at ease, not force him into a corner. He lets the kid stew for a half hour, then pushes against the seat to flex his lower back. The fatigue is catching up with him.

"I been there," he finally says. "On my own. Didn't get thrown out exactly. See, my father was quick with the belt. One word out of line and he'd be whalin' away, especially when he was drunk, which was pretty much all the time. Me, I was too young to fight him with my hands, so I took off." He hesitates for a moment, then says, his tone bitter, "Daddy never bothered lookin'."

"Leastways you knew your daddy."

Johnny-Boy taps the steering wheel. "See, that's where kids without fathers get it wrong. Maybe you watch too much television. Havin' a father can be worse than not. Remember, we both ended up on our own, even if the push came from different directions. I still have scars on my legs."

None of this is true, but the kid eats it up. Most likely he's imagining some kind of bond between them, hard lives shared, battlefield revelations. And why not? The kid's whole life has been a battle.

"So, you got friends in St. Louis?" he asks.

"Can't say I do."

"You tellin' me you're goin' in cold? Man, I lived in St. Louis. Tough town, Sloan. No mercy, if you know what I mean."

"What could I say. I had to get out of Indian Hills."

"Cops?"

"Worse."

Johnny-Boy manages a short laugh. "Been there, done that, too. But why St. Louis?"

"Gotta go somewhere." He stares out through the windshield for a moment before asking the question Johnny-Boy's been waiting for him to ask. "And you? Where you headed?"

"Little city called Baxter. Opportunity heaven."

"Never heard of it."

"Well, you need to get around, Sloan. Nissan's buildin' a factory in Baxter. Thousands of jobs, thousands of men and women away from home with money in their pockets. Like I said, opportunity heaven."

Another pause while the kid thinks it over. "Is that what you do? Work construction?"

"Nope, my back's in no condition for hard labor. I tend a bar near the construction site. But you? What can you do?"

"I worked in my uncle's lumberyard."

"You cut wood there?"

"Some, but I mostly hauled it. Ya know, loaded and unloaded the trucks."

"How old are you?" Johnny-Boy raises a finger. "That you can prove."

"Sixteen."

"You have to be eighteen to work the site, but there's new construction goin' up all over the city. New construction and a shortage of workers to do the constructing. That's why the contractors aren't all that choosy. They can't afford to be. You'll catch on if you're willing to work hard."

"Work wasn't my problem, Paul. I worked hard when I was at work. Problems came after I went home."

◆

Just outside St. Louis, Johnny-Boy catches I-70 heading west. It's beginning to rain and Johnny-Boy's spent enough time in the Midwest to know he's running straight into whatever system's crossing the country. He'd hoped to tough it out, to drive nonstop all the way home, but the rain and wind prove too much and he pulls into a truck stop that includes a diner. Alongside him, the kid's asleep. Johnny-Boy nudges him awake.

"You hungry?"

"Yeah."

Inside, he waits until Sloan drops onto a chair, then says, "I'm heading to the john. If a waiter shows up, just ask for coffee. We'll worry about the food when I get back."

Locked inside the diner's tiny bathroom, he drops a blue tablet pulled from the inside pocket of his jacket. Adderall's an amphetamine, to be sure, but the dose is small relative to the handfuls used by the tweakers. Johnny-Boy avoids drugs, but there are times when he just has to be awake.

Back in the van twenty minutes later, Sloan falls asleep almost immediately. That leaves Johnny-Boy to stare through the windshield, the rain forcing him to focus as he listens to the hiss of the tires and the steady thump of the windshield wipers. There are more semis on the road than passenger cars and they throw up fountains of spray that obscure his vision as he passes. The only good news is that Cammy was right about the Caravan. The van is rock steady, its suspension firm, its steering tight. Computer-assisted brakes allow him to slow without skidding.

The amphetamine also does its work. He's wide awake, a bit jittery, but sharp enough to consider his immediate future. Just as well, because he won't have more than an hour with this one if he wants to be in place at the construction site by eight o'clock. There's no question of keeping the boy imprisoned, as he'd done with Case Dixon.

◆

Johnny-Boy hadn't been Garrison Granger's only . . . Johnny-Boy can't find the right word. Victim doesn't sound entirely right. His own targets, Johnny-Boy's, are true victims, unwilling, unwitting. But if any of the boys Granger seduced were either, Johnny-Boy never saw a sign. Garrison used to regularly lecture the boys on the Spartan warrior tradition, where every fighter was paired with a lover who would never abandon him in battle. The truth, the way Johnny-Boy now views Granger, is that his foster father liked to fuck adolescent boys. The rest was no more than a smoke screen, but a smoke screen that worked until one kid's parents got wind of Granger's adventures and called in the cops.

That was the end of Johnny-Boy's relationship with Garrison Granger, but he's often wondered if Granger thought he'd get away with his little game forever. Had he never measured the risks? His arrest was inevitable. The boys who frequented his gym were local, the children of conservative Christians always on the lookout for sin.

Johnny-Boy's not in a hurry to condemn his foster father's risk management. Yet he often returns to a question: Did Granger know his time was limited? Had he been willing, all along, to accept his thirty-year sentence, a sentence shortened by his murder in prison? Was the reward worth the risks? Or had he been captured by his own perversion, a prisoner even before his arrest?

◆

The rain quits with Johnny-Boy an hour from home, replaced by a cold wind hard enough to rattle the van from time to time.

Sloan's still out of it, but Johnny-Boy wakes him up. He wants the kid fully awake. Awake and aware. They're off the interstate, in a drive-through line at a fast-food restaurant. Johnny-Boy settles for coffee, but the kid orders an egg sandwich and a large chocolate milk.

"Listen, man," he tells Johnny-Boy, "I really appreciate this. I mean . . ." He pauses long enough to laugh. "I didn't know what the fuck I was gonna do."

"Hey, don't sweat the small shit. Like I said, I've walked some hard roads too. What I learned? There's times you gotta reach out."

Back on the road, Johnny-Boy tunes the radio to an all-news station, KGBT, operating out of Baxter. Crime comes first, if it bleeds, it leads. But the crime report soon gives way to progress on the Nissan plant. Behind schedule for the past few months, the contractors are now on track. At the same time, construction outside the plant has reached new heights. With more than a hundred projects already in progress, construction workers are being recruited from as far away as Denver.

The kid's paying close attention, the claims made by his benefactor now confirmed. Johnny-Boy wasn't lying. Hope is in the air, hope that's magnified when Johnny-Boy chooses a route that leads them up Main Street in Boomtown. The enormous plant, even on a Sunday night, is still impressive.

"Now, look," Johnny-Boy says, "you can stay at my house for a while. Not a long while, right? Just long enough to get started."

Next to him, the boy hesitates, probably wondering about the cost, nobody, in his experience, offering something for nothing.

"You wanna pay a little rent when you get on your feet, I wouldn't complain," he tells Sloan as he pulls into the driveway of the small farmhouse. "I'm not livin' in a mansion, which you can see for yourself." He gestures toward the house before tossing Sloan a final piece of reassurance. "One other thing, no drugs in my house. Not even weed, Sloan. Nada, nothin'. I had enough trouble in my life with drugs and I don't make any exceptions."

That Sloan will never violate this mandate goes without saying. Still, as Johnny-Boy leads the kid into the house, he experiences a moment, if not of compassion, at least of reflection. For most people, wins and losses even out over a lifetime. But luck only runs in one direction for some small number, from their first day until the day they die. Like poor little Sloan here. Never caught a break, not a single fucking one, from the hour of his birth until this very minute. And now he never will.

CHAPTER TWENTY-TWO

DELIA

Early October usually carries a hint of winter, even on warm days, but this morning's just plain cold. We're parked, me and Blanche Weber, at the edge of a harvested cornfield twenty miles west of Baxter in Maryville County.

"Mornings like this, I start applying to departments in Florida," Blanche tells me. "You think there are any Minnie Mouse security guards in Disney World?"

Minnie Mouse? I'd have an easier time imagining her as a superheroine at a Universal theme park. But I understand where she's going with her comment, because it isn't only about the cold. There's a body thirty yards away from us, a young male dumped amid the dry cornstalks. Four men stand between us and the body. Sheriff Elvin Morrow, first, unmistakable at six-five, then three of his deputies. Morrow's sporting his customary black Stetson, the rest wear standard police caps with high peaks and polished brims.

I'm in Maryville County because Sheriff Morrow favored the Baxter PD with a courtesy call. Morrow and my boss, Vern Taney, are on good terms, and at one point following the murder of Case Dixon, Vern briefed Morrow and the sheriffs from the other counties surrounding Baxter. Had there been any homicides or assaults in their counties that revealed evidence of torture? The answer in all cases was no, but the briefing served another purpose. Be on the lookout for a sadistic offender.

The heads-up came into the house early this morning. Two men hunting grouse in a cutover cornfield had found a body, an adolescent male, who appeared to have been tortured before he was murdered. I'd taken the call, at work early because I need to attend a birthday party this afternoon. Little Emmaline's all of five years old.

"Sheriff says he'll hold the body," a deputy told me, "but he'd appreciate you comin' out as soon as possible."

"That bad?"

"Worse."

◆

Ten minutes later, I picked up Blanche and headed into Maryville County. I took a BPD cruiser, lights flashing, siren screaming, but now that we've arrived, neither of us seems anxious to get out.

"You're the boss," Blanche remarks. "You first."

I'm wearing a wool coat, too light for the sudden chill, and I pull up the collar as I open the door and step out. Sheriff Morrow turns to us as we approach. This is not our case and we have no jurisdiction here. Respect is the order of the day.

"Mornin', Delia." The pits on Morrow's face betray the remains of what must have been a truly awful adolescence, but the man's genial, his voice deceptively gentle. Like every sheriff in the state, he's elected, not appointed.

"Morning, sheriff. This is Detective Weber."

Morrow nods to Blanche, then says, "We're waitin' on the state CSU. Gotta leave the body how it is for now. You wanna take a quick look, go ahead. Me, I already had my look, so I hope you don't mind if I remain where I am."

◆

There's a clear path to the body, courtesy of the Maryville cops who followed in one another's footsteps, minimizing damage to any trace evidence. I lead Blanche along that path, maybe twenty yards into the stubble. The remains of the cornstalks rise in parallel rows, straight and rigid, as though in shock. The boy lies between two of the rows. Maybe fifteen, maybe even younger, his body is thin and frail. Naked, he's lying on his left side, in full rigor, with one arm extended at an impossible angle. A deep, narrow impression on his wrist indicates the use of handcuffs or zip ties. From where I stand, I can only see one side of his face. It's unmarked except for bruising on the neck, but that's not what captures my attention.

I count eight round wounds on his back, maybe three inches in diameter, burns almost certainly, one so deep I can see his ribs. I want to turn away, but I can't, just as I can't prevent myself imagining the pain of these injuries. And I'm suddenly grateful. This isn't my case. It belongs to the Maryville sheriff and somebody from his office will have to attend the autopsy, will have to watch as these wounds are individually measured and analyzed.

"A hair dryer," Blanche says, her voice seeming to come from a great distance.

"What?"

"That's how he did it. With a hair dryer. He held it tight against the kid's back, pressed down hard. That's why the edges are sharply defined." She pauses briefly, before adding, "It must've taken minutes to . . ."

She lets it go there and turns away. I need to follow, but I can't take my eyes off this child. And that's what he is, a child. Tortured, murdered, and dumped. I make the leap, of course, to Case Dixon, noting the differences. These wounds appear to have been delivered one after another with no gap between them, whereas Case Dixon was tortured for days. The instruments of torture were also different, but consistent in one respect. A pair of pliers and a blow dryer are likely to be found in virtually every household. And the leather or canvas cuff used to bind him has been discarded in favor of a more common restraint. Do the variations indicate two actors, somehow equally sadistic, operating within a few miles of each other? The likelihood is too slight for a working cop to consider. The victims were both boys, half-grown and too small to put up much of a struggle. And both were dumped, naked, close to a little-used country road.

"Captain?" Blanche calls to me, using my rank as she does when other police personnel are present. The message is obvious enough. The case belongs to Maryville County. Undoubtedly, they'll offer a morgue photo, along with a photo of the boy's one tattoo, an elaborate songbird, to media outlets. If he's local, he'll be identified. If not, his name may never be known.

◆

Sheriff Morrow's waiting patiently. I've always found him to be a taciturn, almost placid man. Not this time. Like the deputies standing behind him, his grim expression, the compressed lips, the narrowed eyes, advertise emotions he's trying to hide.

"You think they're related?" he asks. "Him and Case Dixon."

"I do, sheriff."

"And that boy they arrested?"

"Bard Henry."

"Yes, Bard Henry. I believe he's still in jail."

"He is."

Morrow shakes his head. "Wouldn't wanna be in your shoes, Delia. I surely wouldn't."

CHAPTER TWENTY-THREE

DELIA

We're in the car, me and Blanche, when she takes out her cell phone and shows me a text message: *Man hatin' bitches don't have no place in a man's police department. Get out or get fuckin' dead, you pig.*

"There's more." She reads the next one aloud: "*You and that fat dyke you call a boss think you're gonna make the department all bitches all the time. Go back to New Jersey, you whore.*"

"Fat? Is that what it says?" I shake my head. "I know I've put on a few pounds, but that really hurts." The remark draws a short laugh, too short to milk. "What about a number, a phone number for the sender?"

"Right there, easy to read. I didn't answer. I'm thinking it was sent from a burner. If I answer, it'll probably turn the freak on. You wanna run it through the database when you get back to the house, feel free."

"Won't help if it's a burner."

"I'm crossin' the t's, dottin' the i's. Like I'm gonna forward the texts . . ." She pauses long enough to smile. "To you, Delia."

I shrug. If the crap was falling on my head, I'd do the same thing. That way, if the asshole turned up at my door, I could kill him and get away with it.

◆

We're within a few blocks of headquarters before either of us speaks again. Then Blanche lowers the window, lights a cigarette, and leans outside. She inhales, lets the smoke go, finally turns her head to face me. The cigarette's still outside the window.

"I have a bad feeling, Delia. I think the asshole's getting ready to run."

"That would explain the variations between the two murders."

"Yeah, I think he's very nervous. Maybe he saw the witness as he drove away, but even if he didn't, a panel van without the name of the business on the door or sides? That's distinctive, a mistake because he didn't anticipate that scream. A fatal mistake if we trace the van to wherever he held Case Dixon. Any drop of blood that fell on that dry wooden floor was instantly absorbed. There's no scrubbing it out. He'd have to tear up the floor. Which, by the way, is exactly what we'll do when I track him down."

Not if, but when. Blanche has always been an optimist, but in this case her optimism is supported by her own efforts. Working door to door, Blanche finally recovered video of a white van passing Liberty Federal Savings Bank at 4:41 A.M., six minutes before it appeared in the parking lot outside the laundromat. The bank is only five blocks from the mall and the van, if driven straight through, would've passed the laundromat in less than two minutes. Blanche knows because she timed it in her own car. The bad news is that the security camera outside the bank didn't catch a glimpse of the license plate or the driver.

"If he's decided to move on, then why is he still here?" I ask.

"At a guess? He came here to do something specific, something unrelated to his sadistic hobby, and it's yet to be done."

I guide the cruiser into the parking lot and slip into a space designated for BPD vehicles. I'm about to open the door when Blanche stops me with another question I can't answer, at least for now.

"Bard Henry?"

"What about him?"

"Cut the crap, Delia."

"Okay, straight answer. I'll go to our boss, Commissioner Taney, and tell him what I witnessed in that cornfield. Maybe it'll be enough, maybe not. Either way, your job doesn't change. Find the place where Case Dixon was held and you'll find his killer. The rest is above our pay grade. We're cops, not commissars."

Blanche's quick nod seems more defiant than anything else. But she's technically on paid leave and can't follow me into the house. I watch her walk away before I head inside, thinking now of the texts Blanche received. Trolling seems to be an American art form these days, making it impossible to separate serious threats from mere harassment. I'm going to assign one of my detectives to investigate, hoping the assholes will back off when news of the investigation gets out.

Sergeant Vince Trentino's behind the reception desk when I enter, nodding to a middle-aged woman seeking assistance of some kind. Not my business, really, not yet anyway, and I'm held up for a moment by four uniformed cops in the muster room to my left. I can see them clearly through the open door, but I don't recognize any of them. The BPD's been on a hiring spree for almost a year now, and one factor has been obvious throughout. The City of Baxter, in the middle of nowhere, isn't first on any applicant's list of preferred jurisdictions. So, how closely were these four cops, all men, scrutinized during the hiring process? Never part of the recruitment effort, I don't have an answer, but I intend to find out.

◆

Four hours later, I'm walking into the Taney's backyard. Vern and Lillian are throwing a party for Emmaline. I don't know what I was expecting, but the Taney's backyard is a virtual madhouse. Accompanied by assorted mothers and one father, a dozen kids dash about. They wear sweaters and jackets, red, green, blue, and pink, pink, pink, as they dash about, shrieking wildly. It's all technicolor chaos as nobody seems to be actually playing with anyone else. Instead, they move from one to another, from cluster to cluster, like electrons jumping from atom to atom. One little girl, no more than three, pushes a miniature baby carriage over the lawn. I'm too far away to hear what she's saying, but when the carriage tips onto its side and a small doll falls onto the grass, she rights it, picks up the doll, and shakes a finger at it. I can't help but think she'll become a lawyer when she grows up. Or a cop.

My partner, Zoe, walks up as the doll is returned to the carriage. She gives me a hug and says, "Rough day?"

When it reaches the point where your partner can read your mind, is it time to get closer? Or file for the divorce you don't need because you're not married?

"The worst."

Before Zoe can demand any details, I hear Emmaline call out to me. "Aunt Delia. You came to my party."

I hadn't known the issue was in doubt, but I scoop Emmaline up and plant a major kiss on her cheek. She's still young enough for that.

"Where did you think I'd be?"

"Chasing the bad guys."

"I am. And you're the bad guy."

She shrieks when I tickle her, but a moment later wriggles out of my arms and rejoins her companions. On the other side of lawn, beneath a tall maple shedding red and orange leaves, Lillian holds Cora, now a year old. The mothers (and one father, two if you count Vern) have gathered to form a pack of their own. They're all smiles, all good cheer as parents generally are when they see their children happy. Not me, though. The boy remains with me, the boy in the cornfield, the stalks rising from the bleached earth, the bare bones of the harvest. No happy birthday for him, not now, not ever.

◆

Mike and Danny are sitting at a picnic table, eyes fixed on an open laptop. I can't make out the images on the screen, but I suspect they're watching a baseball game. It's playoff season, with a lot of teams competing, not one of which I can name except the hated Yankees. Whatever teams are playing, it must be the end of the inning because the two kids look up at the same time. Danny spots me and smiles, not the thousand watter, but warm enough. I want to drag him home and lock him in a closet until it's time to celebrate his eightieth birthday, but I know I can't protect him. It was easier to sustain the illusion when he was little, illusion though it was.

Zoe and I drift across the yard to join the adults. A group like this, with so much in common, can gab about anything in their lives, from their unappreciative husbands to the hottest cable network series. Yet somehow, as soon as I turn up, the conversation turns to crime. Bard Henry at first, then after I refuse to discuss an ongoing case, to a rising wave of home burglaries. Vern's standing a few feet away, but he just smiles. I'm on my own.

◆

After the birthday cake and the soda, after the presents, so carefully wrapped, are torn open, after the *ooohs* and the *ahhhs*, after Georgina smacks Robbie on the head with a slice of cake, I find myself seated next to Vern on the steps of a small porch at the front of the house.

Time for show and tell? I hand him my phone and a series of photos, then watch as he studies them carefully.

"These are burns?" he finally asks.

"Yeah, and that one is down to the bone. Literally."

"You know how this was done?"

I start to mention Blanche and her opinion, then remember that Blanche is on paid leave. Theoretically, sitting at home watching reality TV. "Best guess? A blow dryer pressed against the skin and held there. For a long time, Vern. Pressed and held, one injury after another."

"Not like Case Dixon, though. And not with the same . . . tool."

Vern's grasping at straws, while me, I'm trying to hold his head underwater. "You wanna take it a step further, the kid's wrists, both of them, bore narrow ligature impressions, probably handcuffs or zip ties, not the kind of cuff used to control Case Dixon. But, so what, Vern? Both kids were murdered by sadists, both endured terrible pain, both were dumped in a field by the side of a farm road. You think there are two sadists operating in the area? Because if this city has ever seen a sadistically motivated killer in the past, it was before my time."

Vern straightens one leg. He stares at his foot for a moment, then asks, "Those wounds, were they the cause of death?"

"That's another problem. Maryville County doesn't have a medical examiner or a coroner ready to perform the autopsy. They're dependent on the state police to send someone. We're lookin' at a week. But the prominent bruising on the side of his neck indicates manual strangulation, only don't hold me to it. I wasn't allowed to roll the boy onto his back. He might've had a dozen bullet wounds in his chest."

"Another difference." He hesitates before adding, "Here's the problem. We have two witnesses putting Bard Henry outside the party at the time Case Dixon left. Sitting in his car, Delia, after telling his girlfriend he going to find Case Dixon. I can't see Tommy Atkinson walking away from that testimony. My guess? At the moment, he considers the case a slam dunk."

And that's another problem. We have a kid, Malcolm Bridger, under arrest. He puts Bard Henry outside the party when Case Dixon left, a claim verified by Benny Cooper while Bridger was still in custody. According to jail personnel, Bridger refused his free call and had no visitors between the time he was arrested and the time we approached Cooper. Seemingly, and the way prosecutors will play it, Bridger and his buddy couldn't have colluded.

"The defense will point out that Case Dixon was held for several days," I point out, "and that Bard Henry has alibis for much of that time. And where, if the case is so cut-and-dried, was Case Dixon held? Given that Bard Henry is a high school student living with his mom." I wave away Vern's response. "Forget that. The bigger question, which I've yet to answer, is simpler than all the rest. If called to testify and asked, point-blank, 'Do you believe that Bard Henry murdered Case Dixon,' how will I respond? And I don't mean this as a threat. You can ask Blanche the same question."

"The answer to that one's really simple, Delia. Tommy Atkinson will never ask you that question."

CHAPTER TWENTY-FOUR

BLANCHE WEBER

I don't give up until the bars are ready to close. Armed with a generic photo of a white commercial van with no signs to indicate a business, I move through Boomtown, from bar to bar, showing the photo, asking the same question: Have you seen a van similar to this one, anywhere, at any time? Boomtown is booming, as always, with prostitutes crowding the sidewalks in the southern part of the main drag. Bad pennies all, they return no matter how many we arrest. The same can be said for the mini-casinos and the drug dealers who haunt the bars, and who I ignore though several are known to me.

I can't say I'm the most popular girl in the joints I enter, especially as the night grows long and the patrons grow more inebriated. There are people in the world who don't like cops (for reasons I can't imagine), and a few seem ready to voice that dislike, but mercifully don't. A good thing because I'm in a foul mood, with no appetite for male aggression. The text messages keep coming, every fifteen minutes. They grow more threatening too. One guarantees that I'll be raped within a week, then describes what will be done to me in detail as graphic as it is repulsive. Another threatens children I don't have, another promises to "learn you right with the whip your daddy shoulda used." After I'm chained to a tree.

The content doesn't really concern me, the essential threat being the same in all cases. More important, there are three cell phones being used, with several texts from each, and the style differs from one to another. This is bigger than Jake Nurine. Is it also bigger than Blanche Weber?

With no answers, I press on. Along the way, I receive a few positive responses from working men who remember seeing the van somewhere or other, but can't name a time or a place. I hand these potential witnesses my card, along with the usual exhortation: "Call me if you remember, or if you see this vehicle again."

I'm aware of the drawback in my approach. My target might hear of my search, perhaps from a friend in any one of the bars, or even be present himself. If so, he's likely to run. But if there's a better option, a second avenue of investigation, I can't name it. The van is all I've got. Plus, even if he leaves the city, I'll track him down sooner or later. Assuming he's identified.

◆

Come four o'clock, I give it up. I'm tired, no doubt, but I can't quit without another effort, the biggest of all. I find a parking spot near the entrance to the Nissan site. A few hours from now, more than a thousand workers will enter the site, hundreds will leave on their way home after working all night. I have to be there and I need sleep, but there's no shutting the engine down. It's far too cold. I nap, sitting up with a window cracked. I'm assuming the arrival of the worker hordes will awaken me, but in fact it's a cop who knocks on my window a little after six. I've clipped my badge to the lapel of my jacket, so I'm not finding any hostility in Sergeant Rowan Krauss when I let the window down. Krauss has been with the Baxter PD for ten years.

"You good?" he takes a quick sniff as he asks. Just to make sure I'm not drunk.

"Never better." I glance at his companion, a kid, really, and I suspect Rowan's breaking him in. He's leaning against the cruiser, looking away, arms folded across his chest. "Call it a stakeout, Rowan," I say as I open the door and step out.

Rowan's short and broad, a smart guy who generally gets the best from patrol officers under his supervision. "I heard you were on leave."

"I am." I gesture to the gate and a pair of security guards standing just inside. "I'm here for a little show-and-tell."

"This isn't about the business with . . . the asshole?"

"Nope, it has nothin' to do with Patrolman Nurine."

Suddenly, he leans closer and drops his voice. "We should talk. I'll text you my number."

◆

A block to the north, I find a food truck already open. I order coffee and a fried egg sandwich, carrying both to my car. It's colder, colder than yesterday, with a rising sun bright against the factory's roofline. I warm myself in my Jeep while I wolf down my breakfast, then head for the gate. Workers are already arriving.

I'm still wearing my badge on the lapel of my coat, but I pay a courtesy call on the security guards. There are four now, three men and a woman. I show them a photo of the van, which they can't identify, and hand out business cards. From there, I take up my station just outside the gates.

They come first in ones and twos, then a steady trickle, finally a deluge as eight o'clock approaches. At least as many will arrive each day once the plant's turning out cars.

The factory must be built. That's the refrain and you hear it every day and everywhere. It's the excuse for ignoring the many code violations inside Boomtown. The infrastructure's been patched up, but there's no way any piece of it would survive if city regulations were to be strictly applied. They're not because the factory must be built.

◆

I manage to briefly engage a small percentage of these mostly male workers as they pass. "Have you seen this van? With no windows? And no business sign?"

A middle-aged worker, carrying a battered hard hat with an American flag above the bill, stops longer than most. He holds his chin as he stares at the van.

"That's ringin' some bells for sure, but I can't put a finger on just where and when," he finally announces.

I pass him a business card. I've brought a hundred along and will run out soon. "If you should remember, you can reach me at this number."

"Will do."

The scene's repeated often enough to have me fearing that unmarked commercial vans are more common than I'd like to believe. I have no idea how many are out there, but I only have this single lead and I don't stop until I've passed out every card. Then I approach the four security guards and thank them for their cooperation. "You've got my card, so if anything turns up, give me a call."

They're polite, but indifferent, and I walk back past the entrance and dig out my cell phone. The early chill's left my fingers half-numb, but I manage to enter Owen's number. On Tuesdays, Owen opens the office at noon and works until eight. He's still home.

"Hey, honey." He half slurs the last word and I'm sure I woke him. But he doesn't complain. Owen never complains, a character flaw if there ever was one.

"I'm on my way home. Are there eggs in the house?"

"Last time I looked."

"All right, I'll pick up some bacon, maybe a few oranges."

"See you soon."

◆

Even as I hang up, I hear a voice behind me: "Hey, detective, hold on a minute."

I turn to find the worker I spoke to early on, the man with the hard hat tucked under his arm. He's walking fast, his determined expression that of a witness who's sure of himself.

"Just remembered where I saw that van. Bar named Coolwater down at the foot of Baxter Boulevard. I drank in the Coolwater near every day once upon a time." He pauses to take a deep breath, slowing noticeably. "Okay, so I was in front of the bar one night about five thirty, grabbin' a smoke, checkin' out the traffic, when this van backed into a parking space. The van didn't have windows on the sides or the rear, which caught my attention. The driver had to use the side mirrors to park, which ain't easy unless you have a lot of practice. The van's back tire hit the curb three times before he got it right."

"Were there any signs on the van?"

He shakes his head. "Nope, which is another thing I noticed. But what really made it stick was the man drivin'. Fellow named Paul. He was the regular bartender at the Coolwater."

"You say he *was* the bartender. Does that mean he no longer works there?"

"Only means I haven't been inside the Coolwater recently. See, I was tight with one of the bar girls. Name of Glory." He shrugs. "Didn't work out, so I moved on."

"Tell me about Paul. Was he there every day?"

"Yeah, and that's another reason I remember the van. Paul mostly opened the bar. That'd be about three or four in the afternoon, but he was late that day. I mean the guy was steady as a rock. Never missed a shift." He pauses here, maybe expecting me to fill in, but I let it ride. After a moment, he says, "Paul, he was always quiet, ya know. He'd listen to anything came out of a customer's mouth, didn't matter how drunk, but he kept his opinions to himself."

That's about all I can expect, but I take a shot anyway. "You have pictures of yourself inside the bar, say with your girlfriend?"

"On a laptop that's back where I'm stayin'. I like to keep my phone clean. Just in case."

I didn't ask just in case what. I wanted the man on my side. "You mind telling me your name?"

"Nat Bronstein."

"Take my card. If you should come across a photo taken in the bar that happens to show the bartender, give me a call." I hesitate for just a second before adding, "You think you might give me your phone number?"

My request prompts a quick grin. "Not a problem, detective. I was military police back in the day."

◆

I make two calls in quick succession, the first to Owen. He's not happy when I tell him that I won't be home for breakfast, but my erratic hours are part of the package. I call Delia right afterward, an update that she eagerly absorbs. Of course, even if Paul the bartender owns an unmarked van, that doesn't mean he killed Case Dixon or the boy in the cornfield. Or that he attacked Mila Wegson. But when you've been flailing away as long as we have, any lead, and this is a good one, brightens your day.

I forward the new texts. Especially the one that identifies Delia as "the fat ass." She takes it well, knowing, as we all do, that a cop's life is filled with disrespect.

"Mila Wegson's still in a coma," she tells me. "The docs plan to keep her there until the swelling in her brain resolves."

I'm not disappointed. Severe head trauma almost always results in partial amnesia. It's likely she'll never be able to identify her attacker.

"Did you check out the bar?" Delia asks.

"Yeah, I passed by. It's almost invisible, just a small blue sign above the front window. The bar's not open yet, but I peeked through the window. It's strictly low rent."

"A dive?"

"More like a drinker's bar. No pool table, not even a dartboard."

"I assume you'll be going back later."

"Maybe not. I'm gonna take a look at a few business records in city hall. If I can find the Coolwater's owner, I may be able to pin down the bartender's home address."

CHAPTER TWENTY-FIVE

BLANCHE WEBER

The city's updating its records department, as it seems to be upgrading everything in Baxter except Boomtown. In the case of our records, that means scanning decades of paper forms, including liquor licenses, into a server. According to local regulations, every license application must contain the name of the owner, be it a corporation or an individual, and must be updated if ownership changes hands.

All that's in theory. Records were often neglected when Baxter was in decline. The evidence locker, for example, was a study in chaos theory. And while things have improved over the past year, navigating the system without a guide is a near impossibility.

My guide, in this case, is Audrey Heffen. Audrey's been managing the city's records department for the past thirty-five years, enjoying a tyrannical rule over employees, who sometimes quit on the day they were hired. No fool, I approach with a Lena's Luncheonette takeout bag in my hand.

"Howdy, Blanche." Audrey accepts my offering, stashing it on the floor behind her desk. She's quite thin, with sharp features augmented by cat-eye glasses that were out of date twenty years ago. "You here to annoy me?"

"I am, Audrey."

"Annoy away."

"The Coolwater Bar and Grill. I need the name and address of the owner."

A computer monitor fronted by a keyboard sits on the desk. Audrey turns to it, her fingers tapping away for a few seconds. "No-go. We're workin' on this material now. The paperwork's in the basement, room 674, waiting to be scanned into the system." Audrey lifts a pointy chin, a dare I greet with a stony silence until she finally yields. "This a big deal, Blanche?"

"Yeah, the biggest."

Another stare off, this one shorter. "Okay, I have my nephew, Hal, working on this batch. You find your way to room 674. I'll call ahead."

◆

From the outside, city hall is divided into three parts, the main building in the center with narrow towers on its flanks. The courts, the city council, and the mayor's office are in the center, the various bureaus in the towers. Belowground, I find a maze of storage rooms and corridors that run the length of the block. Tough shit. With my target likely to abandon the city in the near future, I'm in a hurry.

I wander for near fifteen minutes, sometimes following directions that lead to a dead end, before I more or less accidentally stumble on room 674. Inside, I discover a smiling cherub named Hal. Maybe twenty years old, but looking much younger, the beardless Hal can't be more than an inch or two above five feet tall. The good news is that his smile doesn't fade when I introduce myself. Evidently, he's heard from his aunt.

"Already pulled the paper," he announces. "The Coolwater Bar and Grill is owned by an outfit calling itself JBK, LLC."

"That's it? No list of corporate officers?"

He shakes his head. "Corporations have to register with a state agency, the Division of Corporations, and they have to list their officers when they file."

◆

If I was still allowed inside Baxter PD headquarters, accessing state records wouldn't be a problem. As it is, I have to call Delia, which I can't do because I'm not getting enough signal to make a call. That's what happens when your cell phone is seven years old.

I emerge through city hall's front doors to face a park most people simply call the Green. Officially named City Hall Green, the park virtually proclaims the Baxter miracle. A rectangle twice the size of a football field, a year ago it was more weeds than shrubs, more dirt than grass. Now a blacktop path meanders around and between well-maintained flower beds. Most of the flowers have had their day, but a cluster of yellow chrysanthemums glow beneath a bright October sun. At the far-left corner of the park, three maples planted only this spring are crowned with crimson leaves that flutter in the breeze.

As any Baxterite will readily confirm, it's all about the hope. I'm hopeful myself as I call Delia, a beggar once again. I describe the dilemma, then make my pitch.

"The Coolwater's not open, and according to a sign on the door, it won't be until two o'clock this afternoon. I could wait, obviously, and just walk through the door. But like I said, if I do and the bartender's there, I can't ask questions without alerting him. Now you remember how we spoke about the wood floor where Case Dixon was held absorbing blood, how you couldn't scrub the blood out?"

"Yeah."

"What if you set all that super-dry wood on fire?"

Delia sighs. "I have a lot on my plate this morning, so I'd owe you one if you'd get to the fucking point?"

I drop down on one of the benches along the path, instinctively waiting for a pair of joggers to pass before responding. "First thing, I've already pulled the Coolwater's liquor license. JBK, LLC. No help because the corporation's officers aren't listed. For that you have to access the articles of incorporation and they're held by the State Division of Corporations. If I wasn't on leave, that wouldn't be a problem. As it is . . ." I hesitate, but Delia can do the pregnant-silence bit as well as any cop I know. "If the officers are local, I should be able to get the bartender's home address. That'll give me a chance to survey the place before he knows I'm coming."

"Good thinking. I'll check it out and get back to you, probably in about an hour. Something else, though. I took those texts to Saul this morning." Saul Rawling is our chief of patrol and Jake Nurine's uncle. "Seems that Nurine left town a couple days ago. He's living with his mother in South Dakota and won't come back until workers' comp dumps him."

◆

I have a little time to kill and I drive south on Baxter Boulevard to the Coolwater. As it's still morning, the Coolwater's unlikely to have anyone inside, but an out-of-the-way parking spot allows me time to check my texts. The threats have stopped for the moment, but I'm still intrigued by the news about Jake Nurine. Intrigued and a bit depressed. Jake Nurine made it simple. Now it's complicated. Not only the who, but the why.

The Coolwater's as empty as I expected and I'm left to watch a parade of cement mixers line up on the southern end of the work-site. They've revved up their engines to keep their drums turning. The noise, even from a hundred yards away, is loud enough to inhibit thought, the stink of diesel exhaust pervasive. After a few minutes, I drive farther uptown, past city hall and Baxter PD headquarters. I've almost reached the mall when Delia calls.

"You have a pen?" she asks.

"Wait a minute, I'm on the move." I pull to the curb next to a convenient fire hydrant, shift into park, and reach for the pen in my jacket. "Ready, Delia."

"All right, JBK's treasurer is Zack Butler. My old buddy."

"You're kidding."

"Nope, the man has his fingers in too many pies to count. I wouldn't be surprised to learn that he owns Nissan. But I know him well enough to call him directly. Zack has nothing to do with the bar's day-to-day operations, which isn't surprising. The man has a way of keeping his hands clean no matter what's going on with his investments. Anyway, Zack's already called ahead to the bar's manager, a man named Matt Browner. You can find him a couple doors away from the Courthouse Diner at Scanda Flooring."

◆

The flooring at Scanda seems to be mostly tile and vinyl, with a few rolls of carpet dangling from brackets on the wall. Two men stand together near a roll of black-and-white checkered flooring. They're not doing much of anything, something of a surprise given the construction frenzy gripping the city.

I flash my shield as I approach. "Looking for Matt Browner."

For a moment, I think they're gonna put me off. The older of the pair, tall and thin with a shaved head and a cruel mouth, fixes me with a pair of blue eyes as contemptuous as they are frigid. "In the office," he declares.

I don't bother thanking him as I cross the room, knock on the only door, then open it without waiting for an invitation. I find a man in an oversized swivel chair behind a cluttered desk. As a matter of habit, I explore the items on the desk without finding anything special. Files, a laptop, an open ledger, fast-food wrappers, and more fast-food wrappers. Matt Browner is obese, the lower part of his face somehow joining his neck to form a curtain of flesh. He's angry at my intrusion, but I need to make my position clear. I'm not here as a beggar.

"Matt Browner?"

"Yeah." The words are followed by an audible wheeze, as though his lungs were having second thoughts.

"I'm Detective Weber. I assume that Zack Butler told you I was coming."

"Yeah, he did. And before you get goin', I wanna be on the record. I don't allow anything illegal to go on at the Coolwater, not even little shit. Couple weeks ago, I had a drug dealer eighty-sixed. Permanently. And the whores, when they come around for a drink, know we'll toss them out on their asses if they hook up inside the bar. Zack told me to work the place clean and that's what I'm doin'."

I wait until he runs out of breath, then lay the photo I've been carrying on the desk. He stares at the white van for a moment before tapping the photo with a finger.

"So, what about it?"

"Do you know a man who drives a van similar to this one?" I'm expecting him to withdraw a bit, but instead find genuine relief in his expression. Whatever I want, it's got nothing to do with him or the bar.

"Yeah, man named Paul Ochoa. Used to tend bar for me."

"But not anymore?"

"This asshole, he practically begs me for a job, then quits after maybe two weeks. Just like that. No warning. I'm still lookin' for a replacement."

"When did he quit?"

"He wanted to quit on Saturday, but I got him to work his shift."

"When did that end?"

"Around two." He skips a beat, maybe waiting for another question. "Okay, so that was it, gone, goodbye. Except that I owe him a couple days' pay, which I'd mail out if I knew where he lived."

"He's an employee and you don't know where he lives?"

"He told me that he was new in town and that he saw the ad I ran in the *Bugle*. Only he didn't have a place to stay yet. He was supposed to get back to me when he found a place, but he didn't." Browner shrugs. "In case you haven't heard, there's shortage of workers in this city. Beggars can't be choosers."

"You must have a phone number, a Social Security number, too."

The look Browner throws me is distinctly hostile, but I hold my ground until he shakes his head and goes to work on the laptop.

"I got a phone number." He gives it to me.

"You mind givin' him a call? Maybe ask if he'd consider coming back? I wanna hear his voice." I lean across the desk. "I'd owe you a favor, say down the line."

Browner grunts, the offer catching him by surprise. "I already tried him, like three times. I mean, help is hard to come by, so if I gotta beg, I gotta beg, even if I hate the prick. But the calls went right to voicemail."

"C'mon, one more shot."

He sets the phone to speaker, dials the number, but the phone on the other end doesn't ring. Instead, a computerized voice urges the caller to please leave a message after the tone. Has he ditched his cell? Does he know he's under suspicion?

"Tell me again. What was . . ." I struggle for a moment to pronounce his last name. "Paul Ochoa, what was he like?"

"Quiet, but not a guy you'd mess with. I told you how we eighty-sixed a dealer? Paul was the one did the eighty-sixing. Myself, I think he probably did time somewhere. You don't learn patience in prison, you end up doin' your time in the hole."

"But you don't know that he went to prison?"

"Like I said, Paul wasn't the chatty type. Kept his past to himself."

"What about his co-workers? Who else worked at the Coolwater?"

"Two girls, Glory and Sharon." He snaps his fingers. "Hey, wait a second. I remember now. Sharon, like she lives in Revere County, real farm country, and she told me once that she saw Paul's van goin' past her house."

CHAPTER TWENTY-SIX

JOHNNY-BOY

There are times, like right-the-fuck now, when Johnny-Boy feels as though he's absorbed a part of his victims. His sacrifices, as he commonly thinks of them. In the case of little Sloan, it's Sloan's bad luck. The kid never caught a break and now Johnny-Boy can't catch a break. The slide began yesterday, Monday, and hasn't slowed since. Like he hoped it was gonna be a snowball and it turned out to be an avalanche. Whoops.

That his Monday began with such promise makes his current situation all the more frustrating. He'd been outside the worksite when Theo Diopolis drove through the gates in the morning, and back outside when Diopolis made his exit in the afternoon. Two cars back in a long line of slow-moving vehicles, he'd followed Diopolis north on Main Street in Boomtown, their progress steady until a worker carrying a stop sign on a wooden pole stepped in front of Johnny-Boy's van. A moment later, an access gate to Johnny-Boy's left swung out and a gigantic tractor-trailer, a flatbed, revved its engine as it emerged, spewing twin streams of diesel exhaust into a leaden sky.

Up ahead, the brown Accord driven by Diopolis maintained its slow progress toward the northern end of Boomtown. In another minute, it would disappear. That minute and several more passed before the rig finally made the turn, nearly taking out Johnny-Boy's front end in the process. Diopolis was long gone, of course, and Johnny-Boy was forced into another night of wandering.

The bars, two brothels, a casino where a pair of bouncers took on a worker, a giant, who insisted the dice were loaded. The giant more than held his own until slugged from behind with a baseball bat by the woman who ran the casino. A few desultory kicks followed, brought to a halt by the advance of a patrol car, sirens screaming. To Johnny-Boy's surprise, two male cops, both young, rushed inside, spoke to the woman for a moment, then dragged the giant out of the casino, tossed him into the patrol car, and drove away. Sirens off.

Johnny-Boy stood there for a few minutes after the cops left. Three people beating on one, a baseball bat for a weapon, the target of the attacks bleeding badly from a scalp wound? And the cops drive away? From an illegal casino after a brief conversation with the woman running it? Was it just this pair of cops? Or did the corruption climb up the cop ladder, maybe to the top rung?

Either way, it really had nothing to do with him. He'd witnessed cop corruption many times in a life spent on the edge, but had never known cops to overlook murder. Not unless they committed the murder themselves.

"I was in fear of my life!"

Usually from an unarmed man running away.

◆

Finally, a bit after one, Johnny-Boy decided to take another look at the possible girlfriend's house in the Westside neighborhood. He'd been here several times over the past week, the effort fruitless, but this time he hit pay dirt. The brown Accord belonging to Theo Diopolis was parked in front of the two-family home. Upstairs, the windows were lit and two silhouettes, one a man, were visible.

The calculations came automatically. Risk, reward. Kill Diopolis and be gone from Baxter in less that twenty-four hours. Untraceable, never to return, free to pursue his personal agenda. He spied a parking space just a block away that offered a clear view of the two-family home's front door. Suppose he stationed himself in that space, suppose he remained hunched down in the seat behind a darkened window, suppose he simply waited until Diopolis emerged, then lowered the window? Barely two hundred yards away, he couldn't miss, not with the silenced Sig Sauer.

Only one problem. The rifle wasn't in the van. He'd tucked it into a cubbyhole back at the house. Being caught with an unregistered handgun in an open carry state wouldn't amount to much. But a suppressed rifle designed for military snipers would be a red flag for any cop.

Johnny-Boy heard a persistent voice in his head. "Fuck it. Kick the door down, kill everyone in the house, and anyone outside when you leave. The sooner you get it fucking done, the sooner you get out of this fucking hole that passes for a city."

◆

Johnny-Boy ignored the voice, as he'd learned to ignore other suicidal impulses, but he still had a choice. He could simply wait for Diopolis to emerge, which Diopolis had to do if he intended to report for work a few hours later, then shoot him down in the street. From there, twenty minutes back to the house, ten minutes to pack essentials, then gone.

The thing about rejected possibilities is that you can never know what result they might have produced. Johnny-Boy rejected his first impulse. He headed back home to retrieve the rifle, then returned to discover Theo's car gone.

Now it's almost eight o'clock and he's parked outside the worksite, waiting for Diopolis to show up. From his position, he can see the gates clearly, see the security guards, the men and women passing through those gates, see a cop approach the arriving workers. She's showing them something, probably a photograph. Of him? No, that can't be right. Meanwhile, he's not about to walk up to those gates and find out.

◆

Six hours later, only a short time before the day shift ends at the construction site, Johnny-Boy drives past the Coolwater Bar & Grill to discover guess-who parked across the street. The same bitch cop he saw only a few hours ago. Johnny-Boy barely glances her way as he passes, but somehow recognizes the grim determination he's already noted on the face of the other one. That would be the dyke, Captain Mariola.

As he heads back to the house he rents, Johnny-Boy calms himself. Paul Ochoa's been identified. That much is obvious. Does the how matter? Not really. Have they located the house and the little shed and the bloodstains soaked into the floorboards? That's what matters and he's buoyed at what he doesn't find when he drives past the house. No cops, not a one. They know who he is, but not where he lives.

Johnny-Boy turns around in the driveway and heads back to the city. His heart's slowed a bit and his adrenals have finally stopped pumping. The ID, he tells himself, must have come from the witness living across the street from the mall. Almost certainly. Almost. But Johnny-Boy and his van weren't inside the mall lot when the curtain moved. He was on Baxter Boulevard. So what do the cops have? A crime committed, an attempted kidnapping perhaps connected to the murder of Case Dixon and the boy, a van spotted shortly afterward, a van traveling on the city's main drag. Suspicious enough to warrant investigation, but surely not enough for an arrest.

Unless, of course, blood residue found in Johnny-Boy's house of pain is matched with Dixon's.

Burn the building? Johnny-Boy's home is relatively isolated, but not so isolated that a fire large enough to consume the building wouldn't be noticed by a passing car or truck. Responding firefighters, even the asshole volunteer firefighters working in Revere County, would know an obvious arson when they saw it.

Again, the obvious seized Johnny-Boy as he drove toward the Nissan gates along Main Street in Boomtown. His best move? Head for the house, pack his shit, set fire to the outbuilding, make his escape before the firefighters arrive. Leave Mariola and the other one to nurse suspicions they'd never prove, even if they identified him, even if they tracked him down. Instead, with the cop nowhere in sight, he again follows Diopolis north on Main

Street, then west over the top of the worksite, and into Oakland Gardens. Not the deserted streets where Case Dixon partied, but closer to Baxter Boulevard on Caseman Avenue, where he parks in front of a small house, gets out, and heads inside. The Greek's almost certainly sharing the house with others. There's a car parked on the lawn and a man sitting in a rocking chair on the small porch. He smiles and raises a can of beer in greeting as Diopolis walks into the house.

Johnny-Boy can't settle down to wait. Too much going on. He's sure to be noticed. He's got to drive past, as painful as that may be. Or maybe he should simply kill everyone in the house, including Diopolis. That can't happen, way too risky, but he's thinking that Diopolis will probably leave the house, maybe after dinner, and Johnny-Boy needs to prepare. Two blocks farther east, toward the worksite, he discovers an abandoned, partially burned house. There's a window on the second floor of the house, glass and frame long gone. With a view of the home Diopolis entered? Probably, but there's only one way to find out.

The rifle came with a soft-bodied backpack designed to securely hold the weapon, broken into its components. Suppressor, scope, bipod, and the rifle itself, with its stock folded, were individually tied down with small straps. Now, Johnny-Boy slips on the backpack and examines a small jungle of shrubbery, thigh-high grass and trees, extending onto the vacant lot to the east. When he's reasonably sure he's unobserved, he slips into the little forest, bent forward, continuing on until he reaches to within ten feet of an open front door held to the frame by a single hinge. He stops then, crouching beneath a tall dogwood tree, its lower branches bare, and listens. Abandoned doesn't necessarily mean unoccupied. Five minutes later, he moves to the doorway, then stops again to listen as he pulls a short-barreled .38 from his belt. He plans to use it if he finds someone inside, to subdue, not kill. A gunshot is too likely to attract the attention of residents in the houses across the street.

To his left, a small, quick shadow and the skittering of tiny claws on a wood floor, a rat, probably, or a squirrel. Johnny-Boy doesn't react. After sweeping the living room and what he can see of a kitchen behind it, he's back to listening as he examines the stairs to his right. Most of the fire damage is on the other side of the house, good news, but the stairway, what with the banister missing, appears rickety. If he's to have a view of the Diopolis house, he'll have to reach the second floor, which he surely will not do if the stairs collapse beneath him.

Well, no choice, really. He crosses the room, supremely alert and climbs onto the first step, keeping his weight to the outside. There's some wobble, not much, along with a squeak loud enough to be heard upstairs. Now he climbs quickly, no more point in stealth, reaching a hallway at the top of the stairs. To his left and ahead, a bathroom and a bedroom, both with their doors open. To his right, a closed door leading into the room with the window he needs to access. Johnny-Boy hesitates for just a moment as he centers himself, then turns the knob, pushes the door open, takes a step inside before pulling back. He blinks as something hard and heavy slams into the floor, only a couple feet from where he stands. Then he's inside the room, turning right to slam the revolver into the face of a tall, thin man who joins a red brick on the floor.

There's some light in the room, cast by working streetlights, enough to reveal the bloodied face of an elderly man, his sparse hair and scraggly beard completely gray. *Kill him quick.*

Johnny-Boy's first thought, an impulse he resists, at least for now. The man's bleeding from his nose and mouth, and Johnny-Boy kneels to turn him over so the blood doesn't run into his lungs. He frees the man's arms from the heavy sweater he wears and pulls the sweater over his face.

"Old man, I don't know if you can hear me, but if you haven't confessed your sins recently, you'd best not pull off that sweater. You get a look at me, the next thing you'll see is an angel carrying the book of your life."

Johnny-Boy steps to the window and finds what he expected, an angled view to the entrance and front yard of the Diopolis house. One for the money. The room's been lived in, probably the old man's residence. There's a table and a chair, both serviceable, and he pulls each to the window. The rifle's assembled in a little more than a minute. Practice making perfect, there are no fumbles. Johnny-Boy can disassemble and return the rifle to its case just as easily. He doesn't bother with the bipod. He'll have to stand to acquire a target, but even handheld, he won't miss an unsuspecting target, a target making no evasive moves, not from two hundred yards away.

No longer in a rush—the brown Accord is still parked in front of the house—Johnny-Boy settles down to wait. He'll wait all night if necessary, but he does let a small part of his mind wander. To Case Dixon at first and the hours they spent together. The boy had often cried, at least when he wasn't screaming, and begged, at the end, to be killed. By that time, he'd faced the obvious reality. Despite the many promises, he would never be freed. Finally, he'd taken matters in his own hands. Not Johnny-Boy's fault. No way.

CHAPTER TWENTY-SEVEN

DELIA

I'm in the living room with Zoe and Danny. Danny's shrugging into a hooded sweatshirt, preparing for a morning run. It's barely six o'clock and cloudy-cold, but my son's nothing if not dedicated. Train harder than anyone else, then train still harder. Zoe and I maintain nurturing, parental smiles until the door closes behind him. Then we're all over each other.

I need this, need the escape, not to mention the orgasm that Zoe seems to effortlessly induce. I had a dozen things to do at work before Detective Patrick O'Malley called me at five thirty, interrupting sleep I desperately needed. O'Malley's a cover-your-ass cop who runs it up the ladder whenever he happens on an assignment even slightly controversial.

But not this time. This time I had to know.

Last night, shortly after eight, a man was shot as he left the house in Oakland Gardens that he shared with four men who worked on the Nissan site. The bullet passed through the victim's right arm, midway between his elbow and shoulder, nearly tearing his arm off in the process. Only the quick application of a tourniquet by a roommate trained as a paramedic saved his life.

The extensive damage caught O'Malley's attention because ordinary handguns simply lack the power to cause an injury this severe. But even more startling, although the attack was witnessed by three of his roommates and several neighbors, nobody heard a gunshot.

Could it get any worse? Yes, it could, because when O'Malley finally traded the crime scene for Baxter Medical Center, he first learned that Theo Diopolis would lose his arm, but survive. He then examined the ID of Theo Diopolis in search of kin to notify, only to discover that Theo's driver's license was an obvious forgery, as was his Social Security card.

One too many mysteries for Detective O'Malley. He called me right after a uniformed cop found the bullet, badly damaged but far too large to have been fired from a handgun, embedded in the earth behind a rosebush.

"Jesus Christ, captain, nobody heard the shot. That's an assassination, right? With a suppressed rifle in fucking Baxter."

Diopolis was in the operating room when O'Malley called, enduring the amputation of his right arm. He'd remain in the hospital for a few days, assuming he had family to offer support while he rehabbed. I told O'Malley to collect the victim's cell phone, secure a warrant, lift the prints on the screen and find out who the hell he really is. In that order.

"Last thing, post a uniformed officer to stand outside wherever Diopolis is sent following his surgery. I'll make arrangements for relief when I get to the house this morning."

◆

That's work for later, Zoe's for now, a treat made all the sweeter by the need for haste. Danny will return in forty minutes. Thus, hands fly, not to mention mouths, tongues, and in Zoe's case, toes. We know each other's bodies well, when to touch, when to pause, how to tease until curses fly. In the end, I force the issue, persisting until Zoe twists away, curling into a protective ball. As Roberto Durán, the boxer, once said, *"No más, no más."*

I'm back to being Mom by the time Danny comes through the door. Standing by the stove, flipping slices of bacon with a pair of wooden tongs.

"Bacon and eggs and sliced strawberries. How's that?"

"Great, Mom."

I'm not fooling Danny and he's not fooling me. It's pretty obvious, from the looks they exchange and the small touches, that he and Fetchin' Gretchen have consummated their relationship. Technically a crime, maybe on both their parts, Danny's fortunate to live in a don't ask / don't tell household.

◆

Weekday mornings are always a rush. Zoe and I off to work, Danny off to school. A good reason to make sure we share a meal, brief though it may be. A meal and the latest legal gossip.

"So, Mom, anything new?"

"Case Dixon's funeral."

"I heard. You goin'?"

"Nope. The mayor's gonna represent the city. No cops. Our commissioner doesn't want to risk a confrontation with James Dixon."

Case Dixon's father hasn't stopped criticizing the investigation, even though we've made an arrest. Personally, I think the arrest is bogus, but James Dixon doesn't know that. So, what does he want? After long study and deep analysis, I've concluded that an asshole is an asshole is an asshole. James Dixon's an asshole in need of a platform and now that he has one, he doesn't intend to give it up.

Maybe I'm not any better, because I can't resist saying, "There is one other piece of news. For this table only."

Danny grins. "I won't speak a word. My lips are sealed."

"Have you ever heard of ViCAP?"

"Sort of."

I pause long enough to butter a slice of rye toast and take a bite. "ViCAP is the FBI's Violent Criminal Apprehension Program. They link killings that take place in different parts of the country."

"How do they do that?" Zoe asks.

"By the number of common elements in the various homicides. Anyway, I ran the Case Dixon homicide and the killing of the boy in Maryville County through ViCAP and guess what?" When neither of my breakfast companions answer, I quickly add, "Links, my children, and now I'm expecting a visit from the FBI. A consultation. Like this morning."

Now it's Danny's turn again. "Will they take over the case?"

"You've been watching too many movies. Murder is a state crime. The FBI plays whatever role we allow it to play."

"And what role will you allow?"

I look away for a moment, as though giving the matter careful thought. "Well, if they're very, very respectful, I might recommend the doughnuts at Lena's Luncheonette. Maybe."

◆

I'm at my desk by eight thirty, sifting through routine updates on investigations in progress. Burglaries are killing us, as are thefts from construction sites. The justification for families spending a hundred grand to build a house, but not a few hundred dollars for a security system to protect it escapes me. The general belief, apparently, is that cameras do not deter, but even a desperately addicted burglar, like any predator, will seek the easiest prey available. They avoid houses with large growling dogs, or CCTV cameras conspicuously posted at entry points. Or so they've told me over the years.

My sometime-assistant Marcia Blackstone arrives at nine o'clock, late as usual. I call her into my office, but don't bother with a lecture. Technically, Marcia's not a Baxter PD employee. She's here on a temporary assignment from Baxter's near-moribund Office of Opportunity. The good news is that once she does arrive, late for work and later returning from lunch, she's competent.

"Mornin', captain, what can I do for ya?" Marcia's smile fills her round face.

"Last Friday. That would be October 11. I want the names of anyone in the drunk tank that morning, along with the names of the officers on jail duty. Complete, Marcia, and as soon as possible. In addition, I want to review the applications of any hires in the past six months."

"Righto, captain. Have the first part in an hour or so. The rest by this afternoon." She hesitates, tilting her head slightly. I could do this myself and she knows it. But I have nothing to add and she turns with a swish of her pale yellow skirt and walks out the door. Good news because I've only got a few minutes to spare. At nine thirty I'm scheduled to meet with Vern and a pair of FBI agents.

I use the house phone to call an administrator named Callie Urman at Baxter Medical Center. I want updates on Mila Wegson and Theo Diopolis, and Callie obliges. The swelling on Mila's brain has gone down, Callie explains, though she has a long way to go. Until then, probably another three days, she'll remain in an induced coma. Assuming she survives, the severity of any brain damage can be determined only after the coma is lifted. Diopolis, postsurgery, is stable, saved by the quick work of his roommate. He's currently in the ICU and heavily sedated, but assuming no complications arise, he could be released in two to three days. He'll need rehab, of course, but assuming he has relatives to assist in his care, he can seek it from home. If not, he'll need to enter a rehab facility. Assuming there's a bed available.

I love Callie. She's a master of equivocation, the word *assuming* probably on her lips before *Mommy* or *Daddy.*

◆

I walk into Vern's office to find two FBI agents, a man and a woman, already present. Aside from gender, they might be clones of each other. Both wear dark blue suits with a faint stripe, dark ties that appear black, but might be navy in a brighter light, and pale blue shirts with button-down collars. Augmented by near-identical somber expressions, I find the effect almost clownish, and I have to wonder how much it will change when Vern tells them to back off. We've already agreed, Vern and I, that we're close to the arrest of a target that's easily spooked. The last thing we need is a pair of FBI agents stumbling around.

Vern makes the introductions. "Delia, this is Special Agent Vera Demantovich and Special Agent Lawrence Carey. Agents, this is Captain Delia Mariola, our chief of detectives."

We shake hands, all very dutiful, before I take a seat next to Vern. There's a coffee table between us and the agents. A tray on the table bears four cups of untasted coffee.

"Now," Vern asks, "what can we do for you?" He smiles that folksy smile I know well. "That we haven't already done."

Special Agent Demantovich speaks first. She's older than her partner and probably in charge. "Let me be frank. The most successful serial killers are those who constantly change locales. ViCAP was designed to detect patterns, but, and I'm being candid, it would be a lot more effective if police jurisdictions were more conscientious. Many never report, another factor enhancing the success rate of serial killers."

I tune out for the next few minutes as the sales pitch continues, only tuning back in when she gets to the point.

"We're from a unit that investigates ViCAP-linked homicides occurring in different locales. As a general rule, the first thing we do is review the investigative material . . ."

Vern waves her to a stop. "That won't happen, not at this time." He leans over the coffee table, his bulk imposing, as I'm sure he means it to be. "You have no jurisdiction in Baxter. That means no right, by law, to investigate a state crime. I expect you to back off and leave the investigation to cops who know the terrain. Expect, right?"

Myself, I expect one or the other of the special agents to catch an attitude, but they've been around too long for that.

They glance at each other as Agent Demantovich leans back and crosses her legs. She appears almost relieved. "You're that close?" She smiles when Vern shakes his head. "Commissioner, the goal is to apprehend this scumbag before he kills again. If backing off will help, we'll back off. But if he bolts, you need to bring us in. We have resources you don't have. And of course, if he leaves the state, jurisdiction is ours."

CHAPTER TWENTY-EIGHT

DELIA

Back in my office with work to do. I run the name Paul Ochoa through several databases, state and national, an effort that produces hundreds of names. Pretty much what I expected, but due diligence is due diligence. A few minutes later, Patrolman Rowan Krauss walks into the office. Rowan's not a detective and I have no authority to order him to do anything. Still, he's a veteran, already on the force when I arrived.

I don't have coffee to offer, and I settle for waving him to a chair on the other side of my desk. "When you spoke to Blanche outside the construction zone, you asked her to get in touch. So what's up?"

At this point, Rowan could reasonably indulge in a temper tantrum. He'd confided in Blanche, who promptly betrayed the confidence part. But Rowan's a throwback to an era when cops commonly played judge and jury on the street. A large man, in the gut as well as the shoulders, his eyes are the deep blue of a lapis pendant I once owned.

"Guess Blanche has enough on her plate," he says.

"More than that, Rowan. Blanche is in no position to fight back, no matter what you tell her. I am. Me and Vern both."

Rowan looks up at the ceiling for a moment, then draws a long breath deep into his lungs. "I can't speak directly to what's goin' on with Blanche." He hesitates again. "Two nights ago, I ran into a pimp named Titus Fletcher. Runs three hookers out of a trailer in Boomtown. Myself, I don't care much for pimps, but it's just one of those things. His women won't testify against him." Rowan's smile somehow manages to be sour and amused at the same time, a neat trick. "And the hookers are the ones who get arrested. Not him. But that's how it is and this cop's willing to take advantage of pimps who think they can earn brownie points by snitchin'. Three nights ago, Titus told me that he was threatened by two cops. Seems one of 'em told the pimp, 'Pay up, every week, and keep your mouth shut. You complain, I'll shove my gun up your ass and keep pullin' the trigger until your brains blow out through the top of your head.'"

"But Titus, he's not naming names? That about it?"

"Gotta look at the situation from his point of view. He can't know how many other cops are on the take. Maybe a lot, maybe a few, but not Sergeant Krauss. I've been his buddy for a long time, in his mind anyway, so maybe I'll take the knee off his neck."

"That's it? Just one source?"

"Yeah, in so many words. But hiring all these recruits, all young, at the same time? Thought it was a bad idea from day one. Now they have a regular hangout. A bar called Duke's in Boomtown. In a tent, right? I decided to check it out maybe a week ago. Captain, when I walked inside, the place went as quiet as a mausoleum in a blizzard. Nobody looked up, nobody said hello. In fact, I'd have to say their attitude was downright hostile. And Titus? He's tellin' me that cops are collecting all over Boomtown."

"Only he's not naming names."

"There ya go."

Marcia Blackstone interrupts by knocking softly at the door. She's holding a pair of files, which she offers to me. "The first part of what you asked for," she announces. "Delivered on time."

I thank her and drop the files, face down, on my desk. It's time for Rowan to leave, but he adds another observation as he rises. "These new hires, all young, most still on probation? It's only natural they'd form a . . . a little club. And if there's a few bad apples in that club, you gotta wonder about the rest of the apples. You gotta worry it's gonna be us against them."

There's no disputing the judgment and I don't try. I thank Rowan for coming forward, ask him to keep his eyes open, and shut the door behind him after he leaves. Then I settle down with the files.

◆

The claim made by Malcolm Bridger, that he saw Bard Henry sitting in his car outside the party just before Case Dixon left, is particularly damning. And Benny Cooper's confirmation drives the nail deep. Add two factors. First, Bridger didn't know he'd be arrested. Second, Bridger didn't make a postarrest phone call, and for good reason. He was arrested at home with his mom and dad present. They would arrange his bail and hire his lawyer. Bottom line from the prosecution's point of view: Bridger couldn't have conspired with his buddy to set up Bard Henry for a fall that would likely result in Henry spending the rest of his life in prison.

There's a big fly in that ointment though. My detectives interviewed every kid who attended the party. Not a single one reported seeing Bard Henry that night. Not one.

◆

Being a young and vulnerable adolescent, Malcolm Bridger was placed in a cell by himself pending his arraignment. That cell, the only isolation cell in the system, is right next to our drunk tank. I don't know why or when the arrangement was made, but right now I have a pair of printouts on my desk. One lists the names of every prisoner then in the drunk tank. The second lists the personnel on duty that morning. I start with the prisoners. I'm looking for a familiar name, somebody I've had contact with in the past. A decent rapport wouldn't hurt either.

I recognize several of the names. Out-of-control drunks tend to be repeat offenders. But I need someone special, someone I can lay my hands on in a hurry. I find him in Oakley "Bear" Sawyer. Oakley's nickname fits him perfectly. He's one of those men who'd have to shave down to his collarbone should he one day attempt to remove a shaggy beard that starts just below his eyes. That said, despite standing well over six feet, despite the small glittery eyes, Oakley's a nice enough guy when sober. When drunk, on the other hand, he's a notorious cop fighter, the sad part being that he's usually too drunk to put up much of a fight. The way it generally goes down, one cop distracts him while the other drops down and cracks him across the shins with a steel baton. That brings him to his knees and the rest is usually child's play. Only this time, he managed to connect with a single punch that earned him thirty days in our jail when he pleaded guilty two days later. Which is where he is right now.

◆

Bear's already in a room set aside for lawyer-client interviews when I come inside. He's seated behind a table, not in a corner, and there's a window at the far end of the room. So, not the box, not an interrogation. There's even a can of orange soda and a bag of chips on the table.

Ever the gentleman, Bear stands when I walk inside. "Officer . . ."

"Captain."

"Yeah, captain, so how ya been?"

"Better than you, Bear."

"Well, I'm sorry, ya know, but sometimes . . ." He brightens a bit. "Anyways, I'm goin' right into rehab. Ya know, when I get released."

"I believe I've heard this song before."

"I know, but this time it's all arranged. My daughter, that would be Jenny, she's pickin' me up and takin' me straight to rehab." He pulls at his beard. "Funny thing that. I got two daughters. One, she's livin' in Colorado, won't give me the time of day. But Jenny? She's stuck with me all these years. Don't deserve it no way, but . . ."

I tap the table. Time to get real. "What time were you brought in last Thursday, Bear? I mean locked up."

"Last Thursday. Couldn't tell you the exact time." A smile now. "Wasn't lookin' at my watch. Ya know, the one they took away from me when I was booked."

"But it was Thursday night, for sure?"

"Yeah."

"When did you finally see a judge?"

"Friday, maybe two in the afternoon."

"And you were in the tank the whole time?"

"That's right."

If I put words in Bear's mouth, what with the tape recorder running on the table, I know I'll regret it. Fortunately, Bear heads off that threat when he nods, then says, "This here 'bout that boy they brung in? Gotta be, right, cause ain't nothin' else happen out of the ordinary."

"Then tell me about the boy."

Bear shifts forward on his chair. He's not handcuffed, as per my instructions. "I was still half-asleep when he come down the corridor, but I woke up quick. There was maybe eight men in the tank, all pretty drunk. They most likely figured the boy was gonna be tossed in with 'em and they started callin' out." He stops to look at me and I sense that he might actually be blushing. "Well, I don't s'pose you're unacquainted with what they were threatenin' to do. And even after the officer put that boy in the next cell with bars separating us, they didn't let up. Like fun, ya know, and everybody tryin' to outdo everybody else."

"And the boy, how did he take it?"

"Not good, captain. Like he was about to let go in his pants. He started into beggin' the officer to lend him a phone. Said didn't no one know where he was. How he had to talk to his daddy. How his momma would take it real hard if somethin' happened to him. How he hadda find himself a real lawyer." Bear shakes his head. "Know what, and this here surprised the hell out of me? That officer, he was an older man and I guess he had a soft heart. He lent him his personal phone. Never seen nothin' like it."

◆

It's after noon and I'm hungry, but Vern's press update is only an hour away and I don't want him to embarrass himself. Say if he has to reverse his position a day from now. I head upstairs, to his office, and wait for his office manager to announce me. Vern's sour expression when I walk into the room matches that of Tommy Atkinson, our esteemed district attorney. Tommy's also scheduled to appear at the conference.

I haven't come with good news, and they know it. But I'm definitely here and I repeat Bear Sawyer's tale, keeping it short and concise.

"I want to say good work, Delia," Tommy declares when I finish. "But good for who exactly?"

I'm supposed to quietly accept the rebuke, but I'm not feeling particularly humble at the moment. I've fucked up their morning? So what?

"Sorry to be the bad-news messenger, Tommy, but it never made sense. Bridger had Bard Henry sitting in his car outside the party. In plain sight, no effort to hide himself. So why, with partygoers coming and going, did no one else see him? And remember, we interviewed every kid who attended the party and they all knew Bard Henry well enough to recognize him." I give it a couple beats, then finish up. "All along, we've accepted as fact that Bridger didn't make a phone call between the time he was arrested and the time we interviewed his pal Benny Cooper. That was our mistake, that assumption. Once I stopped assuming, the rest was simple. In this case, the means was supplied by one of ours, but cell phones are routinely smuggled into jails and prisons all over the country."

Vern's first to react. "Have you interviewed whoever was on duty when this phone call was supposedly made?"

"Clyde Norman was on the tier that morning, and no, I haven't spoken to him yet. I wanted to brief you before the press conference. But I'm going to grill Officer Norman as soon as I find him. If I discover Benny Cooper's number on his recent call list, I'll confront Cooper. And by the way, I didn't put words in Bear Sawyer's mouth and I didn't offer him a deal. The man told the truth."

Now it's the lawyer's turn and Tommy Atkinson's never without words. "Malcolm Bridger made a phone call. That's all you have. You don't even know who he called."

"True, and it wouldn't be much if Bridger had disclosed it. Instead, he told us that he didn't communicate with anyone after his arrest." I glance from Vern to our district attorney. I've got their full attention. "First, I need to interview Clyde Norman. He might refuse to cooperate or refuse to give me a look at his cell. But either way, cooperative or not, I'm gonna pay Benny Cooper a visit. The kid's seventeen, old enough to be interviewed without notifying a parent, old enough to understand the penalties for obstructing justice and conspiracy. Cooper also told us that he and Bridger didn't communicate. Worse, he made the claim in a signed statement."

Crunch time. Vern can order me to stand down, or even replace me as the head of the investigation. Atkinson has plenty of juice as well. This has got to be hard for both men. An arrest has been made, with Atkinson assuring the public (and James Dixon) that the perpetrator was in custody. And me, I've taken that assurance away and replaced it with exactly nothing. No arrest, not even a suspect I'm willing to name.

"I can't decide," Vern says after a moment, "whether I want to commend you on your fine work or set a date for your execution by firing squad."

"It's not about compliments or punishment. It's about not allowing a seventeen-year-old kid to spend the rest of his life in prison for something he didn't do."

CHAPTER TWENTY-NINE

JOHNNY-BOY

Johnny-Boy believes there's no why to anything. With him, it's an article of faith. There's a god out there deciding his fate, and everybody else's, only problem being that he's a ten-year-old rich kid with a tiny prick and a bad attitude. But no, he tells himself as he stands in the shower, hot water flowing over his body, that's not right either. It's more mysterious. Like you step through a portal you can't see, feel, taste, or smell. Then you're on the slide, the good luck slide or the bad luck slide. At the moment, he's on the bad luck slide and it's a steep motherfucker with the bottom out of sight.

How could he fucking miss? You'd have to measure the time it took him to pull the trigger, plus how long the bullet was in the air, in milliseconds. Fucking milliseconds. Yet somehow in the course of those milliseconds, Diopolis turned back, probably in response to something said by one his pals, leaving only his right arm in the bullet's path.

And what's the chance of that happening? The man who first said those words to Johnny-Boy had been in reform school, jail, or prison for almost as many years as he'd been alive. Johnny-Boy operated on the flip side of that coin. If there's any chance of a bad outcome, even a tiny chance, sooner or later it's gonna come out. Courtesy of that ten-year-old god with his little dick.

And more bad luck, as if Theo's sudden move wasn't enough. According to Jane Theroux, the KBAX reporter, Diopolis would survive only because of the quick action of a roommate formerly trained as a paramedic. And what's the chance of that happening?

◆

Johnny-Boy needs to slow down. He takes a deep breath then replaces the nastiness in his head, quite deliberately, with the boy, Sloan. The bad luck boy. From that first glimpse when Johnny-Boy walked into the rest area, through the many manipulations as he lured the kid into his den, to the look on Sloan's face when Johnny-Boy drove his fist into the boy's solar plexus. As if he'd been waiting all his life for this moment, for the final loss, the final taking.

As he proceeds, working through the minutes, the zip ties, the blindfold, the breathy rush of the hair dryer, Johnny-Boy's soapy hands drop to an already stiff cock. For the most part, Johnny-Boy's memory is no better than anyone else's. Only when he relives his triumphs does he slide back until he's able to recall every second, every scream, the slow dying of the light as his hands tightened around Sloan's throat. A joyous moment, short as it was.

Johnny-Boy's definitely feeling better as he eats a cold breakfast. His new van is parked behind the house, concealed from the gravel-topped road. He wants the house to appear unoccupied in case an inquisitive visitor happens by, perhaps in search of the place where Case Dixon spent his last days on earth. The modified shed-prison remains where it's always been, untouched. Johnny-Boy's determined to set the shed on fire, but not until he's packed the van.

Time to go? Past time. He'll just have to live with his failure, and if he's lost the patronage of whatever gang hired the job out, there are still others who'll be happy to buy what he has to sell.

That logic goes out the window when his phone pings, announcing the arrival of an email. Most of the emails Johnny-Boy receives go directly into his spam folder. Not this one. It's from Sol Cohen and the message, all caps, is simple: GET A BURNER. CALL ME FUCKING PRONTO.

Johnny-Boy already has the burner, so not a problem. But the demand is a major violation of their basic relationship and his first impulse is to ignore it. Johnny-Boy understands power plays, the application of do-it-or-else, but the power part, in this case, eludes him. Sol Cohen doesn't know the name Johnny-Boy's currently using when he's between contracts, or where Johnny-Boy lives. Sol relies on emails that run from Sol's computer to a server in Malaysia. He can't back up his threatening tone. He has no power to play.

With the packing still unfinished, Johnny-Boy returns to work. He stays busy for almost an hour before a truth, so obvious only willful ignorance prevented it from hammering at his brain before now settles in. The cutouts, Sol and an agent named Braulio Montez? Yeah, they insulate him, but in doing so, they've become the source of all wealth. Without them, no contracts.

Johnny-Boy's occupation will never make him rich. He rarely takes on more than three contracts a year. But his income is sufficient to pay his bills and to provide the free time he must have to find his victims. Commonly, he puts more than two thousand miles on his van between captures.

◆

Ten minutes later, Johnny-Boy's sitting on a lawn chair in a dilapidated, roofless barn that leans far out over its foundation, like it's only waiting for an excuse to collapse. With him inside, the way his luck is running.

Johnny-Boy laughs to himself, imagining his final words as the barn's walls crash around him. And what's the chance of that happening?

He sobers up quickly, glancing at the phone in his hand. He's sitting in deep shadow with a good view of the road. His rifle lies at his feet and there's a handgun tucked into the waistband of his jeans. Johnny-Boy's long decided never to suffer the fate of his mentor, Garrison Granger. Go down fighting is the story of his life.

Quickly, before he can change his mind, Johnny-Boy taps out the number in Sol Cohen's email, blocking his own number. Cohen answers on the first ring. Johnny-Boy assumes that Cohen's phone was bought for this purpose only, because he doesn't bother asking Johnny-Boy to identify himself.

"You fucked up big time," Cohen announces.

Johnny-Boy's having none of it. "How's that, Sol?"

"You missed. The asshole's still breathin'. And if he's breathin', he can talk."

"Talk about what?"

"Is that supposed to be funny?"

"Listen close, Sol. You sent me to this shitpot of a city with a photo. There's a thousand out-of-town workers here. Some of 'em livin' in tents. What I should've done is shut it down right away. Only I didn't. I wandered around the city every fucking night until I found him. Then I set up the shot from the perfect position. But you can't control everything."

"So?"

"So, he moved at the last second, just when I pulled. Not far, right, but far enough that I caught his arm instead of his chest. That's part one. Part two is an asshole buddy of his just happened to be a trained paramedic. He put a tourniquet on the guy and saved his life."

There's nothing more to be said and Johnny-Boy waits patiently for Sol Cohen's response. He's unsurprised when Cohen mutters, "Yeah, well, I guess shit happens. Only it don't matter. Now you gotta finish the job you took."

"Or what, Sol?" Not an idle question, Johnny-Boy's most pressing need at the moment being a quick exit.

"Or Braulio's goin' in the ground. Me, too, if Braulio gives 'em my name. Then they'll come after you." A hesitation now as Cohen sucks it up. "The guy, Diopolis? I don't know what he knows, but he's got major people scared shit he might talk. He's also got major time hangin' over his head, like the rest of his life and a couple lifetimes after that."

"Come after me? Why should I care? Unless you plan to give them my name and a description."

"I don't fuckin' know your name and I never laid eyes on you."

"My point, Sol."

Cohen laughs. "Maybe you're right. Maybe they'll never find you. But they won't stop lookin' either. And maybe there ain't all that many independent contractors out there you could be." A pause here, but Johnny-Boy has nothing to say. "It's not all bad, okay? These people, there willin' to go another fifteen large if you complete the job. Otherwise, nothing, ever again. You hear? Ever again."

◆

Johnny-Boy hangs up before removing the SIM card and crushing it with a rock. True, he'd blocked the number, but not being all that tech savvy, he'd rather be safe than sorry. That done, he straightens on the lawn chair and looks off down the empty road for a moment. What to do, what to do. The main threat, that he'll be hunted, doesn't bother him all that much. He's changed his identity and residence too many times. But that other part, which he predicted, the part about the end of his little contracting business, is a lot more troubling. What would he do? Get a real job, maybe driving for Uber, maybe flipping hamburgers, maybe a job without bathroom breaks at Amazon? Maybe rob a fucking bank?

The sad part, Johnny thinks, is that I brought it on myself. If it wasn't for Case Dixon and the other kid, Sloan, if it wasn't for that bitch screaming at the mall, I'd finish the job. Or at least make an attempt. As it is . . .

One thing sure, he can't stay in this house. He's got to get out and he has to destroy the evidence in that shed. Destroy it by fire.

There's some good . . . well, not exactly good, but encouraging news. There are no photos of him for the cops to pass around, and he has another set of IDs tucked away. The problem will be finding another place to live in a wildly overcrowded city. In fact, if his luck finally turns, the cops will assume he's left town once they examine the shed. They'll find his fingerprints inside the house, of course, but although he's been dragged into police stations a few times, and even charged with misdemeanors that didn't stick, it's unlikely that his prints have made it to the FBI's database.

◆

After he finishes packing the van, Johnny-Boy decides to clean as much of the house as possible, despite the little pep talk he's given himself. He quits shortly after noon, retrieves a five-gallon container of gasoline from behind the house, and crosses the front lawn to the shed. Starting in a far corner, he soaks the floor, board by board, covering every inch, finally running a trail from the shed to the van. He lights the trail, but doesn't stand around to admire his work. He's in the van, driving toward Route 23, almost before the shed bursts into flame. Ten minutes is all it takes to reduce the shed to smoldering charcoal, the dried wood in the walls, floor, and roof adding to the intensity of the fire.

The Baxter Fire Department, alerted by a neighbor, gets lost twice before arriving an hour later to find the neighbor and his son posed by the shed. The neighbor is pouring water from a hose onto the embers when they come up the road, sirens screaming.

"Just in time to take the credit," he tells his son.

Captain Homer Leonard doesn't take credit, or try, but he does recognize an arson when he sees one. The isolated building, the intensity of the conflagration, and the conveniently absent resident? No question in Leonard's mind. He calls the arson into the Baxter PD, but leaves the remains of the shed undisturbed. Leonard's not an arson expert, determining points of origin, scorch marks, and burn patterns beyond his abilities. There's no trained expert at the Baxter PD either, but that's fine with Homer Leonard. A seasoned veteran, he's not big on taking credit, but extremely skilled at passing the buck.

The responding cop's name is Tony Mellone, a new hire. He arrives only a few minutes after Lena Pullan, the property owner, who's not all that upset. The house is still intact and she intends to sell the property as soon as she finds a contractor who'll meet her price. She does tell Officer Mellone that her tenant, Paul Ochoa, paid his rent in cash, rent that included cable, electric, and gas. There was no signed lease, and no trace of the man left behind.

"He was really a very polite man."

Mellone takes a few notes after making sure there are no hidden bodies beneath the ashes, but then loses interest. He'll include the incident in his daily activities report, but that's enough. He's got better things to do back in the city. Five minutes later, as he closes his notebook, a Jeep pulls up and the woman he calls Jersey Girl steps out. As arrogant as ever.

"We need to close off the house," she tells him. "Nobody in or out until the CSU arrives."

Mellone stares at her for just a moment. "Glad to hear it," he declares before sliding into the cruiser and driving away.

◆

Johnny-Boy's long gone by this time. He's wandering along twisting streets on the western edge of Mt. Jackson, the city's wealthiest neighborhood. The houses on this side of Baxter Park aren't as fancy as the houses on the other side, but that's of little mind to Johnny-Boy. He wants to find a place to stay as far from Boomtown as possible, figuring that if the cops are looking for him, that's where they'll start.

The pickings, unfortunately, are few and far between. The first, above a Chinese restaurant on Eagle Street, he rejects. He'll be seen every time he enters or leaves his tiny apartment. An hour later, he finds another in a hastily renovated garage that's guaranteed to admit the soon-to-come winter winds. The children playing outside are equally unencouraging. Too many eyes.

It's after three o'clock when Johnny-Boy finds his lair on a dead-end street that backs into the old border between Baxter and Maryville counties. This close to the edge, the lots are large, even if the houses are small. No big deal, Johnny-Boy's attracted by a sign in a picture window on the first house, a dilapidated ranch that reminds him of an abandoned trailer.

Undaunted, Johnny-Boy parks the van and walks up to the door, which opens before he can knock. The skinny old man who faces him is already scowling, probably his habitual expression. As he checks Johnny-Boy out, he scratches at a thin beard, making no effort to disguise his disdain. Meanwhile, he can't weigh more than 120 pounds.

"You here about the room?"

"I am, yes."

"It's around the side of the house." He snorts. "Name's Morrison, in case you're interested."

The old man leads Johnny-Boy to a doorway facing away from neighboring homes. "You come in through here. Private entrance."

The tiny room Johnny-Boy enters is spare enough to be called barren. A single bed with no headboard, a table, a wooden chair, a narrow recliner, an attached bathroom with a shower stall and no tub.

"Seven hundred." The old man smiles, revealing a missing incisor on the right side. "A week." When Johnny-Boy doesn't respond, he adds. "Livin' space is hard to find and winter is comin'."

Money isn't really a problem for Johnny-Boy. He tells the old man to wait, strolls to the van and digs out his stash. Returning, he peels off seven C-notes and hands them over. The old man smiles again, probably wondering why this asshole doesn't quibble. But Johnny-Boy's all smiles, at least for now. He only needs a day, two at most. Accommodation is the order of the day.

"Here ya go, Mr. Morrison. And thanks."

CHAPTER THIRTY
BLANCHE WEBER

I watch the cop start up the patrol car and drive off. His name tag read MELLONE and he's young enough to be a probationary cop. But there's not much I can do about his attitude, though I technically outrank him. Or I would if I was still on duty. As it is, I turn to the ruins of what was once a farm outbuilding. Homer Leonard, a firefighter I've known for several years, joins me without commenting on Mellone's insolence.

I point to the remains of the fire. "Something off here, don't you think?"

"You mean besides a stand-alone structure suddenly catching fire without human intervention? Me, I'm thinkin' spontaneous combustion."

"That how you're gonna write it up?"

"Hell, no. I'm gonna write it up as a probable arson."

The homeowner, who's been standing to one side, approaches at that moment. She introduces herself as Lena Pullam and I ask the appropriate questions. The answers are as expected. Her tenant paid the rent, which included utilities, in cash. There was no signed lease.

"Did you at least get his name?"

The woman's offended by my sarcastic tone. She should be glad I don't ask her if she's reported the revenue to the State Division of Taxation.

"Paul Ochoa," she finally announces. "And I didn't ask for ID."

"You don't know where I can find him?"

"Told me he worked at some bar in town." Her mouth tightens as she prepares her defense. "The man seemed decent to me. A regular guy, right. He wasn't gonna run women or sell drugs out of the house. Me, I don't want trouble with the cops. I'm gonna sell the property as soon as I get my price."

I thank Ms. Pullam for her cooperation and turn to Ochoa's neighbor, the father and son who reported the fire. They introduce themselves as Lars and Jimmy Saarin, farmers. Unlike Pullam, they don't have an attitude.

"Did you know him?" I ask.

"Never stood face-to-face," Jimmy says. "Few times past, I seen him drive by. I waved and he waved back. That's about it."

"Did you notice what he was driving?"

"Yeah, come to think of it. A van, white, but like commercial. No windows in back. But he ain't drivin' it now."

"You sure?"

"Well, I saw him come past yesterday. Another van, a Dodge, but regular, not commercial. Had tinted windows on the sides."

"You notice the color?"

He looks up at the sky for a moment, then nods. "I'm thinkin' green, but don't hold me to it."

◆

Before calling Delia, I take a moment to examine the charred lumber in the remains of the fire. There's too much. Too much for a building that might have been used to store gardening tools and a snowblower. I'm probably looking at the place where Case Dixon, and the other boy, too, the one found in Maryville County, spent their last moments. Short of a confession, though, I'll never prove it.

Delia answers her phone on the third ring. I'll need a search warrant for the house, a warrant I can't secure while I'm on official leave.

"I have some good news for a change," Delia announces before I get started.

"Love to hear it."

"The boy in Maryville County? Sheriff Morrow called a little earlier. The pathologist from the state found traces of semen on the boy's ankle. Not much, right, and it hasn't been tested, but I have a good feeling about this. The way it is now, you only need fifty millionths of a gram."

It is good news, a lot better than mine. I lay out the details, the all-consuming fire and the landlord identifying her tenant as Paul Ochoa.

"First thing, I need a search warrant for the house."

"You don't think he cleaned up?"

"I think he probably tried. Whether or not he was successful remains to be seen. The house is small, but to leave it free of any trace evidence, DNA, or fingerprints, you'd have to burn it down. On the other hand, the shed is tiny. It's completely gone, along with any blood evidence."

"Okay, got it. Anything else?"

"Yeah, there was a cop here when I arrived. Named Mellone." I spell it for her. "When I told him we needed to seal off the house, he told me 'Glad to hear it' and drove away. Young guy, probably a new hire."

Delia takes her time, but finally answers. "I'll deal with Mellone at another time. But if the tenant's moved out, you only need permission from the landlord to search."

"And how will I know if Ochoa's moved out?"

"Simple, Blanche. Get permission, go inside and check the bureaus and the closets. Look for personal possessions. If you can't find them, it's safe to say the tenant's deserted the premises. And by the way, if he hasn't left, you can stick around and grab him when he shows up."

◆

Personally, I have my doubts, but she's right about one thing. No way Ochoa would leave anything personal that could be traced to him. Once I receive permission from Lena Pullam, I head directly to the bedrooms, ignoring the penetrating odor of disinfectant. The first bedroom I enter was probably unoccupied during Ochoa's tenure. The room is empty, no bed, no furniture, not even a lamp. There's an unmade bed in the second bedroom with the bedclothes pulled back. A thin wool blanket, top and bottom sheets, a pillow, and a pillowcase. The disinfectant's telling me that Ochoa made an attempt to clean up, but maybe didn't have time to do laundry, assuming there's a washer and dryer in the house. There'll be DNA on those sheets, on the pillowcase, too. Cast-off skin cells at the least.

The closet and the small bureau in the room are both empty, as are the closets downstairs. I don't find anything, not even a supermarket receipt. That establishes the fact of nontenancy and I call for the Crime Scene Unit before leaving the house. Not being a wiggle-room kind of cop, I not only want a professional search of the residence, I want the search videotaped.

Okay, time to relax. It's chilly, but the sun has come out and I angle my car so the sun pours through the windows on the passenger side. A small cooler packed at home sits on the passenger's seat. There's a thermos of coffee, two soft peaches that have to be eaten today, a handful of napkins, and a wet wipe.

As I eat, I admit the truth about what I might find in the house. DNA from the occupant, Paul Ochoa, probably. But evidence linking Ochoa to either homicide? The question gives rise to another. Was Case Dixon ever in the house?

The way it's shaping up, the semen sample on the boy's ankle will decide Ochoa's guilt one way or the other. And if the sample isn't semen, or the DNA can't be tested, or there's no DNA to test? Then nothing the Baxter PD recovers here today will make any difference. Nevertheless, we'll go through the house, room by room, drawer by drawer, and we'll work our way through the ashes left by the fire. We'll do our jobs.

◆

I'm running the wet wipe over my mouth and chin when our Crime Scene Unit rides up. I get out of the car, wave hello, and brief the sergeant in charge, emphasizing the need for video. Then I'm left to wander through the house while five trained professionals do their collective job. They bag the bedclothes first, the obvious being the obvious, but I'm impressed when they swab the sink, an attached porcelain toothbrush/soap holder, and the bathtub. I'm even more impressed when they open the sink's trap and remove a mass of hair and grease that reminds me of what you find in a blocked sewer pipe.

"We'll recover the DNA of whoever lived in the house, count on it," Sergeant Tomaselli insists. "You'd have to start a fire to destroy everything, and you'd have to stick around long enough to be sure the burn was complete."

I wander outside, light a cigarette, and have another look at what remains of the shed. As a professional, I'm supposed to focus on the basics, the how, when, what, and where. But I'm again seized by what actually happened, with Case Dixon, with the boy, and with Paul Ochoa as well. The hunt, the capture, pain for pleasure. I've taken down numerous killers who finally confessed. They've always had reasons, even if it's the spurned boyfriend proudly declaring that if he can't have her, nobody will. Or the woman who insisted that her three-year-old daughter was possessed by the devil. But this? A man pressing a hair dryer into the flesh of a boy, watching as the boy's flesh burns away, listening to the screams, becoming erect as a result . . .

My phone interrupts these thoughts. Thank God? It's Owen, with news, bad news, and just when I think it can't get any worse. His voice is cold, icy cold.

"I'm home, Blanche. Someone's been inside. You need to see. Now, Blanche. You need to come home right now."

"Are you sure the house is empty? Have you called it in?"

"Yes, and yes."

"Then tell me what happened."

"Come home and see for yourself." Owen's spitting the words out. He's pissed and unwilling or unable to conceal it. "Dammit, you're not even on duty."

Nothing I can say will do any good, I know that, but I don't get a chance to say it anyway as Owen hangs up. At this point, I have no choice. I brief Tomaselli, reminding him to do it by the book, no shortcuts. Then it's home to face the music. I know I'll be blamed, blaming the victim is an American right. I think it's in the damned Constitution. That doesn't matter right now. What matters is that I'm forty minutes from the house I share with a man I love.

There's no siren on my Jeep, no flashing lights to warn traffic that I'm traveling at a high rate of speed, and I'm forced to stay reasonably close to the speed limit and at least slow for the occasional traffic light. I call Delia as I drive. She's already dispatched a patrol car to the house, just in case somebody's hidden inside, or the intruder returns. She'll be on her way as soon as soon as she informs our commissioner.

"This is a big deal," she tells me. "A lot bigger than pranks in a locker room."

Thanks for sharing. I don't say it, but I can't help but think it. What's happening here is a declaration of war. And I'm not fooling myself. It's not about me. I'm simply a target of convenience, a female cop with a big mouth.

◆

A pair of cruisers sit in front of my house, blocking the driveway. I pull to the curb, nose first, get out, and approach a pair of uniformed cops by the door. As I pass, I search their faces, almost hoping for a smirk. It takes me a few heartbeats to recognize my paranoia. Both are veterans who've worked with me on numerous investigations. I find regret on their faces, and sympathy. They're not part of the insurrection. In fact, in the long run, they might even be targets.

I discover Delia standing in our living room, and she jerks her chin toward the stairs. Owen's in our bedroom—packing a bag as it turns out—and my heart drops in my chest, the pain as sharp as it is unexpected. Is he leaving me?

"I can't take this," he says.

"Owen, I never dreamed . . ."

"Delia tells me I need to get out of my own house because it's no longer safe." Owen's barely able to restrain his anger. The same Owen who prides himself on his calm and collected attitude. He's jamming T-shirts into an almost-full bag. "You attacked this cop, Jack something . . ."

"Jake. Jake Nurine."

"And why, Blanche? You didn't know he was the one who messed with your locker. You still don't know. And now you're running around Baxter when you're supposed to be on leave. Forced leave."

I'm trying not to crumble. Yeah, I've fucked things up. The assault on Jake Nurine should never have happened, deserve it though he did. But there's still a murderer out there, a sadist named Paul Ochoa, and an asshole, Bard Henry, charged with committing Ochoa's crime. Maybe I should explain this to Owen, but I can't get the words out of my mouth.

"I just want a normal life," Owen explains. "Go to work, come home, weekends with the kids, two weeks in the summer. Did you see what they did downstairs?"

I did see. The spray-painted words JUSTICE FOR JAKE cover one wall. Owen's Thomas Hart Benton lithographs lie atop each other in a pile of broken glass. A crude map of New Jersey bears the legend, also spray-painted, HOME SWEET HOME. I've seen a lot worse, but not Owen. It's all new to him.

"They've finished renovating the Skyview Motel. That's where I'm headed." He closes the suitcase and zips the cover before standing up. "Maybe it can't work, Blanche. Maybe our worlds are just too far apart. I'm a dentist, not a warrior. I don't want to fight."

I'm almost paralyzed, my jaw trembling as he walks past me. He's at the head of the stairs before I find my voice.

"Owen, I can't quit now. But later . . ."

Without turning he interrupts me, "Whatever you're doing, there's a whole police force to do it. You're not the Lone Ranger."

CHAPTER THIRTY-ONE

DELIA

On the one hand, I'm not prepared for the Blanche Weber who comes down the stairs. But the enraged Owen Walsh who just passed me came as no surprise. The house belongs to Owen. It validates his middle-class ambitions. Having responded to many burglaries, I know that Owen's home, now violated, will never again be a sanctuary. I have to believe that he's bright enough to know it as well.

It's different with Blanche. She's always been a bulldog, leading with that chin of hers, ready for combat. She seems weary now, almost resigned, another losing relationship in a long string of losing relationships. And me, I have to say something, but I can't make myself believe the words will have any real effect.

"I've already given orders to have the neighborhood canvassed. These assholes were crazy to do this during the day."

"You think they were gonna to try at night, while I'm in here, armed?"

When I don't answer, she crosses the room and begins to sort through the glass and the artwork on the floor. I'm pretty sure the black-and-white prints are valuable, though I don't recognize the artist. Their importance to Owen is apparent from the torn plaster on the main wall of his living room.

Blanche holds up a torn print, a farmer milking a cow as big as a whale. The distorted landscape surrounding them rolls in waves across the paper.

"These lithographs are by Thomas Hart Benton. Owen's maternal grandparents bought them at a time when they were affordable. But they aren't a simple inheritance. They belong to the family and Owen's supposed to care for them until he passes them to his own children." She glares at me for a moment, but I'm not dumb enough to comment. "Why, Delia? What's the game here? Because I'm not thinking this is about Jake Nurine's family jewels."

I take the print out of her hands and lay it on a coffee table. "Are you sure you don't want to follow Owen?"

She shakes her head. "What could I say to him? That I'll change? I can't be someone else. I know because I've tried."

"But are you ready to be Blanche?"

"What's the difference? I'm on mandatory leave, remember?"

"Vern wants to see the both of us, so maybe, maybe not." I take a step closer to Blanche and lay a hand on her shoulder. "But I want you committed, Blanche. I need your head in one place, impossible as that may seem."

Blanche takes one more look around her living room, at the graffiti on the walls, the torn print on the table, the overturned chairs. Finally, she releases the breath she's been holding and her mouth tightens.

"Yeah, you're right. I can't let the scumbags get away with this."

"And you can't kill them either. Keep that in mind."

◆

We're quiet as we ride back to the house in Blanche's Jeep. I'm watching Blanche out of the corner of my eye and she's watching the road. I know she really believes that she and Owen are through, but I have my doubts. She's right, though, about one thing. Blanche and Owen not only come from different worlds, but the worlds they hope to visit in the future are on opposite sides of the solar system. Any decent relationship counselor would probably tell them to shut it down and move on.

Not me.

If humans were truly rational, we'd live in a calm and cool, nonviolent world. They're not, though, and I've known couples even more incompatible who've stuck it out for decades. Zoe and I had Blanche and Owen over for dinner last year, and they returned the invitation a few months later. I was struck by the casual affection they showed each other, the quick hugs, the intimate smiles they exchanged. So, while Owen, always timid, has been deeply affected by the invasion of his little castle, I'm hoping he'll realize that Blanche was the victim, not the perpetrator. I'm hoping.

In the meantime, there's work to do. I brief my detective on the conversation I had with Bear Sawyer, the phone call made by Malcolm Bridger, and the need to follow up. The implications are obvious, but the briefing has another purpose. I need to remind

Blanche that the invasion of her home isn't the only meal currently on our plates. Me, I'm half hoping that Paul Ochoa has left town, what with the fire at his residence. That would make freeing Bard Henry the most pressing need.

◆

I'm expecting Vern to be as deflated as the championship football he keeps in his office, but I've misjudged him entirely. He's standing when we come into the room, and he's not alone. Saul Rawling, our chief of patrol, is with him. Rawling's a survivor, always has been, a large man with a drinker's complexion that includes the broken veins that line his nose. I don't know how he climbed to his current position—he was already in place when Vern was appointed—but he exudes the confidence of a man with serious connections as he takes a seat.

"Blanche, I can't tell you how sorry I am that you have to go through this bullshit," Vern begins. "I'm sorry for the department, too, and seriously enraged by our procurement committee. But that's the problem with contracting out. They're supposed to be HR experts, but I can't make myself believe they did more than rubber stamp the applications." A smile follows, obviously forced, before Vern looks over at Saul Rawling. "Any ideas, Saul? About who might be responsible for these . . . these fucking crimes?"

Saul's face becomes even redder at Vern's sarcastic tone. "Are you looking to put the blame on the patrol division, Vern? Without the slightest proof?"

"Well, Saul, being as you've never been a detective, let me explain it to you. Investigations don't begin with solutions. They begin with the most likely of the possibilities. The detective division is staffed with veterans, men and women I've known for years. Men and women who've earned my trust. On the other hand, more than thirty percent of the patrol division is staffed with men and women who were hired less than a year ago. So where do you suggest we start, if not with patrol?"

Rawling shifts his weight from one buttock to another as he bites at his lower lip. His blue eyes, normally twinkling, have turned the color of winter ice beneath a cloudy sky. "You gonna blame cops, Vern? That's how it's gonna go down?"

"'Justice for Jake'? Spray-painted onto a wall? You think I should start looking at civilians?"

"Okay, I got it." Rawling taps his index finger into the palm of his left hand. "But what about real justice for Jake Nurine, who's currently disabled after an assault by . . ." He points to Blanche. "By this detective. Look, you wanna fire me, you're gonna have to find cause, which you don't have. In the meantime, when it comes to the cops under my command, I intend to have their backs."

I raise my hand, bringing Rawling to a halt. On the way to Vern's office, I stopped by my own to retrieve a narrow briefcase stuffed with employment applications. I take them out and drop them onto Vern's desk.

"Forty-three hires since September of last year. That's when the city council came up with the money to expand the department. I've been working them all morning. Looking for patterns, or a pattern. Call it a logical place to start."

Vern nods at the pile. "Don't keep us in suspense, Delia."

I glance at Blanche. Her eyes are fixed on the pile, her focus intense. At some point, I'll probably have to restrain her, but for now I'm satisfied with her commitment. "Seven hires, all in

January, former deputy sheriffs from three counties in Missouri. They would be Humphreys, Overton, and Bledsoe. And guess what?"

Blanche comes in first, her eyes on fire. "They border one another."

"Exactly right, but there's bad news too. The seven were hired in January. They're a few months past their probationary period. You want to fire them, you have to hold a hearing and prove specific violations of our professional code."

"Like breaking and entering?" Blanche asks.

Vern raises a hand before delivering the ultimate humiliation. "You're dismissed, Saul. We won't be needing you."

◆

With Rawling gone, Vern nods as he draws a breath. "You gonna leave those with me?"

"Yeah."

"So, what next?"

"There's somebody we should approach, me and Blanche." I hesitate for a moment, then add, "Rowan Krauss spoke to me yesterday. Off the record, Vern. The rumor on the street, which he got from a reliable informant, is that some of our cops are dirty."

"And this person you want to contact would be?" Vern asks.

"A man who seems to know everything about anything happening in Baxter. Zack Butler."

"Yeah, that would be about right. In the meantime, I'll be calling a few sheriffs in Missouri. And you, Blanche, are returned to active duty."

CHAPTER THIRTY-TWO

DELIA

Zack Butler's still-green lawn is as immaculately manicured as ever, each blade of grass the same height and standing at attention. Burlap covers his azaleas, protection against the winter winds to come, and the garden itself is weed free.

Blanche shows her appreciation with a muttered, "Wow."

"Zack's a control freak. He needs to manipulate every actor in the play. Not to worry, though. He's a professional charmer, a master."

But not this time. Miranda, his longtime aide, meets us at the door. "Señor is not having a good day," she explains.

"I called ahead, Miranda. You said he wanted to see us."

"This is true, captain. Only please it should be as short as possible. *Por favor.*"

As we don't have a lot of time anyway, a quick visit is fine with me.

"Okay, Miranda, I'll let Zack point the way. If I see him straining, I'll come back at another time."

Zack's in pajamas and an embroidered silk robe covered with red and gold dragons chasing one another through an impossibly blue sky. I'm tempted to lead with a joke, but Miranda's right. Zack's complexion is pale, despite the oxygen being fed into his nostrils, and the pouches under his eyes are dark and heavy.

"A cold. These days, they hit me hard." Zack's voice is hoarse, his breathing shallow. His words appear one phrase at a time, with a pause for breath between them.

"Sorry to hear that." I point to Blanche. "This is Detective Weber, my partner."

"Pleased," Zack says. He touches a scar on his throat, site of a former tracheostomy, and says, "What can I do for you?"

"Seems we have a cop problem. We're wondering if you've . . . gotten word."

"Dirty cops, that about it? A pack of dirty cops."

"Yeah. What are you hearing?" I smile. "I'm askin' because I know your stake in the city is as big as mine."

"Could you flatter me a little more while I ponder the question?" He waits for me to smile. "Can't name names, Delia, but you might wanna talk to Frankie Minter."

"Minty?"

Francis Minter's a small-time dealer who moved his operation outside the expanded city boundaries after he narrowly escaped arrest. A matter of pure luck, our narcotics team raided his operation just after he unloaded the last of his product. We walked away with egg on our faces and a promise to return. Minty pulled up roots a day later.

"Yeah, Minty. What I hear, Delia, he's recovering at home."

◆

A place to start, but there's a lot of work ahead and it's time to split it up. Outside, as we come down a flagstone path that's as flat as the rug in Zack's living room, I lay it out.

"I'm gonna give this to you, Blanche, being as you have a personal stake in the outcome. Grab someone you trust and head out to Minter's place. No uniforms and don't use a marked car. Minty spots a cruiser gliding up his driveway, he's liable to open up. We didn't find any dope in his house, but as I remember, we did find a pair of shotguns."

"I was there, Delia. But I get the point."

"Then get this too. The cops we're after? They're embedded. We're not gonna clear them out in a day, or a week. This is cancer and cancer travels. You cut off one piece, it's already growing somewhere else."

◆

Every police department I ever worked in has at least one. A cop past his use-by date whose private life is so bleak that employing him amounts to suicide prevention. Clyde Norman is one of these. In his early sixties now, he was in his forties when his wife passed. Not long after, his only child, a daughter, moved to New Hampshire. She remains in touch, according to Norman.

Most men or women with a similar history would have moved on, would have remarried, or developed a close relationship with their church, or some club, maybe even a political organization. Clyde Norman didn't do any of that. Instead, he put all his eggs in a cop-basket that loneliness and alcohol blew apart. Until, finally, the Baxter Police Department assigned him to its small jail as a shift supervisor. Originally, the position had no concrete responsibilities, but Clyde was good at the job and comfortable with computers. Even better, he didn't head from work to the nearest cop bar. He earned his pay.

I find Clyde in his tiny office. A large man, well over six feet tall and heavy in the chest and shoulders, he projects authority despite an extra forty pounds. Not that he usually spends much time on the tiers, which raises a question. Bear told me that Clyde Norman led Malcolm Bridger to his cell, not one of the prison guards, who normally do this job.

That's the first thing I touch on when I confront Clyde. And I make myself clear from the outset. I haven't come to socialize.

"Yeah," Clyde responds, "I remember the kid. Officer Garranos wasn't . . . wasn't available, so I took him myself."

"Wasn't available? That's bullshit, but I'm not here about Officer Garranos. I'm here because you lent your cell phone to Malcolm Bridger."

"Yeah, I . . ."

Clyde's brown eyes are close to glowing and I sense the onset of panic. Prisoners are allowed a phone call, said call to be made during the booking process with cops present. Calls to lawyers are private, of course, but we still make sure the person on the other end is, in fact, a lawyer.

"Am I in trouble, captain? Because he was just a kid, and scared to death. He told me he couldn't reach anybody when they gave him a phone call. Ya know, they can be real pricks out there."

"I don't wanna jam you up, Clyde. Seriously, I don't. But I need to see your phone. I need to know who Bridger called. It's important."

Clyde's under no obligation to comply. I have no more right to seize his phone than to seize the phone of a civilian. Instead, he looks down at the phone lying on the desk, then says, "Lemme find it for you."

Thirty seconds later, he points to an entry in his *Recents* file. The day and date stamp are both right, but I really don't need them. The name alongside the phone number is, as they say, plainly writ. Benjamin Cooper, Malcolm Bridger's good buddy, good enough to get Bard Henry indicted, was the recipient of the call.

"Ya know, Clyde, I should keep you here until I get a warrant for the phone. It's evidence and I'm supposed to secure it."

"Delia, how long have you known me? I mean, I'll give you the damn phone. My phone calls are mostly spam anyway. But . . ."

"But nothing. I'm gonna pay a call on Benny Cooper. You hang on to the phone for now. But if I need it, I expect you to hand it over. And let me say it again. I'm gonna do everything I can to keep you out of it."

On my way out, I call over to the squad room. Detective Marcus Goodman picks up. I don't ask if he's busy because he might say yes. I tell him to head to Coolwater Bar & Grill on the lower end of Baxter Boulevard. "I want a likeness of a former bartender named Paul Ochoa. Two employees there worked with him, Glory and Sharon. Use an Identi-Kit, take a laptop."

"And don't take no for an answer?"

"Yeah, this I need. Like right away."

◆

I meant what I told Clyde Norman. He should not have lent his phone to Malcolm Bridger, but he got played, not with a bribe, with a sob story. Just now, as I leave the yard in an unmarked Ford sedan, I'm hoping that Benny Cooper will revise his written statement, the one where he claimed he didn't speak to Bridger after Bridger's arrest. But I want more than the boy admitting his lie. It's the lie about seeing Bard Henry outside the party just before Case Dixon was kidnapped that most needs correction.

A small accident a few blocks from city hall slows me. Neither car looks badly damaged, but the drivers, both men, are standing in the road, two strutting roosters. I put an end to the game with a few whoops of my siren, but the vehicles are still in the middle of the street and it takes me a few minutes to get past. I use the time to call home, where Danny answers. No, I tell him, I won't be home for dinner, and perhaps not at all tonight. His response, "Okay, mom, I got it," does nothing to relieve the guilt.

As I pull out, a thought emerges from somewhere in a part of my brain I can't reach. As usual, it's something I might have considered a week ago.

We've been asking ourselves why Ochoa didn't run after Case Dixon's body was discovered. But let's say he decided that he was safe enough for now. That's possible. The close call with Mila Wegson, on the other hand, was enough for him to lose the van and acquire another vehicle. Time to go? Past time, so why did he return?

Good question, but not entirely to the point. We should have been asking why he came to Baxter in the first place. Did he throw a dart at a map of the United States and happen to hit my little city? Too remote, way too remote. Ochoa came for a reason, and not to pursue his favorite hobby, which he might have done anywhere. And whatever that reason, it was compelling enough to bring him back after the encounter with Mila Wegson.

◆

I leave it there as I approach Benny Cooper's home. It's after six o'clock and I'm hoping to find the Coopers at dinner. Shock and awe, the punch Benny doesn't see coming.

The Coopers live in a well-maintained two-story home that lacks the obsessive order of Zack's place. There are bare spots on the brown lawn and two bicycles on the porch, one full size, a racer, the other pink with chrome training wheels in the back. The effect is homely, a working family, prosperous but not rich, looking to a bright future that I'm about to punch in the face.

Stell Cooper answers the door. In her early forties, she's a trim brunette, likely a working mom given the blue skirt and relatively heavy makeup. Her dark eyes, at first welcoming, quickly grow wary. She knows who I am even before I flash my shield and announce myself. This can't be good.

"Afternoon, Mrs. Cooper. I need to speak to Benjamin for a few minutes." I don't have to ask if he's home. I can see him sprawled on a sofa in the living room. He's wearing a Baxter High Tigers sweatshirt, the letters curving over the top of a basketball. Benny's got the height to go with the sport, along with a dismissive smile I associate with a few of Danny's teammates.

"What's it about?" She looks behind her, perhaps for a husband who's not there at the moment.

"Follow-up, ma'am. From the interview we did a few days ago. Your husband was present."

"But didn't Benny answer your questions?"

"I didn't conduct the interview." I don't have time for a negotiation and I make that clear. "I have to speak with your son, Mrs. Cooper."

Over her shock, apparently, Stell Cooper straightens. "I assume that I'll be present."

"Absolutely."

"Good." She hesitates for just a moment, maintaining eye contact, perhaps to show me who's the real boss, then calls her son onto the porch. He lifts himself from the couch and slouches toward us, the dismissive look on his face instantly relieving me of any guilt about what I'm doing.

"What's up?"

"First thing, Benny, I'm not recording this conversation, but I have to advise you of your Constitutional rights anyway." I do so quickly, and Benny deflates noticeably, as does his mom. "You're not under arrest, Benny. It doesn't have to come to that, and I'm not recording this conversation, like I said. For the moment, we're just talking."

"Yeah, so what do you want?" He's trying for high school tough guy. A little defiance before the hammer falls.

"I'm sure you recall being interviewed by Detective Meacham. That would be last Friday."

"Okay, sure."

"And do you recall telling him that you didn't speak with Malcolm Bridger between the time he was arrested and the time of the interview?"

He pulls back, glancing at his mom. No help from that quarter, a scowl instead. "I think . . . no, I'm not sure."

"Then allow me to remind you that Detective Meacham asked you to write out your statement and that you made that claim in the course of your statement." I shake my head. "There's no escape and you won't help yourself by lying."

"Okay, if I said it, I said it."

"But it wasn't true, was it?"

Stell Cooper finally breaks her outraged silence. At her son, thank God, and not me. "What's wrong with you, Benny? Did you lie to the police? Are you crazy?"

"Mom . . ."

"Just tell the truth. No more crap."

"All right, I lied about not speaking to Malcolm. I shouldn't have done it. I'm sorry."

My turn now. "What else did you lie about?"

"Nothing."

"So, you're still claiming that you saw Bard Henry outside the party?"

"Yeah, we saw him."

"Okay, but here's the thing, Benny. We've interviewed thirty kids who attended that party, kids who knew and mostly feared Bard Henry. They came and went, and even returned. A few actually partied in the yard outside the house. How is it possible that none of them, not a single one, saw Bard Henry, who you claim was sitting in his car right across the street? How likely is that?" I give it a couple beats. "Your buddy, Malcolm Bridger, is going away. Given the lie, prosecutors will never put him on the witness stand and that means no deal. You can't protect him and you have nothing to gain, but a lot to lose. The lie you told amounts to obstruction of justice, a felony in this state. I can charge you right now, and I will if you don't tell me the truth. How is it possible that of all the kids who attended the party, you and Malcolm are the only ones who noticed Bard Henry sitting in his car?"

Benny Cooper doesn't answer immediately and I can almost see the alternatives rolling around in his head. Me, I don't want to arrest this kid, but I'm not willing to leave Bard Henry on the hook for a crime he didn't commit. Without Malcolm Bridger's and Benny Cooper's testimony, our district attorney's case amounts to a threat and a few wood splinters. I'm hoping that Cooper will voluntarily alter his claim of seeing Henry at the party. If not, I have to make sure any testimony that Benny or Malcolm are prepared to give will be thoroughly tainted.

The contemptuous smirk that slowly comes to dominate Benny Cooper's mouth reveals the punch line before he speaks. He's decided to stand up for his pal, to take one for the team, to ruin the rest of his dumbass life. For nothing.

"Maybe," he tells me, "they weren't looking."

Stell Cooper shakes her head as tears form in the corners of her eyes. I'm moved, truly, but the job is the job.

"Benjamin Cooper, you are under arrest. Turn around and put your hands on the wall."

CHAPTER THIRTY-THREE
JOHNNY-BOY

What he should do, and he knows it, he *fucking* knows it, is stay in his room until he's ready to act, which won't be until later in the day. But he can't, he can't sit around with no TV, not even a radio, and only his phone for company, a burner without internet access. Meanwhile, his laptop's been charging for two hours with nothing to show for it. So, what now, being as he already took a shower, already finished a forty-minute workout, already jerked off? Take a stroll? And make sure everybody in the neighborhood has a good look at him?

Johnny-Boy manages to walk to his car and drive away without being spotted. He's wearing a well-used corduroy jacket and a Detroit Tigers baseball cap, just another working Joe, no need for scrutiny. He dumps the jacket as the heater warms the van, but keeps the cap pulled down low on his forehead. Johnny-Boy's not foolish enough to approach downtown Baxter. He'll take that risk eventually, but not yet.

Maryville County to the west is only a few blocks away. That's where he heads initially, but it's also where he dumped little Sloan. The kid's death has been reported in Baxter, in the newspaper and on local news outlets, but it's still Maryville County's problem. And just maybe the sheriff is compensating for an investigation that's going nowhere with random stops designed to produce a fall guy. Call it the drifter gambit.

Johnny-Boy is unaware of the DNA sample found on Sloan's ankle, but he's pretty sure the cops have found his own DNA in the farmhouse he abandoned. That's not what's bothering him, because he's been very careful over the years and he's sure his DNA's not on file in some data bank. No, it's the possibility that somebody with a sketch pad visited the Coolwater and assembled a likeness of Paul Ochoa. Maybe not a possibility, maybe a certainty. The two bitch cops, Mariola and Weber? Dumb isn't on the agenda for either one.

As he drives north, then east, into Revere County, Johnny-Boy listens to the news on KBR, the local radio station. Bard Henry remains in jail, charged with Case Dixon's murder. And Sloan? The kid hasn't even been identified. So the cops might grab Johnny-Boy based on a sketch. They'll surely grill him if they do, but Johnny-Boy's committed to basic legal strategy. Never talk to the cops. Ask for a lawyer right away and if they slap you around, take it. The bit about anything you say can be used against you? Anything means anything. They don't need a confession.

All very rational, all very Boy Scout Be Prepared. Meanwhile, that little voice continues. Get out, get out, get out . . . sounding like a demented child that won't stop until it gets its way. Get out, get out, get out.

◆

Johnny-Boy doesn't map his journey. His turns are pretty much spontaneous. At times, he zips along on four-lane state roads, at times he cruises over county roads that wind between oddly shaped farm lots. An hour into his drive, he stops outside an electrified fence to watch a small herd of buffalo grazing in a meadow. The herd is dominated by a gigantic bull, a hairy tank with horns. He's off by himself, peacefully grazing, while the rest, cows and calves, mill about. A few are lying on the ground, obviously asleep.

For a very short time, Johnny-Boy worked on a cattle ranch in Oklahoma. With rare exceptions, bull calves never became bulls. They became steers early in life and joined the grazing cows. A single bull, kept for breeding, fathered every calf.

This bison rancher appears to have a different approach. Mostly likely, bull calves are slaughtered before they grow big enough to mess with daddy. Good news for this bull. Lots of in-season sex, every calf bearing his genes, and peaceful grazing the rest of the year. He'll never know the slaughterhouse, never take the blood-smell into his nostrils before the hammer falls. At some point, when he's too old to play stud, the rancher will lead him off to a side pasture and put a bullet in his head. Good night, sweet bull.

Fascinated by his own thoughts, Johnny-Boy almost forgets the urgency that preceded his stop. Now he urinates into a narrow ditch at the edge of the field. He's wondering if he should be jealous, at least of the bull. He's not, though. No, he'd rather be in charge, despite the possibility of making a mistake. Johnny-Boy figures that most likely he'll be killed, too, the difference between him and the bull is that he'll be shooting back when a bullet punches through the top of his skull.

◆

Johnny-Boy's headed back to his car when a tractor pulling a hay wagon slowly approaches. Without thinking, Johnny-Boy assumes his nonthreatening posture, mouth, brow, and jaw relaxed, his gaze neither timid nor bold. Nor does it shift when the tractor slows to a stop and the elderly man behind the wheel nods once, then smiles.

"Say, you ain't about to rustle my buffalo, are ya?"

Johnny-Boy returns the smile. "I'm just tryin' to decide whether I can stuff that old bull in the back seat."

The farmer's face is the color and texture of aged leather despite a straw hat with a wide brim that leaves most of his face in shadow. "Friend, you are welcome to try. Save me the trouble of shootin' him myself. That's how ornery he's gotten."

Johnny-Boy's turn to laugh as the old man puts the tractor in gear and pulls away. Then he's back in his car, driving again, his thoughts turning to his special needs. Throughout what he likes to call his career, he's avoided home invasion. Too many unknown unknowns, a dog, a handy firearm, family members or even guests in different parts of the house, maybe a hidden alarm system.

Still, the possibility was always out there, especially after weeks of fruitless trolling. He's even developed a strategy. First extensive surveillance to determine who's likely to be present at any given time, then a surreptitious entry at night, then kill every family member except your special target. After that, it's off to Johnny-Boy's chamber of horrors.

Johnny-Boy's never actually begun a surveillance, but the chronology makes for a pleasurable fantasy as he drives past the isolated farmhouses. He imagines creeping into the bedrooms of the younger children, dispatching them silently. Then the parents, shot dead, before making off with a barely pubescent teen. Boy or girl, it doesn't matter, nor does race, nationality, or religion. Johnny-Boy's an equal opportunity killer.

◆

Johnny-Boy enters the city at three thirty in the afternoon. His nerves are running close to the sizzle point, but it has to be done. He drives south along Baxter Boulevard until he reaches Baxter Medical Center, then circles the block, memorizing the entry/exit points before parking on the street. Outside, he melts into the heavy foot traffic, stopping at the hospital's main entrance to buy coffee from a street vendor. Taking his time, alert at every minute for danger.

It's after four when he heads inside, at the height of the four o'clock shift change, finding three security guards behind a counter in the lobby, but no cops. Workers, many wearing nurses' scrubs, arrive and leave, everybody rushing. Johnny-Boy's hoping to blend in, a face in the crowd, as he makes his way to the elevator bank unnoticed. He gives that up when a security guard behind the counter, an older man, locks eyes with him. Now he's forced to approach.

"Afternoon," he says, that small smile appearing out of nowhere.

"What can I do for you, sir?"

"Well, my buddy, that would be Ted Marron, was hurt on the job this afternoon. Not bad, or at least it didn't look bad, only he went off to the infirmary and didn't come back."

"You want to know if he was brought into the hospital?"

Johnny-Boy's smile broadens. "Right, yeah. It ain't like Ted to just disappear, but he's not answering his phone and . . ."

The guard taps at a keyboard for a moment, then says, "Nope, not here."

"Could he be in the emergency room?"

"That's possible. Sometimes it takes a while before they enter a patient's data. Especially if the patient's not communicating."

"He had a head injury."

"That might explain it, but you'll have to check at the emergency room entrance. Around the back on Tyler Street."

◆

Johnny-Boy's not stupid enough to argue. He nods once before heading back on foot the way he came, circling the block until he reaches the emergency entrance. As he threads his way between haphazardly parked ambulances, he glances through the glass doors into a relatively narrow corridor with open doors on either side. A pair of security guards stand outside the doors, puffing away on cigarettes despite signs indicating the hospital is a no-smoking zone. Meantime, a successful entry is only the first part of the problem, with locating Diopolis inside and killing him without being discovered the second and third.

Johnny-Boy's never considered suicide, not even when he was seventeen and sleeping on the street. If losing Diopolis will mark the end of his basic livelihood? Well, he gave it his best.

Resigned, he continues along Tyler Street, heading back to his van. His path takes him past the main entrance to the hospital as a black Chevrolet Malibu pulls to the curb. Two people, a man and a woman, exit. Both men wear dark suits, dark ties, and pale blue shirts.

Feds. No doubt, not a scintilla. Johnny-Boy's grateful for the lucky break. If he'd found a way inside, he'd still be there when they came to call on Theo Diopolis. That wouldn't do, not at all. They've found their treasure and they'll guard it until the treasure's well enough to travel.

Johnny-Boy turns the facts over as he approaches the van. At some point, they'll have to transport Diopolis to a federal facility, a jail, a prison, or a hospital. In an ambulance if he's discharged in the next few days. And if he's not, if they hold him at Baxter Medical Center until he's fit to travel, well that's it for Johnny-Boy, mission over.

Never a pessimist, Johnny-Boy's always had a nose for the main chance. Let's figure, he tells himself, that Diopolis comes out in the next day or two. Let's suppose he exits through the emergency entrance and into a waiting ambulance. Ten seconds, start to finish? Plenty of time, assuming he can find the right perch with the right view.

Hope? Not exactly. But it's something, which in Johnny-Boy's universe, is better than nothing.

CHAPTER THIRTY-FOUR

BLANCHE WEBER

It's getting toward evening and I'm driving out to Frankie Minter's home in Revere County. Cade Barrow's sitting beside me. He's going on about his daughter, Maddy, a distraction but a welcome distraction. It's already been a long day and it's almost certain to get a lot longer before I lay my head . . . actually, I don't know where I'm going to lay my head. The house, invaded and violated, seems a choice that's not a choice. Could I really fall asleep with the graffiti still on the walls? Just drop my head to the pillow and maybe pretend it didn't happen?

"Maddy's crawling now. Well, not crawling exactly. She's learned to scoot along on her behind, which looks weird, but works for her. It's like her first lesson in life."

"How so?"

"Well, go back to before she could get around on her own. Something would catch her attention, something, say, across the room, and she'd reach for it. That told us that she wanted whatever it was and sometimes she'd get it. Like if it was one of her toys. But mostly, we ignored her because the object wasn't suitable for one reason or another."

"Like a bottle of laundry detergent?"

Cade grins. "That shit's so locked away, I'm gonna have to hire a safecracker if I want to do the laundry. No, more often, it was one of our cell phones. We used them often enough to make her wonder what the fuss was all about." He pauses to look out the window as he organizes his thoughts. Frankie Minter's home in the boondocks is fifteen miles from the city. Not far enough, assuming we can take Zack Butler's word for it, to escape the Baxter Police Department.

"Anyway," he continues, "I think she figured that all these wonderful things that she could shake in her fist and put in her mouth and throw on the floor would be hers if she could only get to them. Now that she's mobile, sort of, she's learning a hard lesson. Your little world is just that. It's little. I mean, she hasn't started throwing tantrums. She's too young for that, but every time we move something out of her reach, she gets this puzzled look on her face. Like maybe her world isn't as big as she thought."

As we leave town, I turn away from the Minter household. I'm just outside the city limits, but there's still the possibility of being spotted. If cops are putting the heat on Minter, who lives in Revere County, there's no predicting where they might be operating. I intend to approach Minter from the north and I've got the route memorized.

◆

There's a lot on my plate right now, but I can't stop thinking about Owen. Delia told me to remember that I'm the victim here, that it's not about Jake Nurine, that it started before my confrontation with Jake. "I think we're lookin' at a hostile takeover, Blanche. If Vern can't handle his cops, maybe the mayor will decide to find someone who can. Or the pressure might come from the city council. We can't afford to look bad. Nissan is watching."

Delia's always been sharp, and she may well be right. If Vern goes down, Chief of Patrol Saul Rawling would be a logical replacement. He's been around a long time and he knows everyone. But at this moment, I don't care. I keep bouncing from depression over Owen to the need for payback. I have to hurt these bastards.

"After Maddy started moving around, we had to put up barriers. Gates, right? At the head of the stairs and in the kitchen doorway. She watched us install them, intent, riveted. What's going on? And when we put her on the floor, she bounced her way over to the one on the stairway. For a while, she sat there, staring, then she began to pull on the wood slats. She'd probably still be at it if we hadn't picked her up and carried her downstairs."

I know I'm supposed to comment, but Cade's doting tale only reminds me of Owen's parting comment. Like all he ever wanted was a family with kids doing exactly what Maddy's doing. Growing up, exploring, learning life lessons. And there's the other thing too.

Minty Minter got his ass kicked recently. By cops, if you believe Zack Butler. Now me and Cade, two cops, are gonna drive right up to his house. I've dealt with Minty in the past. He's not a knucklehead. He doesn't resort to violence at the drop of a hat.

But he's been running a midlevel drug operation on his own for several years. If he wasn't prepared to defend his operation, he'd have been ripped off years ago.

So, how will he react when I come up his driveway? As we approach his front door? Cade and I are wearing vests beneath our suits, Level II body armor barely strong enough to stop a round from a handgun. I don't know what Frankie Minter has in his house, but the last time we looked, we found a .12-gauge shotgun.

◆

There's more tar on Minty's roof than shingle, and his chimney is missing several bricks. Probably cheap from day one, the vinyl siding has pulled away from the small house in several places. There's no lawn, only bare dirt with a refrigerator standing guard in the middle. A pink tricycle and a child's baby carriage with three wheels rest beside a pair of lawn chairs with torn backs.

"One for the money," Cade says as we step out of the car. "Look at the bright side. Nobody shot us as we drove up."

Small comfort. Our weapons are tucked away, mine in a shoulder rig, Cade in a holster behind his right hip. How many seconds to get to them? Ten? fifteen? My eyes are jumping from window to window, but I'm not kidding myself. If Minty decides to put up a fight, I won't be the first to shoot.

I'm feeling it with every step, on full alert, and I'm sure Cade's right with me, if not ahead. From inside the house, I hear rap music. I can't make out the words, but if there's a nonviolent rap tune out there, I haven't heard it. Suddenly, a curtain over a small window to my right jerks to the side and a woman's face appears behind the glass. A couple seconds later, the door opens, and she steps outside.

"What do you want?" She's short and blocky, with her arms folded across her chest and her chin tucked against her throat. Her eyes are dark, her glare ferocious. If she carried a weapon, the effect would be noticeably enhanced, but her hands are empty. Nevertheless, I hope to avoid a violent confrontation. We're far from our jurisdiction, with no authority whatever, and cooperation is the order of the day. I produce my identification and give the woman a long look.

"We'd like to speak with Frankie Minter," I tell her.

"About what?"

"How 'bout the weather," Cade says.

"You gettin' funny?"

I jump in before the exchange can escalate. If left to his own devices, Cade will brush her aside, a strategy not likely to result in cooperation.

"Tell Frankie that Detective Weber would appreciate a few minutes of his time. We're not investigating him, or anything he might have done. Our interests lie elsewhere."

The comment elicits a sneer. "Elsewhere? Oh, that's good. But this ain't Baxter and you got no authority here. Plus, unless you got a search warrant, you got no right to enter this house."

"True enough. You can turn us away and wait for the others to come back." I'm taking a chance. I don't know that Minter's been visited by crooked Baxter cops, not for sure. Then the woman flinches and I know I've hammered the right nail. "Why don't you just ask him if he'll talk to us? If he says no, we'll drive away. You'll never see us again."

◆

The woman, still unidentified, walks back into the house, closing the door behind her. Do or die, now, as we wait outside in the cold. With the sun almost gone, the temperature's dropping and a sharp wind easily penetrates my suit jacket. Tomorrow morning, the fields and a small woodlot in the distance will be silvered with frost.

Leave? Wait? Kick the fucking door down? Five minutes later, I'm pondering all three possibilities when the door opens and the same woman appears. She's still scowling when she says, "Yeah, he'll talk to you."

The living room we enter is a mess, but I'm drawn immediately to Frankie Minter. He's sitting on a couch against the far wall, a shotgun by his side. His face is a swollen, discolored mess, his eyes mere slits, a wide bandage covers his forehead. Whoever started on him didn't stop for a long time.

"Fucked up," he tells me, his voice reduced to a mumble as his words pass over a swollen mouth. He looks at Cade, then asks, "Who's this?"

"This is Detective Barrow."

"What, you needed a bodyguard? We don't know each other?"

I smile and point to a pair of suitcases, one closed, the other half-full. "You leavin' town, Frankie?"

That's enough for Frankie's protector. She puts herself between me and Frankie. "Like you don't fucking know, right? Like you ain't part of it."

"Take it easy, Carol," Frankie mumbles.

I don't wait for Carol to reply. I step around her, locking eyes as I pass, then gesture to the toys scattered across the floor. "Were the kids here when . . . when it went down?"

"Nah. They're Carol's kids. Her mother has custody."

I nod once, then return to the question. "I see you're packin' up. That means you're about to run, correct?"

Cade breaks off at that point, moving to one side as he examines the room. That wakes Carol up. "Where do you think you're going?"

"Wherever the hell I want."

I step closer to the couch. Minter's left arm is tucked against his side, a sure sign that his attackers worked his ribs. "Got no choice," he explains. "No choice whatever."

"You do now."

"And how's that?"

"Why don't you start by telling me who did this to you."

That brings Carol into the fray. "If you don't know, what the fuck are you doing here?"

"A tip. Dirty cops, talk to Minty. See if we have common interests."

Carol looks over at her . . . partner? There's no wedding ring on her finger. "You really wanna do this?" she asks him.

"Stay out of this, Carol. We got nothin' to lose." He waits a moment, then continues. His speech comes slowly and I suspect that he's taking something for the pain, probably his own product. "Three days ago, two cops showed up. Baxter cops in uniforms. Just pushed their way inside. So, me, I'm slow, and I tell them, 'You're off your turf. This is Revere County.' That was all it took. I got slapped in the face with a blackjack and couldn't fight back, so they took their time. Hurtin' me, right, but not so bad I passed out. No, they couldn't have that."

Carol's sitting in an armchair with one arm, her elbows on her knees, her chin in her palm. She's used up the anger that met us at the door. "Wanna hear a good joke? They left off on Minty, I think because they got tired. Big men get tired quick. 'You wanna stay in business,' the one said, the blond guy, 'you gotta pay up.' A grand, okay. They wanted a thousand bucks a month, no exceptions, pay or you'll think what happened to you was a kiss." She finally lifts her chin, angry again. "Look around, detective. You think we're livin' in this dump because we're savin' for our retirement?"

Minty interrupts, "Business has been goin' downhill since you guys drove us out of the city. Nobody wants to come this far when you got a dealer on every corner in Baxter. Why burn the gas?"

I get the point and I don't doubt the accuracy of Minty's complaint. We lost the war on drugs a long time ago. I mean the whole country. Now we're in the management business. I nod agreement and Minty continues.

"I tell 'em I don't have the money and they go back to work. These are big guys, detective, and they're not holdin' back." He stops suddenly, his right hand going to his side. Broken ribs? Minty should be in an emergency room. "They don't stop until I promise to get it. The money, I mean. Three days and I'll have it."

It's Carol's turn again, her comment flowing so naturally from his, I have to assume they've been together for a long time. "Tomorrow's the third day, but there ain't gonna be no payin' off. We don't have the money and we're not gonna get it." She raises a defiant middle finger. "You scumbags drove us out of Baxter and now you're gonna drive us out of the state. Thanks heaps."

Minty and Carol are drug dealers, but it somehow doesn't stop them complaining about government harassment. In fact, I have zero sympathy for either, Minty's condition notwithstanding.

"You didn't by any chance get a name?" I ask.

"They weren't that stupid."

"What about name tags?" Name tags are required by the Baxter PD, but I'm not surprised when Carol shakes her head. I am surprised, though, when Cade Barrow makes eye contact, asking an unvoiced question. I don't know what he's going to do, but I nod. Though it's my case, I don't outrank him.

Cade crosses the room to sit beside Minty. "So, what?" he asks, "you're gonna tuck your tail between your legs and run? You gonna be a punk-ass bitch?"

"Fuck you."

"Now, now, don't get past yourself. But I never made you for a punk. Before now."

Minty glances at the shotgun beside him. "I got two choices. I can kill the both of 'em and spend the next ten years on death row before I'm executed. Or I can head on out." He looks at Carol for a minute. "I'm walkin' through door number two."

"Door number two?" Cade asks. "What was the show called, Minty? Door number one, door number two?"

"*Let's Make a Deal.* Carol likes reruns."

"So, correct me if I'm wrong, but my grandmother also watched that show on cable. There were three doors." Cade looks at Carol. "Three."

"Fine, I'll bite," she responds. "What's behind door number three?"

"We wire this room for audio and video, all concealed. We give you a thousand dollars in fifties, twenties, and tens, all marked. You pass the money to whoever shows up tomorrow, resigned to your fate. We take them as they return to the city, wrapped in a pretty bow."

"And then what?" Minter asks. "Wait around for the cocksuckers to get bail? Or for their friends to come around?"

"Nope. You give a statement and head off to wherever you're planning to go. And, yeah, if the case goes to trial, you'll have to come back to testify. Only it won't go to trial, not with video and audio evidence to show to a jury. They'll take a plea and you'll go on with your life." Cade leans closer to Minty. "Revenge, payback, call it what you will, but I'm tellin' you from personal experience, it feels real fucking good."

◆

I'm trying to count the number of things wrong with Cade's scheme, but I'm having trouble with the final number. First thing, the cameras and recording equipment he so casually mentioned are locked away and it's after six o'clock. We'd need authorization, at least from Delia, and probably from Vern. Even with authorization, we still have to install the equipment and test it. This is a job that will take hours, assuming we get it right on the first try. And the money doesn't make it easier. Yeah, the Baxter PD maintains a slush fund, but again we'll need authorization, no certainty in light of the fact that we're operating outside of our jurisdiction. And the part about taking them down as they head back to the city? I'm imagining me and Cade standing in the middle of the road with our palms out. Stop, or I'll . . . what?

Cade heads our SWAT team. In theory, all we have to do is assemble the unit and deploy them as soon as our bent cops enter Minter's house. Sounds simple, but it's not. The SWAT team is made up of cops from the detective and patrol divisions, and there's no reason to suppose that one or more of the SWAT patrol cops aren't part of the bullshit that's been going down in Baxter. If they can't be trusted, they can't be used, which leaves me and Cade in the middle of the road with our hands up.

Every objection, however, pales beside the biggie. We're conducting an investigation outside our jurisdiction. Yeah, we can chase a fleeing felon into Revere County, but anything beyond that requires us to at least notify the Revere County sheriff. Worse yet, the extortion is happening inside the county. If these cops are prosecuted, it'll be in a Revere County courthouse by a Revere County prosecutor.

I'm still considering these issues when my phone rings. It's Owen. On another day, I might let the call go to voicemail. Not today.

"I have to take this outside," I announce before leaving the house.

◆

"Owen?"

"Yeah, it's me." Owen sounds weary, which is worse than pissed, and I'm thinking he's gonna ghost our relationship. He doesn't. "Look, I'm sorry I freaked out. You never asked for any of this to happen. Even that bastard Nurine, he only got what he deserved. When I saw what happened inside the house, I just lost it."

"I'm sorry too, Owen." I hunch my shoulders against the cold. "I should have controlled my temper. But it's gotten bigger now. Much bigger."

Owen takes a few seconds. "Look, I don't want to go back to the house yet. Maybe not until we get the living room painted.

But I'm at the Skyview, like I said, in cabin 278. I'm hoping you'll come by."

Yeah, that'd be great. The tender reconciliation, the makeup sex. Yeah, that'd be just great. "You know I want to, Owen, but the way it's looking now, I'll be working all night."

CHAPTER THIRTY-FIVE

DELIA

With Benny Cooper tucked away in the isolation cell once occupied by his buddy, I head for my office, picking up a mug of coffee on the way. There's a likeness of Paul Ochoa on my desk and I stare at it for several minutes. Top-of-the-line, computerized Identi-Kits produce images as detailed as a photograph. Needless to say, our software is several grades below top-of-the-line, but the image before me is much better than the charcoal sketches we used when I first became a cop. I'm looking at a human being, trying to extract some obscure information that probably isn't there.

Inoffensive, that's the best way to describe the round, almost serene face staring back at me. Nothing demonic in his eyes, small mouth relaxed, don't be afraid, I only want to help you. And once in the van, the demon appears out of nowhere, as if he'd yanked a mask away to reveal the fangs of a werewolf.

The Identi-Kit sketch is accompanied by a concise note. The sketch was created with the cooperation of Glory and Sharon, who work at the Coolwater, and the bar's manager, Matt Browner. All agree that Ochoa's likeness will be recognized by anybody who knows him.

The larger question is what, exactly, am I going to do with the sketch? There's no warrant out for Ochoa and there won't be until we tie him to a specific crime. We could still release the sketch to Baxter's media, calling him a person of interest. But if we do that, I'm sure he'll run. Good for Baxter, bad for wherever he goes. The local news is just that, the local news.

I'm taking the Ochoa problem to Vern, along with the lies told by Malcolm Bridger and Benny Cooper. I make two calls first, to Baxter Medical Center and to Sheriff Morrow in Maryville County. Mila Wegson's condition has improved, but she's still in an induced coma. They'll bring her up within the next forty-eight hours. Will her brain be damaged, perhaps severely? Will she remember the attack, even if she's neurologically sound? We'll see.

Sheriff Morrow's friendly when I finally reach him, as usual. "Evenin', Delia. How's your day goin'?"

"Seen better, seen worse. And you?"

"Been fieldin' complaints about a speed trap on Route 43. Seems we caught the wife of a county supervisor. Thirty-eight miles an hour in a twenty-five zone. Said supervisor's claimin' we trapped his wife because he voted to cut our budget last time out. Me, I'm claimin' that nobody is above the law. Plus, it couldn't have happened to the wife of a nicer guy." He chuckles. "So, what's up, Delia?"

"Just wondering about the stain you found. Any results?"

"Now, Delia, you think I'd have the results and not let you know?"

"Not really, but I'm meeting with the boss in a few minutes and he's sure to ask."

"Okay, no DNA results yet, and don't ask how long till they come through. There's good news, though. We did a Christmas tree stain on the recovered material and it's definitely semen. Fresh, too, almost sure to produce a strong DNA profile. Eventually."

Christmas tree stains are especially useful in identifying sperm cells. A pair of reagents stain the heads red and the tails green, making them easy to spot under a microscope. So, yeah, good news, and another reason not to release Ochoa's likeness. We can match DNA found in Ochoa's rented home to the DNA on the murdered boy, but we can't prove either came from Ochoa. For that, we need Ochoa himself.

◆

I thank Sheriff Morrow for his time and head upstairs. Bad news for Vern. I know he's hoping against hope that Bard Henry murdered Case Dixon. That would make every important player happy, like the mayor, the district attorney, the city council, and Dixon's asshole father.

As I enter Vern's office, I'm steeling myself. I find him on his cell phone. He waves a hello, but continues his conversation.

"Yeah, yeah. Got it." Ending the call, he lays his phone on his desk and turns to me. "Theo Diopolis has been identified by the Feds. Real name Andrei Abrescu, a naturalized Romanian brought to the United States as a child. Also, a well-connected member of the Russian mob in Chicago. According to the FBI."

"The same pair I met in your office?"

"Yeah, Vera Demantovich and Lawrence Carey. And don't ask me how they identified Diopolis, or Abrescu. Turns out that he's an indicted fugitive and they're taking over and fuck off."

"Sounds like they really want him."

"And the FBI aren't the only ones. Somebody tried to kill him, if you remember. Anyway, they're takin' him out tomorrow. By ambulance first, to Windstorm Airfield in Coombs County, then by helicopter to the prison hospital in Leavenworth. With his consent, of course. Seems the man's anxious to leave town."

"He's okay to travel?"

"They're using an air ambulance, so . . ."

◆

My turn now. I share the good news first, offering the sketch and the note. Vern studies both for a moment, then asks, "You let the media see this, Ochoa's gonna run."

"Yeah, I know that. But think about it from another angle. Ochoa's not from Baxter and he's not a skilled worker. So what's he doing here?"

"Killing."

The observation's so obviously true that I have to smile. "Let me rephrase, Your Honor. Why did he come in the first place? And why didn't he flee after the close call with Mila Wegson?" I hesitate until Vern makes eye contact. "Within a day of the attack on Wegson, Ochoa's ditched the van and bought a new car. He must've been spooked, but he doesn't leave town, even though he could pursue his passions anywhere in the country. No, he continues to live in his rented house, at least for a day. The sequence only makes sense if he originally came intending to accomplish something specific and the murders were crimes of opportunity."

Vern's sitting behind his desk, in a chair he swivels to the right, then to the left, taking his time while his brain works on my theory. Finally, he says, "I know what you're gonna suggest."

"So, tell me."

"Andrei Abrescu."

"And you're thinkin' it's a long shot."

"Like winning the lottery. Three hundred million to one." He grins and I return the grin. "How 'bout a plan? You've got the sketch. What will you do with it?"

"Our evening shift's already in the field, but tomorrow morning, I'll distribute copies of the sketch in the muster room before the day tour hits the street. Emphasizing how dangerous the man is. For tonight, since there's nothing else to do, I'll stop by Baxter Medical Center, talk to the Feds, show the sketch around." I lean forward in my seat. "If I don't check it out, long shot be damned, I'll be nagging at myself for the next two weeks."

◆

Now for the bad news. Malcolm Bridger lied, and his pal Benny Cooper also lied. They claimed not to have had contact after Bridger's arrest. In fact, they did.

"There's no record of what was said," I tell Vern, "and Cooper's holding firm. He and Bridger saw Bard Henry outside the party on the night Case Dixon was kidnapped. Unlike the thirty other kids we interviewed, who also attended the party." I look down for a minute before adding. "I arrested Cooper. He's sitting in our isolation cell right this minute."

"On what charge?"

"Obstruction of justice."

Vern shakes his head. He jumped at the chance to become commissioner. Now it's *be careful what you wish for.* He's tired and strained and it shows.

"Tommy's not gonna like this," he says.

"Neither will the man who murdered Case Dixon." I pause, waiting for a response from Vern. When it doesn't come, I add, "We can't allow an innocent man to be convicted. We just can't."

A waste of breath because Vern already knows it. "Tommy Atkinson met with Bard Henry's attorney this morning. Henry's still not talking, but he's not offering an alibi either. Tommy's eager to prosecute, very eager. Given the torture, he's calling it his career case."

"True, Vern, a career case, one way or the other. Like make or break. That's why I decided to charge Benny Cooper. I want their bullshit on the record."

CHAPTER THIRTY-SIX

DELIA

On the way back to my office, I make a phone call I've been making every day. In fact, a call I made only two hours ago, announcing that I wouldn't be home for dinner. Now I make a second call. I have work to do in my office, case reviews I've been neglecting, followed by a stop at Baxter Medical Center, a stop I'll repeat tomorrow morning if I come up empty tonight.

Danny answers and he's not happy with the news. I won't be home until after nine, if then. "All right," he tells me. "But, Mom, you need to slow down. You're not as young as you think you are."

My guilt is instantly replaced with a middle finger Danny can't see. My darling son's ready to ship me off to a nursing home. Like being called fat hasn't been bad enough. I make my goodbyes as I reach my office, totally unprepared to find Blanche Weber and Cade Barrow inside. Blanche is sitting on one of the chairs in front of my desk. When she twists in the chair to face me, I read her expression as a mix of pride and caution. She's accomplished something she's proud of, but I'm not gonna like it.

"Hope you don't mind, captain," she says. "It's been a long day and probably a long night to come."

Cade's standing, his face unreadable, a man prepared for whatever comes his way. "Evenin', captain," he says, his tone matching his expression.

I take the chair behind my desk and fold my arms. "Let's hear it, Blanche."

It's all good, right up to the point where she convinces Minty Minter and Carol, his partner, to set up the cops who attacked him. Where Blanche offers to provide concealed surveillance equipment to record Minter as he passes a thousand dollars to a pair of unidentified cops. Our thousand dollars.

"Stop a second, Blanche. You didn't think to call me before you committed the Baxter PD to investigate a crime taking place in Revere County?"

"Minter and Carol were packing their last bag as we pulled up. Prepared to flee, like right now this minute. So it was one of those now-or-never situations. But look, say we don't make an arrest on the spot. We'll still have the identities of two bent cops. Our cops."

"And Minter? If you don't make an arrest, he's still on the hook."

"Minty and Carol are leaving town even if we make the arrest. For Minty, this is about revenge. Which is what he told me."

Cade finally chimes in. "Minter was beaten systematically. No emotion, right, not even anger. His face is swollen up till you can barely see his eyes and the way he keeps grabbing his side, I have to figure that ribs were broken. He can't let that go. Not if there's anything he can do about it."

Now it's Blanche's turn again. "What I'm thinking, set up the surveillance overnight, then confront Sheriff Autrey in his office. He gets the bust, we provide the evidence, and the witnesses. All we need is enough firepower to take the criminals into custody. And the best news? The criminals are Baxter cops, so double kudos for the Revere County sheriff's office." She grins now. "A chance to embarrass the Gomorrah of the Plains? It's an offer he can't refuse."

I don't like the idea, in fact I hate it. We're not supposed to investigate outside Baxter without at least notifying local law enforcement. And Sheriff Autrey, who's held his office for at least two decades, is famously volatile. He might view Blanche's work as an opportunity. He might tell her to go fuck herself. Nobody who knows him would bet against either possibility.

Misgivings be damned, there's no way I can factor Vern out of this equation. Blanche isn't authorized to pull the equipment or the cash she needs. I could grant the authorization myself, but I'm not that stupid. The Baxter PD as I know it, and as I want it to remain, is under attack. Is this the way to defend it? I'll let Vern decide.

◆

It's almost nine and cold enough to draw goose pimples when I park outside Baxter Medical Center. On the way over, I listened to KBR, hoping a little music would mellow an intense day. Instead, I heard a newscaster report the FBI's arrest of Andrei Abrescu, formerly Theo Diopolis, at his bedside. Worse, word that Abrescu will be released into the custody of the Feds tomorrow has also leaked. The leak might have come from any of the doctors or nurses who tend Abrescu, or from a worker in the administrative wing. All I got from the reporter was the inevitable "respected source" attribution.

Essentially, Baxter Medical Center is a box sided with dull, blue panels. Built at a time when funding didn't allow for embellishment of any kind, utilitarian is the first word that comes to mind. Maybe that's changed. The city council, with the aid of the state and a dip into federal funding, has released plans for a major expansion. Sometime in the future.

It's too cold to linger outside and I push through the door to face a reception desk thirty feet away. I've got Ochoa's sketch with me and the security officer behind the reception desk stares at it for moment, then dons reading glasses and checks again before shaking his head. A pair of clerks working with him take their turns before confirming the guard's response. "Sorry, but we haven't seen him, and by the way, visitors are always screened before they're allowed inside. Screened and issued a visitor's pass."

"Okay, good," I say, all smiles. "Please tell me Andrei Abrescu's room number."

All three hesitate and I have to assume they've been told not to reveal the man's location. I'm thinking I'll need to reassert my authority, but the security guard nods to himself and half whispers, "Room 408. Fourth floor."

I expect to find a platoon of FBI agents when I come off the elevator, but I spot only two, Demantovich and Carey, at the end of a corridor on the far end of the unit. They're sitting outside what is surely the door to Room 408.

Vera Demantovich smiles as I approach. She's a tall woman, taller than her partner, tall enough to have played basketball in college. If she stood, she'd tower over me. She doesn't.

"Captain . . . Mariola," she says. "It's our turn now."

"Didn't you come here in search of a serial killer?"

Agent Carey speaks up. "Sometimes you gotta roll with the punches. Do we have a problem, captain?"

"Nope. You're welcome to Mr. Abrescu. Just curious, though. Whoever took Abrescu's arm? What makes you think he won't make a second attempt? Being as your plans are all over the news and this guy's obviously a professional."

Carey rises to open the door to his prisoner's private room. Abrescu is in bed, asleep. On a chair alongside the bed, a mannequin sits upright. The mannequin's wearing a hospital gown.

"Come tomorrow morning, we'll be joined by a pair of agents. That should be enough to engineer a dry run without endangering hospital personnel." He gives me a few beats to absorb the info, then says, "Abrescu was already talking to us when he took off. If he testifies, we'll roll up eight or ten of the biggest scumbags in Chicago. Like you said, the shooter who took his arm is a professional. Abrescu needs to recover in a safe place, and that's not Baxter."

◆

Outside again, I circle the block, coming finally on the emergency entrance. Abrescu's gurney will eventually be pushed through a pair of doors to a waiting ambulance, but there's no getting inside unless you're a patient. Even family members who accompany a patient must be screened at the main reception desk and issued a pass. Or so a pair of uniformed security guards insist.

Back on the street, I pause long enough to take a breath. It's still too cold to linger, but I look around anyway. Abrescu's assassin positioned himself so far from his target that we've yet to determine his post. Given the near impossibility, at this point, of getting close to Abrescu, he'll have to use the same strategy. Fire from a distance and vanish. So, where? The buildings on this block of Tyler Street are commercial and mainly occupied by doctors, some offering outpatient services. Come tomorrow morning, they'll buzz with activity. They're too close anyway. An assassin might get a shot off, but escape would be unlikely.

In the distance, I hear a pile driver pounding on something metallic, probably an I-beam. I assume the resonant clang is coming from the Nissan site, but with the sound bouncing off the surrounding buildings on the narrow street, I can't be sure. And that's enough, more than enough for one day and a gamble Vern compared to winning the lottery. I take out my phone and call Zoe.

"Hey, babe, you on the way home?"

"Yeah, should I pick up something?"

"Nope, your dinner's in the oven, dry as unbuttered toast. You'll love it."

"Can't wait. Danny still up?"

"Uh-huh. Watching YouTube videos on throwing the perfect knuckleball. Gretchen keeps kissing him on the neck and he keeps pretending he's unmoved. Don't ya just wish you were still a teenager?"

CHAPTER THIRTY-SEVEN

BLANCHE WEBER

I show up at work expecting to find Cade Barrow waiting for me in the parking lot. He's there, all right, but he has company. Detectives Laura Udell and Stu Harrington stand alongside him. Harrington's tugging at the end of his mustache, a habit he'll never break. Laura's square face is set in stone, but she's holding a lit cigarette in her left hand. Call it a redeeming act. I light my own as I cross the lot.

"Volunteers," Cade explains. He doesn't add, volunteers you didn't ask for.

"Never thought to call me first?"

"Nope."

It's Laura's turn. Thankfully, she's more articulate than Cade. "Cade filled us in last night. Me, I've dealt with Sheriff Autrey. The man's an asshole. I mean of the first fucking magnitude. For example, there's only one female deputy in his department. She works in the office and he calls her 'Honey.' Maybe you should skip the part about notifying the locals."

"Can't do it." It's finally my turn. "No matter who arrests them, the two cops will be tried in Revere County. Consulting Autrey is a given. Besides, we need the help if we want to avoid a miniwar. You saw how bad they hurt Minty. Hard to believe they'll assume the position if there's just the four of us."

◆

That's enough for me. In fact, I'm glad for the extra firepower, though I was too stubborn to ask for it myself. It's also too cold to stand around and argue. The pair of Chevy patrol cars we'll use are already running. The frost that covered their windshields and rear windows, now melted, needs only a sweep of the wipers to clear away. Then we're off, the tension building, to our first stop on a dirt road a half mile from Minty Minter's dilapidated home. Both sides of the little road are lined with brush and small trees, aspen mostly. We're invisible here.

Last night after installing the bugging equipment, Cade and I ran a field test. We couldn't receive video, not from this far away, but the audio was clear enough. Now we'll retest the system, just to make sure. As I set up the receivers, tying them to my Chevy's electrical system with HDMI cables, I keep a careful eye on my squad. Cade appears almost bored, a man waiting for the war to begin, but Laura and Stu give me their full attention when I turn on the receiver. Both smile when a woman's voice, indignant, shouts, "The goddamn toilet won't flush again."

I call Minty, who answers on the first ring. "Yeah?"

"Calling to let you know we're in place. Have you heard from the extortionists yet?"

"Not a word."

"And you still have the money we gave you?" Along with a warning about what I'd do if he took off.

"It's lyin' on the table in front of me."

"Good, but I have a word of advice for you."

"And what's that?"

"Fix the goddamn toilet."

Minty hangs up and I straighten for a moment, then light a cigarette. The rising sun is already burning off the night's frost, producing a thin blue mist that hangs over the surrounding fields. Behind me, I hear music pouring from the receiver, rap music, which I hate.

"You good, Blanche?"

I look up to find Cade standing a few feet away. Yeah, time to go. "Never better, never better." The words, as they come out of my mouth, are punctuated by a series of pings. Incoming text messages I don't bother to read.

◆

The Revere County sheriff's office sits dead center on a county road that bisects the town of Revere. Except for Sheriff Autrey's personal office, it's plain as dirt inside. By contrast, Autrey's office contains a desk that Noah might have used as a foundation for the Ark, with a massive leather chair behind it. Four smaller chairs, much smaller, surround a table covered with folders. On the walls themselves, photos of Autrey shaking hands with various athletes at numerous Super Bowls dominate. Leaving me to wonder how he came up with the money to attend the events. Even basic Super Bowl tickets run three thousand dollars, with hotel rates to match.

Autrey himself is as small as his office is large. He's wearing a tan uniform that might have been filched from a Boy Scout jamboree. I don't laugh, don't even smile when I walk into the office to find him dwarfed by his own chair. But that's only because his Stetson with its curled, ten-inch brim is hanging from a hook by the door. Instead of perched on his bald head.

"Don't have a lotta time, detective," he tells me. "Best make this quick."

I do make it quick. Crooked Baxter cops, attempted extortion taking place in Revere County, a first-degree assault on a Revere County resident, the victims' home wired for audio and video.

"I expect the perpetrators to arrive this morning, as they promised to do. At that point, Minter will hand over a thousand dollars in marked bills. There's only one way out because the road leading to the Minter house dead-ends a quarter mile farther up. I intend to block the road from below and take them into custody."

Autrey places his hands on his belly and gives his gut a little push, producing a soft belch. "And what exactly do you want from me?"

"Manpower, enough to arrest them without a fight. You take physical possession of the evidence and you take credit for the arrest. You'll have video, audio, and a statement from a victim who's had the crap beat out of him. A slam dunk, good for Revere County."

"And bad for Baxter, these miscreants bein' Baxter cops?"

"Yeah, that's it."

Autrey's face is a mass of saggy wrinkles, excessive even for a man in his sixties, but it does hide his expression. I can't read him as he looks down at his lap while his options run back and forth in his mind. Finally, he lifts his chin and stares at me for a long moment.

"Now let me see if I got this right. You came into my county to conduct your investigation without giving my department so much as a courtesy call. You wired this drug dealer's home, using your own equipment instead of ours, likewise without notifying me, and you handed this same drug dealer a thousand dollars. Now you expect me to back your moves by placing my own deputies in harm's way. And what's in it for me? I get to embarrass the Baxter Police Department by arresting a pair of dirty cops?" He pats his stomach before opening a desk drawer to retrieve a bottle of antacid tablets. He looks at the bottle for a moment, then lays it on his desk.

"Well, guess what, little lady, you've already embarrassed the Baxter Police Department, and it'll continue to be embarrassed after you make the arrest. Without my help." He makes his final point as I open the door on my way out. "Cops don't bust cops."

◆

I take the news back to my team. Laura Udell nods, her mouth tight. Autrey's reaction comes to her as no surprise. Stu appears a bit disappointed, but not Cade. The man's always up for a fight and it's becoming more likely that he'll get one. If all goes as planned, we'll be stationed a hundred yards beyond a bend in the road. A pair of dirty cops in a marked patrol car negotiating that bend will find two marked patrol cars blocking the road.

Then what? Fight? Flight? Maybe a realistic evaluation of their position leading them to conclude they have nothing to gain by either option? Just as our targets have options, so do we. Patrol officers are assigned a car before they begin their tour and that car is numbered on the trunk lid, on the roof, and on both sides. We need only get the number to identify the cops who drive it. So, capture the number as the car passes on the return trip to Baxter, gather the audio and video evidence, present it to Vern as a courtesy, make the arrests as they finish their tour.

This is not just an idea whose time has gone. When I present it to my team, it's an idea that should never have existed. The best detectives are hunters by nature. It's in their blood and always has been. Patrol cops, by contrast, respond to crimes as they're happening or shortly after. They collect evidence and make an arrest if a suspect is immediately available. Then it's back in the car, on patrol, waiting for the dispatcher to assign them another job. The more ambitious may seek promotion to sergeant or lieutenant, but they don't hunt.

"I want them," Cade tells us. "I can taste it. I want them on the ground, handcuffed. I want to push their heads down as they're shoved into the back seat of my patrol car. I want to be watching when you read them their rights."

In that case, better to be prepared. I open the trunk of the Chevy I drove on the way up. Our jackets come off first, replaced by Level III body armor. We're carrying standard-issue 9mm Glocks and we pull loaded magazines from a metal box and slide them into pouches on our body armor. The shotgun comes out last, a Mossberg 590 with a pistol grip. Stu gets the shotgun and I watch him stuff his pockets with spare shells.

So, now it's waiting time. Time to drink coffee from the thermos in the trunk, to munch on doughnuts from Lena's Luncheonette, to watch the mist burn off and the morning grow warm. Last night before we left, I asked Minty to keep the music coming in order to monitor the equipment. Minty's obliged with rap artists loudly proclaiming their embrace of violence in all its many forms, along with their hatred of cops. As there's nothing to be done, we bear the insults and turn the volume down.

Time drags, as always. Call it stakeout time, counting the seconds, Laura smoking one cigarette after another with me not far behind. A red-tailed hawk soaring a hundred feet above the ground is irresistibly fascinating, although hawks in this part of the country are almost as common as the small rodents they hunt. No place to hide for the ground squirrels, the voles, the mice, the rabbits. Not on a sunny morning after the harvest. Stu and Cade make a bet, Stu on the hawk finding a target, and both watch until the hawk finally glides out of sight.

◆

Funny thing about waiting for a battle. You know it's coming, but when it finally arrives, you still feel unprepared. As I'm somehow unprepared when the music stops, replaced by Minty's voice.

"They're here. Same two."

I take a deep breath as we pile into the cars, Cade and I in one, Stu and Laura in the other. The plan calls for us to block the road and wait for the quarry to arrive, hoping a show of force will lead to a quick, peaceful arrest. That plan goes the way of the red-tailed hawk when a gigantic boom nearly blows out our receiver's single speaker.

"Shotgun," Cade observes, too calm by half. "Minty's gone rogue."

The blast is quickly followed by three sharp cracks fired from a handgun. Then a voice I don't recognize calling, "Andy, Andy, Andy."

We're flying up the road by then, me in the lead. It's all guesswork from here, but I'm most worried about our targets meeting us head-on as we come around a bend. It's not happening, though, and the front yard with the empty cruiser parked on the grass offers no clue as to what's happening inside. I pull to a stop in front of the parked cruiser, blocking it in, then pull the key from my own.

"Set up a blockade and hold your position. Don't charge the house."

No, that's my job, though I'm not stupid enough to crash through the door. I sprint for the side of the house, propelled by adrenaline. I'm anticipating gunfire from inside, but I reach the house intact. Behind me, Cade, Stu, and Laura take up position behind our vehicles, now parked bumper to bumper. If whoever's inside decides to run, they're gonna have to do it on foot.

I find a window on the side of the house and I rise to my full height, weapon in hand, to peer inside. I'm ready to jump away, but again, our presence has yet to be detected, and I can understand why. A cop in a Baxter PD uniform lies face up in a pool of blood on the wooden floor. Minty Minter sits on a couch pushed against the wall. Four holes in his white T-shirt, closely spaced, explain his motionless state and the odd tilt of his head.

A second cop, also in uniform, kneels beside the dead cop's body, administering CPR in a hopeless attempt to raise the dead. His weapon lies on the floor beside him. I recognize him as a new hire, but can only recall his first name, Todd. A woman standing against the wall to my left, probably Carol, appears to be in shock. Her lips are moving, jaw opening and closing, but there's no sound. I have to tread carefully here. I can't just shoot Todd, though I'm sure he killed Minty. At the moment, he's unarmed.

I have my Glock in my right hand. I bring it up and point it at the kneeling cop. I raise my left hand to make a fist, reminding myself that Todd's wearing lightweight body armor beneath his uniform. I hesitate for only a second as I harden my resolve. If the asshole's hand moves toward his gun, I tell myself, don't hesitate, shoot him.

"Police," I shout as I knock on the glass, "show me your hands."

Carol moves first. For reasons I'll never fathom, she decides to make a run for the front door, coming between me and Todd. I watch his hand drop to his weapon, but I can't shoot, not yet. Then he surprises me. I'm expecting him to send a barrage of 9mm bullets my way. Instead, he leaps to his feet and dashes toward the back of the house.

I make my way alongside the house to the back and peek around the corner. Again, I'm expecting a gunfight, but Todd has other ideas. He's running through a cutover cornfield, any possibility of rational thought off the table. He'd come to collect a thousand dollars, and maybe to deliver a few warning slaps, no limit to his confidence. Now his world has been turned on its head and his panicked brain can only devise a single response. Run, run, run.

Shoot him in the back? I can't do that, not legally. At the moment, he poses no threat to me and there's no proof, as of yet, that he shot Minter. Or if he did, that it wasn't self-defense. But I can't just let him go, sure that I'll find him later. He represents a threat, especially to anyone living close by. Right now, he probably thinks he can run at full speed forever. When that illusion ends, when he finally tires, he'll seek more realistic solutions, like stealing a car from one of the farms scattered about, or worse yet, taking hostages.

I pick up the pace, continuing on for another fifty yards, until he finally looks back, as if only now remembering that he might be followed. I stop as well, long enough to say the wrong thing.

"Give it up, Todd. There's no place to go."

Todd's mouth curls into a sneer. "I should have known it was you. Fucking bitch." He snaps off three shots, quick, the crack of his Glock propelling a flock of crows skyward. Panic inspired, the bullets don't pass near enough for me to hear them go by. I drop to one knee, fighting the adrenaline pouring through my veins, and raise my weapon. By the book, I tell myself. Line up the sights below the vest he's wearing, take a breath, slide my finger through the trigger guard, release the breath slowly, squeeze . . .

That last part, the squeeze-don't-pull, is rendered moot when a bullet slams into Todd's forehead, exiting through the back of his skull, the effect like someone cut the strings on a marionette. Every muscle in his body relaxes at the same time and he seems to melt into the ground.

I'm confused for a few seconds, then I turn to find Cade Barrow with his weapon in his hand. Stu Harrington is sitting on the ground, one hand pressed into his side. Not in sight, Laura Udell's probably sitting on Carol, an eyewitness we'll surely need at some point. That's because I can already hear the sirens. Sheriff Autrey and his deputies, late to the party, but ready to cover their asses.

Cade drops to one knee and pulls Stu's hand away from his side. A missing chunk of flesh just below his rib cage bleeds profusely.

"Am I dead yet?" he asks Cade.

"Nope." Cade rips the sleeve off Stu's uniform, folds it, and presses it hard against Stu's side, producing a groan that has me wincing. "But there's still hope."

CHAPTER THIRTY-EIGHT

DELIA

I wake up wanting to call Blanche. Last night, I contacted Cade Barrow, swearing him to silence. "I don't want the two of you up there alone," is the essence of what I told him. "Find help."

"Blanche won't like that, captain."

"That, Cade, is why I'm calling you." I hesitated before delivering the punch line. "You and Blanche try to handle this alone, I'm going to order Blanche to stand off. We'll make the arrest in Baxter and deal with the jurisdiction problem later."

I'm playing Cade and he probably knows it. Cade lives for the arrest, the takedown. Cuffing a pair of bent cops will keep him high for a week.

"I'm already on it, captain."

◆

That got me to sleep, but it didn't keep me asleep past five this morning. Too many things can go wrong. Sheriff Autrey, for one, is a pompous fool who's been in office so long he's come to think of himself as a genius. In fact, he's an impulsive jerk working in a rural, low-crime environment. Successful? Only at pleasing the Campbells, the Steubens, and the Picketts, who control Revere County politics, as they have for generations. No shock, as their farms run north of ten thousand acres.

At the same time, we need to make these arrests. The Baxter PD is under attack on several fronts. Excessive force complaints, for one. They appear in the media with escalating frequency, and I know that Mayor Venn has received an inquiry from Nissan questioning our "heavy-handed" policing. I suspect it won't be the last inquiry, not with cowboy policing the order of the day.

The more I think about it, the worse it gets. The demands on Minty can't be an isolated incident. He lives outside town and he's small fry in any event. These two bent cops, whoever they are, must have followed a trail to find him. A trail leading from one extortion to another.

Our job, Vern's and mine, starts with turning over the rock, no matter what crawls out from underneath. We have to move against this assault. Vern and I agree on that, and on strategy as well. If the cops who attacked Minty are presented with a Revere County indictment that could put them in a cage for a decade, there's every reason to hope they'll cooperate. And that means naming names.

◆

Without disturbing Zoe, I take my thoughts into the kitchen, where I continue to juggle them through two mugs of coffee. Finally, unable to sit any longer, I start breakfast. I begin with the remains of a baked ham. I'm going to make western omelets with ham, onion, and green pepper, along with small bowls of strawberries and blueberries topped with a pinch of sugar. Even better, when I look in the refrigerator, I find pomegranate juice. Just last week, Zoe told me how pomegranate juice would prevent my arteries from thickening. I didn't know, at the time, that arteries were able to thicken. Now I sprinkle an ounce or two over the fruit.

Danny wanders in as I'm whisking the eggs in a bowl. He pours coffee for himself and takes a seat at the table. I'm used to a morning kiss, a peck on the cheek, but Danny's mood is running in a different direction. He remains silent until Zoe, his other mom, pours her own coffee and joins him at the table. I'm wildly curious, of course, but for now I content myself with dropping the ham, pepper, and onions into a hot frying pan.

Zoe's starting on her fruit salad when Danny coughs it up. "I got a C minus on a Chem quiz," he announces. "And please, Gretchen pounded on me for an hour last night. I don't need another beating."

"Too much time in the gym, not enough time with the books," Zoe says.

Danny shakes his head. "I have to maintain my schedule."

"Somehow," I tell him, "I don't think the admissions department at Stanford will be all that sympathetic."

"Stanford isn't the only college with a baseball program. It's not even the best. Vanderbilt's rated number one." Danny flashes that little-boy grin I know so well. The one that melts my heart, every time. "Besides, Vanderbilt's a lot closer."

"How close?" I dutifully ask.

"Nashville."

I don't know how many miles separate Baxter and Nashville to the south, but it's gotta be a lot less than the fifteen hundred between Baxter and California. I give the eggs a final whisk, pour them into the pan, finally mix the ingredients. As I lay the whisk on my cutting board, a text message reaches my phone. It's from Blanche and it's simple.

On our way.

◆

Cards on the table, we eat breakfast in peace. Zoe supplies most of the conversation. She's dealing with a girl removed from her family by court order. Zoe's placed the girl with three different foster families and she's run away from all three. Not back to her family, but to an abandoned house in Oakland Gardens occupied by a rotating menagerie of stoners.

"Emily's fourteen." Zoe tells us. "She's throwing her life away."

In many ways, Zoe's job is uglier than my own. I rarely have to deal with children. She deals with children every day, children carrying psychological wounds that will never heal. But my mind keeps drifting, first to Blanche and her little squad. I'm now thinking that Vern should've given Sheriff Autrey a courtesy call. But last night, when it counted, I argued that Autrey might take charge of the operation, pushing Blanche and Cade to the side. Would Minter trust Autrey enough to cooperate? Or would he revert to his original plan and head for the hills? We didn't want to take the risk, but now I'm having second thoughts.

And there's Bard Henry, along with a sadistic killer on the loose. So far, it's all surmise, a logical guessing game. Paul

Ochoa the assassin, arriving in Baxter from parts unknown, his mission to assassinate a gangster named Andrei Abrescu. Paul Ochoa the sadistic killer, remaining in Baxter, despite a close call. Even Ochoa murdering Case Dixon and the still-unidentified boy in Maryville County. What do we have besides a burned-over shed on a back road? The whole investigation's no more than a guessing game with almost every fact plucked from thin air.

An honest assessment, more than reasonable. That's what I tell myself. But my little brain can't avoid the obvious. If our guesses are on point, if we have it right, Ochoa will abandon our fair city as soon as the FBI leaves town with their prisoner. Gone for good, free to kill again. And again, and again.

◆

This point becomes all the more relevant when Vern's red Audi follows me into the Baxter PD parking lot. He glides into his designated space, but waits for me to find a space of my own.

"I spoke to Tommy Atkinson last night." Vern gets right to the point. "He's not buyin'."

"Not buyin' what?"

"Not buyin' Bard Henry's innocence, or that Malcolm Bridger's bullshit dooms a successful prosecution. As long as Bridger and his pal claim they saw Henry outside the party, he's willing to put them on the stand. Yeah, they lied, but, hey, they're kids. Bridger only wanted to give his pal a heads-up because the cops were sure to knock on Cooper's door."

"And Bridger gets to keep whatever deal he cuts with Tommy?"

Vern spreads his hands. "Tommy's gonna dismiss the obstruction of justice charge against Benny Cooper. In fact, he wants us to release the kid before arraignment."

"You gonna do it?"

"Fuck Tommy. He can ask for a dismissal when Cooper appears before a judge. I want the obstruction on the record."

Vern pauses, but I have nothing to add. Tommy Atkinson's a dependable ally, and an equally dependable enemy if you get on his bad side. Reward your friends, punish your enemies. The secret of success in politics according to our district attorney.

◆

I head up to my office, passing through an empty squad room on the way. I've got four detectives up in Revere County. I'm assuming the rest are in the field. Baxter's been plagued by a series of burglaries over the past six weeks and we've been working the cases hard. A couple days ago, Detective Marcus Goodman, who believes that most of the burglaries were committed by a single offender, promised an imminent arrest. From his mouth to God's ears. One of the invaded homes belongs to the *Baxter Bugle*'s chief editor. The paper's been reporting any burglary complaint in the city ever since, often on the front page.

For the next hour, until eight o'clock, I busy myself with reviewing investigations and arrests. Though I doubt my squad appreciates it, I keep an eye on my detectives and their individual productivity. Slack off and you'll hear from me. Persist and you'll find yourself directing traffic on game day at a local high school. In the rain.

When I come out of my office, I find the Dink sitting at his desk. Detective John Meacham is the exception to every rule I have. His aunt being Gloria Meacham, president of our city council, he's protected, though not invincible. Meanwhile, unlike Cade Barrow, he's not a hunter. Meacham never does more than he's asked to do.

"John."

He looks up from his phone. "Captain."

"You're my partner for the next hour, at least. Come with me."

I'm remembering my call to Cade Barrow last night, demanding that he and Blanche find backup. Although I don't expect much from a visit to Baxter Medical Center, better safe than sorry. Considering Meacham's policing abilities, his presence won't produce all that much safety, but he's the only game in town.

We reach the parking lot before my cautionary approach implodes. My phone rings. It's Vince Trentino, our duty sergeant.

"Hey, captain, we got a body in Oakland Gardens." A pause. "No one's answering the phone in the squad room, but the uniforms on the scene are asking for a detective."

"Not a natural death?"

"Found behind a house, advanced decomposition, who can tell. That's why they're passin' the buck. They want a detective to detect the true circumstances behind the woman's death." He pauses and I can almost see his grin. "What they're tellin' me, you need to send a detective who likes maggots."

◆

With no option, I dispatch Meacham to meet Arshan Rishnavata, our coroner. Knowing the Dink, he'll turn the assignment into an all-day project. I watch him leave, then head for Baxter Medical Center.

I've been to the hospital many times, including a few as a patient who needed her cuts and bruises attended. Back when I was in uniform. Now I recognize the security guard behind the reception desk. His name is Neil and he's working with a pair of much younger security guards. Neil's probably in his sixties, a tall man with sharp blue eyes that radiate suspicion.

Neil smiles as I approach. "Morning, captain. What brings you to Baxter Medical Center? You ailin'?"

"In perfect health, Neil. And you?"

"Ready to run the marathon, assumin' our little city should decide to host one."

"By the time that happens, you'll need a wheelchair to compete." I reach into my purse and remove Ochoa's likeness. "Were you behind the desk yesterday?"

"Six days a week, exceptin' Sundays when I take my family to church."

"So, tell me, Neil, you happen to spot this guy anywhere?"

Neil looks at the sketch for a moment, then takes out his reading glasses and looks again. "He came in here yesterday, late afternoon. Spotted him right off."

"Why is that?"

"Walked halfway to the desk, then took himself a long look around. Mostly down the hall to the elevators. Me, I think he woulda turned on his heel and walked back out, only we locked eyes and that must've changed his mind. He come to the desk, told me his friend was missin', and was he brought into the hospital? Don't remember the friend's name, but he wasn't admitted." He touches the sketch. "Then he asks me what about the emergency room. Could someone come in through the emergency room and not be admitted right away? I told him it's possible and he left."

"But you're sure it was him." I hold the sketch up and one of the younger security guards glances our way. He stares at the sketch for a moment, then says, "I saw him too. Something about him looked wrong, but he didn't raise a fuss. Just turned around and left the way he came in."

CHAPTER THIRTY-NINE

DELIA

As my heart rate accelerates, my focus sharpens. Get to work, by the book, one step at a time. Procedure, I tell myself, keeps you calm. I head up to Andrei Abrescu's room on the fourth floor. The FBI contingent has doubled, from two to four. They're sitting on chairs in the hallway, drinking coffee and working their cell phones. I'm wearing my badge on the lapel of my jacket, so I don't bother to introduce myself to the newcomers. Instead, I peek through the open door. Abrescu, with the assistance of a nurse, is eating his breakfast with one hand. He glances at me, glassy eyed, before returning to his meal. Alongside the bed, still in its hospital gown, the mannequin stares at the opposite wall.

"Agent Demantovich, we need to talk."

Vera Demantovich looks at her partner. I don't know what passes between them, but she gets up and leads me down the hall. The agent has to be over six feet, but her gait is smooth and graceful, the stride of a confident woman.

"Captain, what's up?"

I show her the sketch. "This man is a suspect in a pair of homicides. Without getting into the details, our investigation produced a theory, far-fetched, that he came to Baxter looking for Abrescu. Or Diopolis, as he called himself."

"Forgive me, but I'm homing in on the far-fetched part."

"Can't blame you, agent, but I stopped at the security desk in the lobby before I came up." I tap the sketch. "This man calls himself Paul Ochoa. Two security guards identified him. He showed up yesterday afternoon with some bullshit story about a missing friend."

That gets her attention and she stares at the sketch for a moment. It's not gonna help, though. Abrescu was shot from a distance by a concealed sniper. If Ochoa's out there when they wheel Abrescu to the ambulance, they won't see him. Of course, if Abrescu was really important, if he was a politician, the Feds would dispatch a small army of agents to sweep every potential sniper's nest within sight of the emergency room. In Abrescu's case, a store mannequin will have to do.

"Just promise me this and I'll go away. When you take Abrescu to the ambulance, or his facsimile, no medical personnel will be present. Just you, your colleagues, and the gurney."

"And as much body armor as a human being can wear." Demantovich finally smiles. "There are three ways out of the hospital. Through the ambulance bay, through the main entrance, and through a service door that feeds into a narrow alley. As for the alley, you block one end, it's a trap. Likewise, the main entrance is off the table. Too many citizens coming and going. That leaves the ambulance bay. We'll be leaving in an hour, an hour fifteen at the most."

◆

If I had more time, I might beg patrol for enough cops to search nearby buildings. But I can't arrange it in an hour, even assuming that Saul Rawling's persuadable. Or that I can trust whoever he's likely to supply. I make a quick call to the squad room, hoping to catch a detective back at his or her desk. Nothing doing. I'm on my own.

Outside the main entrance, I walk to the corner and look west along Polk Street. I have to assume Ochoa has eyes on the emergency bay, whether or not he actually does. But he can't know that he's been connected to Abrescu or identified by the security guard. More than likely, he feels safe.

So, where? I'm looking for a building significantly taller than the low-rise buildings on Tyler Street, for a window or a rooftop that provides a view of the emergency bay. The Feds will have to cross twenty feet of open space to reach an ambulance prevented from backing all the way to the door by concrete slabs. And Ochoa won't have any trouble identifying Abrescu when he exits. Every other patient in a gurney will be entering.

The day has warmed, autumn reasserting its early October primacy. The skies directly above are a luminous blue, the sun a blinding white disk to the east. It's nine thirty and I have an hour. At this point, I'm not worried about Abrescu. One way or the other, Abrescu's going to Leavenworth Prison in Kansas where he's unlikely to meet Dorothy or the Wizard. Ochoa's the quarry now, the target on the other end of my sights. If I catch him with that suppressed sniper's rifle, I can hold him.

Again, I sweep the buildings on the north side of Tyler Street. The block is as busy as the main entrance to the hospital. Nissan's coming has produced a major upgrade to Baxter's medical services. Eight thousand workers with quality health insurance for themselves and their families? Owen's decision to establish a dental practice in the city was based entirely on Nissan's decision to build its factory here. The prospect also inspired doctors, including multi-physician practices, to set up shop as close to the hospital as possible. From podiatrists to oncologists, from radiology labs to dialysis centers, every space is fully rented. Ochoa can't be looking out from a front window, not without taking everyone inside prisoner. He can't be on the roof either. This close, he'd be immediately visible if he stood high enough to fire down at a gurney leaving the emergency room.

I think I'm trying to convince myself that Ochoa wasn't able to find his sniper's nest, that he's given up. That would mean Ochoa's gone, more than likely forever. Good for Baxter, bad for some unsuspecting adolescent. The only certainty here? Ochoa can't stop killing any more than I can stop breathing. Death, for him, is life.

Two buildings on Tyler Street, south of Baxter Boulevard, catch my attention. The first is maybe two hundred yards distant, the second perhaps six hundred. Both rise above surrounding structures and both are set far back on their lots. The upper windows and roofs should offer clear lines of sight to the east side of Tyler Street, including the emergency room.

I head down Tyler Street, staying close to the buildings on the side opposite the emergency entrance until I reach the first building, the home of Prairie Moving and Storage. Half the lot has been given over to their lime-green trucks, two of which are in the process of unloading. Ochoa's presence seems unlikely, but I remind myself that Lee Harvey Oswald assassinated Jack

Kennedy from a perch in a book warehouse. Suppose Ochoa made an entry last night and found a dark spot on an upper floor.

Suppose . . .

But, no. A sign attached to a chain-link fence surrounding the property reads: PROTECTED BY SULLIVAN SECURITY. The claim is backed by cameras positioned on the wall overlooking the lot where the trucks are parked. Ochoa's a cautious man, a necessity given his obsessions. Even if he got inside without being observed, he'd have to get back out after firing. Suppressed rifles are quiet. From hundreds of yards away, if loaded with subsonic ammunition, they can't be heard. But they're not silent. It would require a near miracle for Ochoa to assassinate Abrescu, then escape without detection.

I pass on, walking another block and a half, past Adams Street, until I reach an eight-story brick building, again set a distance from the edges of the lot. Only this building is empty. A sign attached to another chain-link fence is succinct. On top: FUTURE HOME OF. On the bottom: HOLIDAY INN EXPRESS. A few yards away, an upright case fronted with a clear, acrylic window reveals city-issued demolition permits. That's the future, for this site and it seems for the whole city. But for now, the building, with its upper windows offering a clear view of the emergency room, is deserted.

There's a sign painted on the side of the building, so faded by wind and weather it can't be read. Someone's pride and joy back in a day that's long past. The fence surrounding the lot has been cut or kicked away from its posts in multiple places, and many of the plywood panels that covered the windows are lying in the rubble. Access and egress, entry and escape. No problem, with multiple points available.

These observations don't mean that Ochoa's inside. Nor does leaving the building necessarily mean escape. Not if he's on foot, and there's no green van parked on the street. Has Ochoa acquired another vehicle? Was the neighbor who described the green van mistaken? On impulse, I walk a block north, to Coolidge Street. There, thirty feet from the corner, a green minivan beckons. I walk up close and lay my hand on the hood. Still warm.

I call into our dispatcher, requesting backup. I don't know anything about Ochoa's training, but I estimate the distance between the abandoned warehouse and the emergency room to be about six hundred yards. A special forces sniper like Cade Barrow could probably make the shot. I don't know about Ochoa, but the real possibility that he'll miss only makes it more likely that he'll hit someone else. I'm sure the agents who push that gurney through the back door of the emergency room will be wearing body armor, but body armor provides only so much protection. Nor does Ochoa missing Abrescu mean that he'll hit one of the agents. If the round should strike the concrete driveway or the side of the building, the ricochet could take it anywhere.

The dispatcher comes back on three minutes later. My backup is ten minutes away, at least. I look at my watch. Forty minutes since I spoke with the Feds on the fourth floor. I can't wait, but I can definitely make life harder for Paul Ochoa. I carry a folding knife in my pocket when I'm on duty, like every cop I know. The knife's rarely used, but when you need it, you really need it. Like right now when I slash the front tires on the van. The act brings forth a little shot of dopamine, a mini-high that vanishes when I turn to the warehouse.

I make a final call as I walk toward a broken section of chain-link fence, this one to the duty sergeant, Vince Trentino. I state my location and the basics of my mission.

"Are you serious, captain? You're going in alone?"

"There's nobody else and time's running out. I have to find the asshole before I can stop him."

"Or he stops you."

And what can I say to that except, "Ten-four, sergeant."

CHAPTER FORTY

JOHNNY-BOY

Johnny-Boy awakens early, at six o'clock, from a dream he's dreamed too many times to count. He's running through a forest of longleaf pines, the soil beneath them blanketed by saw palmettos. The name, saw palmetto, tells its own story, each thin leaf edged with thorns that cut into Johnny-Boy's flesh, from his calves to his waist. He can't avoid the thorns because it's night, and he can't see them or the blood running in streams along both legs. He can't stop running either, because each time he does, his mother's voice draws closer. She intends to kill him this time, for sure, absolutely. God knows she's threatened him often enough, to murder him and leave his body for the vultures.

In his dream, vultures circle overhead, describing lazy circles as they patiently await the chance to feed.

◆

Once upon a time, the dream haunted Johnny-Boy through the following day. It had him glancing over his shoulder, avoiding middle-aged women of any size or race, keeping a weapon, usually a knife, close at hand. The paranoid part ended about fifteen years ago, fading gradually, though the dream remained vivid. Now he calms himself as he opens his eyes, the nightmare, if not an old friend, a toothless enemy.

Morning rituals follow, always helpful. Emptying his bladder and bowels, brushing his teeth, showering, shaving, slipping into a pair of faded jeans and a hooded sweatshirt. Nothingburger is the look he's striving for, and the bedroom mirror confirms his judgment. Head to toe, he's the guy you don't notice.

Johnny-Boy's long believed that some part of the human brain—his human brain, at least—continually monitors threats. Everybody's evaluated, even kids on bicycles, babies in swings, moms on park benches. Mostly, unless the brain finds a threat, the assessments never reach the part of his brain that's aware. But that's okay with him, as long as some part of himself keeps watch.

On this day, Johnny-Boy intends to appear so safe that he's dismissed immediately. No awareness necessary, the invisible man.

◆

Johnny-Boy packs his few possessions. There's not much. A couple suitcases, two boxes, a backpack containing his rifle, scope, and suppressor. Fifteen minutes later, he's ferrying a box to the van when his landlord makes an appearance. It takes Johnny-Boy a few seconds, but then he remembers the man's name. Morrison.

"You leavin'?"

"Yup."

Peering over a pair of reading glasses, the old man's small dark eyes project a hostility far beyond mere suspicion. He's got no use for his tenant, or for anyone else.

"You paid for a week."

"That's right."

"Seems funny, you're not askin' for a refund."

"Asked for a week, paid for a week."

"Only you're not comin' back and it ain't been a week."

The only good news here is that the old man lives alone. "Sounds like my business, not yours."

"True enough," Morrison responds, his tone somehow menacing despite the age and frailty. "You mind if I check inside? Make sure there's nothin' missing?"

"Nope."

As Johnny-Boy follows Morrison into the house, he's reminded of an old television commercial. Something about cockroaches walking in, but not walking out. And that's exactly how it works for his elderly landlord. With the door closed behind him, Johnny-Boy grips Morrison's throat with both hands. This is not slow strangulation. Johnny-Boy's fingers reach deep enough to crush the hyoid bone, the epiglottis, and the thyroid cartilage. At this point, he can let Morrison go because there's no recovering from these injuries. But he only tightens his grip, until he can feel Morrison's vertebrae against the tips of his fingers.

Johnny-Boy hangs on until his landlord's struggles end, until his body goes limp and he releases his bladder. Then he deposits the body in the apartment's single closet, folding Morrison's knees against his chest. The man will be found eventually, but he's an immediate problem solved, a factor taken off the board. Johnny-Boy stops in the living room to collect his breath, then lifts a final box from the floor. He was really pissed for a few minutes, but he's okay now.

◆

Johnny-Boy starts the minivan and leans back for a moment. He doesn't know when Diopolis will leave the hospital. In fact, he might already be gone. A fool's errand? Johnny-Boy can't wait all day and all night. At some point, he'll have to cut his losses, but not before he fires off a round or two. Just to prove he gave it his best. And if one of those rounds finds the body of a security guard, so much the better.

As he backs out of the driveway, Johnny-Boy tunes the radio to the local news station. More than likely, he's been identified. In fact, he's surely been identified, what with the fire and the cop turning up at the Coolwater. How far has it gone, that's the question. A BOLO handed out to cops as they begin their shifts? His likeness—and the bitch cops would have no trouble securing Sharon's and Glory's cooperation—released to the media? Or maybe a quiet search, necessary because there's no evidence that he committed a crime.

The anchor's voice drones on. Two assaults, three burglaries, all in the same neighborhood and likely committed by the same perp. A small fire in Boomtown that didn't kill anyone. A city council meeting scheduled for the evening to discuss the creation of a Baxter crime lab.

The name Paul Ochoa is never mentioned.

◆

Three blocks away, Johnny-Boy stops at a corner grocery store and buys a copy of the *Baxter Bugle* and a container of coffee, light and sweet. He thumbs through the paper after restarting the van, looking for his face, but the paper's all about the same bullshit he heard on the radio. Good. Especially because he has, beneath the sweatshirt, a .45-caliber handgun, a Colt Commander. The man who sold it to him described the weapon as a "manstopper." Which, in fact, is the whole point.

Johnny-Boy's prepared to use that weapon the moment he's threatened with arrest. Maybe Mariola and the other one, Weber, don't have real evidence now, but there's a goody in the back of the van that will send him away for a long time. The rifle with its suppressor and scope, neatly stored in the backpack. If they've recovered the bullet fired at Abrescu, the one that took off the man's arm, a ballistics comparison will connect gun and victim. But even if they can't do a comparison, because they haven't found the bullet or it's deformed, there's the matter of his phony license and registration, neither forgery good enough to survive close scrutiny. So, if he's not Paul Ochoa, who is he?

The bitches won't cut him loose until they find out. Something like his momma. On the few occasions she got her hands on him before he left the house, the beating was long and merciless. Like she was making up for lost time.

◆

There's no going back. That's what Johnny-Boy tells himself. If this is the day, it's the day. He recalls something he read a long time ago: any day's a good day to die, as long as you go down fighting.

Johnny-Boy continues to drive, scrupulously complying with every driving regulation. Full stops at stop signs, signal every turn, don't follow too close, and never, never, never hit the horn. Johnny-Boy's looking for signs of increased police activity, maybe a patrol car sitting close to the hospital, or cops on foot searching nearby buildings. He only happens on a single patrol car. It's parked behind a gray Toyota on Baxter Boulevard. The door to the Toyota's wide open, the passenger bent over the trunk, passive while a uniformed cop searches him. A small crowd of gawkers, two holding up their cell phones, has gathered on the sidewalk. They gasp when the cop withdraws his hand from the man's pocket, then holds up a large folding knife. A simple flip of the wrist and the blade snaps into place, fascinating in its way, but not Johnny-Boy's business. He keeps his head down as he drives around the two vehicles.

The slow reconnaissance continues for another thirty minutes as Johnny-Boy traces a shrinking circle. He's not foolish enough to drive by the emergency room, only close enough to demonstrate that there's nothing to demonstrate. His route isn't centered around the emergency room in any event. The Feds could put an army outside the emergency room and it wouldn't make any difference. Johnny-Boy's focus is on an abandoned factory that runs from Tyler to the next cross street. He's almost hoping to find police activity at this location.

Overnight, Johnny-Boy acknowledged the trap he's dug for himself. His methods reduce any threat from law enforcement to a minimum. At the same time, he's put all his eggs in one basket. From the client to Braulio Montez, then to Sol Cohen, then to Johnny-Boy via an email address on a server in Malaysia. For the cops, there's no way forward. For Johnny-Boy, there's no way back. And always the possibility that the next contract he takes from Sol Cohen will be a setup.

So, what's he gonna do if he doesn't take another shot at Abrescu? Apply for a job in the Nissan plant? Tightening the same bolts, day after day, month after month, year after year, praying only for the promised pension and a six-pack in the fridge? No, that's not gonna work. He needs the kind of leisure that a Nissan wage will never buy. He needs his fun.

◆

Johnny-Boy finally parks on Coolidge Street, the street west of Tyler. Both sides of the street are lined with small apartment buildings and there's no way to eliminate the possibility that he's being observed. He slides out of the van, stretches, then opens the van's side door. Slow, casual, safe. He reaches into the van's interior for the backpack and slips it on, shrugging his shoulders to settle it against his back. Then he uses the remote fob on his keychain to lock the doors.

Just another workday.

◆

Johnny-Boy takes a few strides on Coolidge Street, then strolls north to Adams Street, which runs along the south side of the factory. He notes a fire escape that clings to the weathered brick. The fire escape's not a way inside, though it passes open windows on the upper floor. He'd be too exposed. On the other hand, it could be a way out. Say if the operation went sideways. Something to think about. For now, though, he's reached the point of maximum risk, the entry. And he's wishing he'd made it in the early morning hours when there was little chance of being spotted. He'd considered and rejected that tactic last night. Cops are a lot more likely to make random stops at three o'clock in the morning than at nine o'clock. So, yeah, here he is, approaching a break in the fence. Beyond, two small structures, storage sheds, stand between him and the warehouse. Both will offer cover once he's inside the perimeter.

CHAPTER FORTY-ONE

JOHNNY-BOY

One for the money, he tells himself as he ducks through the break and strides toward the warehouse, putting the sheds between him and the street. An open doorway twenty yards ahead beckons and Johnny-Boy draws the .45 as he enters, stepping to his left, into the shadows, then freezing. The smell hits him first, of flaked concrete and mold, of animal waste. He shakes it off, an unnecessary distraction. Ahead of him, a startled rat dashes across the floor. Three equally startled pigeons turn circles below a ceiling twenty feet above Johnny-Boy's head. Johnny-Boy's not worried about rats and pigeons. He's listening for humans, squatters or junkies, or both.

The quiet is profound, a kind of shroud, like the odor of abandonment. A pool of rainwater that must have taken years to accumulate covers much of the floor. It adds enough humidity to call forth small beads of sweat on Johnny-Boy's forehead and scalp. Thirty feet away, a thick chain, the remains of a hoist, rests on a wooden platform beneath an opening in the ceiling. This is how the warehouse, or factory, or whatever it was, moved material to the upper floors. No use to him, of course, but to his left, an open door reveals a metal staircase. Johnny-Boy moves toward it, stopping twice on the way, head cocked, testing the silence.

◆

Johnny-Boy rests his left hand on the railing, pushing gently. If the staircase is defective, maybe clinging to the wall by a few screws, he'll be forced to retreat. He can't fly, after all. Slowly, Johnny-Boy increases the pressure, then suddenly yanks hard on the railing. Nothing, not a sound, the welds connecting the steel parts, railing, risers, and treads, are solid despite the years.

The first set of stairs rises twenty feet, long and steep enough to present a problem if he has to come down fast. Johnny-Boy files the insight. For now, it's only about up, about what's ahead of him. The second floor, like the first, is one large room, the ceilings here about twelve feet high. Again, he disturbs several pigeons. He listens to their wings slap against the air while he sweeps the room. A thin mattress lies on the floor, fifteen feet from where he stands. A refuge for some homeless fool once upon a time, it's been torn to pieces by rats in search of nesting material.

Johnny-Boy draws a breath as he starts up the next flight. On the landing, he faces a corridor with offices to either side. He listens carefully, but that's as far as he's willing to go. Clearing every space on the floor would take more time than he's willing to spend.

Two more steep flights to the top. Johnny-Boy takes the first quickly, thinking there must be an elevator somewhere in the building. On the second, now just a bit careless, his foot lands on a loose tread that bangs hard against the riser. He instantly brings the .45 to bear as he listens for footsteps, approaching or fleeing, but hears only the faint beating of wings. Does that mean he's alone? Not necessarily, because someone might be crouched in an alcove, prepared to defend his territory.

◆

Minutes pass, until Johnny-Boy admits that he has no choice. He has to go forward, but now he places his weight carefully, testing each tread as he makes his way to the top floor. The ceiling here is fifteen feet high and the room mostly open. Johnny-Boy moves toward the Tyler Street side of the building, to a pair of tall windows. The closest leads to the fire escape. The second offers a clear view of the Baxter Medical Center's emergency room, as Johnny-Boy knew it would. Both windows are broken, the first from outside. An intruder gaining entry after climbing the fire escape. And the second? Well, it's not just the second. It's every window on the floor.

Johnny-Boy can imagine himself enjoying the same wanton destruction at one point in his life. And maybe the endless hunts in the forests of the Panhandle amounted to the same thing. His mom draining the bottle, dropping the pills, snorting the powder, growing meaner and meaner. Johnny-Boy generally fled before she went off, but he carried the outrage with him, projecting it onto every small creature that passed his way.

◆

Moving quickly now, Johnny-Boy drops the backpack and assembles the Sig, attaching the scope and the suppressor. He rises to his feet, presses the stock to his shoulder, and peers through the scope. Just a check, but it's there, the ambulances, the doors, all in his line of sight. Johnny-Boy returns to the backpack and removes a Bushnell Rangefinder. The device uses a laser to determine the distance between itself and any motionless object out to thirteen hundred yards. The emergency room isn't thirteen hundred yards away. It's only 603 yards.

Johnny-Boy laughs to himself. He has about as much chance of making the shot as he does of going to heaven. His mentor, Eitan Levy, had trained as a sniper with the Mossad in Israel. He could slam a bullet up a mosquito's ass from eight hundred yards, or so he claimed. But Johnny-Boy never developed Eitan's skills. So, yeah, from three hundred yards out, he can put a bullet in the center of a stationary target. Not at six hundred yards. From six hundred yards away, it's more like guess your best.

Johnny-Boy's unsurprised, though he originally estimated the distance at four hundred yards. That was more hope-and-prayer than science. Still, he's not ready to abandon ship. Gravity begins to act on a bullet as soon as it clears the barrel of a gun. Two factors play a role here, the speed of the bullet and the distance. The faster the bullet and the shorter the distance, the less the drop from rifle to target. In the field, Eitan worked with a spotter trained to calculate these factors, along with elevation, wind speed, even humidity. Johnny-Boy's on his own, firing downhill with slow-moving subsonic ammo. He figures he can put a round somewhere inside a ten-foot circle surrounding his target. Will that be good enough? The important thing is that the attempt be reported, proof that he tried his best. Maybe the effort, along with an offer to refund his fee, will be enough to appease the client. Johnny-Boy's not sure, but any chance, even a small chance, is better than no chance at all.

One more chore. Some wooden crates rest against the wall on the north side of the room. Johnny-Boy kicks each, in case they conceal a rat or two, then drags a pair to the window and stacks them. He lowers the biped on the rifle, props it on the top crate, takes a quick look through the scope. All good.

Now he settles down to wait, his thoughts beginning to drift, an inevitability and probably to his benefit. Last night, as sleep eluded him, he'd given a lot of thought to the Feds and how they'd play their hand. Abrescu's to be transported by ambulance to an airfield. An ambulance parked in front of the main entrance would be too conspicuous, and the alley in back is a death trap. So, if Abrescu comes out at all—and Johnny-Boy's not discounting the possibility that the info leaked to the media is a ruse—he'll come through those double doors.

Johnny-Boy slows his heart and breath rates but doesn't take his eyes off the killing zone. An ambulance arrives, a patient's removed and wheeled into the emergency room. Hospital personnel, doctors, nurses, janitorial workers, security guards leave the hospital, two or three at a time. They walk to the edge of the sidewalk and light cigarettes. Not kosher, probably, but tolerated by the hospital authorities.

Johnny-Boy drops the scope to the center of the group. If he fires now, he'll very likely hit someone, more proof of his devotion to the contract. But, no, better to wait until Abrescu comes out. Then, if his primary target's shielded, he'll settle for an innocent bystander.

Unfortunately, the Feds are a step ahead. A security guard emerges and walks directly to the smokers. A few seconds later, the addicts take a last drag before tossing their butts into the gutter and walking back inside. One for the money, two for the show. Made all the more apparent when an ambulance backs as close as it can get to the emergency room doors. On cue, three men in scrubs push a gurney through the front door. Johnny-Boy sights on the unmoving body lying on the gurney, but doesn't pull the trigger. Instead, he laughs.

Unmoving? And why should that be? And why, when he thinks about it, would Abrescu need a gurney? He's lost an arm, not a leg. No, this is a bullshit attempt to draw fire.

Johnny-Boy's assessment is confirmed only a moment later. The gurney's pushed to the waiting ambulance, but not hoisted inside. Instead, after a pause, it's wheeled back into the hospital. Johnny-Boy's eye never leaves the scope as he contemplates the endgame. Take the shot, down the stairs, into the van. So long, sayonara, and good-fucking-bye. Let the future take care of itself.

That last thought turns out to be prophecy as a loud clang in the stairwell reaches Johnny-Boy's ear. The clang is followed by another, then another and another. They're coming for him, as he always knew they would, closing in. Driven into a near panic by the shock coming so close to the triumph, he fires three silenced rounds into the head of the stairwell. He's rewarded by another silence, this one more ominous. There's no way he can go back down those stairs, no fucking way, and no way the cops are gonna charge him either. That's because the first one or two won't be going home to the kiddies tonight.

Johnny-Boy lays the rifle on the ground and draws the .45. The Sig only holds five rounds and he's expended three of them. The Colt, by comparison, with its extended magazine, holds ten rounds, plus one in the chamber. The switch calms him. Yeah, most likely he'll die this morning, but not certainly. There's a way out that doesn't take him into the center of the storm and he instinctively turns to the second window and the fire escape beyond. Untested, it might pull away from the building when he steps onto it, leaving him to prove that gravity defeats every attempt to evade its effects.

He's through the window, onto the platform, and heading down within seconds. Sliding on the railing from one landing to the next, until he finishes ten feet above the sidewalk. There's supposed be a ladder here that he can lower, but it's long gone. Still, he doesn't hesitate, dropping to the sidewalk and into a crouch, already considering the best route to his van.

◆

"Police. Drop the gun."

Johnny-Boy freezes first, then slowly turns his head to find one of the bitch cops, the dyke, standing fifteen feet away, all by her lonesome. She's holding a semiautomatic in a two-handed, shooter's grip. No waver, no tremble, and no fear in her eyes.

"You alone?"

"Backup's on the way."

Johnny-Boy remains silent long enough to be sure that she's not gonna just pull the trigger. A by-the-books cop, she'll give him a chance to surrender. "That was smart," he finally says. "What you did on the stairs."

"If I was smart, I wouldn't have stepped on that loose tread in the first place. But once I did, I stomped on it a few more times. I wanted you to panic, and you did."

"And if I didn't?"

"I'd seal off the building and wait for you to come out." A smile now. "Or kill yourself."

"Why would I kill myself? You have nothing on me."

"We've got DNA from the boy you dumped in Maryville County. We've got your DNA on the bedding you left in the house you rented in Revere County. If you surrender, I'll get DNA from your mouth on a cotton swab. If you don't surrender, I'll take it from your corpse."

◆

Johnny-Boy tries to make himself believe that she's lying, but he can't do it. So, is it a good day to die? Or is it more like kill or be killed? Johnny-Boy's only sure of one thing. Surrender is off the table.

Despite his basic cylinder of a body, Johnny-Boy's quick. When he whirls and pulls the trigger, it's impossible to determine who fires first. The more accurate shot, on the other hand, is never in doubt. Johnny-Boy feels the bullet hit him just below the ribs on the right side of his body. An abdominal wound, tearing through flesh and organs, the pain overwhelming. He drops the gun as he falls to one knee. From a distance, he hears a male voice, a shout, "Captain? Captain? Where are you?"

Delia doesn't answer, doesn't react as Johnny-Boy stares up at her. She's uninjured, though. "Tell me the name," she says.

"What name?"

"The name of the boy you left in Maryville County."

Johnny-Boy thinks it over for a minute. His hand is pressed against his wound and blood runs between his fingers. "Sloan."

"Sloan what?"

"No fucking idea. But you wanna identify the asshole, I picked him up at a rest stop two hours north of Indian Hills, Arkansas. On the run." Johnny-Boy looks down at the .45. "Him, not me."

Again, a shout, this time closer. "Captain? Where are you?"

"What about Case Dixon? Did you kill him?"

"He killed himself, actually. But you could say that I encouraged him."

"And you're proud of that?" When Johnny-Boy responds with a shrug, Delia adds, "Kick the gun away. With your foot, not your hand."

Johnny-Boy drops his hand to within a few inches of the Colt. For just a second, he watches blood drip from his fingertips onto the weapon. "I had a pretty good run when ya think about it. I mean that I lived this long. The way it was supposed to go, I should've died by the time I was ten." He pauses, expecting the cop to respond, but she doesn't. Now he knows. Knows that she wants him dead. Dead by her hand. Johnny-Boy lays his own hand on the Colt, but doesn't try to close his fingers around the grip. No point, really. No point at all.

CHAPTER FORTY-TWO

THREE MONTHS LATER

DELIA

It's twenty degrees outside and damn near twenty degrees inside the Nissan factory. I'm wearing a down coat and I'm still cold, despite a pair of enormous space heaters that are more noise than heat. But here we are, me and two dozen of Baxter's most notable. Vern's present, of course. He's brought his family, as I've brought Danny and Zoe, both of whom are probably wishing they'd begged off. Just now, Vern's schmoozing Gloria Meacham, president of the city council, and four of her colleagues. Not fifty feet away, Saul Rawling, our chief of patrol, is huddled with several of the semiloyal opposition. When it comes to Baxter politics, Gloria's been at the top of the pyramid for twenty years. Mayors have come and gone, but Gloria's always seemed eternal. Probably because she's been sharp enough to support winners. But past success doesn't guarantee the future. Come November, a general election will decide the fates of Mayor Venn, Gloria

Meacham, and every member of our city council. A new mayor, of course, will mean a new police commissioner, who will then appoint the heads of his own departments.

Zoe slides her arm through mine. I think she wants to ask me how I'm doing, but that topic, after many, many discussions, is off the table. Yes, I killed a man, and yes, it shook me for a time. A short time. The analyst I was forced to see, Dr. Phyllis Demeter, cut me loose after four sessions. I was "processing the trauma well," she decided, "and okay to work."

Zoe and Danny, on the other hand, weren't buying. I'd been through a terrible ordeal. I must be in (well-disguised) distress.

A family sit-down was in order.

◆

I held it in a restaurant, the River, specializing in Thai fusion, a concept so Baxter-foreign it would have been unthinkable only a few years ago. Now California rolls were served alongside drunken noodles by servers wearing silk dresses that hugged their very slender bodies. I think Zoe was a bit jealous, afraid I might flirt. For my part, I was more envious than anything else. Thus far, my sort of diet had produced no discernible result.

Me, Zoe, Danny, and Danny's fierce protector, Fetchin' Gretchen, arranged ourselves around a table off in a corner where we couldn't be overheard. But there was no way to avoid the stares of the restaurant's other patrons. By then, Paul Ochoa's DNA had been matched to the DNA found on the boy named Sloan, validating the pair of confessions Ochoa made to me. Bard Henry was released as a direct result, much to the chagrin of James Dixon, Case Dixon's father. James wasn't satisfied, but then satisfaction was never in the cards for James Dixon, now a declared candidate for mayor.

I waited until I had a glass of wine in front of me to interrupt the small talk. "This is the last and final forever conversation about Paul Ochoa's . . . about my killing him."

"Mom, you don't have to . . ."

"No." I waved him off, the gesture more abrupt than originally intended. "I want it over with, Danny. As dead and gone as . . . as Paul Ochoa. No more worried looks. *Is she all right? Is she traumatized?"*

Zoe put her hand on mine. "Just do it, Delia. Say what you have to say."

"Fine, here goes. Maybe three years ago, I interrogated a man named Patrick Prince. Prince was a burglar. He'd been at it for years, despite numerous convictions and prison sentences. Then one night he invaded a home in Norwood through an unlocked window at the back of the house. The family was on the second floor of the house, presumably asleep as Prince searched the lower floor. There wasn't much to find, but Prince managed to snatch an expensive laptop and a jade figurine before he was interrupted by a child, a five-year-old boy. Prince strangled that child."

Gretchen's eyes widened, but Danny's attention never wavered. Zoe laid her hand on my elbow, offering support I didn't need.

"Prince was caught two blocks from the house with the laptop and the figurine in his possession. A matter of luck really, but there was no escaping responsibility. He confessed two hours into the interrogation." I leaned forward, looking from Zoe to Danny to Gretchen. "As he explained it, he murdered a five-year-old boy only because he feared the boy would cry out or identify him in the future. Killing the boy, for him, was just part of the job. He took no pleasure from it, and felt no pain. That's wasn't true for Paul Ochoa. For Paul Ochoa, the more pain he inflicted, the greater the pleasure he derived. And me, I'd hoped to rid the earth of his presence long before I caught up with him."

"And that's what you did?" This from an open-mouthed Gretchen.

"No. I gave him a chance to surrender." I sipped at my wine. "We exchanged gunfire when I confronted him. He was hit and dropped his weapon, a Colt forty-five. We spoke then, long enough for him to admit that he killed Sloan and Case Dixon. Then he knelt and let his hand move toward the Colt. I told him to stop, but he didn't. As for regrets, I can't say that I have any." I lifted my wineglass again, this time for a longer drink. "Technically, any death caused by another human being is a homicide. That's fine for pathologists. It makes life easy. But there's another cause of death you won't find in official reports. It's called suicide by cop. Paul Ochoa knew I'd kill him if he didn't surrender. It was an end he preferred to life in a cage. And that, my darlings, is the last chapter of this story."

◆

Vast doesn't begin to describe the interior of the Nissan assembly plant. Cavernous, either. I've driven along Main Street in Boomtown with the construction alongside, block after block after block, but somehow the scale eluded me. Now the far wall seems only a vague presence, a mountain clothed in morning mist. Our host for the tour, Marty West, is aware of the effect, and slick enough to let it sink in before speaking. Nissan's representative in Baxter, Marty's perfect for the job. He's tall, but not that tall. His shoulders are broad, but not that broad. His belly's pronounced, but not that pronounced. A full head of light brown hair (short, but not that short), and a pair of large (but not that large) eyes complement a ready smile.

Did I mention that his voice can only be described as booming, a verbal clap on the back?

"Eventually," he tells us, "the factory floor will be partitioned into three departments. Just now, we're standing in the domain of the robots." He shakes his head as he chuckles. "Nobody's favorite word. Robots. Ugh. But in this, the first step of the assembly process, robots will fashion the bodies of the vehicles we'll sell throughout the country. Floor, roof, hood, trunk, and doors. Robots will place each piece, then weld, glue, and caulk, moving with a precision and speed that humans simply cannot match. Human participation at this stage—and it gives me no pleasure to say this—will be limited to supplying the robots with the parts they need to get the job done. Only when the body is complete, and meticulously inspected, do we move to the domain of the worker. Now, please understand, we won't manufacture anything in your fair city. Every item, from tiny screws to the engines and transmissions, will be manufactured somewhere else, then brought to the plant by truck or rail. The logistics, of course, are daunting."

◆

I tune out at this point, looking around the room to find most everyone fascinated. Like Marty West's a traveling preacher describing paradise. It's not here yet, but it's a'comin'. In truth, I miss Blanche Weber. She's gone on to bigger and better things. Or maybe it's just love conquers all. After the confrontation in Revere County, she admitted that she couldn't keep Owen and remain on the job. The shoot-out was too much, and Blanche left the job three weeks later. They're engaged now, Blanche and Owen, the wedding set for the first week in June.

The date, six months from now, will allow Blanche the time she needs to establish Weber Security. Blanche, it appears, like many entrepreneurs, has uncovered a need and decided to exploit it. Her only competition, Sullivan Security, amounts to little more than a storefront. They install cameras in homes and stores, but anything larger is beyond their abilities. Blanche took it many steps further when she partnered with Al Granville, Owen's cousin, who brings fifteen years of security work in Las Vegas to the game. Al specializes in new construction and Weber Security has already placed a bid on a pair of hotels yet to break ground. That includes the Holiday Inn where Paul Ochoa came to his well-deserved end.

Both bids await action by the hotels, but the partnership is already working simply because Blanche and Al embody complementary skills. Al Granville has a master's degree in electrical engineering from Duke. His work credits include designing security systems, top to bottom, for two casinos. At the same time, he's arrogant, rude, and defensive about his geeky persona. That leaves Blanche to front for the company. Blanche's people skills are much improved, and her detective background, along with the small celebrity flowing from the shoot-out in Revere Country, hasn't hurt either.

Our lives, mine and Blanche's, weren't made easier when a hot-dog reporter at the *Baxter Bugle* dubbed us the Cowgirl Cops. I would have preferred Cowperson, but the name's taken on a life of its own. For my part, I've been around long enough to deal with the attention. Not Blanche.

"I've had enough," she told me only a few minutes before she handed in her papers.

"Give it time, Blanche . . ."

"It's not just the killing." Blanche stared at me for a moment. "Three dead and it comes to exactly nothing."

"You couldn't know that Minter would open up on Andy Kehoe. Not even Carol knew that."

Andy Kehoe died at the scene, as did Todd Framingham and Francis Minter. Case closed. True, Kehoe hailed from Bledsoe County in Missouri, as did another recruit. True, five more recruits came to the Baxter PD from nearby Overton and Humphreys counties. True, all were questioned by a review board that included Captain Mariola.

The responses were predictable. Individually and collectively, they heard no evil, saw no evil, and were keeping their big mouths shut. One of them, Jeff Greentree, is currently present in the Nissan factory, part of a small contingent of uniformed guards providing security.

"What I know or don't know hardly matters. The harassment is ongoing, Delia, and it won't stop." She waited for a response I wasn't prepared to make. "Our home was invaded. That's a big step, a big risk. So, what next?"

As I said, I miss Blanche. I miss her, but I can't fault her. The harassment ended less than a week after she quit.

◆

An hour into the tour, Marty West suggests that we move on. His suggestion confirmed by voice vote, we adjourn to the dining hall in nearby Goldman High and a loaded brunch table. I suspect the brunch would be held at a convention center if Baxter had one. Baxter doesn't, but it's definitely on the way.

I fix a plate and carry it off to one side. Saul Rawling's still working the room. For good or bad, he's been defending his patrol officers. In his version, Andy Kehoe died a hero's death at the hands of a vicious drug dealer, while Todd Framingham was a hero for killing that same drug dealer. The confrontation behind the house generally goes unmentioned, along with exactly what Todd and Andy were up to in Revere County. Vern hasn't been pushing the issue either. Nor has the city council. A black eye to be sure, but left to themselves, black eyes heal. And wasn't it lucky the two bad apples were eliminated before they spoiled the barrel.

Gloria Meacham joins me after a moment. "I'm not sure I needed to see what I saw today." She smiles. "But the apple turnovers are excellent. The coffee too. French roast. Funny, but I remember a time when I would have been obliged to call it Freedom roast. Then, again, coffee back then was that stuff in cans you found on a supermarket shelf."

"Times change."

"Yes, they do, but other things, like scapegoating, never change."

"And I'm the scapegoat?"

"In fact, you are. What with Blanche retired, you're the only target left."

"And the scapegoater? Would that be Saul Rawling?"

"It would. He's claiming that the . . . the disorder in Revere County might have been prevented if you'd consulted him beforehand."

"That's probably because he would've tipped them in advance."

"You're being overly harsh."

I shake my head. I'm out of chitchat for one day. "The patrol division's dirty, Gloria, and Saul Rawling has to know. He should have asked me to investigate. Instead, he protected them. Which he's still doing."

"You're not telling me anything I don't already know." Gloria's a grizzled veteran, literally. A farmer's daughter, she spent enough time in the sun as a child to produce a mass of fine wrinkles that somehow convey dignity. Now she stares at me for a moment before leaning forward to almost whisper in my ear.

"I don't want to hear a list of grievances, Delia. I want a solution. I want commitment too. I admit to a personal dereliction of duty. I should have seen it coming a long time ago. Now the corruption's entrenched. Now we're talking about a long, hard slog. And you, Delia, you might be able to preserve your position, no matter who wins the election next year . . . if you go along to get along."

I have a one-word response, which I utter without thinking twice. "Never."

◆

Two days later, I'm sitting on the passenger's side of Gloria's sedan, a Nissan Maxima. I happen to know that Gloria traded in her Lexus for the Nissan a few months ago. Driving a Nissan in Baxter is equivalent to flying the flag on the Fourth of July. Like every member of the city council, Gloria faces reelection come November.

I don't know what Gloria wants, or why she chose to hold our meeting in her car. We're driving along Main Street in

Boomtown, behind cars that suddenly pull to the curb whenever the driver spots something he wants. Something female.

It's early evening and the day shift at the worksite punched out an hour ago. The prostitutes along this stretch call it the evening rush. I've been here many times before. And I've seen half-naked women, wearing makeup so garish it wouldn't be out of place on a circus clown, jammed into already packed holding cells.

"Saul Rawling," Gloria tells me, "brags about the arrests his patrol cops make whenever he appears before the council. And he's not lying. Baxter cops made almost three hundred arrests last month. Better still, they took an illegal substance from more than two hundred. Sounds great, yes? We're fightin' the good fight?"

"And getting our asses kicked." I gesture toward the sidewalk. "Jails full, courts so jammed they couldn't provide a speedy trial for littering. And still they come."

The traffic thins as we head north, out of Sin City, onto blocks dominated by restaurants and taverns, including a pair of fancy sports bars that function as virtual betting parlors. Workers from the plant flow in both directions on the sidewalk to our right, in search of anything from a decently cooked meal to a bag of cocaine. I read nothing hangdog in their expressions. Maybe that's because there are so many pleasures available.

"I have dinner here from time to time." Gloria taps the steering wheel. "Mind you, in one of the more respectable restaurants. No casino, no prostitutes, and only one or two drug dealers hanging out by the bar."

I manage a brief laugh, and I can understand what brings her to Boomtown. There's energy to spare, a vibrancy I associate with big cities where the streets are never quiet. Great, but I'm becoming impatient. I've got Danny, Gretchen, and Zoe waiting at home. It's pizza night. And I don't entirely trust Gloria, or any other politician. Politicians are masters of the ulterior motive.

"Hard to imagine," I say because I have to say something, "that Boomtown will be gone a couple years from now. Like it never even happened."

"You think so? Because I'm seeing a hangover. Like the day after, when the bottle's empty, but not forgotten." Her mouth tightens as she adds, "I knew we'd pay a price when you turned down the job. I'm talking about commissioner."

Gloria's statement takes me by surprise, but I maintain a neutral tone. "You have a problem with Vern?"

"I love the guy, Delia. He's great at one part of the job. Say you're trying to coax money out of the state or the Feds, a grant here, a subsidized loan there. Vern's your guy. Charming, handsome, a high school football hero. He's great. Management, though . . ." Gloria shakes her head, setting every wrinkle into motion. "I can't tell you how far the corruption goes, but I can assure you, relying on closed-door hearings, that it runs deep."

"We're working . . ."

Gloria stops me with a wave of her hand. "That's not where I'm going. Look, the BPD needed to expand as the city expanded. In the council after numerous hearings, and after consulting our mayor, we decided that the police department lacked the expertise and the personnel to vet new candidates. You with me so far?"

"Yeah, I remember agreeing with you . . . at the time."

"There's the Delia I know and love. But your sarcasm isn't misdirected, given the end result. We did farm out the vetting to a private contractor who maximized profit by minimizing scrutiny. They contacted former employers and used a federal database to check for arrests . . . and that was that."

"And the result is the result."

"No, Delia, that's where you're wrong. Vern Taney was specifically delegated to supervise the contractor. He should have handled the assignment personally, but he re-delegated the job to a subordinate. That would be Saul Rawling." Another pause, but I have nothing to say. "I have faith in Vern's integrity. He's as honest as I am." Now a smile. "Don't they call that damning with faint praise?"

"I believe they do."

"Be that as it may, the bottom line doesn't change. We've been invaded, literally, and Vern's not the one to fight them off."

"And I am?"

"There's nobody else, Delia. Nobody."

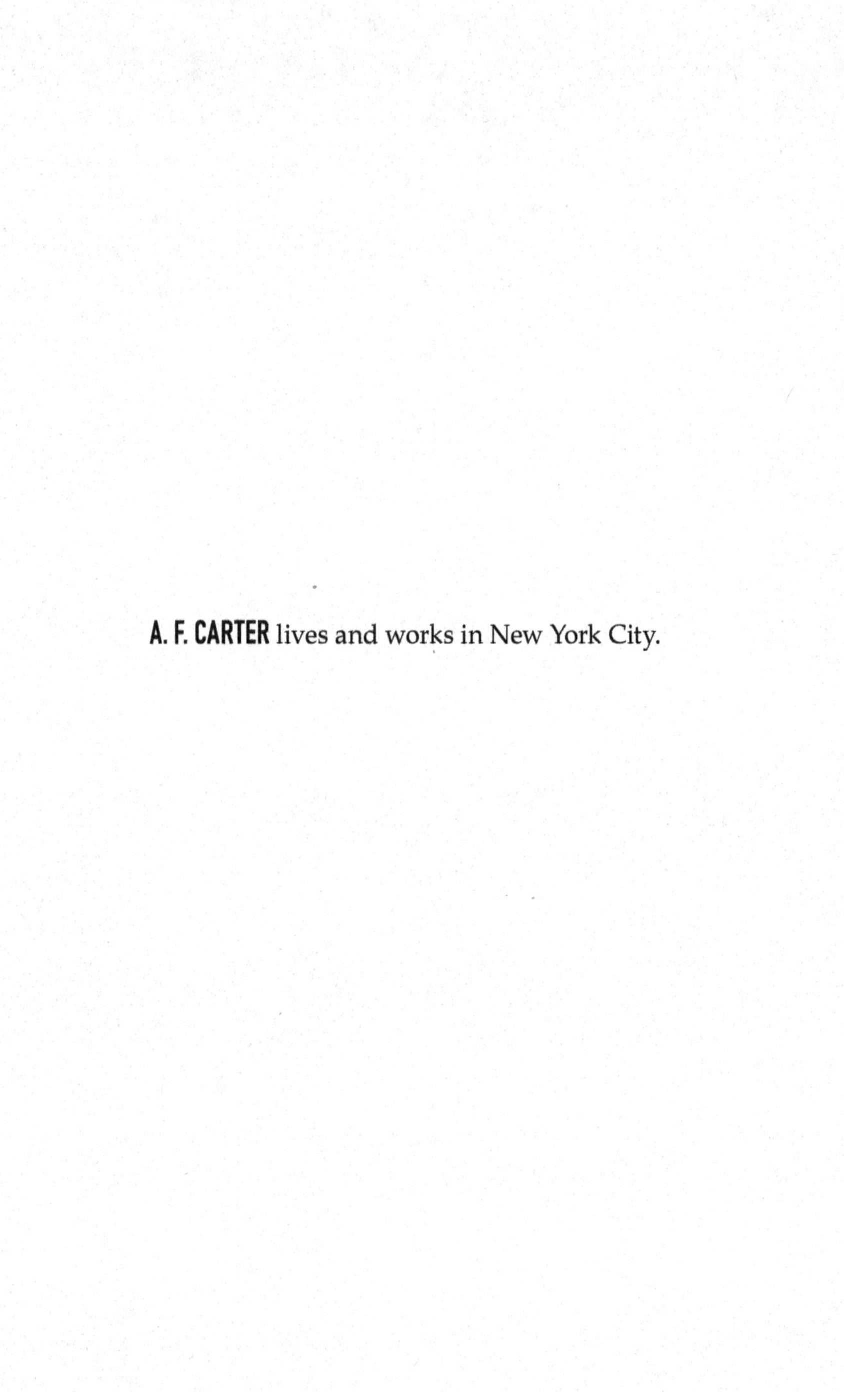

A. F. CARTER lives and works in New York City.

Other titles in A. F. Carter's Delia Mariola series are available now from The Mysterious Press

"A breathless suspenser that's also a painfully acute evocation of the wrong side of the tracks."
—**KIRKUS**

THE YARDS

Git O'Rourke is from the wrong side of the tracks—even if, in the depressed Rust Belt town of Baxter, it's not always clear where that designation begins. A single mother, she works hard to support her daughter Charlie, but still finds time to cut loose every once in a while, to go to a local bar, drink martinis, and find a companion for the night. Which is exactly how she ends up in a hotel room with a strange man passed out on heroin, and how she comes to possess the bag of money and guns that he left open as he got his fix.

When the dead body is discovered at the Skyview Motor Court, a bullet through its forehead, officer Delia Mariola is one of the first on the scene. She recognizes the victim as the perpetrator in an earlier crime—a domestic violence call—but that does little to explain how he ended up in the situation in which they find him. She knows he's connected to the local mob, but the crime scene doesn't exactly resemble their typical hit. Instead, all signs point to a pick-up gone wrong. Which means that all signs point to Git.

"*The Hostage* will keep you absolutely nailed to your page or screen. Smart, urgent, and sneakily deep."
—**C.J. BOX**, #1 NYT Best-Selling author of *Shadows Reel*

THE HOSTAGE

A new Nissan plant is coming to the depressed Rust Belt town of Baxter, and Captain Delia Mariola has been busy cleaning up the crime-addled city ever since the deal was announced. But when the 15-year-old daughter of the lead bidder on the construction project—a wealthy out-of-towner—suddenly disappears and it becomes clear that a professional kidnapping ring may be responsible, Delia realizes that the factory's influx of cash could bring with it an entirely new sort of danger, never before considered in this working class milieu.

Though Elizabeth's abduction was well-planned and bearing the mark of an experienced team, her captors could not have anticipated the quick and clever brilliance of the exceptionally smart teen. From the trunk of the car where she is held, she soon devises a clever trick to get cryptic messages to those who love her back down the highway in Baxter. The only problem is that the messages might be too cryptic even for their recipients to decipher. If Delia has any hope of bringing the girl home unharmed, she'll have to crack the code and discover the meaning behind the message. And unless she does it fast, there may be nobody left to save…

A 2024 EDGAR AWARD NOMINEE

"Striking … A rich and reeking swamp full of exploitation, despair, violence, and summary justice."
—**KIRKUS**

BOOMTOWN

Police captain Delia Mariola is still struggling to drive the predatory drug dealers from the rustbelt town of Baxter, before the new Nissan plant owners lose faith in this forgotten corner of America. It doesn't help that a boomtown has grown up just outside of city limits—a wild west designed to feed every unsavory desire of the workers building the plant. And like vultures homing in on the weak, criminal gangs from the big cities have also been drawn to the boomtown, knowing how freely money will flow to those willing to supply drugs and women to these workers far from home, looking for comfort and distraction. With no police actively enforcing the rule of law in the unregulated town, the criminals have turned on each other as they try to claim control.

In the midst of this drug war, a young prostitute's body turns up on the streets of Baxter, well within Delia's jurisdiction to investigate. Hoping this might be the case that allows her to finally be able to crack down on the boomtown, Delia is relentless in her pursuit of the killer and the group she believes is behind the criminal enterprises plaguing her streets. But Delia isn't the only person looking for the murderer. Two strangers have arrived in town, claiming to be the family of the deceased and possibly looking for a version of justice that has more to do with back hills vigilantism than the court of law.